Family Secrets
A San Francisco Saga

Family Secrets
A San Francisco Saga

Edward J. Dumke

Hot Chili Press

ISBN: 978-0-9862046-4-7

First Edition

Library of Congress Control Number: 2015944025

Cover images:
Front cover image ©iStockphoto.com/mactrunk, photo: 36262878
Back cover image ©iStockphoto.com/pawel.gaul, photo: 18663303

For Bernie and the city he loved.

My San Francisco on her seven hills is smiling beside an opalescent sea.
— George Caldwell

No city invites the heart to come to life as San Francisco does.
— William Saroyan

Chicago is the great American city, New York is one of the capitals of the world, and Los Angeles is a constellation of plastic; but San Francisco is a lady.
— Norman Mailer

Table of Contents

Table of Contents

$\mathcal{S}$TANLEY McMASTERS REACHED into his locker, took out a small leather case and removed a syringe.

"Joey!" he barked impatiently across the room. In a matter of seconds, Joey Chang appeared, carrying a stainless steel tray covered in a white linen towel.

McMasters unbuckled his belt and dabbed his thigh with rubbing alcohol.

"You have good game?" Joey asked politely.

McMasters ignored the question as he took the vial off the tray, carefully inserted the needle through the top of the bottle and drew 25 icu of clear fluid up into the syringe and then tapped the edges to remove any air bubbles. He smiled to himself. It had been a good game. A forty-two on the first nine with a long putt on the eighth green to give him a birdie and an extra $5.00 from a side bet. He liked nothing better than to win at golf, at business, at anything. It fed his sense of superiority especially when he could claim the results were due to his own skill or cunning.

"O.K., that's all," he said, dismissing his hesitant attendant. He hated giving himself shots in front of anyone, even a locker boy. He thought of it as a sign of weakness and in the six years he had been injecting himself he had never grown comfortable admitting to the need.

Without expression Joey carefully put the tray on the nearby bench and retreated. A few other golfers came into the locker room to pick up sweaters or change clothes for a late start, but aside from the opening and closing of a few lockers, it was quiet.

McMasters slipped the needle under his skin, pushed down the plunger and returned the syringe to its case. He pulled up his pants, zipped his trousers and buckled his belt.

"Goddamn it!" he swore under his breath as he reached for some extra tees. He felt a strong sensation like a hot clamp at the top of his stomach, high up under his ribs. A reaction was his first thought, but it wasn't the same and he knew it. He remembered he was supposed to be on the tee and was annoyed. The thought of letting another foursome play through made him angry. He felt dizzy. The pain grew intense and he reached back to find the bench. He never made it. Joey Chang heard him hit the opposite row of lockers and knew from the direction of the crash who had fallen.

"Get Dr. Whitmore! He's on …" McMasters' voice trailed away. He writhed in pain. His face twisted in a grotesque grimace. The cramps were so severe that he involuntarily drew his legs up to his chest and screamed. A few golfers came down the row of lockers and stood peering at a distance. Tears streamed down his face, which was already drenched in perspiration and distorted in pain.

But even more terrifying than the visual agony was the sound coming from deep within his chest. It was an inhuman gurgling, like some foolish creature whistling to be born, and it carried the horror of death to those who watched the involuntary jerks and foamy salivating, to those who never contemplated death except in abstract terms.

By the time his doctor and golfing partners arrived, Stanley McMasters was throwing up yellow-green bile and the muscle fasciculations had spread so that his whole body was wracked in violent spasms.

"Call an ambulance!" Whitmore ordered as he tried to restrain McMasters. He could not find a pulse. "Help me hold him!" he yelled. The onlookers were paralyzed in fear. Trying again, he thought he found a pulse—very rapid and irregular. "Christ!" Someone timidly stepped forward and attempted to take hold of McMasters' legs, but his limbs flailed wildly and his back arched as he suffered a full-blown seizure. His head bashed uncontrollably into a locker door, producing a loud hollow wooden sound that made the scene even more macabre.

"He's arresting," Whitmore said as another doctor arrived on the scene and attempted to help. They tried for some time to revive the incontinent ghostly figure that lay on the locker room floor and stared blankly up at the ceiling, but they knew it was futile.

ᴋATHERINE LAY BACK in the fragrant water watching the light play through the iron filigree that enclosed the bathroom window. Shifting patterns of quivering gold light, she thought. Like a butterfly's wings on unseen currents.

"Señorita?" The voice followed by a knock on the door interrupted her association.

"Sí?"

"Señorita, un telegrama para usted."

"Gracias, Concepción," she replied feeling her body grow tense. Ponlo Sobre el buró."

"Sí, Señorita."

"Aunt Gloria," she thought. They can't be coming back! Not until the end of the month! She took a sponge, filled it with warm water and squeezed it out along the back of her neck. It must be about ten, she guessed, emerging from the bath. The sun was well over the irregular tiled roof. She dried and wrapped herself in a soft green towel. At the dressing table the telegram lay beside her morning tray. "Thank God. It's not from Gloria," she reasoned, noticing by the markings that it was from the States. Perhaps father? Or Trixie? She opened it.

San Francisco   29 August 1953
Deeply regret—Your father, Stanley K. McMasters—died Saturday Aug. 29—2 p.m. P.S.T.—Heart attack—Funeral pending—Contact Philip Addison McMasters Shipping—San Francisco—Yukon 51525 or Tuxedo 72835.

She read the message twice, folded the thin sheet of paper and placed it carefully back into the envelope. She began watching herself from the outside as if she were the focus of a camera. I wonder if? Will I? She tried to identify her feeling. They eluded her. "There must be a memory that will produce an emotion," she thought searching for something. There was nothing. Nothing but the telegram, which lay carefully folded on her lap. She reopened and read it again.

"Father dead!"

"August 29th at 2 p.m." Today? No, yesterday.

"Two, three, four, five, six," she counted. Six o'clock yesterday Buenos Aires time. I was? The reception. Yes of course. The Hungarian trade delegation at the Museo Nacional de Bellas Artes. Aunt Gloria and Uncle Otto's ploy to get me back from Europe. Philip Addison? Yes, Father's President. The gentleman with Father in Brussels. Yes, I remember now.

"Funeral pending." Good Lord! Gloria? She felt herself recoil imagining her Aunt's reaction to the news. The hysteria! So dependent on Father in that strange way she never understood.

She closed her eyes and put her hand to her forehead searching the possibilities that beckoned from the edge of her imagination. Yes of course, San Francisco. At last San Francisco! She smiled absorbing what it meant. "I better be careful! Do Gloria and Otto know? That's the important thing! Perhaps not?" She found their itinerary. "St. Tropez, August 31st. They probably will know tomorrow."

Within the next few hours she had arranged everything. She told no one of her plans except her friend Christina. "I can't risk being delayed," she explained. "Uncle Otto has the necessary political connections. He can be ruthless." She took care folding her black dress. "I wore this to the ceremonies marking the first anniversary of Eva Peron's death. Now it will" She did not finish, but lay the dress on top of her other clothes and shut the last suitcase. "I'll tell the servants we're going to the country for the weekend," she said.

It wasn't until her plane was airborne that Katherine allowed herself to think about anything except getting out of the country.

As the Boeing Strata Cruiser banked over Buenos Aires and headed north, she felt a strange exhilaration mixed with unqualified relief. Then a great net of emotions enveloped her and she put her head into her pillow and wept. Somewhere after Rio, Katherine awoke from a deep sleep, drank strong coffee and began to place things into perspective. She had learned over the years to tidy up her emotions, putting them away in neat manageable compartments. Now more than ever she realized the necessity of taking control. "At last San Francisco," she reflected. "To bury Father. Ironic!" She closed her eyes. "Not the way I have always imagined it would be. My life's ambition and now …"

The times Katherine's father had refused to bring her back to San Francisco to live were too numerous and painful to remember. "I'm a very busy man. I don't have time to look after you," was his usual excuse. "You are better off with your Aunt."

"I wanted so much to go with him, to have him want me to live with him," she recalled, remembering the dreadful scene during one of his infrequent visits. She was sixteen at the time and had pleaded with him to take her out of the convent school where her Aunt had sent her. When he refused, all the years of hurt and rejection came pouring out in an angry tirade. His reaction was swift and imperious. "I forbid you to mention the subject again," he ordered before turning his back and walking out of the room. She could still hear the sound of splintering crystal as the vase she had thrown crashed against the door he had slammed in her face. It had been her first act of open defiance. Within a week, she was sent off to school in Switzerland.

The sun came up as the plane flew across the endless stretches of the Amazon Basin. Memories of her childhood played across her mind like the light on the forest canopy below.

"Strange to never really have a parent's love. Manolo was more like a father," she thought, remembering the old gaucho who had taught her to ride. "Manolo, Carlos, José, Angela and Isabelle. They were more like parents than Aunt Gloria or Uncle Otto. They made my life on the estanciero bearable." The brave, self-reliant gauchos were

Katherine's first heroes. Their families were her family. From them, she had learned a passion for freedom and a love of the land.

"It wasn't until I was eleven that I began to miss having a mother and father," she concluded, remembering how lonely she had been when she was packed off to the hated convent school. "How desperately I missed the pampas! I was so ugly and awkward. 'La Rhea' they called me. 'The Ostrich'." She recalled how the other girls, spoiled and haughty, would brag about their families. She ached remembering how she would create a fantasy world for herself. "A world where I had a place to be with my own parents," she sighed. But reality was different. Mother was dead and Father was always far away.

"Mother?" she pondered, still experiencing the old anxiety as she turned the spotlight of reflection onto that mysteriously dark corner. "Why was I sent away just before she died? How did she die? Where was her family?" She could hear her Aunt's standard answer to all the years of questioning. "Your mother died when you were too young to remember. That is all you need to know." Gloria's subtle suggestions had been that Katherine's mother had abandoned her or that Katherine had somehow been responsible for her mother's death. These were horrific thoughts for a girl who had been deprived of all parental affection. For years they gnawed at the edges of her subconscious like a terrifying little creature that was secretly being fed under the table by her aunt.

Katherine shuddered, reliving the time she had dared press for information about her mother's family. You're an ungrateful little bitch just like your mother!" Gloria had screamed after slapping her across the face. "You're damned lucky you've never met any of them."

"At last," she thought jarring herself back to the present. "Perhaps now I will find out for myself." She found herself worrying for fear that her mother's relatives would not consent to seeing her. "I'll have to handle that the best I can," she concluded.

She slept for a while before the plane touched down in Caracas to refuel. It was good to walk across the tarmac and stretch her legs and have the few hours away from the constant droning of the propellers.

As she flew on towards Florida, Katherine thumbed through the *Life Magazine* she had bought in the airport. In the Fashion section she recognized the black velveteen pajamas and gold-trimmed jacket. "Schiaparelli! He wanted me too!" She smiled, reminiscing how in Europe, she had undergone a metamorphosis. After three years of success at St. Georges in Montreux she had gone to Paris to work on an advanced degree at the Sorbonne. By then, "La Rhea" had become the proverbial swan and she was offered a job modeling for Pierre Balmain. "Fantastic! Alluring!" he had shouted after discovering her flawless complexion and emerald green eyes. For two seasons Balmain dressed her tall, perfectly formed figure and made her a sensation. "For once Father seemed proud of me," she thought, remembering a business trip that brought him through Paris. "Proud of my looks and modeling, if not my academic achievements. And how jealous Aunt Gloria was when she joined us. It didn't take her long to engineer my return to Argentina or my ill-fated romance with Ricardo. And Father let her get away with it!

"Poor Ricardo, such a reckless handsome devil. The typical Latin playboy—rich, romantic and obsessively jealous." She shook her head, remembering how she had ended their engagement by telling him she was in love with a French zoologist. "Aunt Gloria was furious when she found out. 'One of the best families in Argentina,' she had screamed, Dios Mio, I would have been shackled for life!"

The stewardess brought some wine and a meal and Katherine found herself wishing for her friend Trixie, her roommate at St. Georges. It had been Trixie who had helped make up the story about the French zoologist. "Wonderfully daring outspoken Trixie! 'Madcap Metcalf' we called her." As she ate alone, Katherine visualized the Metcalf family gathered around their large dining room in Geneva, everyone arguing and joking and then spilling out onto the lawn for an impromptu game of touch football. "I owe a lot to the Metcalfs," she mused. "Trixie's dad was the first man who ever listened to my opinions. And Dorothy, Trixie's mom, always delightfully cheerful, with her boisterous family and her hundred and one projects. They made me feel at home. As different from Gloria an Otto as sunshine from frost."

In Miami she changed planes and then slept until Denver. As she flew across the rugged terrain of the American West, she found herself becoming anxious. Her nerves seemed to twitter along her limbs like impulses along a high-voltage wire. There was the funeral, the business of the estate and the terrible uncertainty of her Aunt. "Did they know yet?" she kept asking herself. Would they be there to meet her?

She sat staring out the window at the Nevada desert. "Mother," she thought. "Will I be able to find her family?" The Sierra Mountains appeared below and she wondered what awaited her just beyond the vaulted cloudless blue sky that stretched towards the horizon.

𝒮OMEWHERE AMID THE 1,000 smiling dragons of his subconscious Albert Edward Devonshire heard the familiar sliding of draperies as Chow-Ling began the morning ritual, letting the light filter in to replace the darkness. He fought momentarily to regain a dream, attempting to call back the experience of Deirdre's soft warm breast, but his mind would not surrender itself. The coffee tray was set on the table, and the rich aroma brought him closer to that wonderful semi-awake state in which he always considered it a great luxury to linger.

Yet as Chow-Ling went about his duties there was something in his movements that triggered a sense of urgency. Chow-Ling had been in his family for over 50 years and with Albert alone for ten. Their relationship stretched back Albert's entire life and so accustomed were they to each other that they often did not need words to communicate. It was as if their spirits shared the same raft on the stream of consciousness. As he stretched, fighting for consciousness he could feel his fox terrier Windsor stretching too. Then Windsor jumped down and followed Chow-Ling towards the door.

"Messages in morning room. Many calls. Newspaper waiting. You getting up?" Chow-Ling said in his quiet precise manner.

Now Albert knew something was out of the ordinary. Chow-Ling never spoke until well after his second cup of coffee. Messages were always in the same place on the Regency writing desk and, the newspaper was always waiting. Every detail of their domestic existence had been worked out and refined into an orderly routine, and the morning ceremony did not call for verbal communications of any kind. That Chow-Ling had chosen to quietly mention the ordinary meant that the ordinary must have some extraordinary consequence. Messages, Albert thought, as he pulled himself up. What messages? Then he remembered he had been in Sausalito for a couple of days and had only come back late in the evening in order to attend a Sunday concert. Gaetano Merola was conducting and as much as Albert loved being with Deirdre, any performance by the great maestro was worth a run back to the city.

Reaching for the Camel, he still could not fathom what message would be that important, or why Chow-Ling would refer to the newspaper. He pushed his dark wavy hair off his forehead and lit the cigarette. He had a strange sense of foreboding mixed with more than a little curiosity and his normally calm countenance took on a searching look that made his fine steady features look almost scholarly.

As soon as he felt the first few swallows of coffee he seized the moment, got out of bed and fumbled for the dark blue robe Chow-Ling had carefully laid out. He went to the window. The fog was still in, but the morning sun which was already well above the Berkeley hills was casting great shafts of cold light on a rusty old freighter which slithered past Alcatraz on its way towards the Golden Gate. "What a day for a concert in Stern Grove!" he thought as he felt the stiffness in his leg from old war injuries. He went downstairs and across the living room watching his feet move over the floral abstraction of the blue and ivory Persian Senneh carpet that formed the soul of the room. He forgot to exchange the usual greeting with Hector, his mynah bird. Taking offense, Hector screamed an unknown Chinese saying followed by the proclamation: "life is dust." Ignoring Hector's rude behavior and continuing on towards the morning room, he contemplated the interconnecting patterns woven into the rug.

The morning room was a small cozy room off the pantry with a splendid alcove that overlooked a corner of the Bay. Its proximity to Chow-Ling made its location ideal, since Albert preferred to let

12

Chow-Ling screen his telephone calls, thereby giving him a flexibility and privacy so necessary for sanity in the modern world.

As Chow-Ling arrived with the second cup of coffee Albert's eyes caught the headlines, "Stanley Talbot McMasters Dead at Sixty-Four". Instantly he knew why Chow-Ling had forced him out of bed! "How many calls?" he asked." Chow-Ling shuffled to the Regency desk and produced a list of well over fifteen calls, seven of which were from Albert's great-aunt Louisa, and several more from his parents.

Stanley Talbot McMasters was Albert's uncle by his marriage to Albert's mother's younger sister, the legendary beauty Elizabeth Louisa Templeton Harte, and the father of Albert's cousin who he had not seen since he was ten.

Now McMasters was dead of a heart attack. According to the paper he had died at two p.m. the previous afternoon, in the locker room of the San Francisco Golf Club. The front page of the *Examiner* carried the entire story of McMasters' life including the mysterious death of his first wife, his trial, and his second marriage and divorce. And as one of the most powerful businessmen in the city, significant copy was devoted to Stanley's extensive financial empire, the cornerstone of which was the chairmanship and controlling interest in The McMasters Shipping Line.

Albert finished his second cup of coffee while digesting the newspaper accounts and pondering what McMasters' death would mean for his daughter. Would she inherit the entire estate? Would she return to San Francisco for the funeral? His thoughts were interrupted by Chow-Ling, who quietly placed the telephone at his left and refilled his cup to provide the necessary fortification for the call he knew must be made.

Without hesitation Albert picked up the phone and rang up his great-Aunt Louisa, only to reach her companion, Ivy, who was in a state of great nervous excitement.

"Oh yes, yes Albert!" she gasped, "Miss Harte has been trying to reach you all morning. Have you heard the news? I think she would like you to motor down right away instead of having Andrew pick you up at the usual time. She has already chilled the champagne to celebrate—I mean, for your arrival. Oh dear! She has had two Bloody Marys. Yes, yes, she's in the conservatory laughing and singing. I think you had better come straight away."

Albert attempted to calm Ivy by adopting a firm, directive tone, and was soon able to get his aunt on the line. She was not unsurprisingly in rare form.

"You've heard the news, Albert?" she said with an undisguised note of glee. "The old son of a bitch is dead. I hope the gates of Hell are slammed tight behind him."

"Aunt Louise!" he exclaimed, teasing her for the shameless way she approached the subject. "Let the end try the man."

"Don't be asinine, Albert," she shot back without a moment's reflection, "when can you come down? Do you want me to send Andrew? The Mumms on ice, and I'm not going to wait all day."

"Well, I was planning to attend the concert in Stern Grove. Merolo's conducting." "Preposterous! You can always hear Merola conduct, but how often can you help your old aunt celebrate such a momentous occasion? I hope the bastard turned all purple and lingered long enough to suffer a little. That's the least he deserves."

Albert could tell his Aunt Louisa was on a roll, and that nothing would do but that he should spend his Sunday down the Peninsula listening to her uninterrupted ravings.

"All right, very well, I'll be down within a few hours. I can tell you're not going to take no for an answer. Keep the Mumms chilled and try for a little charity until I get there."

His compliance was not surrender, although he may have given that impression. For although he had looked forward to the concert, he could tell that it was going to be an unusually cold and foggy summer day and the thought of warmer weather down the Peninsula was very appealing. Furthermore he had to admit to himself that eccentric old Aunt Louisa, when all was said and done, was his favorite relative. She was at once very grand and very earthy and despite the difference in their ages, she was always great fun. They shared

14

a similar perspective on people and the art of living much like two radios tuned to the same frequency.

It was already 12:15 when he turned his new Buick Roadmaster off the Bayshore and rolled into The Village otherwise known as Burlingame. Within a few more minutes he was driving through the gates of Treehaven and up the poplar-lined drive around the outskirts of the small deer park. The 400-acre estate originally called Huntsford, had been purchased in 1850 by Aunt Louisa's grandfather but had been renamed Treehaven by Aunt Louisa's father, who took exception to living in a home that bore the name of his father-in-law. Thanks to a fire the original Victorian monstrosity had burned to the ground in 1906 and had been replaced by a more impressive Georgian brick structure, for which Aunt Louisa and Uncle Milt commissioned the famed San Francisco architect Willis Polk. Well sited among the native oaks, rolling hills and formal gardens, Treehaven had all the quiet dignity of an English country residence.

Albert slowed his car as it hit the pea gravel in the central court. By the time he reached the front steps Prentice, Aunt Louisa's old butler, had slowly swung open the massive oak doors and her twin canines, Maggie and Jiggs, came running out barking and nipping at Windsor.

"Good day, Mr. Albert. Mrs. Harte is in the conservatory," Prentice mumbled, without a trace of either humor or displeasure. "Just follow me if you would sir."

"That's all right, Prentice old fellow," he said, "I know the way." Reaching the south end of the main hall, which runs the length of Treehaven's core, Albert entered the conservatory.

There at the end of the great iron and glass structure surrounded by sprays of Phalaenopsis Aunt Louisa sat like a Romanoff grand duchess in her fan back wicker chair, centrally placed on a classical Turkish garden rug. Glazed pink and green pots filled with maidenhair fern, gardenias and cyclamen spread out across the slate floor in a sea of green and white. Cattleyas and dendrobium cascaded from fern baskets suspended at different layers from the ceiling, each displaying its own exotic bloom to delight the visitor. Beside Aunt Louisa's chair stood the superb 1815 Johann Gottlieb Matthias silver stand and wine cooler featuring the god Bacchus and containing a chilled magnum of Mumms Extra Dry champagne.

At eighty-three, Aunt Louisa was an ample woman, and although she had never been beautiful, she had strong features, exceptionally good bone structure, and the most astonishing blue eyes that simultaneously danced across and pierced into the world she surveyed. She had been born Katherine Louise Huntsford Fitzhubert in San Francisco in 1870. Her family history was so intertwined with the city of her birth that she was practically a living symbol of the city itself.

Arriving at the end of the conservatory, Albert bent over and kissed his aunt first on her cheek and then on her hand. It was a form of greeting he reserved only for her, the origins of which were lost to memory.

"You're late, Albert," she scolded, and with a wink added, "You see how good your old aunt has been? I've held the Mumms for you."

He poured the champagne and sat down in the wicker chair next to her. "Here's to Stanley McMasters, may he rot in hell," she said, raising her glass with a dramatic flair.

For the next hour or so they talked about family history.

"You know, Auntie, I was only nine when Aunt Elizabeth died," Albert said after Aunt Louisa calmed down.

"Was murdered!" she interrupted again, becoming agitated.

"Yes, was murdered. I was only nine when Aunt Elizabeth was murdered. Then Father took us off to England for a year."

"That was your mother's idea, a mostly unsuccessful attempt to put some distance between herself and the publicity. She's as spineless as a buttered scone!"

"Yes, well, mother is rather fragile. But be that as it may, I never really understood why Aunt Elizabeth's daughter Katherine was sent off to Argentina and why she never returned."

Albert had heard the story of his cousin's exile a hundred times, but its telling was a ritual, and as with all old San Francisco families, their history was a living reality.

"He literally swept her off her feet and she married him on impulse," Aunt Louisa maintained. "I warned her about the family—most unacceptable—but she was determined to go ahead. You know, his great-great-grandfather stole the shipping line from my grandfather."

"Yes, of course Auntie."

"Two days after her funeral Stanley sent little Katherine off the Buenos Aires with that dreadful sister of his. He never wanted his daughter to meet our side of the family. Afraid of what we would tell her. He sentenced her to be raised by Gloria."

"Sentenced?"

"Sentenced! Gloria McMasters is quite deranged and as mean as cat pee! Always was. She married that Otto Brutmann, an Austrian émigré to Argentina. A fascist, from what I've heard! It is all too distressing for words. Such rubbish! To think of that lovely child being thrown to those wolves. But there was nothing we could do."

"Do you think she'll come back to San Francisco now?"

"For the funeral, you mean? Who can say? We have had no contact for over twenty years. She was in Swiss schools for a while. Friends of your parents, the Bryans, I believe, had a daughter in the same school for a year."

"As McMasters' only child she should stand to inherit the company?" Albert asked.

"I suppose, unless the old devil somehow arranged to keep control of the estate out of her hands. There's just no telling what arrangements that old malefactor might have contrived. Such bunkum!"

"You know, Auntie," Albert said topping off her glass, "I vaguely remember Katherine as an infant. I must say I would be somewhat curious to meet her."

"I doubt they will even tell her that her father died until after it's too late. After all, they've done a superb job of keeping her away from San Francisco for over twenty years now."

"Perhaps we should take the initiative and try placing a call to Buenos Aires."

"A good idea, Albert, but we don't have a number and I hardly know how we would go about obtaining one on Sunday afternoon."

"Yes, I suppose you do have a point."

"As a matter of fact, we don't even know for sure if Katherine is in South America. Nor for that matter what kind of reception we would receive. If she knows anything about us it is quite certain that it is not very positive. Stanley and that witch Gloria have undoubtedly fed her enough lies to sink the Queen Mary. Gloria McMasters von Brutmann is the most unacceptable human being on the face of God's good earth. She truly is. The most peculiarly unbalanced person I have ever met. I remember I had a poor impression of her the first time I laid eyes on her, even before Elizabeth and Stanley were engaged. Then the first thing we knew, she was off and married to that damned Nazi."

Well into the second bottle of champagne Aunt Louisa became easily sidetracked and was rambling on when Ivy appeared, nervously crossing the conservatory with fluttering little steps as if she were one of the finches in the large Victorian brass cage in the middle of the room. Ivy's appearance and manner resembled that of an English sparrow as she flittered along through life with her simple gray suits always in perfect order and her salt-and-pepper hair tightly pulled into a small bun at the back of her head. If Albert had Chow-Ling to shadow his life and fill in the necessary details, Aunt Louisa had Ivy.

"Your father is on the line, Mr. Albert," Ivy informed him.

"Christ, I had quite forgotten about George and Victoria," he said with a sigh. I suppose I really should have called. You know how upset Mother will be with all the publicity."

"Ask them about the funeral arrangements," Aunt Louisa commanded.

Albert's father was short and to the point. "Where have you been? We have been trying to reach you for the last two days."

"Sailing in Sausalito, Father," he said, being careful not to apologize. "I told Mother at the beginning of the week that I would be in Marin. Perhaps she forgot."

"I assume you have read the paper," he continued in a grim tone.

"Yes, I was just discussing the situation with Aunt Louisa and ..."

"Most disagreeable," he interrupted. "Needless to say, your mother is undone by all this. I would have thought that you at least might have had the courtesy to call."

"But I only just arrived and I was going to call as soon as I had talked a little with Aunt Louisa. She is really rather hysterical." At this he waved his hand in a mocking gesture at his aunt, who was amused at being made the object of his excuse.

"Ask them about the funeral, Albert," Aunt Louisa interjected with bulldog determination.

With this remark Albert saw his chance and turned the phone over as his mother came on the other end.

"Hello Victoria, your Auntie Louisa here," she said in a tone of thinly contrived sympathy. Then after exchanging a few pleasantries, she moved in for the kill. "Heard anything about the funeral Victoria?" Albert could tell there was an awkward pause at the other end as his mother tried to gather herself.

"I know Victoria, it would be difficult for you," Aunt Louisa continued, "but please let me know; I wouldn't miss going for all the tea in China." There was another long pause before Aunt Louisa added, "I wonder if it will be an open casket. Perhaps I'll bring a hatpin just to make sure he's dead. Of course, if I had my way, I'd have a stake driven through his heart at high noon." Without waiting for her niece to respond, Aunt Louisa said good-bye and handed the phone back to Albert who, taking the advantage of his mother's apparent state of shock, promised to call later, said good-bye and hung up.

"I think you rather shocked Mother, Auntie," he said with a smile that was a mixture of guilt and satisfaction. "You ought to be ashamed of yourself!"

"Ashamed my foot," Aunt Louisa cried in glee, "those dotty old fools ought to be having a good time for themselves, instead they choose to make a bloody trauma out of McMasters' death. That bastard murdered her sister!"

"I think it's all the publicity that has shaken them," Albert explained, half trying to present his parents' position, and half realizing he enjoyed goading Aunt Louisa on.

"Oh, publicity!" Aunt Louisa said with a discounting wave of her hand as she picked up her glass of champagne. "Who cares what they print in the newspapers? It doesn't count for spit."

Unlike Albert's parents, who assiduously guarded their social position and worried about their image as social leaders in the community, Aunt Louisa viewed her position in society as a source of strength and as a resource for adventure. Where Aunt Louisa often felt exhilarated by challenges, his parents felt vulnerable. Albert had always identified rather more with Aunt Louisa's attitude, finding his parents to be a bit stuffy if not rather full of themselves. As far as he was concerned, the family history, with all of its interesting characters, was a rich tapestry to be enjoyed rather than a religious relic to be worshiped. But therein lay the source of much of the exasperation his parents and he felt for each other.

"I'm afraid you missed an unforgettable performance," Aunt Louisa said when Albert joined her the next morning for breakfast in the East Dining Room.

"Sorry, Auntie, I was just too tired for Sullivan. Who did Ed have on?"

Aunt Louisa motioned for Prentice to bring a copy of the *Examiner* from the side table.

"Merola dead!" Albert exclaimed seeing the headlines. "He died at the concert?"

"Accompanying Brunetta Mazzolini in Un Bel Di from the Madame Butterfly, from what the paper says. I remember when he started in 1923."

"I suppose Kurt Herbert Adler will be the new general director."

"He's my choice!" Aunt Louisa interjected.

"Jeepers! What a way to come in!"

"The papers say that Merola suddenly stopped and fell forward from the conductor's stand so that he landed with his feet up," Albert quoted as he sipped a glass of freshly squeezed orange juice. "I think the Italians believe it is bad luck to die on one's feet," he continued, trying to remember if the superstition was Italian or Greek.

"If that's the case, Gaetano deserved to die bottoms up," Aunt Louisa added thoughtfully. "And conducting one of his favorite compositions with his own orchestra. He could not have planned it better. There are days, perhaps, when the gods do smile."

"Of course, McMasters died the same way," Albert added as he scanned the papers for information on the funeral.

"Don't be absurd Albert."

"I'll stop by the PU Club and see what I can find out. My guess is that they will bury him from Grace Cathedral with as much ceremony as old Bishop Teeter can muster. They were drinking partners, you know. I used to see them getting plastered over lunch at the club. The old Bishop could hardly make it down the steps and back across Taylor to his office."

"I think I'll call Dotty McMasters and see if she knows anything," she said, pondering the possibility. "She just might, although they've been divorced for years. The poor dear married Stanley only five years after he murdered Kate. Of course, she was from Chicago and from what I've heard she hardly knew him at all, which explains why she married him in the first place."

"Do you know her?" Albert asked, questioning the propriety of calling Stanley's ex-wife.

"Of course," she continued, not giving his question much thought. "I've met her several times over the years at parties and she worked very diligently, I must say, for our Red Cross Volunteers during the war. Evidently she married him on the rebound from her first husband, who ran off with some sort of gypsy flamenco dancer from Seville."

"It doesn't sound very civil to me," Albert interjected, pleased with such a clever pun so early in the day.

"Yes it was Seville, I am quite sure," Aunt Louisa continued, taking no notice of his little joke. "I shall call her immediately and see what I can uncover. Strange when you think about it. The Bishop married Stanley to his second wife even though she was a divorcee. I bet that cost Stanley a sizable donation."

Aunt Louisa's call to Dotty McMasters was cordial and provided an intriguing piece of information.

"Imagine the old goat!" she said as she hung up the phone. "He was engaged to be married!"

"Married? To whom?"

"A Monique Somebody, I think." she said, "Morales or Manahan or something like that. Can you imagine? A Monique! And she's only 35! Young enough to be his daughter. Monique my hat!"

"When were they going to be married?"

"Dotty didn't know, but she thought it might have been soon."

"Did she know about the funeral?"

"No, but she was under the impression that the corporation would probably be making arrangements and she suggested giving a call to Phillip Addison's office. He is still acting President of McMasters Shipping. Evidently one of the foursome. They had finished the first nine when Stanley died. He was probably losing and had a heart attack to get out of paying his debts. Monique! Can you imagine, and young enough to be his daughter! I wouldn't be surprised if she's from Los Angeles. I can't wait to see her in mourning."

"She should be in mourning," Albert said sarcastically.

Aunt Louisa looked puzzled for a moment and then laughed. "Yes, I see what you mean … so close to a fortune and yet so far. The poor little femme entretenue. We simply must get that schedule for the funeral!"

Albert began to understand the need to act quickly if he was to get back to the city. Aunt Louisa, like a terrier after a rabbit was on one of her tears, and would not be stopped until she got what she was after. Playing to her focus he seized the moment. "If I don't leave now, Auntie, I won't make the club by lunch and won't be able to find out anything." With this said, Prentice was summoned to have the car brought around.

"Now be sure and call this afternoon, Albert, and don't forget to call your parents. I don't want to be blamed for alienation of affection. I'll call Victoria after you leave and tell her you're on your way. I forgot to call them last night after 'What's My Line'."

"Yes, yes, of course, Auntie," he agreed, slipping Windsor a scone under the table. "I leave you to your plots, coffee and curiosity."

As he stepped out into the central court, he could tell that it was going to be a beautiful warm day. There was not a trace of fog over the hills and the temperature was already approaching a comfortable seventy degrees. The sweet dry smell of California summer had replaced the cold dampness of the day before and as Andrew pulled the Buick around, Albert decided to put the top down and enjoy the sun on the drive back into town. Soon he was motoring up the Bayshore with Windsor perched on the passenger side, his nose held directly into the breeze as if he were in charge of navigation.

As they rolled toward the city on the ribbon of highway wedged between the still-green bay and the soft gold San Bruno Mountains, Albert could not help feeling exhilarated. Suddenly he began to feel that this whole business with Stanley McMasters was a waste of time. Why, he asked himself, should he spend such a superb day trying to find out the time and place of the funeral of a man he never really knew? The whole business seemed a little shabby when set against the freshness of the morning. He watched a lone sailboat making long slow graceful swoops as it crisscrossed the water not far offshore, and he thought of a warm afternoon spent around the pool at Treehaven, or reading on the porch in Sausalito. By the time he reached his apartment on Telegraph Hill, he was convinced he needed to escape. All he needed was a plan.

If there is anybody in San Francisco who could get a scoop, it was his old friend Charlie Cahoun down at the *Examiner*. And by the time Chow-Ling had leashed Windsor for his mid-day walk up to Coit Tower, Albert had Charlie on the phone.

"Charlie, Albert Devonshire here. I have a favor to ask."

"Yeah, I bet you do. What is it? I have a deadline!"

"Can you get me the time of the McMasters funeral? It wasn't in the paper."

"I'll get back to you!" Charlie yelled, slamming down the receiver.

Charlie had worked on the *Examiner* since Hearst hired him back in the 1920s and as far as Albert was concerned, he was the shrewdest reporter around. He had a nose for a good story and the connections to find out whatever he needed to know. Albert was one of those connections and Charlie had long ago stopped keeping track of who owed whom a favor. By the time Chow-Ling and Windsor returned from their walk, Charlie had the date and time. Stanley McMasters would be buried from Grace Cathedral Thursday September 3rd at 11:00 a.m.

Freedom was now within his grasp. All he had to do was relate the information to Aunt Louisa, then go past his parents to make the obligatory call. The thought of the afternoon produced a hundred possibilities. He could go riding in Woodside where he kept his horse Pegasus, or he could return across the Golden Gate to his cottage in Sausalito. Perhaps Deirdre would be in the mood for a sail, or he could relax on the porch with a gin and tonic and watch her paint. There was also Golden Gate Park and the enjoyment of a solitary day walking through the zoo or the De Young. As he pondered the possibilities, Charlie called back.

"I've got some additional info. McMasters' daughter is due in Wednesday at 4:00 p.m. A flight from South America. I'm on this story. I posed as a goddamned airline representative to get the confirmation from McMasters shipping."

"Jesus, you're as clever as an old bird dog, Charlie," Albert said, congratulating him.

"Yeah, well, this is a big story, Pal. The airport will be crawling with reporters. Your cousin's something of a mystery woman, having spent her whole life abroad. Now she's returning the probable heir to one of the city's great fortunes. It's dynamite copy. I would appreciate any little scraps you might throw my way."

"You'll probably be closer to this than I am," Albert cajoled, guarding against any obligation to supply information to the press about a family member. "I'm not sure if she will even see our side of the family. They've kept her pretty isolated from us over the past twenty years. But listen, pal, thanks for the info. I really didn't feel like playing the bloody family detective."

"Oh, just one more thing. It's probably nothing, but it's a little odd. There was no post-mortem."

"Gee, I thought they always had to do an autopsy unless you croaked in the hospital."

"Usually, but evidently McMasters was playing golf with his doctor and he signed off on the death certificate."

"Can they do that?"

"If he had seen him as a patient in the last ten days and the coroner agrees to it. Bit unusual, but it happens."

"Interesting." Albert paused. "Tell me who else was in the foursome?"

"Damned if I know. Why?"

"Oh, I don't know. Just curious, I guess. Listen, I'll buy you a drink later this week."

As he hung up the phone Albert looked at his calendar and then at his watch. It was 11:30 Monday August 31, and his cousin was not to arrive for another forty-eight hours. All he needed was to placate his parents with a short visit and make a call to Aunt Louisa. He changed into comfortable old cords and stared into the closet for the appropriate pair of shoes. His riding boots were in Woodside, but it was going to be a hot. He could not imagine taking Pegasus for a ride in the 90-degree heat. Nor could he visualize a day in the park with the hordes of children not yet back in school. "It's Sausalito," he thought as his eyes passed over a pair of sandals.

There was another reason for going to Sausalito. It lay half formed at the back of his mind. McMaster's unsavory reputation was well known and Albert had the inclination to touch base with an old friend who knew the wharves.

Luck was with him. When he called Aunt Louisa she was having her Monday morning conference with the head gardener, and he was able to leave all the information with Ivy. He had similar luck with his parents. His father was at the office and his Mother surprisingly enough, had gone off for Monday lunch at the St. Francis.

As he headed the car down Lombard his decision to go to Marin was confirmed by the promise of a brilliant afternoon. The bay was as smooth as polished glass in the summer sun. The temperature was climbing towards the eighties, producing what San Franciscans call a heat wave. He could smell the garlic as he passed North Beach and Washington Square was filled with old Italians napping on park benches beneath their wide-brimmed hats and the lofty twin spires of St. Peter and Paul's Church.

Just over the Golden Gate and around the corner from the city, Sausalito always provided a superb sense of isolation. At about one o'clock in the afternoon he turned the car into the narrow parking strip and climbed down the irregular steps of the garden. On the far side of the lot a row of sunflowers stood at attention in the hot afternoon sun. Coming down between the lines of beans and sweet peas, he could see Deirdre painting at the end of the front porch. She saw him too and raised her large dark eyes and smiled knowingly before returning to her painting.

Albert had known Deirdre since meeting her in Berkeley in 1939 when he was a freshman and she was a junior at Cal. After being wounded in the South Pacific and discharged in 1942, he returned home to find her painting in an attic apartment. He owned a seldom-used cottage on Buckley Avenue that he had inherited from his grandfather, and since he was back finishing university, he suggested Deirdre live in the cottage and look after the place. It was not long before they were again lovers and he found himself spending more and more weekends in Marin. By the time he had finished his degree and moved back to San Francisco, Deirdre had become an indispensable part of his life.

Deirdre was not like the thin, refined blonde debutantes that his Mother and Father were always arranging for him as dinner partners. Her strong voluptuous body was beautifully formed and reminded him of Renoir's Nude in Sunlight. She was of Hungarian descent and for Albert she was the unique and irresistible combination of earth mother and fire spirit. She was the synthesis of those primary elements and on foggy nights they would often build a fire, go to bed early and make love for slow sensuous hours. She had the most beautifully formed breasts of any woman he had ever known, and nothing in life gave him more pleasure than to wrap his being within their circumference both before and after experiencing the quickness of her fire.

What made their relationship so perfect was that neither of them were the least bit interested in marriage. Deirdre was a sort of happy existentialist. She saw the universe as essentially meaningless, but she nevertheless rejoiced in the patterns of life as they played and danced through her art. And for Deirdre her life and her art had merged into a workable harmony. Her art was her life. Albert made her art possible by keeping her in the Sausalito cottage, and she made his life possible by being there without expectation or inquiry into his comings and goings. It was an ideal arrangement worked out over time to their mutual advantage and delight.

Life at "Garden Cottage," as they called the place, assumed an unhurried rhythm of its own. Deirdre, unlike Chow-Ling, Aunt Louisa, or his parents, felt that traditions were at best amusingly quaint, and at worst, the sentimental occupation of a decadent bourgeoisie. They slept when they slept, awoke when they awoke. Deirdre painted and Albert either read, or went sailing. They made love and ate at odd hours. Friends stopped in to engage one or both in conversation before wandering off again. Sometimes they gave parties and read poetry. The cats slept in the window seat or hunted field mice on the grassy hillsides,

As Albert came round the porch he stopped to observe the process on the abstract creation Deirdre had entitled "Persephone in Exile No. 11". His favorite cat scooted out the screen door. He reached down, flipped Pedro over and roughed up his yellow undercoat in ritualistic play.

Without a word he went into the kitchen, poured a glass of wine and came back to settle horizontally into the porch swing. He awoke hours later. Deirdre had finished painting and was sitting in her wicker chair looking out at the sun as it caught the western side of Angel Island. She poured another glass of wine and together they sat for several hours, listening to the crickets and frogs and smelling the pungent sweetness of thistle and eucalyptus mixed with the salt breeze off the bay. Finally as the slow night came on, he broke the silence. "Did you pick basil this morning?"

"Yes" was the answer.

"I'll boil some pasta," he said, as he rolled off the swing.

"I'll get the salad," replied Deirdre disappearing down into the garden to pick a few tomatoes and greens.

They moved inside and ate dinner by an oil lamp on the old pine table.

After dinner Deirdre took her shawl off the peg and they went down through the garden arm in arm. Within two blocks they were walking along San Carlos Avenue watching the lights reflecting on the bay and listening to the waves as they lapped against the sea wall. After a while, Deirdre spoke from somewhere out of their mutual silence.

"The sea is our soft grave,
An unrecorded history
The womb out of and to which
The agony carries forth and returns

On the currents of time
Terrible. Terrible. Mother Sea
Comfort us in our primitive terror."

Back in the cottage, Deirdre lit the oil lamp and went into the alcove at the far end of the main room. She took off her shawl and draped it over a chair. As she looked back over her left shoulder Albert came up behind her and put his arms around her waist. He rooted his way through her rich black hair and ran the end of his tongue from her shoulder to her ear. She arched her back accepting each caress as she ran her fingers across his forearm. His hands moved to encompass her shapely breasts, which he gently held up and massaged in a firm circular movement. Feeling the urging surge of passion rise through his loins he untied the strings that crisscrossed the front of her peasant blouse, and lifted her breasts free. His mouth closed on her neck and she began to moan softly.

He loved to undress Deirdre and slowly make love to each part of her body as they went along. Sometimes he recited portions of Andrew Marvel's poem "To His Coy Mistress" or other verses in order to slow and extend their passion. Deirdre had taught him much about the art of making love. How to hold back and extend the ecstasy of the moment. How to give and receive pleasure. She had also taught him other forms of lovemaking, but on this night their love was the slow love of known lovers who still found in each other treasured gifts to be consumed slowly as if they were a fine Bordeaux. From the moment he penetrated her, he locked his eyes onto hers. They held each other in a hypnotic gaze. She loved to have Albert inside her, to grasp at his hard, lithe body as they defined the rhythm of their love making. She was after all an artist, and Albert was classically handsome; with distinctively aristocratic features and a body like a sculpture from a Greek temple. But it was his eyes that captivated her. They were at times calm, almost a contemplative blue-green. There was an enigmatic fatherly quality to them that was at once compassionate and coolly discerning. At other times they appeared darker and more mischievous, suggesting that just below the surface there was an irrepressible youth, aided by a creatively playful intellect. Tonight, however, it was the cool, determined father who held her.

"Albert! Oh, Albert!" she sighed as her whole body shuddered with pleasure.

Placing his mind over a void, he held his desire, slowed his pace and remained still. For several moments he did not move as she momentarily slept. Then slowly she stirred, and with her stirring, he resumed again. He moved gently at first, until her body told him she was ready. This time he gave himself up. For a moment their egos collapsed into each other and they were without duality. When they returned, they lay together for a long time, listening to the breath that rose and fell between them, and in his mind her words returned: "Terrible, terrible Mother sea. Comfort us in our primitive terror."

When he woke the next morning Deirdre had been replaced by her favorite cat, Cassandra, who had stretched herself out in a ray of sunlight that fell across the quilted bedspread. He reached for Cassandra and stroked her short black coat to a contented purr. Deirdre was already at her easel and not wishing conversation, he watched her through the screen door as he drank his coffee and finished the end of a hard French roll.

Around ten o'clock he walked down to the village and found Rigg. At 6'6" Rig was the composite image of the rugged longshoreman. His long, tight muscles stretched over his enormous frame, which always seemed a little out of place when he was inside. His balding head was also large and his great broad face sported a thick sandy beard, which he tended to pull thoughtfully with his powerful weathered hands. In addition to working the docks, Rigg fished and wrote poetry on off days, but his real passion was politics. When he was worked up over an issue, he waved his great hands over his head and roared with thunderous protests.

They spent several hours talking about the accusations of the Attorney General that the country's labor unions were filled with Communists.

"The whole damned country is paranoid." Rigg boomed. "They jailed Jack Hall in Hawaii in July. Now this goddamned fool of a Congressman from New York said that if Hawaii became a state the two Senators would be Soviet agents because the longshoreman's union could deliver fifty to sixty thousand votes. I'll be goddamned if any of those apes could deliver fifty votes, let alone fifty thousand."

Albert enjoyed seeing Rigg steamed. He was usually such an easygoing fellow that the contrast was entertaining and Albert added a little fuel to the fire.

"According to the newspaper, the Senate Commerce Committee said the nation's piers are lawless frontiers plagued by corruption, Communism and racketeering," he said, watching Rigg turn red with anger.

"Racketeering my ass!" Rigg shouted, reaching into his shirt pocket and pulling out a pack of Lucky Strikes. He tapped one on the table, lit it and tossed the pack across the table. "Sure there's corruption on the docks, but no more so than on Montgomery Street. Look at those excessive cost overruns Kaiser charged the Air Force to build those transport planes. For Christ's sake, there is enough stock manipulation and double-dealing to embarrass the whole goddamned Defense Department. Corruption and Communists on the piers ... shit!"

"I thought there were more Communists in the Protestant clergy," Albert interjected, trying to disguise the note of sarcasm and a mocking grin.

"Clergymen, longshoremen, Bohemians ... they'll get us all in the end," Rigg said, taking a long drag on his cigarette. "The next thing you know they will be accusing Mamie Eisenhower of being a Communist."

"What do you know about Stanley McMasters?" Albert asked.

"Other than the fact he's dead?"

"Ya."

"He was a son of a bitch. No friend of the working man, that's for damn sure."

"Did he have any enemies?"

"You mean did someone put him on ice?"

"Ya, I guess so."

"I wouldn't be surprised. Son of a bitch. A lot of people hated his guts, and not only Labor."

"Like who?"

"Well, take the Air Force cancellation of the Kaiser contracts. We're talking two hundred million bucks worth of C-119 Flying Boxcars and C-123 Assault Troop Carriers."

"What's that got to do with McMasters?"

"Think! What business is McMasters in?"

"Shipping."

"Ya. And if you can get troops and equipment across the Pacific faster and cheaper in C-119's or C-123's, what does that do to the shipping industry?"

"Are you saying McMasters was responsible for canceling Kaiser's contract?"

"I'm not saying anything, except what's in the papers."

"Kaiser bought a 49 percent interest in Chase Aircraft after the contracts were awarded. That embarrassed the hell out of the Air Force."

"So?"

"So who got Senator Bridges to start an investigation?"

"McMasters?"

"Your guess is as good as mine. All I know is over 5,600 workers were fired because the contracts were cancelled. The United Auto Workers are not too happy about that. Neither I guess is old Henry Kaiser."

"Interesting."

"Ya I think so, but what's your connection with this, anyway?" Rig asked, a quizzical look spreading across his big face.

"Stanley McMasters was my uncle by marriage."

"No shit!" Rig looked startled and uncharacteristically uneasy.

"That's OK. I didn't know the man. In fact, my family hated him. I was asking more out of morbid curiosity than anything else."

A few hours later Albert wandered back up the hill to Garden Cottage where Deirdre was still absorbed in her painting. He read and napped on and off for the rest of the afternoon before deciding to head back to the city.

As he drove back across the Golden Gate Bridge, a fiery sun was setting to the southwest lighting up the great soaring towers of the bridge. A golden day died, making way for the darkness that would fill in the bay waters with shadows and make the city lights flash and shimmer in the distance. In that moment of September twilight with time caught between opposites not a ripple broke the ageless surface of the bay. A freighter inched slowly through the Gate and out towards the open ocean. He recognized the markings, which identified the ship as part of the McMasters fleet and his thoughts turned toward the arrival of his cousin the following afternoon.

CHAPTER 4

*T*HE NEXT MORNING Albert awoke to a mixed chorus of foghorns from Point Blunt, Alcatraz and Line Point. They were accompanied by diaphones bellowing and grunting bass from Yerba Buena Island to mid-channel on the Golden Gate Bridge. The symphony told him that a great fog bank had penetrated deep into the bay. Chow-Ling brought coffee early so he would have a chance to spend a few leisurely hours with Windsor and the paper before heading over to Pacific Heights for the long-delayed visit with his parents.

Like Aunt Louisa, Albert's side of the family had its roots placed firmly in the rich soil of California history. His mother claimed an interesting array of ancestors, including a Spanish foot soldier, a notorious madam, a Main Line debutante, an Anglo Greek merchant and a founding member of the Pioneers of California. It was said in the family that from this unlikely mixture Albert inherited his good looks. "The perfect balance of the Hellenistic and Anglo" as his mother maintained. Yet despite all the rich diversity of their backgrounds the Devonshires were on the whole as dull as Aunt Louisa was exciting. Like so many in San Francisco society, the family for several generations had taken it upon itself to affect English tastes and attitudes, if not the English appreciation for eccentricity. They all sooner or later became Episcopalians and began to see themselves as a sort of Western aristocracy, trustees as it were, of civilization and culture in their City by the Bay.

Albert, their only son, was a bit of a disappointment. It wasn't that he was opposed to the concept of duty. Indeed, he had a keen appreciation for it and had gladly put his life on the line by answering his country's call during the war. Nor did he lack compassion. There was hardly a worthy cause in San Francisco that had not benefited from his support. He was intensely loyal to friends, kind to strangers and generous with his time and considerable fortune. Yet despite all these positive attributes, there was something in his character that bothered those who put stock in conformity. He enjoyed life a little too much, and while he did not go out of his way to flaunt conventions, he couldn't much be bothered with them either. Perhaps it had been the war, his first-hand witness to the agony of it all. And perhaps it had been the years with Chow Ling, the washing in Confucian and Taoist principles, but Albert had developed an oddly detached philosophical outlook and an inexhaustibly audacious sense of humor. On one level, he believed in the need to celebrate living through engagement and correct action, while at the same time a parallel belief existed that accepted the futility and absurdity in human existence.

Upon his arrival, Daniels, his parents' butler, informed him that he had missed his father, but that his mother was waiting for him in the upstairs sitting room. Relieved that he had only one parent to confront, Albert made his way up the great mahogany staircase under the watchful eyes of the ancestors whose portraits encompassed the central hall. As remote and impersonal as ledgers, these were the dead who had left him a comfortable fortune and now seemed to sit in judgment. He found his mother in her blue lace dressing gown, sitting quite still in her favorite chair, which on a good day commanded a sweeping view of the Bay from the Marin Headlands to Treasure Island. Today however, was not a good day, and his mother's mood matched the weather. Her whole body seemed tense, except for her hands, which methodically worked a piece of needlepoint. He could tell she was still upset about the attention the family had received as a result of McMasters' death.

"How are you doing Mother?" he asked sympathetically as he leaned over and kissed her cheek.

"We are surviving Albert," she answered in a flat, weary tone. "God will always supply the strength to surmount every misfortune."

It was characteristic of Victoria Devonshire to sum up uncomfortable situations with a piece of general triviality and since he did not particularly wish to discuss the matter with her, Albert quickly moved to change the subject by inquiring where his father was, although he knew very well that he had gone off to the bank.

"Your father has gone to the office, Albert. We must all go on. We cannot let ourselves be overcome by something that happened twenty years ago. Your father must go on and I must go on. We all have our responsibilities in life."

Albert detected the slightest degree of recrimination in the way she talked about responsibility and he decided to move the conversation back to safer ground. "Yes Mother," he said, trying to sound sincere. "I have some information about the funeral and about Katherine," he continued in an attempt to prepare her. Her expression did not change. Her lips remained tightly drawn and her pale blue eyes soft and undirected, but she did put down her needlepoint and slowly turned her head toward him as he slid into the armchair adjacent to hers. "Katherine is arriving today at four p.m. The funeral is set for eleven o'clock tomorrow morning at Grace Cathedral."

At first his mother did not respond. After a pause, which seemed like an eternity, she said, "I see," and turned back to her needlepoint. She had not seen her sister's child for over twenty years and now that she was returning home, she did not quite know what to think.

"I think I'll drive down to the airport this afternoon and meet the plane," Albert said after a while. "After all, she is my cousin."

Such a direct move would never have occurred to his mother who always proceeded in life only after the future had been pre-arranged to assure the maximum amount of predictability. The spontaneity of his proposal caught her by surprise. "Would you and Father care to come along?" he asked, not mentioning Aunt Louisa. He knew that his mother would feel obligated to come if her aunt was going. Such was the nature of the subtle competition between them.

After another long pause her answer came with hesitation. "Well, yes, I suppose so," she said, slowly fingering the yarn. "Although don't you think it might be a little overwhelming if we all go? It might be a bit unpleasant if Gloria and Otto are on the same plane. I shouldn't want a scene."

"I suppose they might be arriving at the same time," he said thoughtfully, "but I doubt they would create a scene with the press out in full force." He knew that he had now ensured that his parents would not go to the airport.

"Oh, I see," his Mother continued. "The press … well, yes, I hadn't thought about the press. I think we need to be very careful. Gloria can be very unpleasant."

"How do you mean?" he sensed a caution based on experience.

"I mean that Gloria has always been a highly emotional person. Very odd, you might say. She never really cared who she hurt as long as her own interests were served. She always was extremely possessive. I remember several years ago when your father and I were in Monteux, I attempted to see Katherine. She was attending St. Georges at the time. I called ahead but when I arrived, I was told she had been taken on an unexpected holiday to the south of France. Gloria evidently was informed. It was midterm. One can only assume."

His mother was not a direct person. Whenever she was faced with a person or situation that displeased her, she simply chose the path of avoidance. Consequently his curiosity was aroused by the intensity of her condemnation. "Would you say Gloria is unbalanced?" he asked, attempting to pursue the topic. There was yet another brief pause as his mother again took up her needlepoint.

"Oh," she said with a sigh, "I really find the entire matter too distasteful. I would rather not dwell upon it."

Whatever impulse it was that caused the brief shift in her personality, her desire to avoid rancor had returned, and he knew it was useless to pursue the topic any further. "I think it more advisable to contact Katherine through a note," she advised after a while. "But you do what you think is right, dear."

He spent another hour or so but they did not discuss Gloria, Katherine's arrival or Stanley's funeral. Instead, she reminisced about her childhood and the family home on California Street. It was as if she wanted to block out all the memories connected with her sister's life after her marriage to Stanley McMasters.

.

CHAPTER 5

*O*N HIS WAY down the Peninsula, Albert began to wonder if going to the airport was such a good idea after all. Perhaps his mother had been right when she had advised a more delicate approach. Deep in these considerations, the hit song "Keep It a Secret" by Jesse Ray Robinson and Johnny Mercer came over the radio. It was a bit uncanny, he thought. The song seemed to answer his doubts about going to the airport. What were the secrets surrounding this mysterious cousin he was going to meet? Her mother had always been something of an enigma and he felt that he had not been told her full story. There was something about her death that he did not understand. Perhaps no one did. It was nothing in particular, but a small something existed at the back of his mind that began to stimulate his curiosity and he was a very curious person. He had only been nine years old when his Aunt Elizabeth had died, but certain vivid images persisted. There had been something brilliant and exciting about her that grabbed at his attention like fireworks on Chinese New Year's. She had been extraordinarily beautiful, with pale silky skin like his Mother's, but with the most brilliant dark blue eyes that seemed to dance to the unfathomable depths of her soul. And her laughter ran like a thread of music through his memory.

Albert had no idea what his cousin looked like. He pictured her as either a nondescript schoolgirl, or a haughty Euro-Argentinian. When he thought of her as being attractive, he saw her as being dark and mysterious, like her mother.

He watched the DC-3 come in over the bay and touch down at the far end of the field. It had turned out to be a hot September day after all and from the airport the golden-brown hills of the Peninsula studded with oaks and eucalyptus stood in dramatic contrast to the deep blue of the sky. He became annoyed with the jostling of reporters as the plane taxied toward the building. He wondered how Aunt Louisa was faring. Her arthritis was bad, and he had insisted she wait in the car with the promise that he would bring Katherine to her. She agreed, principally because she hated wheelchairs. The thought of poor old Andrew waiting with her passed through Albert's mind. "Poor old chap," he thought, "she'll probably make him drive around the parking lot just to keep moving."

Albert noticed a tall, distinguished gentleman in a three-piece pinstripe suit. He had the bearing of a colonel he had known in the Army, for he seemed to be standing perpetually at attention. But when the plane came down the field, the gentleman's demeanor suddenly changed and he began arching his neck from side to side and shifting back and forth on his feet. Albert studied him for a moment and thought he looked familiar. He was about six feet tall, slender and balding. His pale cheeks sagged slightly. Albert judged him to be in his mid-sixties. It was his eyes, however, that caught Albert's attention. There was a sadness there along with a subtle intensity that made him look like a man just returned from the front line of a battle. A lady dressed in a nondescript gray suit and sensible shoes accompanied him, and judging by the leather portfolio she was carrying, she was his secretary. Suddenly Albert remembered having seen him at the Bohemian Club but by now the plane had come to a stop and the ground crew was pushing out the metal steps and securing them to the doors. As passengers started to disembark, Albert sorted through them trying to recognize anyone who might resemble his cousin. He couldn't seem to find a likely candidate. However, he did notice a tall blond-haired beauty in her late twenties wearing a light tweed suit with classic lines. There was a precision and grace to her movements that caused his eyes to return to her again and again. She was extraordinarily elegant. He watched her approach the door, slow her pace and search the waiting crowd until suddenly she seemed to recognize the gentleman in his mid-sixties. As he moved towards her, the press took their clue and rushed in. It was only then that Albert realized that this was his cousin. This was Katherine Louise McMasters and the gentleman was Phillip Addison, president of McMasters shipping. In the crush Mr. Addison protectively flanked her and with his secretary on the other side, started towards the door waving off the reporters with a commanding gesture. In the rapid pace of events Albert stood motionless. The whole scene was like something out of a Hollywood movie. Then he started to run and came around the crowd, until he blocked their path. Once in position he stopped and moved directly at them. He guided several reporters out of his path and recognizing several others, called them by name. Seeing Charlie Cahoun he shouted out a quick "Hey, Charlie!" Charlie returned the greeting. All this had the effect of changing the strategy of the reporters. He'd had drinks with a lot of these guys in the press, and most of them knew him pretty well. They also knew that he was related to the woman they were out to cover, and they helped him get close to her in the hope of getting their pictures or a statement. Within seconds Albert was able to stop the progress Addison was making. When he finally reached Katherine he said in a loud, firm voice, "Katherine Louise, I am your cousin, Edward Albert Devonshire. Welcome to San Francisco."

The use of her middle name jarred Katherine. She had never known anyone to use it before. The unexpected mob of reporters was disorienting after the long flight and she felt like someone awakening to bright lights after an anesthetic.

"My cousin?" she questioned stopping and looking at Albert. His voice seemed kind.

"Yes, your mother's nephew."

Impulsively Katherine held out her hand and found his grasp firm and reassuring.

"Welcome home," he said.

She felt her heart catch itself.

"You've changed quite a bit since you were a baby."

"Spontaneously she embraced him, kissing him on both cheeks before backing away to assess him at arm's length.

The interchange took place so quickly that Mr. Addison was not fully aware of what was happening. He tried to regain his lost momentum but without success. He called Katherine's name, but she ignored him. He had temporarily lost his charge to someone with the claim of family. Indeed it was the claim of family that Albert had instinctively used and it had caught everyone, including Katherine, by surprise.

After their brief greeting, Albert turned to the press, "Fellows, could we give you a statement and then call it a day?"

"Now just a minute," Addison objected, "I don't think we want to make any statements just now."

"Thank you Mr. Addison, but I think we can say just a few words to these gentlemen," Katherine interrupted. Then without a pause, she turned to the crowd of reporters and continued, "I have come home to the city of my birth to attend my father's funeral. I hope you gentlemen in the press will understand."

She was so direct and open that even some of the hard-nosed reporters were touched, not so much by what she said, but by the manner in which she said it. She was at once refined and sophisticated, warm and genuine. Above all, she was very much a woman who conveyed her femininity in every movement. In this she was very European. In contrast to her Continental manners, her looks were in every way Celtic. She was more striking than pretty with well-proportioned features and an aquiline nose that flared just enough at the nostrils to remind Albert of a well-bred and highly spirited racehorse. Her blond hair with red highlights was as natural as a fall leaf and her eyes were the most extraordinary shade of green, very much like Columbian emeralds. Albert judged her to be about five feet ten inches, with perfectly formed long, slender legs.

After taking a few questions from the press, she turned back to Albert.

"I came out today with our great-aunt Louisa," he said, ignoring the few reporters who still insisted upon asking questions.

"I'm afraid I don't know much about my family in California." She replied.

"I'm sorry," he apologized, realizing her confusion. "AuntLouisa is our great-aunt by marriage. Katherine Louise Huntsford Fitzhubert Harte is her full name. She married our grandfather's brother, Austin Jerome. She was very close to your mother. You were named for her."

Katherine felt as bewildered as a cat startled by its prey. These were the people she had always dreamed of finding and they had found her. It was not the way she had imagined. This cousin had simply appeared and after so many years of conditioning she could not help but feel wary. She looked at Albert again with a more critical eye. He appeared very much the gentleman and very handsome—tall, athletic, with wavy black hair and clear wistful blue eyes.

"Yes," she finally said; bringing herself back to the conversation after what she feared must have been an embarrassingly long pause. "You say my aunt is here?"

"She's waiting in the car. She's rather crippled with arthritis at eighty-three, but she would very much like to greet you."

"Of course," was the only reply she could make before turning to Phillip Addison. "I would like to see my great-aunt before we leave."

Addison looked frustrated, but he could do nothing. He followed with his secretary as they walked across the tile floor towards the front door of the small Spanish terminal, the press following at a civilized distance. There outside the building, waiting in her old black Cadillac limousine, was the woman who had waited for over twenty years for this moment. Andrew stood at attention and as they approached the car, opened the back door. Katherine leaned forward putting her head into the back compartment. "Katherine!" was all Aunt Louisa could say and beckoned her to climb in. Albert followed, pulling down the side seat. The door closed and they were momentarily isolated from Phillip Addison and the press. Katherine was immediately drawn to her great-aunt. With an uncompromising candor she looked straight into Aunt Louisa's light blue eyes, only to find a keenness of will that seemed to match her own.

"I am Katherine McMasters," she said, "I understand that you are my great-aunt. It was very kind of you to come out to meet me."

For once in her life Albert thought Aunt Louisa was going to be speechless. Finally, after giving Katherine a steady assessment, she turned and opened her arms. Katherine turned too and leaned forward to receive the embrace.

"I remember you as a child, my dear. I remember your hair. It is still the color of spun gold. You were so loved, so precious; and to think—" she did not finish but simply stared at Katherine, gently shaking her head.

For some reason Katherine felt an odd sort of familiarity. She thought perhaps it was the old lady's voice. It was a deep opulent voice like a fine brandy. Yet it sparkled around the edges like the best champagne. "Yes," she thought, "It is the voice," and for a split second she saw something that had been lost long ago.

"What is it my dear?" she heard the voice saying, and could not find what it was she had momentarily captured and lost again.

"Oh nothing," Katherine replied. "It's just that it was a long flight."

Where are you staying? Did anyone come to meet you?"

Aunt Louisa bombarded Katherine with questions, but finally she stopped long enough to allow her to answer.

"Mr. Addison, my father's president, came with his secretary. They have made the arrangements. I think he is a little agitated that I have not entirely cooperated with his schedule."

"Oh never mind," Aunt Louisa said. "You are welcome to come and stay with us in Hillsborough. You need to rest after your long flight, and—"

"I'm afraid Mr. Addison has me staying at my father's home in the city, at least until after the funeral."

"Perhaps then you will come to dinner. You must. Your mother was so very dear to me, you see, and I want to get to know her daughter."

"Yes of course," Katherine said, reaching over and squeezing Aunt Louisa's hand. "I will want to get to know you, too."

They became aware of Phillip Addison again, for Andrew opened the door to say that Mr. Addison was insistent that Miss McMasters come with him.

"Katherine!" Aunt Louisa said, becoming very agitated, "don't trust any of those cutthroats. Don't trust any of them! There's small choice in rotten apples!"

Katherine felt taken aback. She was not sure to whom her Aunt referred. She wanted to ask but knew it was not the time.

"Might I have a telephone number?" she asked, turning towards Albert.

"Yes of course," he said, taking a card from his pocket. "Let me write down my number in San Francisco and Aunt Louisa's in Hillsborough."

"Thank you. I will call within the next day or so," she said, slipping the card into her purse.

"Also I must mention before letting you go, that my mother, your Aunt Victoria, wanted very much to come and see you today. She would have come, but she is not feeling very well."

There was long pause and she seemed to stare right through him, she felt as if she were removed to a distant time and place.

"My mother's sister," she said, "yes, I must see her."

With these words she climbed out of the car and only when she was out and a few steps away did she turn and go back. Leaning over again, she looked into the car across to where Aunt Louisa was sitting. She gazed at her for a few moments. "Thank you for coming to meet me," she said leaning forward and embracing her again. Then suddenly she turned and with a subtle wink she took Albert's face between the palms of her hands and kissed his forehead, "And thank you too, my cousin." And with that, she left.

It wasn't until Katherine settled into the back of the company limousine that the experience of meeting her relatives began to take full effect. She rested her head against the grey flannel seat and shut her eyes. Gloria's voice, sharp and splintering like broken glass echoed down through long years. "They are not the sort of people you would want to know. They wouldn't want anything to do with you."

"Mother's family," she thought. "They were there waiting for me the moment I stepped off the plane. Waiting for me, embracing me, inviting me into their homes." She felt her heart expanding as if it were a butterfly emerging from a cocoon.

She tried to remember what it was that had flashed through her memory at the sound of her aunt's voice. It would not come back. She heard another voice. It belonged to Mr. Addison.

"You must be very tired after your long flight."

"Yes," she said struggling to bring herself away from her thoughts. "It was a very long flight."

"We will be coming into the city in a few minutes. It won't be long before we are at the house." He seemed concerned and much like she remembered he had been during their brief meeting in Brussels two years before. They drove along the Bayshore and into the city, crossed Market Street and Civic Center Plaza before continuing on up to Pacific Heights. Here were all the landmarks she had known in pictures: The Bay Bridge, The Ferry Building, and the Opera House and City Hall with its classically extravagant Renaissance Architecture. She could not help but feel excited.

But the moment she entered her father's house her mood changed. She felt a stagnant weight in the old Victorian as if a terrible emptiness dwelt there. The dark paneling and heavy drapes made the rooms seem like caves and there was a musty smell like dead cigar smoke trapped in damp velvet.

Mr. and Mrs. Deng, her father's servants, were polite but seemed to operate from behind a thick wall of impenetrable silence. Their appearance, even when anticipated, startled Katherine. They carried her luggage up the long staircase to a second floor room where she bathed and changed into a simple striped corduroy skirt and velvet blouse before rejoining Mr. Addison in one of the double drawing rooms.

"Tell me, how did Father die?" she asked as he handed her a cocktail. For a moment he looked taken aback by her directness.

"It was a heart attack. We had been playing golf and ..." He stopped and took a sip of Scotch. "He went to the locker room after the ninth hole. The rest of us were on the tenth tee when we heard. We rushed in. Dr. Whitmore was there. It was a massive attack, very quick. He didn't suffer."

"Had he heart trouble?"

"Yes, a little. He was diabetic, you know."

"No, I didn't."

"For several years now. He didn't want people to know."

"Yes, that sounds like Father," she said trying to disguise the note of sarcasm she felt in her voice.

"Would you like me to freshen your drink?" Addison asked, moving towards the side table.

"No thank you." She felt a certain awkwardness in his manner.

"There is the matter of your father's will," he said slowly. "I'm not sure if this is the appropriate time but if you would like to know the general outline ... I had the company attorneys prepare a copy for you. It's a lengthy document but I could give you a general idea of its contents." He seemed nervous and almost apologetic and she found herself feeling rather sorry for him.

"Yes well, thank you Mr. Addison. I'm not sure I want to read it right now, but why don't we have a look."

She felt surprisingly calm as she followed him out across the entrance hall and into a dimly lit library. "This is it," she thought. "In the next few moments I will know. I cannot allow myself to become anxious. Whatever will happen will happen."

Addison turned on a green shaded lamp, carefully unlocked the top desk drawer and removed a brown folder. He placed the folder on the top of the desk and bid her to sit in the chair opposite him. "This is your father's will; completed, signed and witnessed October 15, 1947," he said in a most solemn manner. "Needless to say, it is a long and complicated document. In summary you are the chief beneficiary. There are, however, a few bequests. A block of stock to your aunt and a few shares to me. But when all is said and done you will inherit 90% of his estate."

"I see," Katherine said betraying no emotion.

"Conservatively, your inheritance is somewhere in the neighborhood of fifty-eight to sixty million dollars."

"Are there any conservators or trusts?" she asked.

"No, none, now that you have your majority."

"Then I am in no way beholden or dependent upon anyone?"

Addison looked at her for a moment and smiled. "No, you are dependent upon no one." His voice was warm and reassuring and she was sure she detected an understanding expression in his face. "Your Aunt Gloria has not been reached yet."

Katherine sat very still for a few minutes, letting the information sink in. She had known her father's estate was considerable, but she had never bothered to guess at its value. Her only concern was that whatever she would inherit it would come to her free and clear. She got up slowly, picked up the folder, opened it and turned to the last page. There was her father's signature. She took the pages between her thumb and index finger and let them fall away until they had run their course and the first page lay neatly on top of the others.

"We will have a closer look later," she said placing the will in the folder. For the first time since entering her father's house she became aware of his effects. His watch, a bottle of pills, and an engraved letter opener were placed neatly on the desk. "How impersonal his life had been," she thought to herself. There was very little in his private study that said much about the man who had lived there. It was more like a hotel suite than a home.

Katherine moved around the desk, running her fingers along the edge of her father's leather appointment book. A picture frame in matching Moroccan leather sat facing her father's chair. It contained a photograph of women Katherine did not recognize. "Who is this?" she asked picking up the picture and examining it carefully.

A long pause followed, and for a moment she thought Addison had not heard her. "Monique Monahan." His voice was quiet.

"Monique Monahan?"

"Your father's fiancé. I thought you knew."

"No, I did not know," she said putting the photo back in place. "He did not bother to tell me."

"They were to be married sometime this fall after her divorce was final."

"I see," Katherine said turning away and feeling as if the floor had suddenly shifted under her feet.

"I'm sorry. I thought—it never occurred to me that ..." It's all right. My father never shared anything of his life with me." She paused and then added, "Except, I suppose, his money. Why should it be different in death?" She felt angry at herself for feeling hurt, at being shut out this one last time. After so many years of disappointment why should she let his callousness affect her? "Shall we go in to dinner?" Katherine ran her fingers back through her hair and told herself she would be alright.

Dinner was almost as silent as the faded tapestry that hung at the end of the formal dining room. As the Dengs appeared and disappeared with the arrival and departure of each course Addison made conversation about San Francisco. But aside from his general commentary he allowed Katherine time to pursue her own thoughts.

Katherine felt very much alone in the big house after Addison left. She crossed over to the library and turned on the green desk lamp and sat down in her father's chair. There on the desk was the brown folder containing the Will. She did not pick it up. "How very strange this day has been," she thought. She stared at the photo of the fiancé.

"Monique." Katherine said the name aloud. She could tell from the picture what kind of woman Monique was. "No wonder father didn't tell me." Her eyes came back to the folder. "Sixty million dollars!" The fortune suddenly seemed almost a burden. "I will have to be careful." She wondered about Addison. He was certainly kind; but he was also an employee. Perhaps he was maneuvering to consolidate his position in the company. She considered the possibilities. There was something else about Mr. Addison that she had sensed. Katherine was not sure what it was but Mr. Addison seemed permanently suspended in some great sadness, the waves of which washed over his face at odd moments.

Her thoughts turned back to the airport, the press, and her mother's family. "Aunt Louisa! What was it about her voice?" Katherine turned off the light, went upstairs and found her cousin's card in her purse. She looked at her watch. It was nine o'clock. She picked up the telephone and dialed the number.

"Harte's' residence." The voice was fixed and formal.

"Is Mrs. Harte there please?"

"Who may I say is calling?"

For a moment Katherine felt she had make a mistake. "I'm sorry, is it too late? This is her niece, Katherine McMasters. I just arrived today. They met me at the airport. Would it be better to call tomorrow?"

"Just a moment please." Sure she had made a mistake, Katherine waited for what seemed an interminable amount of time. Finally, there was her aunt's unmistakable voice, strong and sparkling.

"Katherine?"

"Yes, I am sorry for the hour but I just wanted to thank you—"

"Not at all. We just finished dinner. Couldn't be better! Are you settled?"

"Yes. I am at Father's house. Mr. Addison just left and I thought I would call and thank you. It meant so much to have you come to the airport. I never knew much about my mother's family and ..."

"Never allowed to know!" Aunt Louisa shot back crisply.

"Yes, well that seems to all be put right," Katherine said hesitantly. "Unfortunately I was always given to believe that—that my mother's family had no desire to see me."

"Oh my dear! Of course! But nothing on God's green earth could be farther from the truth. Now when will we see you again?"

"Tomorrow is Father's funeral. I will be with attorneys in the afternoon and for most of the day Friday, but I should be free Friday evening if that is convenient ..."

"Yes, marvelous, I will send the car for you. Shall we say five or six o'clock Friday then?"

"Five o'clock will be splendid," Katherine said feeling the delight in both their voices.

It took no time for Katherine to fall asleep after concluding her conversation. And as she slept she dreamed that she was a small child again. There was a garden and laughter and the sound of the wonderfully familiar voice.

Eighteen miles to the south Aunt Louisa and Albert sat up late over brandy. "I suppose it's something in her carriage or her manner," Aunt Louisa said as they settled into the big overstuffed chairs in the library. "She reminds me so much of Elizabeth even though she has different coloring."

"Yes, extraordinarily lovely," Albert agreed, thinking of his long-legged cousin, her subtle grace and sophisticated style. "She moves like a light breeze across water." He paused and watched the fire crackling in front of them. "Isn't it strange that neither of the Brutmanns were with her? Do you think they are not coming to the funeral?"

"It is strange," Aunt Louisa agreed. "They might be on another flight. But it is very odd."

"What is it about Gloria that elicits such a strange response in people?" he asked thoughtfully. "This morning when her name came up, Mother was uncharacteristically harsh. It was almost as if she hated Gloria more than Stanley."

"Gloria's a bad hat! Always was. Most selfish unacceptable person I have ever known. She hated Elizabeth from the day she married Stanley. She did everything in her power to make her life a living hell."

"Isn't it strange then that she would consent to raise Katherine?" he asked pushing for more information.

"Not really, I suppose," said Aunt Louisa reflectively as she finished her brandy. "I think she did it out of a sort of warped sense of vengeance. She would, you see, have the power to raise the child of the woman she hated. A sort of final theft, if you will. And then, too, she was devoted to her brother in a very odd sort of way. She undoubtedly did it partly as a favor to him. Before Elizabeth's death, Gloria spent about half her time in San Francisco. She spent as much time here as she did with her husband in Argentina." Aunt Louisa paused for a moment and Albert thought he noticed a very strange expression come over her, a sort of puzzled glee.

"I can't imagine!" She said. "Talk about putting the fox in with the chickens."

"Imagine what?"

"Oh," she said, pulling her mind back from the thoughts that had engrossed her, "I can't imagine what Gloria would have thought about Monique."

"Perhaps she hasn't been told."

"Yes, perhaps," she smiled and with a wicked laugh, added, "Imagine the two of them in the front row of Grace Cathedral. What sport!"

CHAPTER 6

*I*T WAS A cold grey San Francisco morning, and the interior of the cathedral chilled those who had come out of either duty or curiosity to pay their respects to one of the city's most powerful citizens. As she stepped into the transept of Grace Cathedral, Katherine felt as if she were playing a part in a film. With Philip Addison at her side, she proceeded to take her place in the front pew and wait for the service to begin.

"I am the Resurrection and the life, saith the Lord." The sonorous voice of Bishop Teeter echoed up through the great Gothic space. Katherine shuddered at the thought of her father being shut up in the heavy bronze casket that rested beneath the towering stone arches. She had seen him that morning reconstructed and beautifully dressed in a dark pinstriped suit. She had sat for a while trying to say goodbye over the great gulf that is irrevocably fixed between the living and the dead.

"I know that my Redeemer liveth and that He shall stand in the latter days upon the earth." As the service continued, she played her part with stiff dignity, allowing Addison to place his hand under her elbow as they stood for a psalm and knelt for the Benediction. Beyond these motions she heard only the river of words carrying in its current the ordered summary of Western man's hope in the face of death.

On the circumference of the ritual she was aware of the heavily veiled figure across the aisle. It was Monique Morales Monahan who, like a Shakespearean actress, gave herself over to prolonged weeping interspersed by loud cries and groans. Katherine ignored this display which intruded upon the form and dignity of the service. She did not want to know this woman or recognize her presence. Mrs. Monahan could remain a nonentity.

Well toward the back of the cathedral Albert had found an inconspicuous seat from which to observe the service. The cathedral reminded him of a large womb-like cave that he once visited in India. The cave contained a temple to the Hindu goddess Pavati. There was a power in the cathedral that seemed untouched by humanity's feeble attempt to address an infinite God and make him or her manageable for the events of finite lives. According to Chow-Ling, who had studied an old Chinese map of San Francisco, the cathedral was built on the eye of a dragon, the place of greatest power. The head of the dragon was Nob Hill and the dragon's back ran down California to Grant where it became the shoulders and backbone of the beast. Albert could not tell if the cathedral was like the womb of the earth or the eye of a dragon, but the place held something out there beyond his ability to put it into words. "We brought nothing into this world and it is certain that we shall carry nothing out," the Bishop continued. Albert's mind focused on the words rather than the sentiment, and he wondered how they ever got old Stanley to go, since it is certain that he could carry nothing out of the material world. He did not feel his thoughts were irreverent. They were simply his thoughts, and if he was inspired or amused by the service it seemed to be of little consequence.

Aunt Louisa had not come after all. At the last moment she had decided that she might not be able to contain her anger and she did not want to be considered a bitter old fool by people who were too young to know any better. In the end, she stayed at Treehaven content with the mention in the morning paper that Katherine McMasters had been met at the airport by her cousin, Edward Albert Devonshire, and her great-aunt, Mrs. Huntsford Fitzhubert Harte. Nevertheless, she had given very explicit instructions that Albert was to provide her with a detailed account, especially on "femme entretenue" as she had taken to calling the intended third wife. Yet from where he was sitting, Albert had trouble making out the infamous Monique and feared he would be unable to provide the required anecdotes. Indeed, he was beginning to doubt her existence, for she had not been mentioned in any of the newspaper accounts.

The Bishop's eulogy was only six minutes. He made brief mention that Stanley was of pioneer stock and recounted in a few short sentences the gifts he had made to the church and the community. Most of the eulogy was a series of loosely strung religious generalizations. None of them caught Albert's interest, for he knew all too well the sordid McMaster family history. Stanley's great-great-grandfather had used his newspaper as an instrument of blackmail to obtain numerous properties from prominent San Franciscans, including the shipping line from Aunt Louisa's grandfather. A great uncle had been shot by a county supervisor and another, a notorious drunk and gambler, had drowned himself in the Bay. McMasters' own grandfather had kept his cousin as his mistress and had refused to attend her funeral after she died giving birth to their third illegitimate child. "They were all as cruel and spiteful as the Devil himself," according to Aunt Louisa. As the Bishop concluded his remarks, Albert remembered Rig's words: "A lot of people hated his guts!"

Albert could not see Katherine, but at the end of the service as the casket was turned, he saw her step out behind it and stand for a moment as her father's body started slowly down the center aisle, carried toward the back of the cathedral by the directors of his corporation. Then Katherine turned and crossed the chancel steps and disappeared with Philip Addison behind a curtain. As the casket and pallbearers were about a third of the way down the aisle, Albert noticed the procession had been joined by a heavily veiled woman, whose demonstrations of grief were so extraordinary that she appeared to require the support of two young men. Her steady sobbing was punctuated by moans, the frequency of which seemed to Albert all too predictable. This was the long-anticipated Monique and after the casket passed his pew, he discreetly moved to the side aisle and exited by a side door.

Once outside, the procession momentarily stopped while the doors of the hearse were opened. Taking this opportunity, the veiled lady let out a loud wail, broke away from her escorts and threw herself upon the casket so that one end slipped from the unsuspecting pallbearers and crashed to the pavement with a heavy thud. She then began what Albert would later characterize as "a most ungodly and distorted caterwaul," which reminded him of rutting cats. The woman's companions seemed in no hurry to help her from her awkward position, draped as she was across one end of the lopsided casket. When they finally extracted her, she fainted so that they were obliged to carry her to a waiting limousine.

Albert did not go to the cemetery where the interment was private. Instead he walked across Huntington Park, and by twelve noon was comfortably enjoying a double martini in the Pacific Union Club.

With a police escort, it took less than half an hour to reach Cypress Lawn where an open grave waited to receive the body of Stanley McMasters. At the gates of the cemetery, the hearse was halted by a flock of ducks that had wandered up from the small artificial lakes flanking the roadway. The directors of McMasters Shipping became increasingly annoyed with the delay as the minutes ticked by and several geese joined the flock, which crisscrossed the road looking for bugs along the grassy slopes.

"Father was always so proud of his hunting ability," Katherine commented to Addison who was riding alone with her in the first limousine. "It would appear the ducks have formed a picket line in protest to his moving in to their neighborhood."

Addison smiled sympathetically. "I'm sure they will move in a moment," he said looking at his watch. Several minutes went by, and the hearse attempted to inch forward without success as more birds joined their comrades. Finally, a company official emerged from his limousine and came forward to evaluate the situation. Waving his hands, he tried chasing the fowl back into the lakes but only succeeded in slipping on a pile of freshly deposited duck shit.

The entire scene reminded Katherine of a Marx brothers' movie. "Viaduct" was all she could say before bursting into a fit of laughter. She tried to control herself, but the more she tried, the funnier the situation seemed, until tears came streaming down her face. At first, Addison was disconcerted, but realizing Katherine was not coming completely undone, he began to chuckle himself.

Finally, cemetery gardeners were called to the rescue, and by the time the procession arrived at the mausoleum Katherine had recovered. "Are you all right?" Addison asked gently touching her hand.

"Yes, quite. I'm sorry. It was those ducks," she said dabbing her eyes and trying to focus on the casket, which was being slowly lifted from the hearse.

"Yes, a bit of comic relief. Happened all the time in the War. Don't worry, everyone will think those tears are legitimate." Addison smiled and gave Katherine's hand a squeeze, but there was something in his tone that suggested he was enjoying his own private observation of poetic justice.

With great solemnity, the procession proceeded the ten yards to the large stone Victorian family mausoleum, which had been filled for years so that the present generation of McMasters were being buried adjacent to it. Stanley's grave was alone on the north side. The floral displays that had been carefully laid over the displaced earth had already begun to wilt in the autumn heat.

"Man that is born of a woman hath but a short time to live and is full of misery. He cometh up and is cut down like a flower. He fleeth as it were a shadow ..." the bishop began. Katherine for the first time took careful notice of the pallbearers, members of what was now her board of directors. They were all very serious but none exhibited any real grief. Looking down into the dark hole that would hold her father's body she thought how sad it all was. Her father had been very wealthy and powerful, but the only tears shed over him at his grave were hers. And they were tears that came from laughing at a flock of ridiculous ducks.

The service concluded, the party began walking back to the waiting limousines, leaving the cemetery workers to the task of lowering the coffin. For a moment Katherine lingered. She felt suddenly very much alone. There seemed to be no one she really knew well enough to trust and she wished more than anything that Trixie were there with her. She kissed the tips of her fingers and placed them on the head of the casket. "Goodbye Father," she said and turned away. Philip Addison was waiting a few yards off. "Tell me, Philip, do you know where my mother is buried?"

For a moment Katherine thought Philip Addison looked very peculiar. He shuddered and grew pale. He seemed unable to respond. "Yes, of course," he finally whispered. "Would you like to see."

"Yes, very much," Katherine answered.

They returned to the limousine, and Addison directed the driver around to the south side of the cemetery to where the Harte mausoleum stood on a grassy knoll. With its large domed central chamber and three adjoining alcoves the mausoleum held generations of Hartes with room for many more.

Katherine stood a long time in the south alcove looking at the inscription carved into the marble that secured her mother's tomb.

Elizabeth Louisa Templeton Harte
1904 ~ 1930

At the end of the alcove, a stained glass window bathed the cool interior in a soft warm glow. "I'm here, Mother," she thought. "At last, I'm here." Katherine felt a slight tremor throughout her body, and she knew she would weep. Finding a marble bench, she sat and took out her handkerchief before letting the years of doubt and separation dissolve into tears.

Addison, who had remained in the central chamber, left Katherine alone for some time before coming to sit beside her. He put his arm gently around her but said nothing. Katherine was thankful for the gesture. Slowly she stopped crying. She sat very still looking at her mother's name and the small spray of orchids beside it. When at last she was ready to leave, Addison reached over and picked a single flower and placed it in her hand. "Did you know her?" Katherine asked quietly.

"Yes, we were good friends."

"Please tell me about her."

"Your mother," he sighed. "She was very beautiful, talented and kind. She was a loyal friend. She loved you more than anything in the world." Addison gave Katherine's shoulders a reassuring squeeze. "She would have been very proud of you, Katherine." Addison's voice cracked slightly. Katherine sensed he could not go on.

"I will be back," she said pressing the flower to her lips. They walked out of the mausoleum into the warm afternoon sun and down the grassy knoll.

CHAPTER 7

𝒯HE DAY AFTER the funeral, Andrew collected Katherine in San Francisco to bring her down to Treehaven. Fifteen minutes before she was due to arrive, Aunt Louisa was waiting by the front door. This was unprecedented, for Aunt Louisa always had Prentice escort guests into her presence. Today, however, she stationed herself in her favorite armchair in front of the Chinoiserie tapestry and calmly waited, flanked to the left by George and Victoria Devonshire and to the right by Ivy and Albert.

Albert was a bit anxious to again meet his cousin. After reflecting upon their first encounter, he was keen to see if Katherine would fare as well the second time around. Only Victoria seemed a little nervous, but on the whole everyone was in a good mood. The morning papers had finally made mention of a Mrs. Morales Manahan, who was "said to be engaged" to the deceased and who, apparently overcome with grief, had collapsed on the steps of the Cathedral and had to be taken by her brothers to St. Mary's hospital and treated for shock.

"She would have been treated for more than shock had Gloria been there," Aunt Louisa commented as she reviewed the various accounts of the funeral.

"According to the *Examiner*, Mrs. Brutmann was unable to attend because she was in the South of France and had not been reached in time," Ivy added, attempting to fill in the details.

"They're in Biarritz attending a masquerade ball," Albert said. "The Marquis de Cuevos invited them but from what I hear it was organized by Elsa Maxwell—supposed to be an imitation of parties given by Louis XIV. According to Charlie Cahoon at the *Examiner*, the affair was protested by the local communists. They plastered Biarritz with slogans—*Remember the Revolution!*"

"With any luck Gloria was dressed as Marie Antoinette," Aunt Louisa commented out of the corner of her mouth. "How marvelous to have the revolutionaries of Biarritz decapitate her in the town square!"

"Really, Auntie!" Victoria said. "I don't think we should ..."

"Oh, don't be absurd, Victoria," Aunt Louisa snapped, "You'd like to see the bitch's head on a stake as much as I would."

Victoria fell silent, and Albert tried to contain the grin that was creeping around the corner of his mouth. Suddenly Aunt Louisa started to get up. She had seen the glint of sunlight on a car that had turned off the road and was coming up the drive through the poplars. Within a minute Andrew had brought the car around and a very excited Katherine stepped into the central court.

"Katherine, welcome, I trust you had a good ride down," Albert said, stepping out across the entrance.

"Ah, cousin, Alberto, how good of you," she responded, taking his hand at arm's length and looking into his eyes. There was a joie de vivre there that she found devilishly charming, a spirit that made adrenaline bubble in her veins. He was, as she remembered, a very beautiful man, not unlike Tyrone Power, with classical features and thick black hair. She gave him a knowing wink as if they shared some secret familiarity and then tilted her head almost playfully to the side before they embraced.

"Katherine dear," Aunt Louisa started with tears in her eyes as Albert guided her great niece through the front door. "Welcome home to Treehaven."

In leaning forward to kiss her great-aunt, Katherine noticed Victoria hesitantly stepping forward.

"Aunt Victoria?!" Katherine said, catching her eye.

"Yes, Katherine, how lovely. How lovely you are here." As they embraced both started to weep. They realized that the bond as well as the distance between them was rooted in tragedy.

"This is mother's sister," Katherine thought. "How long I have waited for this moment." She looked into the round delicate face. It contained no distinctive characteristics, but the soft blue eyes were kind and the complexion was a lovely creamy white.

After a few minutes of repeated greetings, Ivy was introduced and Aunt Louisa again took Katherine by the hand.

"Come, I think we all need a cocktail," she said leading her out of the foyer and down the Great Hall.

The main hall at Treehaven was truly splendid, with fourteen carved Doric columns marking twelve recessed walnut paneled alcoves. Every alcove contained a work of art. A Monet, a Remington bronze and a pre-Columbian quimdaya gold figure were among the treasures. The hall was arranged so that the alcoves containing large works of art stood across from the alcoves designed for sitting. This arrangement offered guests a quiet place to hold conversations while viewing some important pieces from the Harte collection. The placement and the lighting of the art were arranged by a curator from the De Young Museum, which had long benefited from Aunt Louisa's rotating loans.

As Katherine moved toward the drawing room on Aunt Louisa's arm she felt as if she could remember something from her childhood. There was something about this hall, these people or this old aunt that seemed strangely familiar. She vaguely remembered something from a dream she had had about her mother the night before but could not cleanly bring it into focus. "How odd," she thought. "These people are strangers yet they knew me and held me even before I knew myself."

"Have I ever been here before? When I was a baby, I mean?" she interrupted as Aunt Louisa was explaining a painting.

"Yes, of course dear, you were here many times in your first years," Aunt Louisa assured her.

"It all seems familiar somehow," she said, taking a long, deep breath. For an instant she felt engulfed in the most wonderfully pleasant feeling, as though she were being transfused with gently warmed milk. Then she stiffened and set her head slightly forward. She could not afford to explore too closely a past that might be filled with emotional pitfalls, at least not now.

They proceeded down toward the drawing room. The twelfth alcove contained an enormously fierce dragon from the Han dynasty inlaid with gold, silver and semi-precious stones. The dragon caught Katherine's eye. She stopped cold and whirled around. A quick golden current shot through every nerve in her body as she looked into the dragon's fiery eyes. For some reason she could not identify she felt empowered, but try as she might she could not trace the source of that power. It seemed simply to be there.

"What is it, dear?" Aunt Louisa inquired, having felt Katherine's body tense. "Are you all right?"

Not knowing why she felt so strange, or why this dragon should unsettle her, she gathered herself. "No, I'm quite all right. I think perhaps I remember this piece."

"Yes of course," bellowed Aunt Louisa. "Dragon was your favorite thing. Frightens the spit out of most children, but not my Katherine. You were fascinated by Dragon, or "Dag" as you used to call him."

"Yes," Albert said in an attempt to reassure her. "It is a terribly fierce dragon. It always gave me the willies when I was a child. Provided some copy for nightmares I dare say. Perhaps it has something to do with the way it appears to be in perpetual motion."

"Yes, perhaps," Katherine replied, "but it's not frightening. Not at all." She walked over and touched the dragon on its jade nose.

"That dragon has Chi. I've always said so," Albert continued.

"Oh Albert!" his mother scolded. "You listen to all that nonsense that Chow-Ling spouts. I've had Chinese servants for years and never listen to hint of their superstitions."

"Yes I know, mother. Four thousand years of collective wisdom is a mere nothing."

"Oh Albert, you know what I mean," Victoria insisted.

"At any rate, Chi is a force; something like the Christian concept of the Holy Spirit," he continued, ignoring his mother's objection. "It is the flow of energy from the primordial abyss out into the galaxies and through our very veins."

Katherine turned and gave him a very odd look. His ramblings had just described her intense physical experience, and she marveled at his ability.

Albert had been concerned that after the death of her father, the long plane trip and the ordeal of the funeral that his cousin would not quite be up for an evening, caught as it were, between the outspoken eccentricity of Aunt Louisa and the dotty reserve of his parents. He needn't have worried. By the second gin-and-tonic, Katherine felt so completely comfortable that she began sharing the outline of her life.

"I spent most of my early years on a rancho four hours southwest of Buenos Aires while Aunt Gloria and Uncle Otto stayed mostly in the capital or traveled in Europe," she explained.

"You mean you didn't live with the Brutmanns all the time?" Aunt Louisa asked, obviously pleased that Gloria's influence had been minimized.

"Yes," Katherine replied. "We didn't see much of Aunt Gloria and even less of Uncle Otto."

"We?" Victoria asked, betraying a puzzled look.

"Otto's children from his first marriage. There was Ingrid, Otto and Dieter, and then there are several others niños naturales, if you know what I mean?"

Victoria looked uneasy and stiffened in her seat. Aunt Louisa, noticing her pretense at morality, asked in a voice that was a little louder than usual, "How many bastards does this Brutmann have?"

Victoria put her hand to her throat and gasped, "Aunt Louisa!"

"The bastard has four bastards, unless you count me, which I am sure he does." Katherine replied without sign of embarrassment.

"I see," Albert said, with a chuckle. "It sounds to me like you're not all that keen on your old Uncle Otto."

"A mastery of understatement," she said winking mischievously. "I can see now how we are related."

Aunt Louisa enjoyed a good laugh, George poured another drink, and Victoria, not understanding the verbal interchange, smiled sweetly, relieved that her niece had not taken offense.

"I'm afraid my Uncle Otto has a rather rigid unforgiving Germanic mentality. He was always very stern and aloof. He runs the rancho, his business and his family with an iron hand. We have never particularly gotten on, especially in the last few years."

"How dreadful!" Louisa sighed. "He is most certainly not a gentleman."

"No, Aunt Louisa, he is not a gentleman. He never shows any kindness unless in the most condescending manner."

"And Gloria?"

"Oh, Aunt Gloria has really always been a rather remote figure, too," she replied in a way that suggested she did not want to pursue the subject.

"Actually, much of my early childhood was quite happy," she continued. "We always had an English governess. Several were quite nice actually. Then there were the servants and the gauchos and the families around the rancho. I had many friends, warm lovely people. I learned to ride almost before I learned to walk. The wide open spaces of the Pampa can get into your blood. I still miss them."

"But you were sent off to Europe to school?"

"Yes, that is expected in Argentina, particularly among the Europeans. I was sent to St. Georges in Switzerland, near Montreaux. Then I was at the Sorbonne, in Paris."

"You didn't go back to Argentina then?"

"Only twice. I spent most of my holidays with Trixie Metcalf and her family in Geneva. Trixie is a school chum from St. Georges. The Metcalfs are from Marblehead, Massachusetts, but Mr. Metcalf is an international lawyer working for the U.N. They are absolutely marvelous. Very different from the Brutmanns, I dare say."

"In what way?" Aunt Louisa queried.

"All rather rough and tumble and very bright. The family seems to run as a sort of radical democracy. Mr. Metcalf insists upon being called Stewart. He adores an argument and encourages all his children to state their position on any subject that happens to arise."

"They sound delightfully interesting. How fortunate for you to have been included in their family," Aunt Louisa said, conveying a certain satisfaction that her niece had been exposed to what she considered to be sound American values.

"They are delightfully interesting," Katherine agreed. "I'll never forget the first Christmas holiday I spent with them. Everyone was so raucous and gay. It was my holidays with the Metcalfs that made me realize how terribly autocratic and rigid my upbringing had been. I think I learned more from them than I did from all the tutors and schools I attended."

They dined at eight in the large formal dining room with its rich Venetian renaissance paneling forming the backdrop for the Gobelin tapestry that hung along the side wall and the Bernard Bouted de Monvel portrait of Aunt Louisa that had been painted in the late twenties. Albert had always thought the portrait a little hard-edged but it did seem to capture something of the elegance of that marvelously decadent period. Aunt Louisa had been anxious to have the evening be rather special and by choosing the larger of her dining rooms, she had succeeded in underlining the significance she placed on Katherine's visit. They enjoyed a splendid dinner including Beef Wellington done to perfection, green asparagus tips in a truffle sauce and a very fine 1920 Chateau Margaux with which Albert and his father made toasts welcoming Katherine back to "the city of her birth" and "back into their hearts." For the first time in her life Katherine began to feel connected. These people who had been virtual strangers just a few hours before now seemed to belong to her.

"Tell me, Aunt Louisa," she asked during a pause in the conversation, "I was named Katherine Louise after you, but I have never been sure about the name Harte, except that it was supposed to be Mother's maiden name.

"Your great-great-grandfather's," Victoria interjected.

"Yes, my husband was John Melton Harte the third," Aunt Louisa interrupted, taking the floor away from Victoria. "Your great-great-grandfather came to San Francisco after crossing Panama on a mule. He made a fortune selling dry goods and whiskey to the miners in Sacramento and the City during the gold rush. He would row out into the bay with bags of gold and buy up all the goods off the ships before the captains got ashore and learned how inflated the prices were. He was a character, all right. He married Lily Martin, who was a notorious madam and a great beauty."

"Louisa!" Victoria exclaimed, dropping the title of Aunt to emphasize her displeasure. "You are talking about my great-grandmother, who happened to run a respectable hotel when she married. I don't think you should …"

"Yes, yes, of course, Victoria, you are quite right. They always called them respectable hotels in those days."

"You must remember, my dear, that your great-great-grandfather, Howard Samuel Templeton, was a founding member of the Pioneers of California," Victoria said, nervously fingering her filigreed diamond and pearl necklace and trying to divert the conversation to a less colorful branch of the family tree. "He marched under their banner in the funeral procession we held when President Taylor died in 1752."

"I believe you mean 1850, Mother," Albert said, looking over his wine glass and giving Katherine a wink.

"Oh no, dear, Howard Templeton came in 1830, way before the Gold Rush. You know that, Albert!" She said dogmatically.

"Yes Mother, 1830 for old H.S. Templeton. But President Taylor died in 1850, not 1752."

Victoria caught her son's unconcealed smile and was a bit annoyed, for she knew he always delighted in correcting her dates, especially after a few cocktails when she invariably muddled her history. However, seeing her niece's interest, Victoria decided to relate a second story at which point George Devonshire, not wanting to endure another muddled account of family history, abruptly changed the subject.

"How long do you think you will stay in San Francisco, Katherine?" he asked.

"I don't really know, Uncle George," she replied. She felt comfortable with this uncle. His manner was cordial in a formal sort of way, and his thinning hair and round pink face with its double chin reminded her of a kindly old professor she had known in Paris. "There seems to be so much to go over. I spent all day today with my father's attorney and Phillip Addison, going over his will. Next week I will meet with the company's accountants and board of directors. It's all rather confusing. I told Mr. Addison that I needed a few days to just rest before taking on the corporate problems."

Unknowingly Katherine was skirting the subject in which everyone was vitally interested. Finally Aunt Louisa came to the point. "I hope your father provided for you, dear."

With only a slight hesitation Katherine responded, "Yes, he did. As I understand the will, he left me just about everything. There are a few small bequests, of course, but other than that I inherit everything: fifty-five percent of the stock in the shipping line, and a controlling interest in the subsidiaries, with the exception of one or two in which partners are given the opportunity to buy out my interest."

"Marvelous! Couldn't be better!," Aunt Louisa proclaimed in a note of triumph. "After five generations!"

"After five generations?" Katherine asked, confused by the tone of the remark.

"It's a long story, Aunt Louisa," Albert interjected.

"And a rather confusing one, too," Victoria added sympathetically.

"Nothing of the sort," Aunt Louisa insisted, "Charles Kingston, Stanley McMaster's great-great-grandfather, stole my grandfather's shipping line, and now it's come back to my great niece." She leaned over toward Katherine and with a twinkle in her eye, continued,

"Charles Kingston was a blackmailer. Had something on grandfather, don't you know. And well, there you have it."

Victoria looked down the table at her Aunt. Albert could tell from the smug expression on his mother's face that she had detected a flaw in Aunt Louisa's logic. He tried to head her off, but was unsuccessful.

"I think you are overlooking the fact that Katherine is a descendent of the Kingstons and not the Huntsfords," she proclaimed pedantically.

Aunt Louisa drew herself up in a manner of which only she was capable and fixed Victoria with a strong stare. "I forget nothing, Victoria and it would do you well to remember that both your son and Katherine are Hartes, just as you are."

Victoria could tell by the imperious tone in Aunt Louisa's voice that she was displeased and would brook no argument.

The awkwardness of the moment was saved by Katherine, who, sensing the tension between her two aunts, volunteered additional information that caught everyone by surprise.

"Oddly enough," she said, fingering her wine glass and looking out across the room, "Father was drawing up a new will when he died. He evidently had plans to remarry. Had he lived another month … well, my situation might have been substantially different."

There was a long pause for even the indomitable Aunt Louisa could not think of an appropriate rejoinder to this new revelation. The femme entretenue had discreetly not been mentioned and the thought of her having a claim on McMasters' estate had not really been considered except by Uncle George, who always thought of such things. Yet what amazed those gathered around the table was not only the information, but Katherine's relaxed manner. Indeed, Albert was amazed at Katherine's candor in relating the details of her father's will. She seemed on the whole rather unaffected by having incurred controlling interest in one of the city's most powerful companies or by the possibility that fate might have relieved her of it.

As she finished a general explanation of the will, George Devonshire leaned forward and said in a very low voice intended to convey a certain degree of confidentiality, "I hope you have independent counsel, Katherine."

"Well, no I don't, actually," she confessed. "Mr. Addison seems to assure me that everything has been worked out by my father's attorneys for my best interest. He has been most kind, really"

"All the more reason to have independent counsel," he insisted.

Katherine felt a little confused. "I see," she managed to say, "I will certainly give what you say some careful thought, Uncle George. Thank you for your advice."

Katherine did not mean to close the door to further discussion, but what she said seemed to have that effect on everyone present except Aunt Louisa, who was fidgeting nervously with her spoon at the end of the table. Albert could tell that she was having a great deal of difficulty containing herself. He feared that she was about to enter the conversation in the form of a tirade against Stanley, or a denunciation of the entire McMasters' organization, which Katherine now owned. At this point they had just finished a dessert of vanilla ice cream and black cherries on tuiles, and he moved to head off any unpleasantness by suggesting they all retire to the library for brandy. Aunt Louisa concurred with his suggestion and rang for Prentice.

Over brandy, the tenor of the conversation become more relaxed, as Aunt Louisa engaged Katherine in lengthy discussion of her horses and dogs and Katherine told Aunt Louisa about learning to ride in Argentina. By 10:30 Katherine began to feel rather sleepy, and she caught herself starting to yawn as Aunt Louisa went into great detail about how her uncle Lord Thomas Wiggin Sykes, the eighth baron of Goodacre, had the finest Lakeland terriers in the whole of the British Empire. "I've always kept a Lakeland until just recently, when I lost my Sir Galahad at age seventeen. I keep debating if I should get another male or try a bitch. I prefer the male Lakelands, but it's so much easier to introduce a bitch when you already have five dogs."

As Aunt Louisa described her dogs, she called each one over and talked to it as if she were talking to a human being. She was at once abrupt and very loving with her animals, and Katherine found Aunt Louisa's attachment to be very endearing if not just a little eccentric. When she first arrived at Treehaven, an enormous Irish wolfhound and golden retriever had met the car halfway up the drive and she had been aware of a swirling pack of smaller yapping dogs that had greeted her along with the rest of the family. At the time she had been too preoccupied with her relatives to pay much attention, but now as the evening came to a close, Aunt Louisa gave her a formal introduction, first to Maggie and Jiggs, then to Fergus, the Irish wolfhound, who had spent the evening curled into a huge ball by the fireplace. Only Ginger, the golden retriever, was missing.

"I'm afraid Ginger has taken quite a liking to one of the gardeners," Aunt Louisa explained in a confidential tone. "She sneaks away to spend the evenings in his cottage."

Lord Byron was the last to be introduced, and Katherine thought him the most unsightly mutt she had ever seen. His brindled coat was coarse and stuck out in all directions at varying lengths. There was nothing uniform about him, and it was impossible to tell his breeding. He had spent the entire evening sleeping on the end of the Queen Anne sofa, his white muzzle resting sublimely on a silk pillow.

"Lord Byron is nineteen," Aunt Louisa continued. "He limped into Treehaven just one week to the hour that my husband John died. It was quite queer, don't you know. I was reading a volume of poetry by Lord Byron and I had just finished a poem entitled, 'We'll go no more a-roving' when Prentice came in to tell me that some strange ugly mutt of a dog with a broken leg had wandered into the kitchen garden. Poor old Lord Byron was still a pup. He was half dead with cold and hunger. I think someone had thrown him out on the road. Anyway, I named him Lord Byron and he has been the lord of Treehaven ever since."

"He even gets a biscuit on the morning tray," Albert interjected. "Sleeps on all the best furniture and half the time can't remember whether he's inside or out, if you know what I mean."

74

"That's not a problem anymore, Albert. Ivy sees to it that someone takes Lord Byron out for a walk in the garden about every other hour," Aunt Louisa said, shaking a scolding finger at him while her eyes danced with glee.

Putting his hand in front of his mouth, he leaned toward Katherine and lowered his voice just enough so Aunt Louisa could not hear. "She thinks that old mutt is the reincarnation of our Uncle Milt." This unexpected revelation for some reason struck Katherine as being both very amusing and at the same time, rather sad.

"Don't believe anything that reprobate of a nephew tells you, Katherine," Aunt Louisa scolded before turning to Albert with all the fury she could muster. "I demand you tell me right this moment, Albert Edward Devonshire, exactly what you said to this sweet innocent child."

"All I said," he disputed, "was that you should have called the dog Rover instead of Lord Byron because you were reading, 'We'll go no more a-rovin.' And speaking of roving, dear Auntie, I think we must be roving home. I'll ride back with Katherine and keep her company."

Aunt Louisa extended an invitation to stay the night at Treehaven, but Katherine declined, feeling she should get back to the city. As she stood up to leave, she felt compelled to embrace this old eccentric, fun-loving aunt who had so graciously welcomed her. "Thank you so much for giving me a San Francisco family. I can't express how very much this evening has meant. I hope we will see each other again very soon." She paused and then asked with unaffected sincerity, "May I call you Aunt Louisa?"

"Oh my dear, of course you may," said Louisa, as tears gathered in her adoring eyes. Albert had never seen Aunt Louisa so unspeakably delighted. Victoria also embraced Katherine, told her to call her Aunt Victoria and extended an invitation to lunch the following week.

As the car reached the end of the drive and turned onto the main road, Katherine looked across the back seat to where Albert sat half concealed in the darkness, "Were you serious about Aunt Louisa thinking Lord Byron is the incarnation of Uncle John?" she asked.

He looked across to where her exquisite form was barely visible. "I don't know, really. On one level, I was just kidding, but on another level, I am not sure. Perhaps Lord Byron is the incarnation of John Milton Harte III. Sometimes I think he snores rather like old Uncle Milt, but I really can't be sure."

"Are you ever serious Cousin Albert?" Katherine asked teasingly.

"I am always serious," he said, putting a lie to the answer with a laugh.

"Yes, I can see that," she said mockingly.

For the few minutes it took to drive to the village they sat quietly encased in the comfortable gray flannel back seat of the limousine. It was one of those beautiful September evenings when the Bay had been unable to draw either wind or fog across the hills from the Pacific. The temperature even at 10:30 was a comfortable 68 degrees, and they rolled down the windows to let the air blow directly into their faces.

Katherine tried to formulate the questions she had held for so many years about her mother. But every question seemed trivial in light of the evening just past. She felt in a way that she had found her mother at Treehaven. She was there among this family, in the rooms and through the laughter and easy strong conversation. And what Katherine had found far exceeded all her childhood expectations. "It is all like a fairy tale where the orphan grows up to be a princess," she thought. A beautiful knowledge came over her like the warm California night. Whatever had happened to her mother, whatever dark forces may have entered her life, she had been much loved.

"This is the end of the warm dry season, and California has the subtle sweet smell of dry herbs," her cousin said at last.

Katherine laughed. "You ought to be a poet."

"I am a poet," he replied, making a slow wave of his hand.

"Seriously? You are a poet?" she asked as if she had perhaps discovered another dimension to his character.

"I am never serious," he chuckled.

"Yes, I can see that," she said, amused by the easy interplay of the conversation.

As Andrew drove the car through the village toward the Bayshore, the mood changed.

"Did you know my mother? I rather mean do you remember her?" Katherine asked. "You must have been about ten when she died?"

"Yes, I remember her quite well," he answered in a slow measured voice.

"What do you remember about her? I wanted to ask Aunt Louisa and Aunt Victoria all evening, but I was afraid."

"Why were you afraid?" He was a little puzzled at her confession.

"I suppose I was partly afraid of what their emotional reaction might be, and I suppose I was also afraid of what they might tell me."

Albert leaned forward and pushed the button to roll up the windows. "You should ask Aunt Louisa and Mother, too. But perhaps it would be better to ask them at separate times. They tend to compete. Often get on each other's nerves. Poor Mother never knows quite how to handle Aunt Louisa. But you should ask them because they both loved your mother very much, although I think Aunt Louisa understood her better than Mother ever did. Even though they were sisters, they were really nothing alike."

"How do you mean?"

"Well, Mother was never considered the great beauty your mother was. She is what one calls a 'lovely person'. She wouldn't think of going downtown without a hat and gloves, and her friends are all 'the right people'. She never wears diamonds before five o'clock, if you know what I mean!"

"And Mother? What was she like?"

"Like champagne in fine crystal. Magic! Like a flawless diamond against black velvet. She sparkled in an age that glittered. Most of her friends called her Liz. From what I gather she was the rage of the West Coast in the 20s. Rather than go home from her cotillion she went dancing in the jazz halls of the Barbary Coast. Absolutely scandalized our grandmother Helen. Of course, Grandmama was a Templeton, and they have always been a stuffy lot. My mother inherited the Templeton blood, if you know what I mean."

"Yes, I think I do. But go on."

"About your Mother?"

"Yes."

"Well by all accounts the dancing continued for years. The 1920s was a kaleidoscope of grand costume balls, weekend house parties and endless late night cavorting. It was a fantastic time to be alive!"

"And Mother?"

"She was, as I said, Magic in a magical age."

"And how did she come to marry my father?"

"That has always been a mystery. I was only six at the time. I suppose she may have grown tired of burning the candle at both ends. From what Aunt Louisa has said, your father wanted the most beautiful woman in San Francisco and he set out to get her."

"You mean he was not in love with her?"

"Not according to Aunt Louisa. No. It was rather, a matter of conquest. Once he had her, he ignored her."

"Poor Mother," Katherine thought aloud. She felt a great tug of empathy. Her father had done the same thing to her.

"Yes it was all very sad. I remember her death and the funeral and them sending you away. It almost killed Mother and Aunt Louisa."

"My mother died of an overdose?"

"Yes, barbiturates mixed with alcohol I think. Aunt Louisa always claimed your father was responsible, but of course it was impossible to prove."

"You know, it's really very odd," said Katherine, "I don't know the first thing about my mother. She has always seemed to be a taboo subject. Aunt Gloria never spoke of her, and neither did Father. As a little child, when I would ask Gloria she always was evasive. Then the few times I brought up the subject in the last several years, she became quite annoyed, as if she felt it was some sort of childish interest that I should have outgrown."

"I take it you're not very close to your Aunt."

"No, I'm not close to Gloria. No one it seems is able to become very close to Gloria except Father. She adored Father. Worshipped the ground he walked on."

"Even Uncle Otto?" he inquired, trying to inject a note of humor.

"Yes, even Uncle Otto," Katherine said with a half-puzzled sigh. "He's as cold as a block of ice in Tierra del Fuego. They have a very odd relationship. I've never seen them express any warmth at all toward each other. I even noticed their lack of affection when I was a child. I suspect their marriage is one of financial convenience, although he does provide her with a rather odd sort of emotional support. She can be very erratic. I suppose when you are raised in a country like Argentina that has a strong Latin flavor, Otto and Gloria stand out as being terribly severe. Of course, he had German friends in Buenos Aires and Aunt Gloria, I think, frequently entertained when they were there. But I was so seldom with them that I really couldn't say who their friends are. With a man like Peron in power, one is naturally a little cautious anyway."

Soon Andrew was on the Bayshore, and the car sped on toward the city, just 15 miles to the north. Katherine settled farther back and let her head rest against the back seat. She stared out the window at the string of red and white lights that moved north and south along the edge of the bay. Breaking her reverie, Katherine asked, "What did Aunt Louisa mean at dinner when she said something about 'after five generations?'"

"Oh, she was referring to the shipping line. She claims that her grandfather was blackmailed by your father's great-great-grandfather. One of those old pieces of family history."

"How interesting."

"Yes, well, I think Aunt Louisa rather sees your inheritance as a much-longed-for victory. Rather puts things right after all those years."

"But I'm not even a blood relation to Aunt Louisa."

"Yes but you're your mother's daughter, and the bond between your mother and Aunt Louisa was stronger than any blood tie. Quite extraordinary how those two got on!"

"You know," she finally continued, "It's doubly odd. I didn't know my mother, and I hardly feel that I knew my father. I saw him only about once a year while I was growing up and then sometimes not that often. Of course, the last two years I have seen him a little more because he has been in Europe on business. But when I think of him, he was always coming or going from either New York or London or Amsterdam or some other city. He always talked about those cities, but he never talked about San Francisco. I suppose I don't know the city of my birth, either. And Uncle George, tell me about Uncle George," she asked suddenly changing the subject.

"Father, like Grandfather Devonshire, is a banker. He looks and thinks like a banker. I think he sometimes worries that I have the family wild streak. Anyway, he told me once when I was six that in life one cannot do what one wants but what one must. Rather sad, don't you think?"

"Yes, I suppose. But tell me," she said changing the subject again. "Why did you come to Father's funeral?"

Again he took time before replying. "I am not really sure why I came. I suppose, to be quite honest, it was partly out of a sort of a strange sense of loyalty. I think one has to be loyal to events, to history, as well as to people. Perhaps I had some sense that with your father's death a chapter in my own family history had come to a close. It was a chapter in which I was at most only a marginal character. And being a marginal character allowed me the opportunity to be a witness without an excess of emotional involvement. Does that at all seem to make sense?"

Katherine thought for a while. When she finally spoke, she repeated something he had just said. "A marginal character," she said very thoughtfully. His phrase seemed to capture a definition she could apply to much of her own life. She had been raised much as a step child without any feeling of belonging to either her father or her Aunt Gloria's family. They in turn had seen to it that she was kept isolated from her mother's relatives. By birth, she was an American and a sixth-generation Californian, but she had been raised in Argentina and finished in Europe. She had only second-hand knowledge of her native land and not even that of half her family.

"You know, Katherine," he continued. "What I remember most about your mother was the way she played the piano. She had the gift just to sit down and play by ear. I used to be fascinated watching her play. Aunt Louisa always claims that your mother and I have the same blood. She says we both looked like Nicholas George, our great-grandfather. Old Nick was a handsome devil all right, but I think a bit of a pirate, don't you know. At any rate, I think I rather replaced your mother in Aunt Louisa's life."

"I trust not in the same way that Lord Byron replaced her husband?" Katherine laughed. They were approaching the outskirts of the city and she seemed to be gaining a second wind.

"Tell me, Albert, why do you live in the City as opposed to Burlingame?"

"San Francisco is center stage," he explained, eager to provide a commentary on the relative advantages of city life. "I have friends in Marin County, across the Golden Gate, and I still have a few friends in Berkeley, although I suppose I really don't go over there much anymore. East Bay people have to come to San Francisco to see their friends. Anyway, I enjoy the night life, and I especially like my penthouse on Telegraph Hill. You'll have to see it. It has a rather spectacular view of the bay."

"Oh, I would love to see it," Katherine said enthusiastically. "Why not tonight? For some reason I don't feel tired anymore. I rather dread going back to Father's house. It feels so spooky with only old Mr. and Mrs. Deng there. I don't think Mrs. Deng likes me. I fancy she sees me as an intruder."

Albert was intrigued by his cousin's sense of adventure and he pulled open the glass panel that separated them from the front seat and instructed Andrew to drive them home. At first he thought it was forward of Katherine to invite herself to his apartment at eleven-thirty in the evening. But he sensed that she had an almost desperate need to come to terms with her new position. She was now by virtue of her inheritance, an extremely wealthy woman and potentially a major player among unfamiliar people in a strange town. Nevertheless, Albert could not help but smile to himself. There was the way they looked at each other, that certain something in her movements that betrayed a message he had long been able to read in women. Yet they were first cousins and that alone with the events of the last week placed a certain prohibition between them.

"This is Telegraph Hill," he explained as Andrew turned the car up Lombard. "Goats were the main occupants until the turn of the century when Italians and then the painters and writers moved in. You can still find their little wooden houses tucked away."

"Is it still an artist's colony?"

"Yes, to a degree, but the views are so spectacular all these modern apartments have been added. I'm embarrassed to say that my building violates the forty-foot height limit which was imposed after its completion. It's really too tall for the hill, but there were no restriction when it was built in 1940 and the neighbors lost a campaign to stop it. I suppose I would have been on their side but I didn't move here until I finished University in 1945."

"Is that Coit Tower?" Katherine asked as they climbed out of the car.

"You recognized it! How surprising!"

"From pictures. I've always been keen to know about San Francisco."

"There's a nice park surrounding the Tower. It was one of the things that attracted me. My dog Windsor was only a puppy when I found the apartment and I wanted a place to give him a good walk."

It was about 11:30 when Albert opened the door and Windsor jumped up to greet him. Chow-Ling had long since gone to bed, and he had the freedom to show Katherine around without going through the formal introduction that would have been necessary given Chow-Ling's position.

"C'est magnifique!," she said as he drew the drapes revealing the sparkling lights that ran around the circumference of the Bay like so many strands of precious gems.

"Thank you. I think it's one of the most interesting views in the city," he said as they stepped out on the terrace to capture a better look. "A man's home may be his castle, but for any true San Franciscan a man's view is his treasure. Of course, there are so many views in San Francisco that it is the source of endless arguments which one is the best. There are those who favor Nob Hill, preferring to see the city and the Bay at a distance. My preference is to see the Bay close up so that I can smell the salt and have freighters move along so close to my window that I get the surrealistic feeling that they are moving through my own backyard. But then, no view is a fixed reality. The sun, the Bay, and the winds produce a never-ending kaleidoscope of light and shadow. Nothing ever seems fixed for very long, including the ground into which we sank our city."

They stepped back into the drawing room and Katherine looked around noticing for the first time the way the apartment was furnished.

"This is the most unusually disorganized art form I have ever seen," she commented after a long pause as she surveyed the eclectic jumble of antiques and art objects.

"I'm afraid I have never gone in for interior decorating as such," Albert explained, "I inherited most of the English and Chinese antiques from my family. They've been buying from Gump's since old Solomon opened his doors in the 1860s. Then I've added to it all when I find something that is particularly unusual. Things just get put in various places by chance, although Chow-Ling often has some strange notion of how things should be. It's next to impossible to change them around once he decides."

"Chow-Ling?"

"Ah, my manservant, but he always goes to bed by nine. He gets up at five to do his Tai Chi."

"Tai Chi?" Katherine asked with an incredulous look on her face.

"Yes, Tai Chi. It's a type of exercise rather like a ballet in slow motion. The Chinese claim it promotes harmony and health. You'll see old Chinese doing their Tai Chi in the parks at just about any hour of the day, although most prefer to do it in the morning. He'll give you a lesson tomorrow if you ask."

"It sounds like Chow-Ling is quite a character."

"Yes, I suppose he is. He runs the apartment and my life as well. For example, he insists my mynah is happiest on the refectory table because from that vantage point he can see into the hall and scream obscenities at guests when they arrive. That keeps Chow-Lin amused. He has a very odd sense of humor but I'm used to it."

"Well, Cousin, I must say you have one of the most extra-ordinary apartments I have ever seen," she said, shaking her head at the gold leaf statue of Shiva perpetually dancing on a seventeenth-century Boulle pedestal.

"Thanks, I suppose. I think a person's home should be filled with things that give meaning and pleasure. I have always enjoyed art and good antiques, but comfort comes first. I had the contemporary davenport and chairs designed with relaxation in mind. I guess I'm not a purist."

It was obvious from examining his apartment that Albert had a keen sense of history and a good eye, but what caught Katherine's attention was the Rousseau over the fireplace. "That was a twenty-first birthday present from Aunt Louisa," he explained as she admired the untamed gibbons cavorting through the lavish foliage of a private forest. In the foreground, a leaf monkey feasted on a mango he had unconsciously plucked from the tree overhead.

After lighting the Rousseau, Albert retreated briefly into the kitchen to get champagne, only to return to find Katherine out on the terrace, entranced by the magic of the view. The searchlight on Alcatraz silhouetted stationary ships riding at anchor as the steady stream of lights carried late-night partygoers home to Marin and the East Bay.

"I never thought San Francisco would be so very lovely," she commented. "I was given the impression that this was a rather provincial outpost on the far end of the North American continent. Strange, isn't it? Now that I am here, it all reminds me of Europe. It's like a combination of Naples and Paris and London."

"We are on the far end of the North American continent, but I never thought we were provincial. 'This is the city that was never a town'," he said, quoting Will Rogers. "This is the city by the Golden Door, beyond which lies the treasures of the Orient." He romanticized on about San Francisco for a while, telling her something of its history and color before they moved back inside.

As Albert talked on about his life, Katherine listened as intently as a sister would have to a brother she had never known. His charities, his friends, his intellectual pursuits all fascinated her. When the conversation turned to opera, she was enthralled.

"Del Monaco was slated to sing Otello and Carmen this year, but he cancelled at the last minute," Albert explained. "Now they're substituting Bohème and Traviata, because it's almost impossible to get a good Otello tenor."

"I must confess a passion for opera too," she said settling into the davenport.

"Would you like to accompany us opening night? They are doing Mefistofele, which ought to be rather dramatic. Rossi Lemeni is starring, I believe."

"I would be delighted," she said before thinking for a moment. "Poor old Addison will probably have a fit. He seems so protective. I'm not sure why, but he seems to want to isolate me from …" she hesitated as she caught herself on the verge of revealing what she suspected was Addison's displeasure at her having had dinner with her mother's family.

"You were about to say isolated from us," he said, "It really isn't surprising that your father's chief executive officer would not approve of your mother's side of the family."

"Perhaps," said Katherine, "but I am not sure it is so much a matter of disapproval as it is something else."

"Like what?" he asked.

"I'm not really sure. I have the feeling he wants to protect me from something, but I am not sure what it is. He has this rather paternalistic attitude toward me that is in one sense quite dear but in other ways is puzzling. For example, there was a strange incident the other morning before the funeral when the Bishop came to call. Mr. Addison had arranged for the Bishop to call well before my arrival but didn't bother to tell me until half an hour before. Then much to my astonishment, he introduced me as his goddaughter. I was astounded. I didn't think to ask him about it until after the funeral. Everything has moved so quickly. He said that he had been chosen godfather for my christening which Bishop Street performed at St. Matthew's Church in San Mateo."

"I think you may be correct," Albert interrupted, "I know Aunt Louisa and my mother are your godmothers, but I can't remember who your godfather is. I am afraid all I can remember from that day was that there was a party at Treehaven after the service. It was a scorcher of a day, too. Aunt Louisa let me have some champagne and I got tipsy. Of course, when my parents found out, there was trouble. My mother was scandalized, but I can remember your Mom and Aunt Louisa making up a song 'Tipsy at Ten' and doing an impromptu soft-shoe routine. Poor Mother was always rather like Mrs. Dumont from the Marx Brothers' movies—she was the brunt of their irrepressible humor. At any rate, we can ask about Addison in the morning."

They rambled on for several hours in the way that old friends talk without need to fill in the gaps or frame every statement in an explanation. At two-thirty they fell into a brief period of silence. Albert had comfortably settled into an overstuffed armchair near the fireplace, while Katherine had removed her shoes and had curled up at the end of the Chesterfield opposite him. In the silence, she began to contemplate the feasting monkey in the Rousseau painting. The monkey's expression was at once mysterious and compelling. It seemed to mirror some primal knowledge or primitive satisfaction that had been lost to civilized man. Forcing herself to dispel the trance, she asked Albert what he saw in the monkey's face.

"I'm not sure," he admitted. "Aunt Louisa says that I am the monkey eating the mango." He paused for a moment and took a slow sip of champagne. "I suppose she is right. Sometimes I come in here at night and have philosophical discussions with that ape."

Katherine did not laugh. She felt his cryptic remark revealed something very significant, although she did not understand exactly what it was. Soon she was nodding off to sleep.

When she awoke the next morning she found herself still in the presence of the leaf monkey eating the mango. She thought for a moment that he was smiling at her. She could not remember why she was still on the Chesterfield. She vaguely remembered her cousin asking her if she wanted to move into the guest room, but she could not remember answering. She pushed back the light goose down comforter and surmised that he had simply covered her as she slept. She felt like she could sleep another twenty-four hours. She surveyed the portion of the room in view until she found the Vulliamy clock. It was eleven o'clock.

Katherine heard a telephone faintly ring once from a far room and then a strange voice in broken English. The conversation did not last long, and it was quiet again. She wanted to get up but could not. She felt as if her whole body, which had run for days on nervous energy, had suddenly given up. She dozed off for a few minutes and awoke conscious of movement behind her. She lifted her head as Albert was coming through the dining room.

"Ah! Sleeping Beauty awakens," he said, mustering a cheerful tone. "Did you enjoy the honey-heavy dew of slumber?"

Katherine looked at him for a moment and then smiled. "Alive perhaps, but fully awake, no."

"We have just the remedy for that," he said, as he pulled the silk cord in the corner. Within moments Chow-Ling appeared carrying a silver tray with a yellow rose and a small pot of Italian coffee.

"Chow-Ling, I want you to meet my cousin Katherine."

Chow-Ling smiled, nodding his head several times in quick, attentive bows.

"Honored to have Cousin Katherine as guest. Remember you as little baby. You sleep late. Too much on go."

"Thank you, Chow-Ling. I am pleased to meet you, too. The coffee smells absolutely fabulous. I don't think I would have been able to get off the davenport without it."

Chow-Ling returned to the kitchen, but not before he removed the cover from Hector's cage and greeted the bird with repeated Chinese sayings. When Hector replied in Chinese, Chow-Ling laughed heartily and reached into his pocket for a grape.

Joining Katherine for coffee, Albert fell back into the same chair he had occupied eight hours before. She studied him for a moment. He had showered and shaved, and was wearing white silk pajamas and a navy water silk dressing gown with black piping.

"You look very pristine for someone who was up until 2:00 a.m. drinking champagne," she said.

"Thank you," he said with a broad smile. "On the whole, I feel rather balanced, although I can't say I was greatly enthusiastic when I first got up. I always suffer when I mix brandy and champagne. How's your head?"

"Dios Mio!" Katherine replied, rubbing a temple and sipping her coffee. "I could use an aspirin."

Albert leaned forward and took a small gold and lapis lazuli snuff box off the breakfast tray. Popping up the lid, he leaned forward, placing one knee on the carpet. "Ask and you shall receive," he quipped as he held out the box. Katherine took two aspirin and poured some extra cream into her coffee.

"I am afraid we have been besieged by telephone calls," he reported. "It seems that this morning when you had failed to return, Mrs. Deng called Phillip Addison and reported you missing."

"Madre mia!" Katherine sighed. "You would think I was in Argentina."

"Evidently Addison became very concerned and called Aunt Louisa, who then called here. Of course, Chow-Ling told her you were here, but she didn't bother to call Addison back with that information. About an hour later, he called her again and became exceptionally agitated when Ivy told him where you were but informed him that Aunt Louisa was otherwise engaged reading and could not come to the phone. Anyway, Addison called here, and I am afraid ran into Chow-Ling," he concluded with a chuckle and a shake of the head.

"You mean you didn't talk to him?" Katherine asked, somewhat amazed.

"Not on the first two calls. I was still asleep. But I am afraid Mr. Addison had the misfortune finally to get me after only two cups of coffee and before Chow-Ling had adjusted my spine."

"Adjusted your what?" Katherine asked, dumbfounded.

"My spine. Chow-Ling will adjust yours if you like. I always have mine done, especially on mornings after I have been at the altar of Bacchus."

Katherine could not help but laugh. "I don't know about you, my dear cousin Albert Edward, but you are a marvel."

"Anyway," he continued, ignoring the compliment, "I am afraid I was not too awfully civil to Mr. Addison who is, by the way, your godfather. I checked with Mother."

"What did you say?" Katherine asked, sitting up on the Chesterfield and pouring another cup of coffee.

"I simply said that you were here, safe and sound, and that I would have you call him at the earliest convenient opportunity. He asked if I would awaken you, to which I replied that I felt you needed the sleep, given all the physical and emotional distress of the last few days. I have the distinct feeling that Phillip Addison does not like to be told no."

"Well, he is a retired Navy Captain, you know."

"No, I didn't. But, ah yes, the chain of command and all that sort of thing. Must keep everyone shipshape, you know."

"Well!" sparked Katherine. "I suppose I will just have to call the Captain in a few minutes or ..." she paused, and added with a raised eyebrow and a smile, "at the earliest convenient opportunity."

After coffee Albert showed her the guest bedroom where Chow-Ling had laid out towels alongside a green silk kimono. She bathed leisurely, put on the kimono and rejoined him in the breakfast room for toast, ginger marmalade and fresh strawberries.

Again the phone rang, and Chow-Ling answered. "Oh, Miss Williams," Chow-Ling said, looking at Albert for a signal. He nodded that he would take the call. He knew that this was the third time Aunt Louisa had tried to have Ivy reach him. "Yes, Mr. Devonshire will speak to Aunt. Please hold on," Chow-Ling concluded, handing over the phone. The conversation with Aunt Louisa lasted long enough for a quick recapping of the previous evening.

"I'm so pleased Katherine stayed," Aunt Louisa said, before hanging up. "It's better to be with family."

They spent a leisurely hour over breakfast and while Chow-Ling took Windsor for his midday walk, Albert explained how Aunt Louisa and Chow-Ling were archrivals. "She resents Chow-Ling screening my calls, and he avoids putting her through on purpose by making up stories. I think Chow-Ling derives a perverse kind of pleasure thinking up ever stranger tales. He knows she doesn't believe him, and she knows he knows she doesn't believe him, yet the game has gone on for years. She always is insisting that I get rid of him, which of course, is not within the realm of possibility. He is the only person I can trust to awaken me in a civilized manner. Anyway, I think that beneath it all they enjoy hating each other, if you know what I mean."

Albert could tell by the incredulous expression on her face that Katherine did not understand Chow-Ling's relationship to the family.

She had never been around Chinese and obviously did not understand the Oriental mentality. He could see where this cultural gap might prove the source of confusion, and he resolved to fill her in so she might reap the benefits and avoid the pitfalls of a relationship with Chow-Ling.

"Chow-Ling's father originally came to the country to work on the Transcontinental Railroads and according to Chow-Ling he was in Ogden, Utah when Governor Leyland Stanford hammered in the last spike. The railroads completed, he came to San Francisco, where he was hired as my grandfather's cook in 1873. After six years he had saved up enough money to bring over a wife he had contracted to marry from his native village. She gave birth to Chow-Ling one year later. Chow-Ling raised my father, then me, from the time we were born, and I don't think anyone on earth is more devoted to my welfare," he explained, trying to give Katherine a feeling for the depth of their relationship. "On the other hand, he is a despot when it comes to certain things like the kitchen. Once he gets an idea into his head he is impossible to change. I remember a little battle over potatoes that raged on for years with Mother. If she ordered mashed potatoes with dinner, he would serve spring potatoes. No matter how much she pleaded or how angry she became, the result was always the same. He would listen to her patiently, wait until she finished with whatever she had to say and then serve spring potatoes. I think she would have fired him had he not been so entrenched in the family. Of course she always had to admit that he was a master at keeping food costs down. He always finds a bargain."

"It sounds like Chow-Ling can be something of a tyrant," Katherine said. "He wouldn't last a day in a European household."

"Gadzooks! The tyrannical Chow-Ling," Albert laughed. "But I'd rather cut off my right arm than lose him. I suppose it's more a case of benevolent despotism. There isn't a member of the family except Aunt Louisa who doesn't love and respect him."

"And why not Aunt Louisa?"

"That's difficult to say. They have always had a strange rivalry. She respects him, I think, but at the same time they have a love-hate relationship. She appreciates the care he gives to the family, but she is jealous of his influence."

"Influence?" Katherine asked, still not able to completely understand the position Chow-Ling held.

"Yes, of course. Influence. For example, Chow-Ling would smuggle a tray into my room when I was a boy and my father had sent me off to bed without dinner. Later on, he would cover for me when I came home drunk. One time, my father caught him and delivered a stern lecture on the rules of the household. The result was the same as the potatoes. Chow-Ling just listened, and when Father was through, he shrugged and said, 'No good. Growing boy need food.' Father was furious, but what could he do? He had had his own tray when he was young."

"How did he come to you from your parents?" Katherine asked, obviously intrigued by the strange devotion of both family and servant.

"We have always been close. In many ways, he is closer than my father, and he certainly understands me a hell of a lot better. After coming back from college, I stole him away from Mother by suggesting he was getting too old for their big house. Actually he was getting bored there. Here he has Windsor and me to look after, and he enjoys the excitement of my friends. The damned thing about it is that he owns a store down on Grant and could have easily retired years ago, but he wouldn't ever think of leaving. Sometimes I think he regards the Devonshires as his own personal property."

At about one Katherine finally decided to call Addison. "I think I've given him enough of a wait, a chance to cool off, as you Americans would say."

Albert had Chow-Ling place the call so that Addison was the one who had to wait for Katherine to come to the phone. Her instincts had been right. Addison had had time to cool off.

"I hope you are feeling well. I was a bit worried when you didn't return to your father's house last night," he commented.

"How typically kind of you to ask," Katherine said without really answering his question. "I feel very rested. I think with the ordeal of this past week, I simply needed to spend some time relaxing with my family."

The effect of this remark, like her whole conversation, was meant to remind Phillip Addison that despite his role as president and godfather, she was in charge of her own life.

As the conversation concluded Addison's tone changed.

"I wonder, Katherine, if you would do me a favor. I would like to meet with you for an hour or so tomorrow on a purely personal matter."

"A personal matter?"

"Yes. I don't feel I should go into it over the phone, and I wanted to wait until after the funeral was over."

"Yes, of course, Phillip," Katherine said, sensing a strange tension in his voice. "Shall we say about three in the afternoon?"

As she put down the receiver, Albert looked up from the morning paper and leaned back in his chair. "That was a first-rate performance! Chow-Ling, I think Miss McMasters deserves a bottle of champagne."

"Oh, no, I don't think I should."

"Of course you should. Haven't you ever heard about the hair of the dog and all that?"

"The hair of the dog? Is that another delightfully American expression?"

"An American cure, I should say. You take a little hair of the dog that bit you the night before. In this case, we'll use champagne."

"All right, cousin Albert. I suppose I should apply the old adage, 'When in Rome' and all that. But just one glass. I don't want to be bitten again."

By two-thirty, they had sipped through an entire bottle while munching on cold chicken, crab legs and a pasta salad from a favorite

North Beach deli. Albert then suggested a siesta and showed Katherine back to the guest room. They spent the rest of the day napping and reading—Albert with Windsor on his bed, and Katherine in the red, black and gold San Francisco guest room on the Charles Percies empire bed.

Early in the evening, Albert drove Katherine back to her father's home in Pacific Heights so she could have a chance to go over some papers before her meeting with Phillip Addison. She worked until 10:00 p.m., attempting to gain an overall picture of her father's estate and making a list of questions she wanted answered.

$\mathcal{T}$HE FOLLOWING DAY Addison arrived at exactly ten minutes to three, and Katherine received him in her father's library. Feeling she had already made a significant statement of independence, she was much less distant with him than when they had talked on the telephone. He made small talk, asking how she was feeling and making general references to meetings he had scheduled for the following week. Katherine asked him to reschedule a Monday meeting for Tuesday and he complied. "Other than that change," she said, closing her father's Moroccan leather desk calendar, "I think the week ahead looks very much in order."

"I would like you to do me a favor, Katherine," Addison said, after a slightly awkward pause.

"If I can, I will be pleased to," Katherine again felt the need to be on guard.

"I have something to give you," he continued, "I have kept it in my home for over twenty years in anticipation of the day you would return to San Francisco. I would like you to indulge me and ride over to my apartment. It should only take an hour or so."

There was something in Addison's voice and eyes that was very touching, and she felt suddenly just a little guilty about feeling defensive the moment before.

"That will be fine," she said, "I'll slip on a sweater, and we can go along then."

Addison's apartment building, with its iron balconies and baroque cornices, was reminiscent of ones Katherine had known in Paris. It stood on the corner of California and Mason facing the Pacific Union Club, and it shared the intersection with the famed Mark Hopkins and elegant Fairmont Hotels.

On the drive over Katherine noticed Addison seemed distracted, attempting to make conversation about several unrelated topics. As he parked the car and helped her out, he grew increasingly nervous. They went up the few steps which took them to the beveled glass door of the lobby. Suddenly he became quite flustered and began frantically searching his suit pockets. "I'm afraid I don't have the key," he said. "We always have a doorman on duty, but lately we've had a problem. Mike, who is supposed to come on in the afternoon, has been drinking on the job and then going into the back room to sleep it off."

Katherine noticed Addison's hands were trembling as he searched each pocket and repeatedly rang the bell. Trying to help, Katherine instinctively stepped forward and tried the door which was unlocked. Addison's pale skin blushed into deep shades of red as he apologized. They rode up the elevator together in dead silence. She wondered what he had kept for over twenty years, but she somehow couldn't bring herself to ask. She thought how fragile he seemed and felt that their roles were somehow now ironically reversed.

Once inside the apartment, Addison removed his Borsalino and placed in carefully on the hall table. He stood for a minute as if he didn't quite know what he should do next, like a deer caught in the glare of headlights. Then he led her into the living room. Again he stood for a moment as if confused, but once they were seated, he seemed a little steadier.

"Katherine," he began, his eyes looking off into the distance, "I have something that was your mother's. I have saved it for you because I knew one day you would want it." That was all he said before he stood up again. He reached out and asked her to follow him. He led her back again into the entrance hall, then down a side hall past several bedrooms to a closed door at the end. Reaching into his vest pocket, he pulled out a key and unlocked the door. He stepped back, pushing the door open as Katherine stepped forward.

There, in the dim light that seeped in through the cracks in the venetian blinds, was a splendid Bosendorfer grand piano. On the piano in an ornate silver frame was a picture of Katherine's mother bearing the inscription, "To my dearest friend Phillip with fond affection— Elizabeth." By the picture was a well-cared for slipper orchid in full bloom. A chill ran down Katherine's spine and she felt her legs grow weak. The room seemed like a tomb. There was a timeless quality to the air, as if it had not been stirred for a very long time. Katherine did not faint, although she wondered if she might. Then slowly she moved toward the piano and placed her hand gently on its top to secure support. The picture of her mother was one that she had never seen. It looked as if it had been taken at a party, for her mother was dressed in what appeared to be a long, shimmering silk chiffon evening gown. Katherine studied the picture for a while, noticing how beautiful her mother had been. Her long, rich black hair framed a perfect oval face with high cheekbones and large, dark eyes.

Hundreds of disconnected images flashed through her mind, like sunlight jumping through breeze-ridden trees. She remembered a piano, but she could not place it or recall why it slipped into her memory. She recalled something her cousin had said about her mother. The dragon in the hall at Treehaven passed her memory and then her father's casket retreating down the center aisle of Grace Cathedral. She focused on the orchids and then remembered orchids in Argentina and the orchids at Aunt Louisa's. This orchid was not like any she had ever seen. The front two petals of the flower joined together in a cupped formation resembling a small shoe. She could not seem to bring any of these images into a clear focus or relate them to a pattern of thought. Neither could she begin to understand why her mother's piano was in Mr. Addison's apartment, locked away in a back room like a sacred relic adorned with an exotic flower.

After some minutes Katherine regained herself. "You must forgive me, but I am a little undone," she said, attempting to excuse her apparent astonishment. "I seem to remember something about this piano, but exactly what it is remains somewhat out of reach."

Addison stepped fully into the room and Katherine noticed that his eyes were filled with tears. "This was your mother's most treasured possession," he said. "She asked me when I became your godfather, to save it for you if anything ever happened to her. It was almost as if she had a premonition that she ..." He paused for a moment, because he didn't need to complete the thought. "I frequently stopped in during the late afternoons to leave papers for your father when he was at the club. Your mother would mix a drink, and we'd talk for a while. When you woke up from your nap, she would play the piano for both of us. I think those were the happiest hours of her life. She seemed so calm and ..." Again he avoided concluding his thoughts but focused the conversation to the orchid. "Your mother always had an orchid like this one on the piano. She loved to be surrounded by beautiful things."

"And you've kept it all these years?" she asked, walking over and striking middle C.

"Yes."

She struck another key and another, followed by a few arpeggios. "It's perfectly tuned," she said, looking back at him.

"Yes. Do you play?"

"Oh, yes!"

"Well then, you have inherited yet another of your mother's talents." He managed to smile, but it was a smile that arose out of the encompassing sadness she had noticed her first evening.

"Thank you, Philip," was all she could manage to say. She wanted to ask him a thousand questions. Why had her mother selected him? Why not Aunt Victoria or Aunt Louisa? What had her father thought? Why had he enshrined the piano? Did her mother have some premonition of her death? She wanted to ask but the questions seemed somehow inappropriate for a man who has fulfilled an obligation albeit in an unusual manner.

"How well do you know the Devonshires?" she finally asked. It had been a question that had been on her mind since her arrival, and it seemed safely unrelated.

"I used to know them very well. Years ago, that is."

"And now?"

"Well, you see Katherine," he said as they reached the drawing room. "Since your mother's death, there has been a rift between her family and your father. And of course ... you understand? I worked for your father and naturally I suppose ..."

"Yes, of course," she said, feeling a little embarrassed for introducing a question so out of context.

She stayed for another hour attempting to expand her rudimentary understanding of McMasters Shipping before the scheduled board meeting. The number and types of ships, what they did, how they were chartered and the jurisdiction of international law were all complicated issues, which Addison did his best to explain in a kind and patient manner. But it occurred to her as they drove back to her father's house that perhaps Phillip Addison was a bit too patient and too kind.

"I just can't figure him out," she confessed to Albert when she called him that evening to relate the circumstances surrounding her mother's piano. "There is something about him that is very odd."

"In what way?"

"I'm not sure I can put my finger on it. He's very kind, but I keep wondering if he doesn't want something."

"I'm sure he does."

"What?"

"I don't know, but everyone wants something: power, money, love, control—something!"

"Yes, but with Addison I'm not sure. He's very controlling but I'm not sure that is his end. It's as though he sees himself as my guardian or protector or something."

"Perhaps he takes his role as godfather very seriously."

"Perhaps. It's peculiar. I asked him today if he knew your parents, and he was very honest about the rift after Mother died. But he didn't say anything against anyone."

"Why should he?"

"I don't know, except that if he worked for Father all those years …? Father and Gloria hated Mother's relatives like poison."

"Maybe he's being cautious."

"Cautious?"

"He can see you've made contact with us, and he doesn't want to lose your confidence."

"Yes, I suppose you could be right but …"

"I'm not suggesting that's his motive. It's only a possibility."

"Yes, of course, Albert. I know. You're the perfect confidante. You let me just ramble on without …" She stopped and thought for a moment. "That's it! That's what's so very odd!"

"What?"

"Confidante. It's as if Addison thinks of himself as my confidante. He was that way with the ducks and the will and the piano. Even at Mother's grave."

"Ducks? Your mother's grave?"

"Oh, the ducks at the cemetery. A bunch of ducks held up the hearse. Very funny, really. I laughed so hard I cried. Partly nervous exhaustion, I suppose."

And?"

"Oh, I don't know, but on some level I think Addison enjoyed the ducks, too. At least he seemed to enjoy the fact that I enjoyed them. And with the will. When I asked if Aunt Gloria would exert any control over my estate, there was the odd way he answered. It was as if he had arranged everything or at least understood. Sometimes I have the feeling he really never worked for father."

"Yes, well, I'm not sure what to say. Maybe you're just reading too much into Mr. Addison. If he's an old Navy man, he just could be acting out of a highly developed sense of duty."

"Possibly, but I keep thinking about what Aunt Louisa said at the airport about not trusting anyone—that they were all a bunch of cutthroats."

"I don't think she meant Addison."

"Why?"

"Because I asked her this morning what she thought of him and she said the most remarkable thing. She said that fate had treated him mercilessly.'"

"What did she mean by that?"

"I'm not sure. When I asked her what she meant, she just passed the remark off and said that anyone who worked for McMasters was either eventually corrupted or destroyed. At times she can be untypically cryptic."

"Remind me to ask Mother about the piano," he concluded. "She may have the entire matter in perspective. And speaking of Mother, she has been trying to reach you to confirm Wednesday's lunch and to extend an invitation for dinner for the following Thursday. Just a few family friends. Nothing elaborate," he said, convincing her that it would be an easy evening.

They talked on for a while about the Board of Directors meeting the next day, and she confessed to being a little nervous. "I'm afraid I don't have a firm grasp of just how the company operates. There are so many papers and reports to go through."

CHAPTER 9

*P*ERHAPS MORE THAN anyone else she met in that first week, Katherine had come to feel wary of Chambliss Horsley, who seemed to occupy a powerful position on the board of directors. Along with Phillip Addison and Dr. Whitmore, he had been playing golf with her father the day he died and had been the last person besides Joey Chang to talk to him. At first she thought Mr. Horsley looked like a rather jolly old grandfather, with his fat, round face, jolly grin and jovial manner. But at the reception after the funeral, Katherine had noticed something in Horsley's eyes that caused her to reserve judgment. They were extraordinarily small eyes, and they tended to dart nervously from side to side when she engaged him in conversation. She imagined Horsley as a rat somehow trapped in the body of a pig and try as she would, she could not release that image from her mind.

"Chambliss Blackmond Horsley has one of the most slippery reputations in town," Albert had told her. "And I 'm not saying that just because he owns a bank which is one of our largest competitors. The word is around that he's a bad actor. I wouldn't trust him for a minute. Father claims it's a matter of bad breeding."

"Bad breeding?" Katherine asked, curious to uncover whatever it was her Uncle George had meant by the remark.

"Chambliss Horsley is the descendent of one of San Francisco's most unsavory characters," he explained, pleased at the chance for an oral history. "His great-grandfather, Theodore Greenfield, was an embezzler from New York who came to San Francisco with a large sum of money. His identity was discovered in 1848 and he was sent back to New York, where he was convicted and later died in prison, leaving a wife and daughter. Greenfield's daughter married Chambliss' grandfather, who initially made millions of dollars selling worthless patches of Nevada desert to eager silver prospectors after the Comstock Lode was discovered. He became a notorious federal judge and eventually was tried for graft and political corruption."

"How are you familiar with such a detailed account?" Katherine asked, amazed at the extent of his knowledge.

"I grew up with it. San Franciscans all have interesting histories. Aunt Louisa knows them all. Of course, so do Mother and Father, but they have always been more reticent to talk about them."

"Was Horsley's grandfather ever convicted?"

"No. The chief witness for the prosecution was shot to death before the trial got started. But his career as a judge was through. He retired part-time to Hawaii, where he invested in sugar cane and shipping."

"Quite extraordinary!"

"Yes, well, that's not all. Chambliss Horsley's mother's side of the family wasn't exactly free from corruption either. She was the descendent of David Ford Blackmond, a purchasing agent for the Transcontinental Railroads. He made an enormous fortune by siphoning off public funds, defrauding the United States Congress and issuing fake railway stock."

"With a family like that I'm astounded the Horsleys are even accepted in San Francisco."

"Oh, San Franciscans don't mind that sort of thing. They prefer color to virtue. It's much more interesting."

When Katherine was ushered into the boardroom at eleven o'clock by Phillip Addison, all the board members were waiting. She wore a lightweight Donegal tweed suit with box jacket that made her look dignified and conservative. After a preliminary greeting, the directors moved towards their chairs. The room, designed and carved by Norwegian shipbuilders, was an impressive piece of architecture. It sat on the top floor of the McMasters building and commanded an excellent view of the Bay across to Treasure Island and Berkeley in the distance. The boardroom table, Katherine judged, was made of walnut in the first part of the eighteenth century. Its boldly carved ball and claw feet provided a message of power and authority. Without hesitation Katherine moved to the empty chair at the head of this table. Her decisiveness surprised everyone including herself, for she did not know what to expect next.

"First of all I want to thank each of you," she started after a momentary pause. "Your kind messages of condolence and your support are so very much appreciated. And may I say I will always be grateful for your cooperation in this time of confusion and uncertainty."

As she finished, Chambliss Horsley, who was seated to her left, reached over and placed his hand over her forearm. "Let me assure you, Katherine, that although this is a time of grief, we are not uncertain or confused."

At first Katherine thought he was trying to simply be kind, but there was something very condescending in the way he had spoken, and she found his touch clammy and ungenuine. She withdrew her arm from his grasp.

"I didn't intend to imply you were confused," she stuttered, feeling angry at being forced into a defensive position over such a non-substantive matter.

"Would you like someone else to chair the meeting?" Horsley interjected, taking advantage of Katherine's momentary awkwardness.

"Yes, perhaps Phillip will," she said, turning to Addison.

The meeting continued with a series of complicated reports concerning everything from projected rubber production in Southeast Asia and international insurance rates established by Lloyd's of London. Katherine pretended to study each report and attempted to follow the discussion, but she felt overwhelmed and lost.

"I would think that Katherine might feel more comfortable signing a proxy over to the board as a whole," Horsley suggested when Addison opened the meeting for new business. "She would therefore be relieved of making the various complicated decision that are continually needed to run the company." Then turning towards her he continued in a chauvinistic tone.

"I know, Katherine, that all this is rather difficult for you to grasp. Let me assure you that running a shipping line is a Herculean task. You will not want to be inconvenienced by the morass of details that are involved."

For a moment, Katherine felt stunned. She knew she could not argue with Horsley's contention. She was not equipped to participate in company decisions. Yet, she was also keenly aware that his suggestion was only a thinly concealed attempt to neutralize her. She felt her body become taut and her heart more rapid as she listened to Horsley's proposal.

Finally, he stopped talking. She paused briefly and looked slowly around the table. "I will take your suggestion under consideration, Mr. Horsley, but before I make such a decision, I will require more time to familiarize myself with some of the basic ways in which this company operates. Consequently, I would like to have the financial reports for the last five years, along with a general accounting of all the company's holdings and assets, and a description of how each division in the corporation functions."

The words she used and her deliberately measured response caught everyone by surprise. She was simply attempting to buy the time she needed to sort through her own personal feelings, to say nothing of her new business obligations. With this statement, the other members of the board who seemed to support Horsley's suggestion fell silent. Horsley, however, made one more attempt. Pointing the end of his pipe at her, he said in a blunt, patronizing manner, "I would hate to see a nice girl like you bother her pretty head with the problems of the rough-and-tumble business world. Your father continued to build a business started by his great-grandfather, and I would hate to see your interest in that business endangered."

His words were spoken as a warning, but Katherine felt that somewhere there was an implied threat that she could not quite decipher. Again she moved to cut him off.

"I can assure you, Mr. Horsley, that I have no intention of ever allowing my interests to be jeopardized, and may I further assure you that I will continue to seek the advice of this board as McMasters Shipping moves into the future."

After these remarks Chambliss Horsley leaned back in his chair without further comment, but Katherine could feel his small rodent-like eyes fixed on her with a vitriolic intensity that made her very uncomfortable.

CHAPTER 10

*A*T ELEVEN O'CLOCK Wednesday morning, Victoria Devonshire sent her chauffeur to gather Katherine and drive her back to the Devons, where she waited nervously in anticipation of her niece's arrival. Albert had canceled joining them for lunch, because, as he told Katherine, "Mother may be more honest if the two of you are alone. She never trusts me with anything that is at all irregular about the family history. And since Dad won't be there, it will give the two of you a chance to talk."

Katherine was hesitant about his decision, but he convinced her that he had good reason for making it. So, wearing a light pink suit by Cavanaugh, she climbed into the back seat of the waiting car and was whisked off up Gough to Broadway and into the circular drive of the Tudor mansion Julia Morgan had built in 1912 for Albert's grandfather. "The Devons," as the family home was called, lacked the ostentation of the great nineteenth-century houses built in a more frivolous ear of the city's history. Nevertheless, its' size, combined with superior craftsmanship, conveyed the impression of old family solidarity. Massive beams criss-crossed the structure that rose three floors above Broadway and sank one floor below into the rock of Pacific Heights ...

It was a beautiful warm September day, and her aunt had arranged for drinks in the white Victorian lath house at the end of the small formal garden at the back of the house.

"This is a Tommy Church garden," Victoria explained as they walked down the path admiring the massive blooms of bedding plants. "He is absolutely a genius in landscaping small city gardens. He designed the boxwood and pea gravel walks so that they would make a pleasing pattern from the house as well as from the garden."

"He gives the garden a certain European flair," replied Katherine, trying to seem interested. "I feel the French influence in the way he provides the eye with interesting focal points."

Katherine could sense her Aunt was a little uncertain. Her manner of movement and hesitant speech reminded Katherine of a bird that hesitates before landing on a branch and then is off again before settling. As they moved into the octagonal garden house, which was a pastel world of cascading fuchsias, Katherine wished Albert was there to help guide things along.

While Victoria was relating in extensive detail a war she had fought with fuchsia blight, Daniels, the butler, brought down a tray of enormous pink daiquiris in Steuben compote glasses.

"I think it's such fun to have daiquiris this time of year in the garden," Victoria said with a nervous little giggle. "We can't really enjoy summer fun until August and September, you know."

Not until well into the second daiquiri did her aunt begin to relax and when there was at last a pause in the conversation, Katherine decided to ask the question which had been weighing on her mind.

"You know, Aunt Victoria, I had a rather odd thing happen last Sunday."

Victoria straightened her back, tilted her head and smiled in full attention.

"Phillip Addison gave me a piano that he said belonged to my mother," Katherine continued, stirring her daiquiri with the swizzle stick. "He said that she had asked him to keep it for me in the event that something happened to her."

Katherine could see her Aunt's smile disappear and an anxious expression came across her face. Nevertheless, she pressed ahead. "I don't quite understand why Phillip Addison should have my mother's piano, or why he has kept it all these years in his apartment. Albert said you might know something about it," she said, looking up from the swirl of crushed pink ice to Victoria's soft blue eyes which seemed painfully distracted.

"I'm sure I don't know. Of course, they were close friends. He was a very handsome young naval officer when he came to San Francisco in 1925. Quite the gentleman. Although I have never understood how he stayed with McMasters. I mean, well …" She momentarily faltered, embarrassed by her criticism. "Your mother always loved playing the piano from the time we were little girls. We took piano lessons twice a week. She was so adorable sitting up on the bench with her long braids." Victoria trailed off into a remembrance of her sister as they had grown up together in San Francisco. "You know, Katherine, I can remember the 1906 earthquake. I remember waking up in your grandfather's old Victorian house on California Street, and feeling the bed shaking and hearing the creak of wood and the crack of plaster. I was absolutely frightened to death. I begged my father to let me go up to the observation tower. We watched the fire on Market Street and saw the old Palace Hotel go up in smoke. Father sent us in carriages with our maid and dogs out to Golden Gate Park while he stayed and packed the library and paintings into wagons. The fire hit Nob Hill in the early hours the next morning. It was awful, but as children we found it rather exciting. Of course, your mother was only a baby. You must ask your Aunt Louisa sometime about how she stayed up all night watching the hills of San Francisco burn."

Although Katherine found her aunt's stories about early childhood fascinating, she was aware that she was trying to avoid talking about her sister as an adult. She was obviously guarding painful memories that long ago had been tucked away into some safe corner. Attempting to maneuver her aunt back to her initial question, Katherine asked another. "Was the piano that I received from Phillip Addison last Sunday one of those items that Grandfather put in those wagons?"

"No, I don't believe so," she said, looking at her watch. "I think Cook should be ready for us by now."

As Katherine stood up her aunt reached out and took her by the hand. "It is so absolutely marvelous to have you here in San Francisco," she said as they walked back through the garden. "Both George and I are so delighted that you will be joining us Thursday night for dinner."

They lunched on avocado and crab salad in the newly completed Chinese room which George Devonshire had made over as a fortieth-anniversary present. The room derived its name from the exquisite hand painted Chinese wall paper, which, with its robin's egg blue background and bursts of pink and white peonies, provided a more feminine and intimate setting for small luncheons than did the large formal dining room. The centerpiece on the Sheraton rosewood table was an unusually delicate orchid with an arching flower spike containing ten beautiful white orchids, each about four inches across. "That is the most arresting orchid, Aunt Victoria," she commented, trying to make conversation. "I don't believe I'm familiar with the variety."

"This particular orchid is a species of moth orchid, a Phalaenopsis Amabilis," explained her aunt as she tasted the Chevalier Montrachet Daniels had just poured. "It is a genus of orchid from the Far East. I think it grows mainly in Formosa and the Philippines, so I don't suppose you would be at all familiar with it in South America. Our Madame Ng imports all types of rare varieties from the Far East. You must have Auntie Louisa show you her greenhouses. Over the years, Maggie Ng has acquired some very unusual specimens for her."

Katherine remembered the orchid by her mother's picture on the piano in the room at Phillip Addison's apartment, but she did not ask her aunt any further questions concerning her mother. She felt perhaps she had asked enough questions for one day and she wanted to enjoy the rest of the afternoon simply talking about whatever her Aunt Victoria found most comfortable.

$\mathcal{T}$HE DAY FOLLOWING lunch with her aunt Victoria, Katherine had scheduled a meeting with several directors and top executives of McMasters Shipping including the company's controller, treasurer and general manager. She was nervous but determined to find answers to some of the questions she had on the reports she had received. "I think you should know, Katherine," Addison began when he came to her office in the early morning, "that your aunt and uncle have cabled from France. They will be arriving here next Monday. "Yes, I know," said Katherine, surprised that her aunt and uncle had cabled Addison. "I received the same message yesterday."

"There is something else I think you should know," Addison added hesitantly.

"Yes?" she replied, looking up from the papers she was sorting.

"It probably will not come to anything, but Mrs. Monahan has hired an attorney. She claims your father intended to alter his will in her favor and as a result, is entitled to a portion of the estate."

Katherine put down the papers and leaned back against the red leather chair. "I see," she said slowly. "How strong is her position?"

"Legally? I don't think there is anything to worry about. I checked with our company attorneys and they have assured me that her claim is groundless. He had begun a revision of his will but the process had not been completed. Nothing was signed and there is no evidence of intent."

"I see," said Katherine. "You will keep me informed, then."

She attempted to go back to work but could not concentrate. "So Father was going to change his will. I wonder what control Monique exercised over him."

At ten-thirty, Mrs. Tucker, who had been her father's personal secretary, interrupted to inform Katherine that Mr. Horsley had arrived for their meeting. She noticed that Addison stiffened a little as Chambliss Horsley walked into the room.

Katherine moved to her father's conference table so that they might be accommodated more comfortably. "We were just going over the figures and tonnage for our North American and Baltic fleets," Katherine explained. "Yes, yes," said Horsley, lighting his pipe, "I am sure that is all very interesting for you." And halting only to draw a small puff, he continued, "Has Mr. Addison explained to you any of the details of our offer?" We didn't get to that yet," Addison replied as he hesitantly fingered the stack of paper that lay before him. I thought I would wait until you arrived."

Katherine suddenly felt that she was being treated like a child whose parents had kept a secret from her and were now about to explain something from their adult world. "Is there something I don't know?" she asked slowly, putting down her pen and looking at Addison, whose eyes remained on the paper before him. "We want to present you with what we feel is a very attractive offer," said Horsley. "A group of business people, mostly from San Francisco, but also including your Uncle Otto, want to present this offer for the purchase of McMasters Shipping." He reached into his briefcase and pulled out a thick legal document and handed it across the table.

Katherine was so astonished she had no idea what to say, but simply looked at Horsley's beady little eyes as they narrowed and darted. Reaching out her hand she took the forty-seven page document, and put it down without examination. "You will find, Miss McMasters," Horsley said, now taking a more formal tone, "that this is a very attractive offer. You will, of course, want to go over it thoroughly. There are several alternatives within the offer itself that you may want to consider. But on the whole, I can assure you, as can

Mr. Addison, or any other independent advisor you may wish to consult, that you would indeed be very foolish not to consider what is proposed here."

She could say nothing, but she looked at Addison for a reaction. "I think, Katherine, that Mr. Horsley is right about all this," Addison said, diverting his eyes. "You will of course want to study the proposal carefully, but it is a very generous offer, and I think you will want to consider what it will mean to your future." Addison went on to explain that a syndicate, of which he, Mr. Horsley and her Uncle Otto were members, was offering thirty-seven million dollars for her fifty-four percent interest in McMasters, or eighteen million dollars for twenty-five percent interest, which would leave her still the largest shareholder, with twenty-nine percent of the stock. "Why wasn't I told of this offer before?" Katherine finally asked. "It wasn't in existence before," replied Chambliss.

Katherine quickly concluded the meeting, promising that she would give the proposal her careful consideration. She felt in a state of shock. She no longer wanted to be around these men whom she felt she could not trust. She wanted to retreat into a safe place with safe, kind people, and she sighed with relief when she thought of her Aunt Victoria's dinner party that evening. Her Uncle George had been right about getting independent counsel and she wished she had pursued his suggestion that first night at Treehaven. Now she resolved to follow up his suggestion, but not that evening. She was tired of business intrigues. It all could wait until later.

CHAPTER 12

*W*HEN ALBERT PICKED Katherine up that evening, she looked absolutely smashing. She was wearing a black dress by Givenchy with the most daring bare back. It was slung from the shoulders and anchored with a seven-inch rhinestone gauntlet.

"Your Aunt Victoria has planned the most marvelous dinner party," Albert said, intimating what he knew was to come. "She is having the Charles Whitneys, Dolores a childhood friend of Mother's, and their daughter, Beezie, who talks as if her jaw was permanently frozen at birth. Then there's Edwin and Mildred Klassen, and the Rudolph Waters. Gertrude Waters is very chumsy with Mumsie and Rudy plays golf with Charlie, Edwin and Father. Gertrude is currently president of the Opera Guild, so she will probably be in a lather over the opening. Then they are having Gertrude's niece and second husband, Amy and Douglas Mackie. Amy's great fun, actually. Her first husband was a ski instructor—one of those impossible love affairs. It lasted two seasons, about eighteen months, I think. Her second husband, Douggie, is an attorney and an Adlai Stevenson Democrat. They also invited a business associate of Dad's, a Patrick Barkley, or Bartley, I think."

Katherine smiled. "Thank you, Cousin Albert. Do I detect a note of sarcasm in your briefing?"

"Not really. It's just that some of mother's friends can be a bit much, especially the Whitneys. But if you don't take them seriously they can be fun."

When they arrived at the Devons, the Whitneys were already there. "How marvelous, absolutely marvelous to meet you! I've heard all about you from Mumsie and saw your picture in the paper," said Beezie Whitney as she shook hands. "How do you like our city? I suppose it's very different from living on a ranch in Argentina. Of course, I've never been to South America, but we went to Mexico last year and saw the Mayan ruins. It was ghastly hot. Absolute ghastly hot. I don't know how you can live in that kind of climate. We went to the Temple where they had human sacrifices. It was absolutely ghastly."

Victoria Devonshire smiled sweetly. She knew that she had been right in inviting Beatrice Elaine. "She's such a sweetie and such a good conversationalist. I'm sure she'll make Katherine feel right at home," she had said when her son had groaned upon hearing Beezie's name mentioned on the guest list.

"What would you like for a cocktail?" Victoria asked, after introducing Katherine. "Dolores and I are having old-fashioneds."

"I told Katherine about Father's famous martinis," Albert said as he crossed the drawing room to where Daniels had laid out all the necessary ingredients on a Georgian silver tray with the precision of an operating nurse.

"Oh, Albert," sighed Victoria, "don't be a bad influence on your poor cousin."

"I think I should have at least one," said Katherine. "Albert told me all about Uncle George's famous martinis on the way over in the cab."

"You didn't come in a cab, Albert!" his mother said, aghast at the idea. "Why didn't you drive, or have us send Thomas for you?"

"Father's martinis," Albert said, winking at his father. "Or should I say Father's infamous martinis?"

"Tell me, Uncle George, what is the secret of these infamous martinis of yours?" Katherine asked as she followed him across the room.

"Don't bruise the gin," said George with a laugh as he poured straight gin into a large Waterford pitcher. "Just one jigger of vermouth per quart of ice cold Bombay gin. Pour over the ice and then right into the chilled glass. I never stir the gin. And here you are," he said, popping an olive into the glass and handing it to Katherine.

"I just adore gin, Uncle George," said Beezie, sticking out her lower lip in a dramatic little pout. "But it doesn't like me. Could I please have just a teensy glass of Mumm's?"

"A teensy glass of champagne?" Albert said. "I think, Beezie, if my memory serves me correctly, that the reason gin doesn't like you is that last time we were together in Pebble Beach. You had just a teensy pitcher or two of martinis at the Castles."

"Oh that was that naughty, Howard," said Beezie, "he is always ..."

"... a perfect gentleman," Albert said, finishing her sentence in a voice that could not be heard by the ladies who had moved over to the window to look at the Golden Gate in the setting sun. "After all, he went to all the trouble of undressing you and putting you to bed."

Beezie paused for a second, trying to remember exactly what had happened in Pebble Beach, and then as if searching for something she could remember, she turned to Katherine. "What do you think of Lana Turner's getting married to Lex Baxter this week? I read all about it in the paper. It's her fourth and his third. Of course, he's so handsome and with all those muscles."

Before Katherine could answer, the Waters and the Mackies had arrived and she was co-opted by her aunt for introductions. "Gertrude is absolutely the pillar of our Opera Guild," Victoria said. "Katherine is coming opening night for Mefistofele."

"Oh, how marvelous, Katherine!" Gertrude replied. "With everything else up in the air, I think that at least opening night will be a success. We have absolutely had to throw things together since Gaetano's death, together with the cancellation of Del Monaco. They've had to substitute Bohème and Traviata for Otello and Manon Lescaut and the chorus had already spent so much time on Otello and Manon

Lescaut. Of course, what could they do? It's absolutely impossible to find a good Otello tenor."

"Have you ever been to the opera before?" asked Beezie, who had joined the conversation.

"Yes, I quite adore the opera," replied Katherine, finding Beezie's question rather odd.

"I didn't know they even had opera in Argentina. Is it in Spanish?" Beezie continued.

"Actually, I've never been to the opera in Argentina. I've only been in Vienna and Paris, and of course, once in Milan, which was truly superb. But I've never seen Mefistofele performed, so I am quite keen to come next Tuesday."

As they finished their first martini, Gertrude Waters rambled on about the new soprano, with the flaming red hair, who had been hired as a protégé for $175 a week. "She was supposed to live with the Merolas, but she arrived in San Francisco the day after he died. Her name is Beverly Sills and Herbert Kurt Adler told me she is living at the Whitcomb where she's had to cook frankfurters on the radiator. Can you imagine?"

Gertrude's saga was interrupted by Daniels. "Mr. Patrick Bartley," he announced with his usual reserve. Katherine turned towards the door as a tall, rugged, dark haired man with a broad smile walked down the two steps from the entrance hall into the drawing room. George Devonshire, who seemed to be the only person in the room who knew Mr. Bartley, left a batch of martinis. "I want you all to meet Patrick Bartley, one of our most aggressive young developers," said George as he introduced his guest around. "He's turning all those sand dunes out at the beach into communities, to say nothing of new profits."

As Patrick Bartley shook her hand, his dark brown eyes seemed for an instant to penetrate hers. It was typical of Katherine to form opinions of people very quickly and she always instinctively watched their eyes. With Mr. Bartley, she couldn't tell what she thought. She felt as if she had swallowed a goldfish and felt its tail flipping in the pit of her stomach. He seemed at first impression to be the incarnation of the All-American stereotype she had always entertained. He was powerfully built with extraordinarily broad shoulders and strong features. She could not tell, perhaps she sensed that the force of his personality was just a bit too overpowering and perhaps a little out of place in a room where the trials and tribulations of the San Francisco Opera were being discussed. He exchanged a few words and then went to get a drink, and engage Charlie Whitney and Rudy Waters in a discussion of the World Series, which had, as far as Katherine knew, something to do with the American sport of baseball.

"Who is Patrick Bartley?" whispered Beezie as Albert came to rescue Katherine.

"He was Lana Turner's second husband," Albert whispered in the most confidential tone. "So don't mention anything about Lana because he is very upset."

Beezie didn't seem to absorb what he said. She had already launched into a monologue telling Amy Mackie what a friend of hers told her she had heard about Kay Williams and Adolph Spreckles.

"You know," said Katherine as she returned to where George Devonshire had started a fresh batch of martinis, "I'm not sure. Is Beezie just a little ... a little ...?"

"'Off her trolley' is the American term," Albert said, saving Katherine the pain of sounding critical.

"Is that like the British expression 'gone round the bend'?" queried Katherine.

"I suppose so, but gone around the bend implies that a person is still in the same county, and in Beezie's case, we are talking about long-distance migration."

"You are a wicked person, Albert Devonshire," she said with a quiet chuckle. "Have you always had such sport with her?"

"Always," he said, spearing a second olive for his martini. "It's the only way to ensure one's sanity."

Dinner was served at eight-thirty in the Georgian dining room as Victoria called it in honor of her husband and the English kings who lent their names to the furniture and decor. The dark paneled walls feature carved Corinthian half columns and along one wall a fireplace blazed under a magnificent Georgian mantle with a chalice and grape motif. A splendid mahogany table laid with Staffordshire porcelain and Victoria's collection of eighteenth-century silver was surrounded by George III mahogany dining chairs in the manner of John Cobb. All this was lit from above by a superb early Regency period cut-glass chandelier.

Victoria had arranged the seating so that the younger set were seated towards the far end of the table. Katherine sat in the place of honor next to her uncle George, with Douglas Mackie on her right, and Beezie directly across the table. Albert was seated between Beezie and Amy Mackie.

"I don't know where to put Patrick Bartley," Victoria had complained to her husband. "I guess between Amy and Dolores. After all, Dolores traces her family back six generations. They held land grants from the King of Spain. I'll tell her to talk about real estate if the conversation lags. Do you think he would talk across the table to Rudy? You know Rudy if he starts in on Scotland and one of his golfing holidays. Oh, and he's right in the middle of the table! I'll just have to ask Mildred to keep an eye on him. Gertrude's a darling, but she is so absorbed with her Australian tenor and who's going to take over Calaf that she's absolutely useless."

"Don't worry," George had counselled, "after three of my martinis, old Rudy will volunteer for Calaf and that will solve all the problems."

Victoria had not found her husband amusing and she simply chose to ignore his comment in favor of discussing the menu.

The first half of the dinner went well and Katherine felt comfortable with the easy conversation Douglas Mackie provided. They talked about her impressions of San Francisco and the balance of the Montrachet.

"You know, Uncle George," Katherine said, turning to her uncle, who had been sentenced to hearing Beezie describe the plot of a newly-released film called "Gentlemen Prefer Blondes." "The French say that Montrachet should be drunk kneeling with the head bare."

"Oh that's probably only because they're Catholics," said Beezie, who was obviously annoyed at being interrupted.

"You're quite right," Douglas agreed catching Albert out of the corner of his eye, "all those French Catholics are the same!"

Katherine could not contain her laughter, although she tried successfully to make Beezie think that she was laughing at Douglas. Amy Mackie also dissolved in convulsive giggles which went completely unnoticed by Beezie, who had recaptured the initiative with George Devonshire. "Do you want to play for points, Douggie?" Albert asked, looking Douglas straight in the eye.

"You're on, Albert my friend," retorted Mackie, "and it's one to nothing in my favor. Agreed?"

"Agreed."

Despite this brief departure from the formal rules of conversation that govern dining, the rest of the first half of the dinner went on without interruption. Edwin talked with Victoria about Bernard Davetto's death, Rudy told Mildred about playing St. Andrew's, Albert discussed the newly translated work, Zorba the Greek, while Beezie finished "Gentlemen Prefer Blondes" before overlapping into "From Here to Eternity". Only once did Albert pause to score a point by asking Beezie where she felt she belonged on the spectrum of "From Here to Eternity."

When Victoria turned the table midway through the dinner to engage Charlie Whitney, Douglas and Katherine were discussing the Rosenberg execution and the anti-Communist hysteria that was gripping the country. Picking up on the tail end of their conversation, Beezie turned to Albert. "Do you know I think it's just ghastly. Why, in the paper just today, they reported that Lucille Ball registered as a Communist in 1936. You know, I just adore 'I Love Lucy' and I never knew she was a Communist."

"You must be kidding, Beezie," he said, picking up the challenge and noticing Douglas Mackie trapped and squirming in a conversation with Mildred Klassen. "With all that red hair, how could you think anything else?"

"Oh, you're kidding, Albert! I just never know when you're kidding," Beezie giggled. "You're just a big tease."

He caught the smile coming over Douglas Mackie's face, and he felt infuriated that he had not scored a point. "I couldn't kid you, Beezie, not me," he continued with resolved determination, "why, there are Communist supporters everywhere, even at this table. Isn't that right, Douglas?"

Douglas, who had not heard the question, asked Albert to repeat it, which of course he did.

"Yes," scowled Douglas, "and they all went to UC Berkeley, isn't that right, George?"

George Devonshire shook his head and took a long sip of the 1928 Chateau Margaux he had been trying to enjoy. "Yes," he said, at last with a sigh, "unlike you and my son, I went to Stanford, which is a respectable university."

"And that's why he serves Beluga caviar at dinner parties," Albert said in a quick retort as everyone chuckled except Beezie, who had a puzzled expression on her little face.

"Well," she said, after thinking for a moment, "Howard Castle went to Stanford and his family never served caviar."

"Oh, for crying out loud!," Albert said, "That is precisely the point. Lucille Ball does! You have to learn to look past the immediate facts and coordinate the evidence. It's sort of like the title of your movie. You have to look from here to eternity."

"Oh, I see!" said Beezie as she moistened her lips and reached under the table to run her hand across his thigh. Everything seems so much clearer when you explain it, Albert."

"That, my little chickadee, is what comes from having the advantage of a Berkeley education," he said, leaning forward and placing a conspicuous smack on Beezie's cheek that was noticed by his mother at the other end of the table.

"You know the poem about the caviar, don't you?"

"No I don't," sighed Beezie, "what is it?"

"Allow me to place it in the form of a toast," he said, as he gently tapped his spoon on the Waterford crystal and brought the whole table to attention. "I have already proposed a toast to my beloved cousin Katherine, who we all love and are just beginning to know. But now I want to propose a toast to a very special person who has given us all so much enjoyment over the years. Beezie. As dear Mama always says, Beezie brings an undefinable dimension to every party. So rather than attempt the impossible, I will simply recite the following in her honor."

"The virgin sturgeon needs no urgin'
The virgin sturgeon is a very fine fish
Not many sturgeons ever are virgins and
That's why caviar's a very fine dish.
Once I served sturgeon to my girlfriend
She was a virgin tried and true
Now this virgin needs no urgin'
There is nothing she won't do."

"Oh, I so admire good literature," sighed Beezie.

"I thought you would, my little chickadee, and thanks for the two points," he said, giving Doug a smile across the table.

By this time the entire end of the table was convulsed in laughter, except for Beezie, who with a triumphant smile nodded her head from side to side accepting what she interpreted to be the accolades of all. At the other end Albert's mother turned to Dolores Whitney and said, "I think maybe Albert has sort of a soft place in his heart for Beatrice."

"Oh, yes," said Dolores, "isn't it just too fun!"

At the end of the fruit course, the men escorted the ladies into the drawing room before retiring to the library for cigars, brandy and conversation. "Whatever were you all talking about down at your end of the table, Albert?" his mother asked as she seated herself in the middle of her favorite George I settee.

"The Kinsey Report, Mama," he said, leaning over and kissing her on the forehead.

"Oh," she said, "I don't like that political talk about the Communists at the dinner table. I think it's really very boring."

As they adjourned to the library, Albert took the opportunity to become better acquainted with Patrick Bartley. As his father's friends reminisced about their encampment at the Bohemian Grove, he talked with Patrick about his real estate development in the Sunset District. Albert had not anticipated finding Bartley particularly interesting, however, as they talked over their brandy he found that underneath his rather driving personality Bartley possessed a jocular sense of humor not unlike his own. Patrick was the oldest son of an Irish working class family from the Mission District, but despite their differences in social background, Albert sensed that they shared a similar sense of adventure along with a passionate love affair for the city of their birth.

He had just asked Patrick about the effects the new interest rates were having on the building industry when he overheard a comment Edwin Klassen made.

"Old Henry J blames the cancellation on Fairchild. Seems they were dragging their feet on the C119. He's had a bad time, damned bad time."

Why do you think the government contracts were cancelled?" Albert asked, turning his attention to Edwin.

"Damned if I know. That Senator Bridges is from New Hampshire. You know how damned tight those New Englanders are. Suppose the extra cost just went against good old Yankee prudence."

"Is that what Henry and Edgar Kaiser think?" Albert pressed.

"I think so. Although they tell me the Air Force said the Senate investigation had nothing to do with it, but Edgar doesn't believe that for a minute. Why are you so interested?" Edwin asked, looking up from his brandy.

"Oh, just curious," Albert said.

About eleven-thirty Douglas finished his second brandy. "I think perhaps we'd better see if Amy and Katherine need rescuing," he said. "You're probably right," Albert concurred as he arose from the red leather armchair. "Perhaps Patrick would care to rescue Beezie?"

"I think I'll leave that to you, Albert old boy," Patrick replied. "You do such a magnificent job with her."

As they returned to the drawing room, Dolores was telling Katherine what a source of spiritual inspiration she had found in the new book, *The Power of Positive Thinking* by Norman Vincent Peale. "You really must buy a copy. I think you would find it just too awfully helpful with all the strain in your life now. Reverend Peale shows us how to approach life with a positive attitude. He's absolutely marvelous. I can't tell you how he has simply changed the whole way I look at everything."

Although Katherine was being terribly gracious in attempting to follow the conversation, Albert could tell that she was becoming a little weary.

"I'm afraid we will need to be going," he said, apologizing for being the first to leave, "but I think Katherine should get some rest. She's been under a tremendous strain, as you can appreciate."

"It isn't even midnight, but I suppose that you should get your rest, dear," his mother agreed sympathetically.

After climbing into the taxi, Katherine said, "I am not at all tired. I hope that Aunt Victoria won't think us rude for leaving so soon."

"No, I don't think she will," he assured her, "and anyway, I had to leave. There are only so many of my parents dinner parties that I can take. I can't make polite conversation any more for over four or five hours at a stretch."

"Are American's always so optimistic?" Katherine asked out of the blue.

"Oh, I suppose some are," Albert chuckled. "Our parents' generation still believe that progress is an intrinsic part of reality. Why?"

"It seemed that every time I wanted to ask a serious question, I found the conversation being swept along on a tide of perpetual enthusiasm."

"Yes, well, there you have it! I warned you not to take them seriously. I'll tell you what. Let's go down to North Beach and have an espresso. You can compare American Bohemians to your friends in Paris."

"What fun! I'd love to have an espresso, but I am truly shocked," Katherine teased, throwing her hair back behind her neck.

"Por que, Katerina?" he said, after redirecting the cab to a place called "The Cellar."

"I am surprised you aren't taking Beezie, your chumsie-wumsie dinner partner," she baited in a perfect imitation of Beezie's speaking voice.

"Oh, please!" he chuckled. "You can't say I didn't warn you about From-Here-To-Eternity-Beezie-Darling! But I must say, I beat old Mackie again. He gets so damned mad at me every time I ace him out with Beezie."

"Have the two of you slept with her?" Katherine asked out of the blue.

Albert was a little surprised at both her perception and her bluntness. "For crying out loud, how did you know?"

"Mon Dieu, c'est evident!"

"How?"

"I don't know ... just the way you interacted and competed over her. It was really rather charming. I mean, the two of you are just terrible, but she doesn't comprehend any of it. She just basks in being the center of attention."

"You truly are an amazement, Cousin Katherine. I don't think there's a woman in San Francisco who is as perceptive as you are."

"Oh, not really. I would imagine that Beezie has many lovers and it was a fair assumption that you and Douglas were among them."

"At any rate," Katherine continued, "she is a most extraordinary person. I must say I found her rather amusing and soothing at the same time. After a while I no longer attempted to follow what she was saying, and just listened to each episode as sort of a brief little fantasy, like those children are read before they go off to bed. She is truly quite exceptional. Everything is somehow grounded in reality, but nothing is connected to anything else. It truly is rather amazing."

"Ah, of course, but not if your mother and her mother think you would be the perfect couple. Jeepers! Can you imagine Dolores as mother of the bride playing to Victoria's mother of the groom? They would have the time of their lives!"

"Your mother tittered to Dolores all during coffee about the two of you. She really took you quite seriously." Katherine laughed, grasping his arm as the cab came over the crest of Powell Street and started to plunge down towards North Beach.

"Yes, of course she takes me seriously. They see what they want to see and pay attention to little else." Pausing, he continued, "But I suppose that is the story of all our lives in some way or another."

CHAPTER 13

"*L*IKE THIS IS the scene, man," Albert joked as the cab turned onto Grant Avenue. "This is where my other friends hang out, the Bohemians and the hipsters. I think you'll like this scene. If not, we can split, as they say, and go back to the pad."

As the cab pulled up to the curb and they climbed out, Katherine noticed a man in a tattered pair of jeans and an old sweatshirt leaning up against the brick wall. His heavy lidded eyes had a melancholy look like the subject of an El Greco. First he took no notice of them, but as they moved towards him, he suddenly looked up. "Hey, what's happening man? Who's the chick in the fancy rags?"

"Hey, Jack, what's happening?" Albert shot back.

"Nothing, no thing, no ring. Like, tonight I'm not into heavy poetry. Alan got busted. He wigged out on some leapers. Like the heat netted him naked in Washington Square blowing some far out Tibetan poetry."

"Hey, man, I'm really sorry—if I can help?"

"Hey, like Alan's really fucked up, man. Like Nola says, it's time for the laughing academy."

Albert opened the door and led Katherine down a narrow flight of stairs into a small, dark nightclub. The faint smell of pot mingled with the mystical words and soaring ecstasy of a Beat poet named Angel, as she described the coming holocaust. For a few minutes they stood by the door waiting for Angel to finish. While the audience snapped their fingers in acknowledgement, they moved to a table where a large heavy-set man named Hal sat with a jug of wine and his woman, Ellen.

Katherine thought how much Hal and Ellen resembled the typical image of the eastern European peasant. Hal had a broad, flat face, an exceptionally large head covered with coarse, unkempt brown hair, and he smelled of sweat and tobacco. In his deep-set steel blue eyes, one could see a life ridden with memory. His woman was a big, buxom mama with olive skin and long thick unbound hair that made her full face seem almost moonlike in appearance. Her plump short body was concealed beneath a dark brown caftan and long, beaded Indian earrings dangled to her shoulders.

"Far out," said Hal as he looked up and saw them. "Mister Circumstance has descended into purgatory to blow the circuits!"

"Hey, big Hal!" Albert said, reaching over and squeezing his shoulder. "This is my cousin Kate. We just cut out from one of my parents' parties. I thought I'd turn her on to the good people."

They sat down, Gary and Bruce came over and made fun of Albert's white dinner jacket, they related how Alan got busted for indecent exposure in Washington Square. "Like, the fuckin' heat oughtta go arrest the fuckin' Secretary of State and his fuckin' A-bomb and let Alan blow his mantra," Gary ranted.

Katherine smiled and Albert could tell she did not feel any less comfortable talking to Gary than she did talking to Gertrude Waters or Dolores Whitney. Gary continued to relate Alan's mishap in Washington Square, a saxophonist started blowing out disconnected notes of impromptu jazz, and Katherine was soon telling Ellen about her existential friends in Paris, who all seemed to share the Spenglerian expectation that Western civilization was in the last stages before collapse.

"Far out! Shut down! Shut out! And split!" Gary kept saying, as he listened to what Katherine was talking about. "Like, I can dig this cousin's trip, man," he said to Albert. "She's on to what's happening. She's hip. Like far-out!"

A tall slender girl, Lyric, wandered over to the table and sat down. Bruce pulled out a joint, took a drag and passed it around. Albert took a hit and handed it to Katherine, who was so absorbed with Ellen and Gary that she passed it along without taking a drag. Within a few minutes Albert felt the puff take effect and he found himself talking to Hal about the insubstantiality of all sensory phenomena and how Western man operated under the illusion that he had a separate identity from the universe in which he lived. "The true identity is infinite consciousness. Beneath all this illusion of personality, there is the solitary oneness that breeds the essence of all things," Hal maintained as he took the last hit off the roach and watched the smoke drift upwards as he slowly exhaled.

"A person can never be free until he expands his awareness beyond the boundaries of categorical reality and breaks into the essence of the Un-thing that encompasses and gives birth to both being and non-being."

Suddenly Lyric stood up and, tossing her long, straight black hair behind her head, broke into a recitation of Hindu scripture:

"There was neither being nor non-being
   No air nor firmament beyond it.
   Was there a stirring?
   Where, beneath what cover?
   Was there a great abyss of unplumbed water?"

Hal paused to listen like a bearded sage would listen to a pupil. By the time Lyric had finished, the entire house was quiet, and then suddenly broke into the spontaneous rhythm of snapping fingers. Someone a couple of tables away started shouting, "Albert! Albert! Albert!" And he was soon joined by the entire room.

Albert stood up to recite and the chanting subsided.

"Now is then
   And so is then
   I am so
   Death is when"

Again the rhythmic snapping of fingers renewed, another person's name was called, and another poem was recited. Somewhere about one-thirty, the poetry stopped and the saxophonist began to wail. He was accompanied by a drummer, a pianist and a bass player, and each took turns playing solo, improvising on the basic theme. For a while some of the crowd kept time clapping in accompaniment, like primitives participating in a ritualistic rite of passage.

A cat named Larry approached the table and tried to come on to Katherine, but he was so strung out, he made little sense. Finally, Albert told him to cool it, and Larry, feigning insult, wandered off to another table to drink more wine and eventually pass out.

After a while, Hal decided to leave and invited everyone back to his pad. Albert looked at Katherine, who by now seemed thoroughly engrossed in a conversation with Bruce and Gary. "Sure, let's go," she said, "I'm good for a party".

"Like far-out!" said Bruce as they all got up to leave. "Let's make it, let's make it happen."

By the time they had emerged again into the street, the fog was in and The Beach seemed strangely quiet after the sounds of the club. They walked down Green to Grant and turned the corner. Hal had invited several other friends on the way out of the club, and they had followed with their friends until about fifteen or so hipsters had joined the migration. As they started down Grant towards Hal's pad, Lyric and a cat named Norm started playing an imaginary game of hopscotch while several others sang "She'll Be Coming 'Round the Mountain". They turned a few more corners and soon reached an old Victorian and climbed the narrow flight of stairs.

Ellen went into the cluttered kitchen and turned on the overhead bare electric bulb that hung on a frayed cord, which dangled from the belly button of a large smiling Buddha painted on the ceiling. "Ah, enlightenment," she said as she lit the few candles that sat on the overturned orange crates in the living room.

Hal produced a little bottle of ouzo, a half jug of red wine and about seven or eight jelly glasses.

The flat consisted of a living room, kitchen, and two small bedrooms. There was very little furniture in the living room, save a mattress, a battered old sofa and overturned orange crates. The walls were filled with Ellen's abstract paintings, and in one bedroom, slogans like "If you see the Buddha, kill him" and "Jesus Saves Green Stamps" were scrawled on the walls. The other bedroom was a workroom filled with a clutter of paints, canvases and a bizarre variety of art objects, including a collection of seashells and old bottles.

Albert poured a glass of ouzo and they settled onto the mattresses in the living room, resting their backs against the wall. As the crowd straggled in, some gathered in the kitchen, where an intense argument ensued as to whether the French Communist Party had been justified denouncing Pablo Picasso's portrait of Stalin. Others joined Katherine and Albert by sitting on the floor in a circle. Several joints were lit and passed communally and this time, Katherine took a short hit. Hal put on a Japanese record, and for a while they sat quietly transfixed, sipping ouzo and following the patterns of the Kabuki music. People filtered in from the kitchen and others drifted away, but Katherine did not take notice. She had reached that sense of timelessness that did not require thought about the past or consideration for the future. She was content to be caught in the movement of the music, like a seed in a current of air.

After a while Hal emerged from the back room carrying another bottle of ouzo and wearing a loosely-fashioned orange kimono. He came over and landed his huge frame unceremoniously on the mattress next to Katherine. He was pretty stoned and in a playfully belligerent mood, started to put Albert on about his white dinner jacket.

"Albert, White Angel Aristocrat
Descending to the valley.
Upbeat, downbeat.
Leave the mind behind.
Decisions, revisions.
And the turning of time behind.

Bind the behind time.

Cut out, cool out, fall out, far-out, cop out the cop out

Far-out White Angel."

By the time he had finished, he had gained an audience who took up the beat.

"Cut out, cool out, cop out the cop out." "Cut out, cool out, cop out the cop out." They chanted, snapping their fingers and swaying to the rhythm they had created, which completed and blended with the Kabuki music. "Cut out, cool out, cop out the cop out."

Katherine joined the mantra, directing it as much within as without. "Cut out, cool out, cop out the cop out."

Suddenly Lyric got up and went off, only to return with a tray of Ellen's paints. "We are the Hesperides," she said as she took out several brushes, dipped them in the paints and passed them around the chanting circle.

"We are the Hesperides.

Guardians of apples gold.

From the garden in the western sky."

With those words she knelt down on the mattress and began painting bright yellow apples on the lapels of Albert's dinner jacket. She was joined by the others, offering different colors and designs while the chanting went on. "Cut out, cool out, cop out the cop out."

Soon they lifted Albert up and Katherine collaborated with Siegfried on an abstract representation of the dragon, which according to Greek mythology helped the Hesperides guard the golden apples given to Hera by Gaea. All this time Albert maintained a posture of mental detachment, as if he were Zeus or Brahma. He was only vaguely aware of these lesser gods as they played through the world, which was the incarnation of his body. When they had finished they returned to the circle and fell silent, leaving him standing in the middle. After a moment he spoke:

"They danced around the circle and suppose

But he who sits in the middle, knows."

With this there was a chorus of loud applause accompanied by shrieks and shouts of laughter.

A cat named Mailer brought a pair of bongo drums from the closet. He produced a beat and some people began to keep time, while his chick, Zorba, began what Katherine called, "an interpretive dance beyond interpretation". Within minutes she removed her blouse and danced naked as if to bare her soul.

Jack, who Katherine and Albert had first seen outside The Cellar, appeared with two more jugs of red wine. Hal had called him since it was too late for him to make the run. Gary and Bruce finally slipped off to their pad to ball and Ellen engaged fellow artists in a critical analysis of critical analysis.

Albert finally looked at his watch, it was four-thirty in the morning. And Katherine had fallen asleep leaning on his shoulder as he discussed the Zen principle inherent in the existential moment. He reached over and gently shook her. "The goddess Aurora will soon bring light," he said. "I think it is time to go."

Hal had blasted crap until he was totally gone, so there was no point in even saying goodbye. Albert found a phone and called for a cab. The party had thinned out now. Some had gone, some had fallen asleep, some were still talking quietly through a stoned stupor. The high evening had begun to slide down the opposite side of Olympus.

It was five o'clock by the time they climbed into the back of the cab. "Let's greet Aurora from Twin Peaks as she arrives over your city," Albert said, almost as if to suggest the final absurdity.

"I'm hip," said Katherine with a relaxed yawn, "but I need a cup of coffee for the gig."

They both laughed and then she said, "Do you think we should stop by and ask Beatrice Whitney to come along?"

"Far-out!" he teased, after directing the cabbie to an all-night coffee shop on Van Ness. "Far-out!"

They witnessed the sun come up over the East Bay hills, illuminating the city and azure bay with iridescent pink and gold as if stealing the treasures of the west back from the darkness. They drove home, where Chow-Ling readjusted their spines and provided them with a substantial breakfast of orange juice, scrambled eggs, and Chinese herbal tea, after which they went to sleep.

CHAPTER 14

WHEN KATHERINE AWOKE the next afternoon, she had been in San Francisco for only ten days, but in many ways it seemed like a lifetime. She had buried a father, negotiated to protect her inherited interests, and met a family she had never known. Somehow the turmoil, dilemmas and discoveries of these ten days seemed to have been summarized in the carefree absurdity of her wild night in North Beach. It was as if a calliope had steadily increased its tempo and she had been forced to ride the carousel even faster to keep up with the music until everything had become a whirling blur of disconnecting images and events. The calculated absurdity of The Bohemians had somehow made the music stop and now perhaps life could be placed back into some sort of perspective.

"Ay que vida!" she said as Chow-Ling applied pressure to the palm of her hand.

"What we both need is to take the cure." Albert suggested. "We need to spend the weekend in retreat."

"That sounds divine, but how do you propose to arrange it?"

"Through Chow-Ling," he laughed. "He will screen us from the outside world and supply us with trays of hot herbal tea and fresh fruit. It will be just like going to Karlsbadden before the war. We'll have an entire weekend to purge ourselves from the toxins of city life."

"Very good, let's agree on the logistics of the plan," she said. "I really think the cure may be the answer, but absolutely no dog hair."

"Dog Hair? Does Windsor bother you or do you mean dog hair as in 'hair off the dog that bit you?'"

For a moment Katherine looked completely bewildered and then burst out into laughter. "No, not old Windsor," she cried, realizing her confusion over the idiom and reaching over and giving Windsor a pat.

Besides an initial call to thank his mother and father, and a somewhat longer call to Aunt Louisa, Albert turned the phone over to Chow-Ling, who screened calls and left messages. Chow-Ling told people that they had driven to Pebble Beach for the weekend and would return Monday morning.

"Aunt Louisa wants to know if you want her sparklers for Opening Night," Albert said after hanging up the phone.

"Her what?"

"Her sparklers—her diamonds. She has a sapphire and diamond necklace that's the envy of San Francisco. She wants you to wear it to the opera."

"Oh, the opera! I had quite forgotten. What am I going to do for a gown?"

"I'm sure you can find something at I. Magnin's."

"Good, I usually don't need more than a few alterations. I've never had trouble in any of the Parisian or Italian houses. But I'm not sure about Aunt Louisa's sapphires?"

"Don't worry. They're Van Cleef and Arpel. Very nice, designed in the 30s," he said reassuringly. "I know what you're thinking about old lady's jewelry, but you will like these."

"Very well. I'll trust you. I suppose I don't have a choice."

"Not really. There are implications beyond style."

"What do you mean?"

"To be perfectly frank, you will be making a statement by wearing them," he explained. "Everyone knows Aunt Louisa's sapphires and when you appear with them, San Francisco will know that Katherine Louise McMasters has been reunited with her mother's side of the family."

"I see," Katherine pondered. "In that case, I shall wear a very low-cut gown."

But Katherine knew that dressing for the opera was one of the least of her problems, and she shared with her cousin the new revelations concerning the possible challenge to her father's will, the astonishing offer to buy the company and her decision to hire independent counsel.

He listened carefully as he always did, asking thoughtful questions and helping her sort out the issues.

"You really ought to have a talk with old George Hampton," Albert concluded. "For my money he's the best attorney in San Francisco—wise, steady-on-the-helm sort of fellow. Father uses him. He'll know how to advise you."

"Yes, of course," Katherine said, "we must do that next week." She sighed and reached over the table to squeeze his hand. "For now, I have to think about my Aunt Gloria and Uncle Otto. She can be as unpredictable as a riptide—a very strange sort, obsessively jealous, especially of Father. She'll undoubtedly be outraged she was not left a controlling interest in the line. She always has to be in control."

"And her husband?"

"I'm also concerned about Otto," she said, gazing out the window. "He can be very stubborn and at times cruel. With Peron's policy of nationalization, he may feel he has his back to the wall. His offer may be part of some long-range financial strategy and if that's the case—well—?"

"What are Otto Brutmann's politics?" Albert asked, trying to introduce a subject that held a good deal of curiosity for him.

"I don't know really. I'm sure he had fascist sympathies during the war, but in Argentina, politics are never discussed with women or children. Of course, I've heard rumors."

"Rumors?"

"An old friend told me she had heard he was involved in a conspiracy to hide Nazi war criminals in exchange for gold. She isn't a very reliable source, and those kinds of rumors are very common since the war."

"But if they were true, he might be using that gold," he speculated.

"You mean to back up his share of the offer?"

"Exactly!"

All these concerns ran through Katherine's mind as she tried to rest in her cousin's apartment during the Sunday before her aunt and uncle's arrival.

Early Monday morning Albert called I. Magnin and scheduled an appointment for Katherine with Stella in the Custom Salon. Normally it would have been impossible to get an appointment, but since his mother and her friends were such frequent patrons, he was able to pull the appropriate strings, and they both arrived at ten o'clock. Because time was critically short, Katherine did not hesitate in selecting a Howard Greer gown of black crepe styled with a floor-length straight skirt and a bodice of blue topaz edged in velvet. Aunt Louisa's sapphires and diamonds would complete the outfit and by eleven-thirty, they were headed for lunch at the Iron Horse on Maiden Lane.

At four p.m. Addison arrived in the company limousine to pick Katherine up for the trip down to the airport. New York confirmed that Gloria and Otto had made their connecting flight from London, and were due in San Francisco at around five p.m. The ride down was as still and stiff as a Siberian winter. Addison did not want to bring up business because he sensed that Katherine already felt unduly pressured and he did not want to aggravate an already sensitive situation. But from the moment she saw her aunt and uncle disembark from the plane, Katherine felt the tension in her body increase. Gloria was more emotional than ever. Upon seeing Katherine, she cried hysterically and had to be removed to a private lounge until she recovered.

"We'll have the doctor come 'round and give you something when we get back to Father's," Katherine sympathized.

"I don't need a tranquilizer," Gloria insisted. "What I need is to be told why they buried Stanley without me."

"I told you, Gloria," her husband interrupted, annoyed at his wife's hysterics. "The Corporation decides on such things. It is better to have this past."

Otto's directness seemed temporarily to control what had appeared to be the start of a tangent

It wasn't, however, until they arrived back at the McMasters home that the real trouble began. In the course of discussing their offer to purchase her shares in McMasters Shipping, Katherine mentioned that she felt she needed time to consider all the alternatives. At this point, Otto became very emphatic. "You don't have any real alternatives, Katherine. You cannot assume responsibility for a multi-million dollar corporation you know nothing about. You must be sensible and turn over the running of the company to people who know their business. You will be free then to return to Argentina or Europe and go on with your life as a normal young lady should."

Along with her husband, Gloria became irritated at Katherine's suggestion. "What do you mean 'alternatives'? How dare you suggest to your uncle that the offer you are being made is not a generous one. I can't imagine what you are thinking of, Katherine. I think you owe us an apology at once," she said as she banged her cocktail tumbler down on the heavy marble end table in the drawing room. Getting out of her seat, she turned her back on her niece and moved to the window to register an extra degree of dissatisfaction.

This was the behavior Katherine had anticipated. Gloria in one of her rages. There was a long silence as Katherine sat without moving, waiting for the next affront.

"Well?" Gloria said, finally turning sharply and glaring at Katherine across the room. "What do you have to say for yourself?"

Katherine took a slow sip of the iced tea she had substituted for a cocktail and after a controlled pause, she put her glass gently down and spoke in a quiet, firm voice, "I am sorry if I did not make myself clear. I am not implying that the offer is not a good one. Indeed, I am sure it is. What I am saying is that I need time to examine the offer and the company, and to consider what I might want to do. If that position is unacceptable to you and Uncle Otto, then I am afraid it will just have to be unacceptable."

She got up slowly from the chair and continued in an almost condescending manner, "I am sure you are both quite weary from your long trip. Perhaps we need to discuss this all at some later date, after you have had time to rest and collect yourselves."

With this remark, Gloria exploded. "We will discuss it now. You are being extremely rude, Katherine. We will discuss it now, and we will discuss it for as long as it takes if we have to stay up all night and all day tomorrow. How dare you to talk to us like you were in charge. How dare you! How dare you! Answer me, answer me this instant!" she screamed in an uncontrollable flash of indignation.

Katherine turned and looked at her aunt, but this time the cool relaxed control was replaced by a determined strength that Gloria had never seen in her niece before. "Let me try to explain, Gloria," she said, dropping the familiar "Aunt. "In the first place, Father's will may be contested, in which case the company may not even be mine to sell. In the second place, if I do inherit, I will be in charge. I will own a controlling interest in McMasters Shipping, and I will do what I want when I want with my company. In the third place, as for staying up all night, or discussing the business tomorrow, I am afraid both are out of the question. Tomorrow I am attending the opening night of the San Francisco Opera, so I will not be able to discuss anything with either of you until Wednesday at the earliest. By that time, I hope you will both be in a more agreeable mood." With these words Katherine turned, said good night, and walked out of the room to leave her aunt and uncle and Phillip Addison looking at each other in a state of complete shock. She had never been so openly defiant. As she ascended the stairs she could hear screaming, as if a parrot had just been lit on fire, and she knew that Gloria had just been told about Monique Moralles Monahan and the intended marriage.

The next morning she greeted her aunt and uncle with a cordial but cool reserve. They all had spent a rather fitful night, but Katherine awoke with a new resolve not to be manipulated or bullied. For their part, Otto and Gloria were still agitated at her defiance, but initially seemed somewhat more willing to seek accommodation. They sensed that the niece they had more or less ignored for so long had grown into a strong independent woman capable of decisive action.

However, soon after Katherine had joined them for breakfast, any pretension of civility disappeared when Gloria inquired about the opera. "How did you manage to decide to go to the opera when you have only been in San Francisco for two weeks?" she asked.

"I was invited by my cousin, Albert Devonshire," Katherine said, looking Gloria straight in the eye. "We will be going with his parents and sitting in the Devonshire's box."

Katherine could see a wave of corrosive anger cross her aunt's face, as if Katherine had purposely chosen to thwart everything Gloria had attempted to achieve in raising her. Yet combined with the rage there was an element of consternation, as if she were stunned by the bombshell Katherine had just exploded. When Gloria finally absorbed what her niece had said, her wrath was uncontrollable.

"You have betrayed your father's memory," she blustered. "Your father has not been dead two weeks and you're attending the opening of the season! Do you know what the Devonshires and that bitch Louisa Harte tried to do to your father? Do you know?! Do you know?!!"

Perceiving her aunt to be on the verge of hysteria, Katherine decided that it would be well advised to leave. Without finishing her coffee, she calmly folded her napkin, arose from the table and left the room. Her leaving, however, did not stop her aunt, for she could still hear raving in an irrational diatribe against what Gloria denounced as a great act of hateful betrayal and disrespect.

CHAPTER 15

*O*PENING NIGHT OF the San Francisco opera season is as glorious
as the coronation ball of a Russian Czar and Albert was anxious for
Katherine to enjoy herself. If she still harbored any lingering feelings
about San Francisco being a provincial town, he knew opening night
would dispel them forever.

Katherine had decided to dress at her cousin's apartment to avoid
any further confrontation with Gloria and Otto. As she joined Albert
in the living room, resplendent in the Howard Greer gown and Aunt
Louisa's sapphires, Hector proceeded to scream and whistle insults.
She turned, faced the bird and with a laugh, took her sable coat and
covered his cage. Doug and Amy Mackie soon arrived. They shared
a bottle of Blason de France champagne, which Chow-Ling had
chilled especially for this night of nights. Being thus fortified, they
piled into Doug's old restored Packard and headed across town for
the candlelight dinner in the San Francisco Museum of Art. The
large throngs of spectators who always are drawn by the glamour of
the evening, were waiting outside when their car pulled around. As
they emerged, a reporter shouted to his photographer, "There she
is! Get her!"

"They have probably been waiting to photograph us for hours,"
Albert said, temporarily blinded by a barrage of flashbulbs.
Katherine, however, did not seemed to be startled in the least, and
demonstrating a remarkable degree of savoir faire; she nodded
and smiled at both press and public before slowly moving into the

museum hall where she was warmly greeted by Mrs. Russell, one of the evening's hostesses.

"She seems like a charming lady," Katherine commented as they moved across the hall admiring the decorations, which in fiery shades of red carried out the theme of the opera by resembling Hades. "She's W.H. Crocker's daughter," Amy said, filling her in. "She was hospitality chairman of the charter U.N. conference. Organized hundreds of parties all over town. Kept everyone from the Russians to the Arabs happy. It was all great fun. We all had parties. George and Victoria had a splendid dinner at the Devons for the British Ambassador and Mumsie and Dad did cocktails.

"Geez! The champagne we went through in those days was phenomenal," Albert added, remembering the fun of eight years before.

Amy took Katherine under her wing and introduced her around. They chatted briefly with Mona Miller and Mrs. Lyman before moving on to where the Devonshires and the Waters had engaged Mrs. Esberg.

"That topaz tiara Mrs. Esberg has plunked on the top of her head along with the necklace belonged to the Empress Eugenia," Albert whispered. "Years from now they will point to Auntie's sapphires and say they were worn in 1953 by Katherine, Empress of San Francisco."

"I hope that won't make me a relative of Emperor Norton."

"Very good. You know more about your city than I thought."

Almost before Albert was able to introduce Katherine, Beezie came bouncing over decked out in a bright red sequined gown that came down to her knees before flaring out in yards of tiny pleats. "Are you part of the decorations?" he asked, observing how Beezie's ample bosoms were lifted to the point of almost overflowing.

"Oh, yes!" said Beezie, twirling around breathlessly, too full of herself to process his quip. "Pedro Rodrigues designed this for me in Spain last summer."

"For the bullfights?" he asked, steadying his expression so as not to reveal anything but the most serious countenance.

Again his comment went unnoticed as Beezie Whitney was off in a cloud of busy chatter and seductive posturing.

"I wonder if being crazy is contagious," Amy said as they watched Beezie flit away towards an unsuspecting victim.

"Well, I haven't kissed her!" Katherine said throwing a teasing glance in her cousin's direction.

The dinner, although quite acceptable, was not very enjoyable as meals go. There was always too much electricity in the air on opening night to enjoy the food and Albert speculated that Aunt Louisa perhaps had made the wise decision to have a quiet dinner with friends at the St. Francis. He found himself becoming more than a little annoyed at the seemingly endless flow of acquaintances who jostled by their table in order to meet Katherine. Finally, determined to avoid a last-minute dash across the courtyard, and, anticipating another gauntlet of photographers, he decided they should leave.

Once safely inside the carriage entrance and past the inevitable sea of flashing lights, Katherine had a few minutes to admire the classical design of the opera building, with its great free-standing granite columns and marble promenades.

They joined Aunt Louisa in her box and watched the golden circle fill up with the brilliant array of fashion and excited expectation. This was the annual gathering towards which so many hours of considered preparation had flowed, and Katherine was moved in the realization that the city of her birth could produce an evening infused with such elegance. Yet beyond the glamour was something even more important. It was the underlying sense of solidarity and continuity in the wild sparkling soul of San Francisco. Representatives of the great families who had made San Francisco grand filled the golden circle, as Millers, Zellerbachs, deYoungs, Tobins, Camerons, Kings and Crockers took their places.

Doug and Amy, followed by Albert's parents, joined them just before the curtain went up and Nicola Rossi Lemeni in the title role of *Mefistofeles* transported the audience into the obscure realm of Goethe's mystical drama in which the devil struggles for the soul of Faust against the Lord of Creation.

"You know," Katherine whispered, leaning over and touching his hand, "the first time this opera was performed at La Scala in 1868, there was fighting in the streets. After two performances, the police ordered it closed."

"Let's hope the reception is somewhat calmer tonight, "Albert said, adding drily, "they seemed to be on the verge of rioting over you when we arrived." He knew his cousin had been a sensation and that she would undoubtedly be the talk of the town for the season. This amused him, for he knew that the buzzing among the movers and shakers of society would ensure all sorts of interesting gyrations that would be fun to observe.

Act Two was brought to an end by a chorus of infernal powers celebrating the Sabbath and they strolled through the lobby with Amy and Doug, leaving Aunt Louisa in her box to receive friends. They had no sooner started a conversation with Mrs. Ayers when Beezie again materialized. "How do you like our opera house, Katherine?" Beezie asked haughtily, as if suggesting Katherine was unacquainted with architectural grandeur.

"It's really quite splendid," Katherine replied sweetly, "it reminds me just a little of Palladio's Basilica in Vicenza."

"Oh!" said Beezie, with a quizzical expression, "I don't know the Pallodioses. Do they live in Argentina?"

Albert caught a glance thrown in his direction by Doug. "Yes, Beezie, they are Argentinians, but they don't have a relief of the two Amazons riding twin horses like we do," he said, referring to the sculptures which decorated the side walls.

Beezie smiled triumphantly in the knowledge that her opera house contained such a treasure. "Yes," Albert said, turning to Katherine and with a wink, continued, "and I'll have you know, Katherine, if you look closely, you can see that Beezie was used as the model for our Amazons."

"Oh, Albert, I was not!" giggled Beezie as she nearly spilled champagne down her cleavage. "You're such a silly-billy. I've never even been to Brazil."

Satisfied with scoring a few points, Albert turned the conversation to baseball, while Katherine engaged a group of admiring men in discussing the Grand Prix, which had just been won by her friend, Juan Manuel Fangio. Upset at Albert having scored a point on old Beezie, Doug unsuccessfully tried to persuade him into taking the Dodgers over the Yankees in the Series.

"Not on your life, Douggie old boy," he laughed. "I'll stick with Stengel's winning streak. He'll take Charlie Dressin just like he took Cleveland yesterday. But if you want to put the same money on Mefistofeles in the fourth act, you're on!"

Soon the warning buzzer sounded and they returned to their box, accompanied by Beezie, whose escort had decided to remain at the bar and settle his nerves. She tried to talk through the entire third act, until Aunt Louisa finally quieted her with a stony stare. The rest of the performance went along without interruption until Victoria made the mistake during the fourth act, of attempting to explain to Beezie how the duet between Faust and Helen is symbolic of the birth of ideal poetry in the union of the classical Greek and the romantic German.

"You know, Beezie, darling," Victoria concluded in a confidential whisper, "Albert has both Greek and German blood."

"Yes, I know," said Beezie with a sigh. "Isn't it all too awfully marvelous that this opera is about him?"

Soon the last act was over and the audience began slowly making its way out towards the long line of limousines, which waited to collect them. Albert and Katherine stopped at the bar to have a drink and let the crowd thin out. A few of his friends who always successfully avoid the third and fourth acts were well oiled by this time. "What do you think of the opera, old boy?" said Beezie's date, Joe Pritchard, slapping Albert on the back.

"I found I was somewhat sympathetic to Faust," he replied, assuming an academic tone he had learned from a Berkeley professor. "In the end he found reality to be filled with sorrow, and the ideal nothing but an unsubstantial dream."

"Oh, I did too!" interjected Beezie, who had somehow decided to permanently attach herself to their party. "Wasn't it all just too awfully wonderful!"

Turning around to where she had taken up residence at his right, he continued, "I suppose, Beatrice, my darling, that the difference between you and Faust on the philosophical level is that for you, reality is largely an insubstantial dream, and the ideal has simply never been considered."

"Oh, do you really think so?" she asked, and for the first time during the entire evening, she seemed for a fleeting moment to be halfway serious, and at the same time very proud that Albert had probed her psychological depths.

CHAPTER 16

HE NEXT MORNING, the social column of the city's paper was filled with news of the opening night of the opera's thirty-first season and a large picture of Katherine chatting with the Waters and her aunt dominated the society page. "You were obviously the rage last night," he said as Chow-Ling served coffee. "Listen to this: 'Not unlike the ideal poetry produced at the union of Helen and Faust in the fourth act of Boito's *Mephistopheles*, Katherine Louise McMasters, escorted by her cousin Albert Edward Devonshire, provided something powerfully electric to the opera's opening night.'"

"I wonder who fed them that line," Katherine said smiling knowingly. Albert did not answer but slowly turned the page in search of Herb Caen's column without which no one in San Francisco could start the day thinking they were informed.

They spent a leisurely breakfast pouring over the paper and laughing about the account of Beezie's dress, which was described in great detail.

Soon, however, the opulence of the evening and its memory began to fade.

"I wonder if I should call Aunt Gloria or simply go by father's house and chance to catch them in a more agreeable mood."

"It would be a shame to let your Aunt spoil the glow of opening night," Albert sympathized. "Perhaps you should call first and test out the waters."

"The waters?"

"Check things out," he explained. "Test out the waters, hair of the dog. You'll learn the language eventually."

"Yes," she laughed. "In the case of Aunt Gloria, it's a matter of testing out the tidal wave. But I suppose you're right. I'll call rather than go by. I don't want to become embroiled with Gloria's irrational temperament or Otto's Teutonic one, for that matter."

When Katherine finally did get around to calling, she found her aunt still fuming over the account in the morning paper. "You have betrayed your father's memory," Gloria screamed again and again into the phone. "How could you appear on opening night with those Devonshires? Do you know what you have done?"

She finally paused long enough, for Katherine to answer very matter-of-factly: "You seem to forget, Gloria, that I really never knew Father very well, so I don't have much of a memory of him to betray. And as for the Devonshires, they are as much my relatives as you are, and frankly, they have been most gracious and kind to me. I can only wonder why I was not allowed to have any contact with them as I was growing up." This only served to infuriate Gloria more, and she slammed down the receiver in a fit of rage, which, although it did not surprise Katherine, did tend to mar what otherwise would have been a beautiful morning. "I suppose that I will have to go back to my father's house at some point and try to settle things," Katherine said, "although I am sure that it's not going to be very easy. When Gloria gets into one of her states, it's almost impossible to deal with her in any reasonable manner. I think the news that Father was going to remarry has completely unhinged her and she has decided to take it out on me."

"Perhaps the best course of action would be simply to ignore her for a day or so, and let the whole thing blow over," Albert suggested "We might run by your father's house, pick up whatever you need, and then drive down to Treehaven and spend a day or so taking it easy by the pool and enjoying Aunt Louisa's company.

After thinking about it for a moment or two, Katherine consented. "I suppose you are right. I could use a rest, and I don't see any point in continually subjecting myself to Gloria and Otto's bullying. Asking them to leave Father's house would only make matters worse, although I am not sure that going down to Aunt Louisa's won't just add more fuel to the fire."

Albert made a hasty call to Treehaven, informed Ivy that they were coming, and then helped Chow-Ling load up the Buick. When they arrived at her father's house, they found that Gloria and Otto had gone out making things a lot less complicated. Within a half an hour, they had packed Katherine's clothes and were heading out of the city, talking and laughing about the opera, Beezie, and the midnight buffet supper Albert's parents had given at the Devons.

"You know, Albert," Katherine said, "I think Gloria would be marvelous cast as one of the witches in Act II. I can just visualize her dancing and prostrating herself before Mephistopheles."

It was a beautiful September day, and Albert stopped in Brisbane to put down the convertible. As they sped south and the warm fresh air blew through the car, Katherine unloosened her hair and rested her head against the back of the seat. For several miles they were quiet, and Katherine let her mind wander. Thoughts about her friends passed through her mind: Trixie Metcalf, now studying at Vassar, Ricardo de Valpolicella, who had proposed marriage to her in Buenos Aires. They came to her, not as part of her present, but as a memory from the past. Slowly she began to realize that she was starting to think of San Francisco as the place where she belonged. She had no particular reason to return to Europe other than to continue traveling, and she had grown tired of doing that. And although she at times missed the open pampas and the ranchero where she had spent her youth, she realized that she could not go back and make a life there again. She thought warmly of Ricardo. He had been truly in love with her, and both his family and her aunt and uncle had promoted an engagement, but she was not in love with him, and only saw complications if she returned to Argentina without the intention of marriage. Her mind then shifted to her mother. Why had her father and aunt kept so much from her over the years? She wondered if her mother might not have been somewhat like Margherita in the opera, a victim of forces beyond her control, a pawn in a larger game she had perhaps not understood. But what were the forces, and what was the game? There was something too about her Father and Gloria that she could not quite crystallize in her mind. It was an old impression. Something about remote laughter coming from closed rooms closed off in the lost memories of childhood. She certainly had overreacted to her brother's plans to remarry. Again Phillip Addison came to mind, and her mother's piano preserved all those years in a darkened room of his apartment with a tribute of orchids by her picture. What was she going to do about the piano? She did not want to live in her father's house. It was too cold and impersonal and made her feel very uncomfortable.

As they passed the outskirts of the old Mills estate north of Burlingame, Katherine rolled her head in Albert's direction. "Where can I find an apartment with a drawing room large enough for a grand piano?" she asked vaguely.

For a moment, neither of them realized the implications of what she had just said, and then with a look that registered surprise, Albert turned his head quickly, "You mean your mother's Bosendorfer?"

A long, expectant pause followed as both of them began to absorb what she meant by her question. "You are planning to stay?" he finally said in a half-question, half-statement of fact.

"I suppose I am," Katherine said finally, still a little astonished at the decision she had just made about her life. "I suppose I will have to stay for a while, at least, until I settle the business, and I can't go on bouncing between my relations no matter how much fun it has been."

"You can bounce all you like as far as we are concerned", he said with a smile. "But this is capital! Wait until we tell Aunt Louisa! The old gal will be thrilled, as will Mother and Father. This is capital! We'll get you an apartment. There's no problem in doing that. I'll call old Ross Page as soon as we get to Treehaven. He always knows what's available in town."

They drove through the village in the midafternoon, confident they would have time for a long swim if they avoided telling Aunt Louisa about Katherine's decision until the cocktail hour. Their plans, however, were almost interrupted when Prentice informed them upon their arrival that Aunt Louisa was in the conservatory with her florist and orchid supplier, Madame Ng.

"I think I would like to meet this Madame Ng," Katherine said, glancing at her watch. "Aunt Victoria mentioned her several times and she sounds rather intriguing."

"All right," Albert said, slightly annoyed, "but if we miss our swim because we become entangled with Madame Ng and Madame Aunt Louisa it will be all your fault."

As they proceeded down the central hall, they passed again the jade dragon in the sixth alcove. Again a chill crossed Katherine's shoulders as she looked at the fierce compelling head. They moved on a few yards and through the conservatory door. There at the opposite end in her usual place, sat Aunt Louisa with Madame Margaret Mae Ng. As they approached, Madame Ng looked up slowly and directly at Katherine. Again Katherine sensed a strange chill cross her shoulders as she was introduced and observed Madame Ng's indecipherable eyes. She was, thought Katherine, a beautiful woman for her age, but at the same time, she felt a sense of bewilderment and confusion over something she could not identify.

"I am honored to meet the grand-niece of Mrs. Harte," Madame Ng said with an enigmatic smile.

"I am pleased to meet you," Katherine said politely. "Albert's mother was just telling me at lunch the other day about the fabulous orchids you import. I should like very much to see them sometime."

Madame Ng did not respond verbally, but merely nodded her head in acknowledgement, and Aunt Louisa began talking about a variety of cattleyas she was trying to obtain. Taking this opportunity to excuse themselves, they headed for the pool before it was too late. "She was a rather mysterious sort," Katherine said as they walked across the gardens to the pool house.

"She certainly is," Albert agreed with a laugh. "We always called her the Dragon Lady when I was a kid. She's right out of Central Casting. I don't think she ever liked me, but I have to hand it to her—she has dominated the florist industry in the city for years. No one ever schedules a wedding or an important party until Madame Ng is consulted."

They swam for a while, played a short game of tennis, and then popped back in the pool to cool off. It was a warm, quiet afternoon without a trace of wind, and the sun falling slowly towards the western foothills, cast long playful shadows across the well-manicured lawns of Treehaven. They sat in the pool house for over an hour talking quietly about Katherine's decision to stay in San Francisco and experiencing a profound sense of peace as a covey of quail came out of the underbrush and scurried restlessly through the gardens in search of food.

A little after five o'clock they joined Aunt Louisa and Ivy in the garden pavilion for gin and tonics. Aunt Louisa was still exuberant about the success of opening night, and how well her great-niece had been received. "I had so many compliments, Katherine," she said. "The McCreerys thought you were absolutely charming, and so did Mrs. Clark and Mrs. Blyth. The McGuires even made a special point of coming by my box during intermission to tell me how lovely they thought you were. Florine said you were absolutely the rage of the younger set, and she heard that Susan and Mary thought you were just too amusing for words. She also said Marilyn was terribly jealous. Kay and Helen called this morning and are both vying for an opportunity to entertain you, and so is Mona. Of course, I told them you were terribly busy, but they all just insisted on having a party for you. They're afraid you're going to go back to Europe before they can have a chance."

"Well, you can tell your friends to relax, Aunt Louisa, because I have decided not to go anywhere, at least for a while. Albert is going to try and find something for me in the city. After all, I think it is my duty to keep an eye on him with Beezie around."

For a few moments Aunt Louisa did not absorb what Katherine had said, but continued to ramble on about how marvelous Nicola Rossi-Lemeni had been in the title role. Suddenly she stopped and jerked her head upward and around so she looked directly at Katherine. When she saw the smile on Katherine's face, her own eyes filled with tears and she fumbled for her handkerchief. Katherine and Albert looked at each other, for they knew just how much this news meant to this great grand old aunt of theirs.

Albert's eyes were also filled with tears, as he watched the realization creep over Aunt Louisa's face that the daughter of her beloved Elizabeth had come home to San Francisco to stay.

After a few sniffles, Aunt Louisa suddenly stiffened. "We need another gin and tonic, Ivy," she said, in a very abrupt manner. "Where is Prentice? Albert, you make the drinks. I'll have to have a party! That's it, I'll have the party. Why should anyone else entertain you until I have presented you at Treehaven? You never had a coming out party, so this will be a substitution. Albert, ask Prentice to chill the champagne. We may want some later, but get me some Bombay and tonic now!"

Katherine and Albert just sat and smiled at each other as Aunt Louisa shifted into high gear. The old mind was working a mile a minute, as she began to focus on what Albert already knew would be one of her most memorable parties, and he could remember some lulus.

Soon the conversation changed briefly to the topic of Katherine's apartment, and Albert excused himself to call Ross Page.

"Ross? Albert Devonshire here. Sorry to bother you at Happy Hour. How's the real estate business?"

"Albert old man! Fine! Fine! Gee, it's good to hear from you."

"Ross, I need your help and your confidence."

"You have it!"

"I am looking for an apartment for my cousin. Something spacious with views. On Telegraph if you can find it."

"I think there are several possibilities. Let me check a few out and get back to you tomorrow morning. Where can I reach you?"

"I'm in Burlingame. Diamond 4-3-443. And Ross, please keep this on the Q.T. you understand."

"Right, Al. Don't worry."

Because it was so very warm, they decided to have dinner in the garden pavilion and enjoy the quiet of the evening as it settled along the garden. After a delightful meal of green pepper shrimp, smoked duck, snow peas and an excellent Pineau de la Loire, Aunt Louisa and Albert told Katherine about the parties given at Treehaven over the years. "The masquerade balls are ones I remember most," he reminisced. "Remember the one you gave in the late 1920s, when everyone came dressed in California themes? Mother and Father came as a Spanish Señorita and a forty-niner. I was only eight or nine at the time, and they dressed me up as a little Indian. I had great fun all night scouting the ballroom and conservatory."

"That was the party where Kate Barube and her husband Mike came dressed as an orange and a bunch of grapes," remembered Aunt Louisa. "He fell into the fountain in the conservatory, and broke off the head of the gargoyle. Then Charles Peters got into his cups and thought he was a conquistador. He went out to the stables, got a horse and rode it over into the ballroom. Of course, the horse spooked and slipped on the floor and they had to take old Charlie away with a broken leg. Thank God the horse didn't break his leg, or I would have had to shoot them both."

Before they retired Albert and Katherine took a late-night swim. The still air was pungent with the sweet smell of gardenias and jasmine in the warm quiet night. He could not help but notice how beautiful Katherine was as she glided through the water, fracturing it in reflected moonlight. Her long, slender legs opened and closed in perfect rhythm as they swam the length of the pool, laughing and cavorting through the cool water. There was a carefree playfulness about her that he found exhilarating, and her exquisite beauty attracted him in a strange, unfamiliar way.

160

The next morning Phillip Addison called. He sounded particularly nervous, but was most insistent that Katherine come to a meeting with her aunt and uncle as soon as possible. "I think it's very important to take a serious look at the offer that is being made. In the business world, offers can sometimes be withdrawn as quickly as they are made. I just don't want any personal feelings you may have about your aunt and uncle to color a decision now that you might regret in a month or two."

Oddly, Katherine did not feel particularly pressured by Addison's request, because there was something in his manner that made her feel he was truly interested in her well-being. And the strange devotion he had displayed towards her mother's piano continued to add a degree of mystery to his motives. Yet having made the decision to stay in San Francisco, Katherine also felt she needed to buy some time. She knew Gloria would be furious at her decision to establish an apartment in the city, and she did not want to cloud business negotiations with the strange unpredictability of Gloria's emotions.

"Let me call you back, Phillip," Katherine finally said. "I need to check on a few things here, and I'll be back to you as soon as possible."

Hanging up the phone, she came back into the dining room where Aunt Louisa and Albert were poring over the morning papers. "They want a meeting as soon as possible," she said, sitting down with a sigh. "I'll have to go back to town either today or tomorrow."

"Why do they have to have a meeting so soon?" he asked. "Is there something in the wind? You told them you have no| intention of making a decision until you have had some time for consideration."

"He said that there was the possibility that the offer might be withdrawn."

"That's a high-pressure tactic if I've ever hear one," Aunt Louisa snapped. "My father always used to say, 'If you do business with pigs, you have to get down in the dirt, and just remember that the pigs love it!'"

"Is there any more about Monique Monahan?" Albert asked. "It would seem to me that any transaction concerning the company would have to be put on the back burner until the legality of the will is established."

"Phillip Addison assures me that there is absolutely nothing to worry about. She claims to be upset because there wasn't a post-mortem, but Addison said that the worst that could happen would be that some sort of minimal settlement would have to be made to get rid of her."

"She's a gold-digger. I've asked around," Albert volunteered. "She must be terribly frustrated to have come so close to such a large fortune and then lost out. I know the type. I wouldn't put anything past her." He paused for a moment, then snapped his fingers. "You can use her for an excuse to avoid a meeting."

"Well, I know you're both right," Katherine said, her eyes staring at some non-existent point on the table. "But there is something about Addison that I do trust, at least on some level. Anyway, I suppose it won't hurt to go and honor their request. To do otherwise would completely undo Aunt Gloria and would be, for Uncle Otto, an unforgivable affront. I know how he thinks, and he never forgives an insult."

"Are you going to tell them about your decision to stay in San Francisco?" Albert asked.

"I think not," Katherine said, with a restored twinkle in her eye. "If you think the British are having a bad time with the Mau-Mau terrorists in Kenya, you haven't seen anything until you've seen Aunt Gloria in action. All I'm going to do is listen to what they have to say, be noncommittal, and as polite as humanly possible."

"I wish you would see my lawyer," Aunt Louisa interjected. "Don't do anything without seeing George Hampton, I always say. He's the best lawyer in San Francisco, absolutely tops! George Devonshire uses him, and so does Albert."

"Yes, Auntie," Katherine agreed, "Albert is setting up an appointment for this week. But meanwhile, I'll call Addison back and agree to a short preliminary meeting tomorrow."

They had planned to spend the rest of the day playing tennis and relaxing by the pool, but by eleven a.m., Ross Paige called down.

"I have one of the best apartments in San Francisco. It's not even on the market yet, so I'm not supposed to disclose the address. You understand."

"Sure, Ross. Is there a chance we can see it?" Albert asked skeptically.

"It's an outstanding property. Panoramic view of the entire bay."

"O.K., Ross, O.K. But can we see it?"

"Hey, if you can keep it under your hat, I'll give you the inside track. What about this afternoon?"

"Great! How much will it list for?"

"You'll have to see it. Three-fifty a month. The view is spectacular. One of the best in the city."

"Holy smokes! Three hundred and fifty bucks a month!" Albert said, registering initial surprise to establish a position for later bargaining. "It sure would have to be one of the best in San Francisco for that price."

"It's a penthouse with nine large rooms and servant quarters," Ross continued, dropping key words to keep up the interest. "But as I say, you need to see it. The craftsmanship is superior, the location ideal and the view!—as I say, it's a winner!"

"All right, Ross, sounds good," Albert said again somewhat incredulously. "Let's have a look."

For all his posturing, Albert knew that Ross had always provided him with good service, and he trusted Ross's instincts. "Say about four o'clock. That will still give us time for a few hours by the pool before driving back to the city."

"You've got it, Al. Four o'clock."

From the moment Katherine entered the ornate tile lobby through the wrought-iron-and-glass front door, she fell in love with the building. There was the European flavor to the architecture, which was completed by a marvelous little old Italian doorman with a good-humored smile and enchanting manners. The apartment was on the eighteenth floor and Ross had been correct—it had a commanding panoramic view of the bay from the Golden Gate Bridge and Marin Headlands around to Alcatraz, Telegraph Hill, and the Bay Bridge, with Treasure Island and the Berkeley hills beyond. The apartment consisted of nine main rooms: living room, dining room, kitchen and paneled library, plus four bedrooms and four baths. The living room was particularly spacious, with painted paneled walls and an orchestra loft, which with the servants' quarters and glass sun deck formed a half second floor. The kitchen was small and needed remodeling, but it had a reasonable pantry. The oval dining room was designed for entertaining and it shared a spectacular view of the bay from an outdoor terrace, which ran across the length of the living room and master suite. Ross had also been right about the craftsmanship. The building had been designed by Julia Morgan and the fireplaces, ceilings, moldings, and doors looked like something William Randolph Hearst would have considered worthwhile. Katherine knew almost instantly that she wanted the apartment, and she gave her cousin an approving nod when Ross was not looking.

"Who is the owner?" Albert asked as they stood in the living room's large bay window looking out at the Golden Gate.

"Patrick Bartley, the developer who is doing all that work out in the Sunset," said Ross. "I'm surprised you haven't heard of him?"

"Heard of him!" Albert chuckled. "We just had dinner with him last week at my parents'. You remember, Katherine, the big fellow who sat across and down the table between Amy and Dolores. He seemed to be a hell of a nice guy, actually, although a tough businessman, I'll bet."

"You don't get to be where Patrick Bartley is by being a softie," Ross laughed.

Katherine had said very little. She had been visualizing her mother's piano in the bay window where they stood and she could imagine her mother sitting by a similar window at about four p.m. in the afternoon playing Mozart or Bach, or even a piece of modern jazz.

Spread out below them, the drowsy city looked like a giant sun-swept stage set. The afternoon breeze had not materialized to stir the smooth waters of the bay which seemed like glass, except for the wake of a single red stacked tug that plowed persistently past Yerba Buena Island.

"What do you think, Miss McMasters?" Ross finally asked.

Without thinking, Katherine replied, "I'll put the piano here. C'est ideale!"

Ross looked a little surprised and Katherine, suddenly realizing what she had said, corrected herself. "I mean, yes. It's perfect. I'll take it."

"Perhaps you should wait until tomorrow and think it over," Albert suggested, fearing she was acting on impulse.

"No, it's perfect. I can't imagine anything better. I'll want to talk to Mr. Bartley about a few alterations. The kitchen needs to be completely redone and there are a few minor details, like the floor on the sun deck, but I'm sure we can work things out."

Both Ross and Albert were surprised, but Katherine seemed resolute and there was not much room to engage in the negotiations, which Albert had so carefully anticipated.

"Perhaps it all might be more amicable if we met with Patrick Bartley directly," he suggested after considering things for a moment.

"If you feel comfortable with that, it's fine by me," Ross concurred.

By five-thirty they had left the apartment and Ross had a check to deposit. As Katherine and Albert drove the short distance back to his apartment, he thought how extraordinary fate was. A few short weeks ago, he did not even know this cousin who was sitting next to him, but now she had become the central focus of his life, and he had just acquired her as a neighbor. Katherine was also thinking about her destiny. What awaited her in this beautiful city of her birth, which had greeted her so warmly? The future was not without obstacles, but nevertheless, as she looked towards it a strange sort of calm settled through her, and for the first time in many years, she felt at one with her life.

That evening they went to Sam's Grill on Bush for dinner. "You know," Albert said over the petrale, "you can see Hal and Ellen's pad from the library in your apartment. You won't have far to go to party with Siegfried, Lyric, Mailer, Zorba and the rest."

Katherine laughed. "I suppose that's the one thing I find so utterly charming about San Francisco. Everything is so close together and compact, and there is such a wide variety of cultures and people in such a beautiful setting.

Quietly nodding, Albert did not respond. He knew that his cousin was falling in love with the city, and that once that happened, it would be a love affair that would last a lifetime.

CHAPTER 17

KATHERINE HAD NOT spoken to her uncle or aunt for two days, and she had hardly spent any time with them since their arrival in San Francisco. She felt badly about their estrangement, but she was determined as she drove to their Friday meeting, that she would not be bullied by either of them into concessions.

She arrived at the office to find that Gloria and Otto had requested a short meeting alone with her before the general meeting.

"Show them in when they arrive," Katherine replied as she looked over the reports Mrs. Tucker had handed her.

Within ten minutes, Gloria and Otto were there and Katherine, in a gesture of reconciliation, came to the door of her office to greet them. Gloria looked pale and tired under a large-brimmed hat which made her appear as if she were trying to hide in the shadow of a cave. As Katherine met them in the doorway, Gloria reached out both hands, placed them on Katherine's shoulders, and kissed her on the cheek as if trying to convey an apology. Katherine knew what she was doing, but she was bothered by the way Gloria executed the greeting. There was something indirect and dishonest about it. Her uncle's manner seemed less strident as he started the conversation with what amounted to more of an explanation than an apology. "You must know, Katherine, that we have been under exceptional pressure. The last months have been very hard on the nerves. We are not so sure now of our position in Argentina. This political and economic situation, both are without steadiness. Peron takes dangerous steps. He nationalized the Emberg's holdings. Two hundred million dollars. And the opposition party. Each day he arrests more leaders."

"We just don't know," Gloria interjected melodramatically. "You know, Eva has only been dead a little over a year now, and last spring his mother died, and then there was the assassination attempt."

"That has nothing to do with the situation, Gloria!" Otto growled intolerantly. "The point is that politically things are unsettled, and economically we cannot always be sure of where we stand. Only a few months ago, the government, under an order from Peron, expropriated large tracts of what he called 'idle farmland' and gave it to landless farm workers."

Katherine could not tell if they were trying to apologize for their heavy-handed behavior by explaining the pressures they had been under, or if they were merely attempting to build a framework to explain their offer to buy McMasters Shipping. She thought they might be trying to do both, and so she said very little. Soon, however, Otto showed his hand. "You see, Katherine, you understand that your Aunt Gloria and Uncle Otto want the best for you. I think you know that. If you see us unhappy, you know that it is because now there are many pressures for us to make decisions. When we make you an offer for this company, it is a very good offer. You know nothing about the running of a shipping line. You are so young, and you should be thinking about your marriage and family."

Finally Katherine saw the opening she had been waiting for. "I want you both to know as I am sure you do, that I am always very appreciative of all you have done for me. I know that you have been under a great deal of pressure because things are unsettled now, but you must also realize that I am under a great deal of pressure, too. You can appreciate that, I'm sure." She paused momentarily before she continued to let her words establish an equality with Otto's. "So you can understand that I, too, become impatient and irritable and want to go very carefully before I make any major decisions."

Otto stiffened almost imperceptibly, and Gloria, who had removed one glove, began to fiddle with the other as Katherine continued, "The point I wish to make without anger, is that I assume your offer is a generous one, but I need time. I just can't be pressured right now, until I get my bearings, so to speak."

Suddenly Gloria bristled, "How are you going to get any bearings at all in a city that is completely foreign to you, where you don't know anybody, where you are trying to run a company that you do not understand. This is what I cannot understand. You could come back to Buenos Aires and marry Ricardo, the most eligible young man in South America. You could do anything. We can't understand why you want to stay here. Your life has been in Europe and Argentina, not here."

Katherine could tell that Gloria was not as much angry as she was impassioned. But she also knew that Gloria's passion often turned into anger when it was thwarted, and that was what she hoped to avoid. She did so by agreement. "I think, Aunt Gloria, that you are probably right. I probably will decide to go back to Europe, maybe Geneva or Paris. Of course I will also consider Argentina a special home. I don't know about Ricardo. Perhaps he too, will be in my future. All I am asking is for a little time, a few months or weeks to decide where I am going to go and to learn something about my father and what he did and how he lived."

A strange frantic look came into her aunt's eyes, as if somewhere a nerve had been touched. Otto, too seemed to be aware of that nerve and looked at Gloria to judge her reaction. Katherine could not tell where the source of the panic lay, if it had something to do with the distant past or if it had something to do with Monique Monahan. "The point we are making," Otto said, taking over the conversation, "is that we must do something for our own financial position, to give us some protection in the event Peron nationalizes more industries and appropriates more land. I cannot say, but I think I always get on well with the Perons, so I think that I have nothing to worry about; on the other hand, one can just not be sure of these things." He went on talking about the one hundred and fifty million dollar trade pact Argentina had signed with Russia in August, and another for three hundred million dollars with Hungary. "Now if we were able to acquire McMasters Shipping, we could handle much of this trade, but only if the Perons see a profit for Argentinian interests. If they see an advantage, then they are more likely to use our ships. There are also other advantages for us personally, in terms of placing certain amounts of capital outside Buenos Aires, but this is very complicated. All I am saying is that we need to act now, and I need to return to Buenos Aires in the near future."

Katherine could begin to see that their impasse was essentially over time. She needed more time to make decisions, while her uncle needed her to make the decisions immediately. Of course she had no way of knowing if Otto was telling the truth. She thought it a little odd that McMasters would have any greater advantage in shipping just because he owned more of the stock. Furthermore, she saw no reason, other than a diminished sense of loyalty to her aunt and uncle, to hastily make a multi-million dollar business decision just so Otto and Gloria could ensure their financial position. She understood that things in Buenos Aires were unsure, but then they were always unsure, and she suspected their sudden panic was more fabrication than reality.

In the course of their conversation Mrs. Tucker came on the intercom to announce the arrival of Phillip Addison, Chambliss Horsley and several other directors.

"I just want you to be aware, Katherine," Otto said in conclusion, "that we are not trying to pressure you, but we do need to have an answer from you very soon. If you say no, then we need to do something else to protect our position."

"I understand," Katherine said, trying to be sympathetic without appearing weak.

As they walked into the boardroom to join the company's executive officers, Katherine felt they had at least reached some sort of understanding, if not an agreement.

The meeting with the executive officers was cordial. They spent the better part of two hours going over the offer, along with the corporate financial reports.

"All I can do is give you my word that I will continued to look at this offer very carefully," she promised. "I don't, however, feel in a position to commit to a decision by a specific date. Perhaps we can talk more when we meet next week." As they were preparing to break for lunch, Mrs. Tucker interrupted the meeting. Her expression was grim as she handed Katherine a note.

To: Miss McMasters
From: Charles Cahoun, reporter with San Francisco *Examiner* wants statement.
RE: Court order obtained 9/18/53 a.m. to exhume body of Stanley McMasters.

Katherine could feel the blood drain from her body.

"What is it?" She could hear Phillip Addison's voice. She handed the note over. Addison's face went white, his hands began to tremble and his breathing became rapid. He seemed stunned and unable to formulate a reaction.

"What is it?" Otto Brutmann demanded, but there was no response. Addison dropped the note on the table and got up and left the room. Katherine followed him. Halfway down the hall she could hear her Aunt screaming. She went into her office and closed the door. She sat quietly behind her desk for over half an hour trying to absorb what it all meant. "At last," she thought when the initial shock wore off, "At last any doubts surrounding father's death can be cleared away and I can get on with my life." She could not feel threatened by Monique Monahan or the possibility her inheritance might be threatened. "I suppose I'm just an active fatalist," she reflected as she picked up a report. "Whatever will happen will happen."

CHAPTER 18

*I*T WAS A weary Katherine who arrived back at the Lombard Street apartment after telling her aunt and uncle that she truly needed to be alone and had taken a room at the St. Francis Hotel. To cover herself, she had called Albert during lunch to tell him about the hotel and the autopsy, and he had agreed to register a room at the St. Francis under her name.

"How did it go?" Albert asked when she walked into the drawing room.

"Me siento cansada!" she said with a sigh as she melted into a chair. "I guess this changes everything at least for the time being."

"At least 'til Monday or Tuesday. I called Charlie Cahoun back after we talked and he said it shouldn't take much longer than a few days to get a preliminary autopsy report. How are things at the company?"

"Very strained."

"Does anyone think there is anything to any of this?"

"Oh, I don't think so. It would seem they all feel Monique is just trying to stir up a bit of trouble. Of course Aunt Gloria became hysterical. She has accused everyone from Father's doctors to Monique for being responsible for his death."

Monique?"

"That's Gloria. When she heard the news, she became completely undone. Otto had to take her back to the house and have her sedated."

"I took the liberty of calling Charlie Cahoun this afternoon and from what I gather, Monique Monahan's lawyers were the ones that asked for the court order for the exhumation. They are claiming there is the possibility that ... well, your father's death might not have been due to natural causes."

"That's preposterous! Who would have wanted to ..." She did not want to finish the sentence.

"Only someone who would have benefitted by his death before his will was changed," Albert said. He hated being so blunt, but felt Katherine needed to face all the possibilities that might arise.

"You mean me," she said, relieved that he had at last mentioned what she felt some people might be thinking.

"Well, yes, you for one, but then you would hardly be a likely candidate given that you were over 6,000 miles away and didn't even know about your father's intentions."

"Who else, then? No one else stood to lose anything of significance."

"Except perhaps your Aunt Gloria?"

"Who was also 6,000 miles away and didn't know what Father was up to. She was devoted to Father anyway. She worshipped him."

"Well, there is another possibility that someone wanted him out of the way for retribution."

Katherine closed her eyes and sighed. "I know Father was not well liked but who would—I mean it all is too much to begin to consider."

"The unions, a competitor—anyone might have had a motive. For example, the day before you arrived I talked with a friend of mine who sometimes works as a longshoreman. He suggested that your father might have exerted political influence to have certain Air Force contracts cancelled with the Kaiser Corporation. He didn't say he thought old Henry Kaiser had your dad snuffed, but he suggested that if your father was manipulating Washington to protect his line, a lot of people, including the Autoworkers, might have it in for him."

Katherine shook her head. "I suppose it's possible, but how could any of this be proven?"

"It probably couldn't. Rigg likes to speculate anyway. He always suspects a conspiracy among Capitalists."

"Have you ever seen any of the drafts your father was working on when he died?"

"You mean of the will?"

"Yes."

"No, since I was told they had no legal standing I never asked to see them."

"I think it might be interesting to have a look if you can get copies."

"I'll ask Addison."

"And what does Phillip Addison have to say about all this?"

"I don't know. He seemed to take the news rather more severely than anyone else. I didn't see him after we received the information until much later in the afternoon. Mr. Horsley, on the other hand, didn't seem the least bit affected. He came into my office with Otto about two-thirty and insisted that nothing would come of all this. He said I shouldn't let it deter me from considering their offer. They are both such scheming, despicable men. I don't trust them at all."

"What did you tell them?"

"I told them that under the circumstances, their request was completely inappropriate."

"I bet they didn't like that."

"No, not in the least, but they had to accept it."

"By the way, I made an appointment with my attorney for early Tuesday morning and arranged to drop off some of the relevant documents on Saturday, so that his junior partners can begin an examination of the offer."

"The point is, I suppose," said Katherine at last, "that even if the offer is a good one, I don't much feel like being pressured into selling immediately."

"What's the real reason for the hurry?" Albert asked, attempting to probe for possible motives behind her aunt and uncle's desire to close the deal so quickly.

"Otto talks on and on about how they need to protect their assets by moving them out of Argentina. The political situation, he claims, is uncertain. I can appreciate his position, at least on the surface, but I am just not sure they can appreciate mine. In a way, though, it was all rather strange. This morning before the news, Gloria avoided discussing the offer, or my seeing my mother's side of the family. I think for some reason that both are very emotional issues, and Uncle Otto had to more or less cap her off, so she wouldn't jeopardize the business proposition."

At six-thirty Albert got up and moved to the railing, "I have a surprise for you tonight," he said. "Ross Paige got the key to your apartment and I had Chow-Ling pack a picnic supper. We'll grab a couple of bottles of champagne and go over and watch the sunset from your terrace. What do you say, Cousin Kate?"

"Oui! Certainment!" she said, her eyes suddenly sparkling with delight. "And I say you are one of the loveliest relatives anyone could ever hope to have. Let's go!" She quickly changed into a black silk jacket, which she wore over forest green velvet pajamas and Albert could not help noticing how beautiful she looked as she joined him back at the railing overlooking the bay. She gave him a kiss and they were off with a wicker basket filled with iced shrimp, paper wrapped chicken, onion cakes and several varieties of dim-sum.

They entered her apartment well before the sun began to sink below the towers of the Golden Gate. There were a few pieces of wrought iron garden furniture on the terrace and they set out the delicacies and opened a bottle of champagne. Soon the sun began to plunge like a great igneous disk between the twin towers of the bridge, igniting the western sky in fiery blends of mercuric vermilion and cinnabar. The bay and the eastern sky played against each other, turning in turn a deep azure blue with shades of indigo and turquoise before the waters yielded to a dark slate gray. Against this unfurling display, Katherine was particularly beautiful. Her hair reminded Albert of a Titian painting and he felt that he had never beheld a creature quite so exquisite. The sky turned again into shades of crimson and magenta and they moved to the edge of the terrace to catch the sun as it began to slip over the horizon into the west. Soon the lights of the city and the east bay hills started to twinkle in the on setting shadows and Katherine slowly turned towards him as if she wanted to say something. She could not find the words and only stood staring into his eyes as if bewitched by some mystery. Albert was also at a loss for words. She was, he thought, so lovely, and yet so tragic, so strong and yet so vulnerable. As the west encompassed the setting sun, he reached out and put his arms around her waist. Without thinking, their lips met and their bodies melted together. For several long moments they felt the heat of their passion rise as if to replace the fire that was disappearing far below the erect towers of the golden bridge. She opened her mouth wide and their tongues slowly began to caress each other.

Then a moment later it was gone. And in that indefinable moment which is neither day nor evening they knew that they would not be lovers. They had reached that point in their relationship beyond which they dare not move. For some reason they could not understand, yet knew all too well, their appetite for each other could not be satisfied. Perhaps they needed each other too much to allow their passion to cloud their relationship. Perhaps it was that they were too much alike to carry their relationship into the purely physical realm. Or perhaps it was the deep seated incest taboo that placed a barrier between them. They stopped and looked at each other for a long time. He put his arm around her shoulders and she leaned back, resting her head upon his chest. He bent forward placing his chin on the top of her head, and very gently rocked her in the gray dusk. Finally, he asked softly, "More champagne for my dearest cousin?"

"Merci," she said with a quiet laugh.

They had needed this moment, this confrontation of love, to clarify their relationship. And in that moment, they found that there was somehow a third party. In some way Katherine's mother, was there, and they needed to respect her memory. Her presence seemed to draw them even closer together than they had been before.

After a long time they sat down on the small wrought iron love seat and watched the twinkling lights ringing the dark black waters of the bay. They did not speak for a while. They did not need to. They understood their relationship now. They would always love each other, not as lovers, but as soul mates. It was a bond that transcended the needs of the moment and they knew in the darkness of the terrace above the glittering city, that they would always be friends.

They spent the rest of the evening on the terrace. It was one of those rare nights in San Francisco that usually come in September when there is no fog to chill the air, and they shared more of themselves that evening than they ever had before. Albert told Katherine about Deirdre, his life in Sausalito, and the South Pacific he had seen during the war, and Katherine told him about Ricardo de Valopolicella.

"Ricardo was very romantic," she confessed. "The typical hot-blooded Latin, I'm afraid. He swept me off my feet in the beginning. Of course, I was young and susceptible."

"What happened? It sounds as if you were in love with him."

"I'm afraid he was looking for the perfect storybook romance. He truly was a hopeless romantic. He wanted a wife to love him, bear his children, oversee his home and entertain his guests but he always had to come first."

"He sounds a bit egotistical."

"Yes, very selfish, spoiled, I should say. When he didn't get his way, he became bitterly disillusioned. He exploded in recriminating tirades. I finally had enough. I guess he was just immature," Katherine said, reflecting on their love affair. "At first, I found myself susceptible to his idealism, but after a while, I wanted more stability in the relationship."

Finally the conversation turned back to Elizabeth, and Katherine began to ask questions about her mother's last years, who her friends had been, and how she had died.

Albert felt no need to conceal anything from her now. "I think towards the end, in the last year, she began to use opium. Aunt Louisa said your father was responsible somehow. He was terrible to her, especially after you were born. I think she went through a post-partum depression and rather than deal with her emotional problems, he had her sedated. I don't know how, but I always had the impression that he did it without medical consent."

Katherine listened intently. She was beginning to understand why Albert's side of the family hated her father, and why her father had for so long kept her away from San Francisco. They talked on into the wee hours of the morning about many things that are not shared except between the closest of confidants.

"I was addicted to morphine after being wounded in theSouth Pacific. A lot of guys came home with a habit," he explained. "There are many things that come through the Golden Door from over the horizon," he said, as they got up to leave. "I almost became a victim, too."

CHAPTER 19

COMING TO BREAKFAST Saturday morning, Albert saw a message on the Regency writing desk from Patrick Bartley suggesting that they might meet that afternoon to discuss the alterations Katherine wanted on her apartment. As Katherine was still sleeping, he decided after several cups of coffee, to take Windsor for a mid-morning walk.

"Did you see the message from Bartley?" he asked upon returning and unleashing Windsor in the entry hall. There was no response. Coming into the living room he found Katherine practicing Tai Chi with Chow-Ling.

"Arm forward, one, two, three, around and through," Katherine repeated, imitating Chow-Ling's movements. "Yes, he wants to meet at the Top of the Mark for cocktails at five o'clock."

"The Top of the Mark? Holy Cow! You weren't able to put it off until Monday?"

"No. He can't fit anything into his schedule for Monday and the rest of the week will be difficult for both of us. I hope this isn't an inconvenience. I know you envisioned a quiet Saturday showing me Sausalito."

"Gee, I had half thought of taking you for a sail. I guess we'll have to leave Marin for another day."

"Grazie, Alberto for being so understanding. I would love to go sailing and I particularly want to meet your Deirdre, but I think I should, how do you say? Strike the hot iron on Mr. Bartley's apartment."

"Of course, strike the hot iron," he laughed, mimicking her attempt at American slang. "We'll iron everything out."

Halfway through breakfast Katherine looked up thoughtfully. "You know, Albert, there isn't any reason why you need to come tonight. Why don't you go to Marin? It's been a long week, and I think you need a holiday. The water and the salt air will do you good."

"I wouldn't think of it. I want to be sure you are not taken for a ride."

"A ride?"

"Taken advantage of."

"If I can negotiate with Gloria and Otto over McMasters Shipping, I can certainly handle Mr. Bartley negotiating over a few altera-tions on an apartment," she said, half-mocking her cousin's offer of support.

"You'd better watch out for those Irishmen," he laughed. "They're a bunch of bewitching devils, and according to Father, Bartley's a terrifically tenacious businessman, sort of like a bull terrier, or old Windsor here," he said, roughing up the dog's coat.

Katherine looked over the table to where he sat in his red silk smoking jacket with Windsor on his lap. "You're right. Just like Windsor. When I get through with Mr. Bartley, he'll be a lap dog, just like old Windsor."

"All right, then, you win, but don't say I didn't warn you about the Irish."

Before leaving for Sausalito, Albert drove Katherine over to company headquarters, so she could pick up the necessary documents for the attorneys. Even though it was Saturday, she thought she might find Phillip Addison in his office, but by the time they arrived he had gone and they had to call him at home to inquire about obtaining drafts of her father's new will.

"I don't know where any of those papers are," he said hesitantly. "I suppose they would be somewhere in the legal department or in your father's desk. Why? Do you need them?"

"I'd like to have a look," Katherine said coolly. "I think I should know what my father was planning when he died."

A long awkward pause followed.

"Yes, of course. I'll see what I can do," Addison said at last.

"Phillip acts very strangely," Katherine commented as they drove over to the offices of Hampton, Hampton and Doner. "I often feel like a child when I ask him for something:

"I think it's a matter of intruding on his territory," Albert suggested. "After all, he has been running that company for a good many years."

"I suppose so, but it is strange nonetheless."

Even though it was past noon on Saturday, old George Hampton had his law serfs working in the law library.

"I must admit to feeling a little more secure after explaining the rudimentaries of the offer," Katherine said as they left the Shell Building on Bush Street.

"That junior partner you were talking to was first in his law class at Stanford in 1937. He's been with the law firm for over 15 years. I guess you should feel a degree of confidence."

Back in the apartment at two p.m., Katherine decided to take a siesta and let Albert leave for Sausalito without further delay. "I don't know, Albert, what I would have done without you over the last few weeks," she said as he prepared to leave.

They kissed each other good-bye. Katherine said "arrividerci," and he sang a version of the new hit "Vaya Con Dios", and they were off, Katherine into the arms of Morpheus, and Albert into the arms of Deirdre.

Patrick Bartley had offered to pick her up, but Katherine had called him back and declined. Since Albert was not accompanying her, She did not want to put herself at his disposal when they were going to be negotiating a lease, and they agreed to meet at the Top of the Mark at five p.m. Katherine did not arrive until five-twenty to find that Mr. Bartley had been waiting for her for almost half an hour.

"I'm dreadfully sorry for being late, Mr. Bartley, "Katherine apologized as he helped her into her seat. "I'm afraid I took a siesta and overslept."

"Would you like a drink?" he asked, ignoring her apology.

"Yes, thanks awfully. A scotch and water without ice, if I might."

As they began to talk, Katherine again experienced the uneasy feeling she had felt when they had first met at the Devonshire's dinner party. Yet she had to admit to herself there was something intriguing about this man. He was not like most of the men she had known socially, either in Buenos Aires or Europe. She thought at first that he reminded her a little of the gauchos who ran cattle on the pampas for her uncle. There was something earthy, tough and clear-cut in his manner, and she noticed that his large hands were rough and calloused like a common laborer's. At about six foot three and two hundred pounds, he was much larger than any of the Latin men she had dated, and although he was dressed in a sport coat and tie, she could not help but notice that he possessed a powerful physique with exceptionally broad shoulders and strong neck. His well-formed head and square sun-browned face were forged with strong clearly chiseled features and framed with curly dark brown hair that seemed not to want to stay combed. Yet it was his eyes that commanded Katherine's attention and made her feel slightly unsettled by their riveting intensity. Perhaps, she thought, it was his slightly pronounced brow ridge that gave to his eyes that almost primitive vitality. From the moment she had approached the table, his eyes had locked onto her like an eagle onto its prey, and as they began to talk, she wished for a second that her cousin had come along.

"I understand from Ross Paige, Katherine, that you want to rent the penthouse in my building on Mason," he began after the waitress left the table. After a moment's pause, Katherine responded, "It's a beautiful apartment. The view is lovely, and the craftsmanship is really quite extraordinary," she continued, searching for a way to make the conversation more relaxed.

"Yes, the view is one of the best in San Francisco," he said in a slow, deliberate way as he watched her intently. Again there was a long pause as he settled back in the small chair and crossed his legs. She felt annoyed at his almost arrogant manner. He had not bothered to exchange much in the way of the traditional formalities that usually go with such meetings. He had not mentioned that he had enjoyed meeting her at the Devonshires, nor had he asked her about how she liked San Francisco, or whether she enjoyed the opera. At least he had the courtesy to avoid mentioning the court-ordered autopsy, which had been front page news in all the papers. It was not something she wished to discuss, especially with a stranger. But to start immediately discussing business after ordering a drink, she thought really rather boorish, and his uninvited familiarity in calling her by her first name did not please her either. Then somewhere out of her annoyance sprang indignation followed by anger. "Yes," she said sharply, her eyes darting into his, "I am sure it is one of the best views in San Francisco, and from the research I have had conducted, undoubtedly the most expensive." As she concluded she saw a mischievous grin slowly emerge across his face and break into a broad warm smile that for an instant made him seem like a small boy. "You get what you pay for, I suppose," he said, with a deep chuckle.

Katherine noticed that the hard analytic intensity in his eyes had been replaced with a sensuously playful quality that unnerved her even more. Again she felt herself stiffen with anger. "If you think the price is too high, we can drop it fifty dollars a month," he continued in an off-handed manner.

This offer caught her completely off guard, and she started to fumble for a response, when he again took the initiative. "Ross Paige informs me that you have a list of alterations you would like made on the apartment before you move in. He mentioned specifically the kitchen and the flooring on the sun deck. Do you have any further requests?" As he spoke Katherine finally began to understand what she found so disarming about this Mr. Bartley. He did not make conversation like most of the gentlemen she had known. There were no embellishments. He simply came straight to the point in an unusually direct manner which she found very odd, since he did not seem to be in a hurry.

Katherine thought for a moment before she answered his questions, but this time, she did not feel the pause in the conversation to be awkward. "The two most important things, Mr. Bartley, are, as you mentioned, the kitchen and the floor in the sun deck. Other than that, there are only a few minor details."

"Please, call me Pat, "he said with a confident smile as he took a sip of his Scotch and water. "I prefer doing business on a first-name basis." And again not giving her a chance to respond, he continued, "I had my men start on the flooring today, and I can have the kitchen out and a new one in by next Wednesday or Thursday if you want to trust my contractors and decorator. If you want to choose your own design and colors, it will take as many days longer as it takes you to make your selections, provided we can get the materials from our wholesalers. I'll leave the choice up to you."

By now Katherine was completely confused by what amounted to Mr. Bartley's unconditional cooperation, and she fumbled for a moment before she could find words. "Would it be possible to take out the wall between the kitchen and the pantry and put in all new appliances?" She asked, pushing for the concessions she truly wanted.

"Yes on both counts," Bartley complied. "The wall between the kitchen and the pantry is not a bearing wall. I had my men look at it today. And yes, the kitchen will have all new appliances. Do you want to pick them out, or trust us?"

Slowly Katherine started to understand that Bartley's directness was not a matter of being rude, but merely a matter of wanting to get things done. As they talked, he took a small pad of paper and pencil from his pocket and began to take notes, and she began to feel more comfortable with what she now perceived to be his rather sensible, down-to-earth approach to problems. Within a half an hour everything was decided, and he promised to have the apartment ready for her within a week. "Now that we have our business completed, can I buy you dinner?" he asked, closing up his pad of paper.

Again Katherine was caught completely off guard. But since she had indicated that she had not made any plans for the evening, she was trapped into an acceptance.

"Good," he said, finishing the rest of his drink. "We'll go to Vanessi's. It's an Italian restaurant down in North Beach, where they make the best tortellini in the world. You'll love it!"

Katherine laughed quietly to herself. She had never met anyone so blatantly positive in her whole life. Mr. Bartley had not even asked her if she liked Italian food, or pasta, for that matter, and yet he was telling her that she'd love it. On one level she found his behavior irritatingly unsophisticated, but on another, fascinating. It was so typically American. She also felt something else about Mr. Bartley, but she could not quite put her finger on what it was. It sat somewhere in the pit of her stomach and it bothered her because she could neither contain nor understand it. She thought perhaps it had something to do with power. Not only his unusual physical power, but his ability to throw her off guard and move without hesitation to the place he wanted to be. He was not what she considered a good conversationalist. He had a way of dominating the conversation without saying much. She had felt confident in the beginning of her ability to negotiate with him, but she found that she had become completely confused in discussing the lease and alterations on the apartment. As she reflected on their conversation, she realized that he had essentially led her into all the decisions. He had manipulated her in a way she had never before been manipulated, and she resented the intrusion. But what disturbed her most were the results of this manipulation. She had achieved everything she had wanted and more. He had agreed to everything and in the end, had voluntarily offered to drop the rent in the process. In fact, she could not even remember if they had agreed on the rent. On some level of consciousness, she felt that Mr. Bartley wanted something from her and this made her feel wary, like a switchboard operator on emergency alert.

Their drive to the restaurant in North Beach was one of the most harrowing experiences Katherine had had since being in San Francisco. Without explanation, he took a detour down Lombard Street in the block called "The Windiest Street in the World". But what really scared her was the way he seemed to delight in picking out the steepest hills and then watching her gasp as his new red Cadillac Coupe de Ville came over the crest before plunging down towards the bay like a roller-coaster out of control. He was very proud of his new car, and explained in great detail about the power of its 400-plus cubic inch engine. It was, she commented, an attractive automobile, but with her heart caught in her throat, other than asking him about the novelty of push-button windows, she could think of nothing to say.

Walking down Broadway to the restaurant, she felt unusually small beside him and she could not help but notice the strange way he walked. He walked with an unfaltering assurance and a relaxed, wide gait, as if he owned the street or was walking across his own living room.

"Hey, Pat, how's it going? Where you been?" was the enthusiastic greeting as they entered the restaurant.

"Hey, Joe, good to see you!" Patrick said, shaking Joe's hand, and squeezing his arm. "I want you to meet my friend Miss McMasters."

Joe was effusive in his greeting, "Such a pretty lady! How you like San Francisco? You like our opera? I see your picture in the paper. Such a pretty lady. My condolences for you on your father's death."

Katherine could not help but be charmed. "Lei e molto gentissimo, Signore," she said, offering her hand. Joe's face lit up, and she had the distinct feeling she had made a friend.

"For you, lovely lady, the best table in the house. Come, I show you." After they were seated he darted away, only to return with menus and a wine list for Patrick. "Anything for Mr. Bartley and his lady."

"You don't really have to bother with the menu, unless there is something you particularly want," Patrick informed her. "Just let me take care of it."

"Of course," Katherine smiled, never ceasing to be amazed at how this Mr. Bartley assumed control without apology or any pretense of embarrassment. Normally this would have infuriated her but for some reason, it didn't.

Soon Joe was back with a bottle of wine, and much to Katherine's surprise, pulled up a chair and sat down to join them. "Try this. You like," he said, pouring a quarter of a glass of wine for each of them. "Now what you want to order for the lady tonight, Mr. Patrick?"

"What do you suggest, Joe?"

"I think you like the Fettucini al Burro Dolce?"

"What about the tortellini?"

"Of course, the tortellini. It's always a-good, but if you would allow me, I think you like the fettuccini. Is special tonight."

"I don't know, Joe. I usually take your word, but I think we'll go for the tortellini."

"O.K., you're the boss, but I tell you what I do. I bring you both."

Katherine had to admit that Mr. Bartley had been right. The pasta was superb and the veal piccata was as good as any she had had in Italy. And with each course the wine selection proved exceptionally interesting. "Usually I sit at the counter and watch the chefs cook," Patrick said as he looked over towards the long line of people observing the culinary artistry behind the counter. "It's great fun! Everyone in San Francisco from politicians to entertainers comes here, and sometimes Joe persuades a big-name entertainer to perform and everyone gets a free floor show. You never know what's going to happen, except that you're going to eat well."

Midway through the meal Patrick paused for a moment and then fixed his eyes on her. "Tell me about Katherine McMasters," he said with a warm, big, almost childish smile creeping across his face.

"Why don't you tell me about Patrick Bartley?" she said, raising her eyebrows and tilting her head forward. "I'm rather tired of telling people about myself."

"Okay, one story's as good as another, although I'm sure mine is not nearly as interesting as yours." He told her about how he was raised the oldest of five children in San Francisco's Mission District. His father, a San Francisco cop, had died when he was twelve, which left him the man in the family. He had worked all the way through high school, helping his mother raise his three brothers and a sister. And although he never had time for sports, he saw to it that his brothers always had the necessary equipment to play on the school teams and that his sister went to a good Catholic parochial school for her education. As he talked, Katherine began to feel very differently about him. There was a practical, determined loyalty in his character that she could not help but admire.

"Mother had a very rough time of it after my father died. She had difficulty finding work the first year, but then after that, she became a housekeeper for a family in Sea Cliff and took in some sewing on the side. But we managed somehow, and I suppose I never thought of myself as being poor. I just knew that we didn't have very much money and that I needed to work so that we could at least eat and have some decent clothes on our backs."

His life had been so different from hers that Katherine found it difficult to find the proper questions to ask, but for the most part, she didn't need to worry. He seemed to enjoy talking, and the awkwardness of the cocktail hour had given way to the pleasant ramblings of a man who seemed perfectly at ease with himself and her company.

"It took me three years working as a carpenter to get through two years of college. I would have liked to go on, but I couldn't afford the time. I figured there was more money in construction anyway if you knew what you were doing. I quit school and started building houses. Then the war came along and I joined the army."

"Were you in battle?"

"Yeah, I saw a lot of action during the North African and Italian campaigns. It's something you don't forget but it had to be done."

Katherine wasn't sure, but she sensed that he did not want to talk about the war. "And after the war?" she asked, letting a moment of silence slip by.

"After the war, I came home and started building houses again. There was a lot of construction going on, a lot of construction! All those guys from the East and Midwest who shipped out to the Pacific could hardly wait to get back home and pack up for California. I guess once you see San Francisco, you're hooked."

"I suppose I am finding that to be true," Katherine smiled.

"Anyway, I started a construction firm with a couple of partners and we've done very well. We're one of the largest in the City. I suppose I'm pretty lucky. My mother doesn't have to work anymore and I've been able to help my brothers and sister. That's the main thing."

He seemed to delight in talking about how he had built up his business and the plans he had for the future. However, his delight was less connected to his accomplishments than it was in the fact that he had been able to provide his family with security. Yet Katherine could also detect a certain degree of satisfaction in the power and wealth he had accumulated. He did not brag, but she could sense that he knew that he had power, and she sensed that he would not be reticent about using it to protect what he considered to be his.

Towards the end of the meal, he turned the tables on her. "Now it's your turn, Miss McMasters. I want to hear just a little about the fabulous lady who has captured the press and the heart of the city over the last few weeks."

Katherine laughed at his mention of the press. "I don't know where to begin. I'm never sure what people want to know about me, or what they already know, for that matter. Sometimes I get the strange feeling that they don't really care, just as long as I tell them something."

"Okay, tell me something. Tell me about Argentina. That's a place I've always wanted to go," Bartley said, spurring her on.

Katherine did not want to go into the complexity of her family relations with Otto and Gloria, and she did not want to appear condescending by telling him about the Swiss schools and her travels through Europe. She turned to her early life on the ranchero, where, although she felt it might bore a man from a working-class city background, it was at least safe and simple. She began by telling him about the ranch, how they raised cattle, and how she had learned to ride at an early age. "Sometimes I used to think I was born on a horse, and almost all my childhood memories have something to do with riding." As Enrico brought another bottle of wine, she continued to tell about the different horses she had trained, and the difference between the English and Argentinian riding method. She had now become engrossed in a topic she loved, and it wasn't for some time that she thought of observing Mr. Bartley's reactions. Finally she noticed that he was looking at her in a very strange way, and she had the queer feeling that he had not heard anything she had said. His huge tan hands were folded as if in prayer, and he leaned forward, resting his elbows on the table. His eyes were transfixed on her, and she wondered if he might not be a little drunk. "I'm sorry if I have gone on," she said apologetically, "I tend to do that when I talk about horses."

He did not move, but smiled sympathetically and waited for her to continue. When she did not, he leaned back and smiled again. "Horses are something I never tire of hearing about," he said, twirling the wine in his glass. I'll take you to see my ranch in St. Helena. I keep seven or eight horses up there all the time. I'll take you riding through some of the most beautiful country in the world."

Katherine laughed, "Thank you! It sounds like it would be very nice." She was beginning to find his directness amusing. He had not offered her an invitation—he merely had informed her that he would take her. She wondered how many other women he had approached in the same way, and how successful he had been with them. He was, she had to admit, very attractive, and she was beginning to discover that underneath the masculine prowess and cool business head there was a spark of the impulsive boy which had long been kept in check. Not wanting, however, to be placed in the position of making a commitment, she changed the subject back to her apartment.

CHAPTER 20

Since Albert was away in Sausalito, Katherine spent all day Sunday reading reports. She only left the apartment to accompany Chow-Ling and Windsor on their midafternoon walk up to Coit Tower and down the Filbert Street Stairs where she discovered the lush gardens and little cottages dating from the 1860s. Yet despite this brief interlude, Katherine began to feel the increasing pressure from her meeting schedule and the ghastly uncertainty of her father's autopsy. At first, she had been almost relieved to have a post-mortem. Now the thought of her father's body being removed from its resting place and subjected to the grisly probing of pathologists, weighed upon her. "Such bureaucratic rigmarole," she thought and found herself haunted by the speculation of murder.

"How did your meeting with Mr. Bartley go?" Albert asked when he returned late Sunday afternoon.

"Very well, I think. He was very agreeable to all my suggestions, but I must say he is rather a different sort of man. Quite charming after a fashion. His manners take a bit of getting used to."

"What about the lease? Is he going to up the rent because of the alterations?"

"No. He even offered to lower it. At least I think he did. We went to Vanessi's. Superb dinner!"

"Oh, you've met Joe?"

"Yes, charming. And you? Did you have a good time?"

"Slept, read and dug in the garden a little. Yes, it was just what the doctor ordered."

Albert slipped into his pajamas and robe while Chow-Lin peeled oranges and made tea.

"Is that another report you're reading?" he asked, coming back into the living room and settling into the davenport.

"This is an economic analysis of Pacific Coast Shipping prepared by the Stanford Research Institute," she sighed, laying the document on the coffee table. "The more I read these bloody repots, the more confused I become. It all seems so abstract. I think perhaps I'm approaching the whole thing from the wrong end."

"What do you mean?"

"I keep reading all these statistics on shipping and I haven't even seen the wharfs. I was just thinking about something Mr. Bartley said as we drove home last night."

"What's that?"

"He mentioned he had a friend, a Brian Shaw I think, who supposedly knows a great deal about the waterfront. He said he would arrange for this Mr. Shaw to show me around."

"That sounds like a good avenue to explore," Albert advised. "I should have thought of that before. My friend Rigg also knows his way around the docks. Deirdre said he's out fishing now, but when he gets back, I'll try and get hold of him."

They paused for a moment while Chow-Ling served tea, rice cakes and orange slices.

"When do you think your friend will be back from fishing?" Katherine asked.

"With Rigg one never knows. Why don't you let Mr. Bartley set you up with his friend and then if you want to see more, you can have Rigg show you around later."

"All right, I'll call Mr. Bartley and thank him for dinner and inquire about his friend."

Katherine's conversation with Mr. Bartley was short and somewhat inconclusive.

"He sounded preoccupied," she reported, coming back from the phone. "He can be very brusque, but he said he would see what he could do. Perhaps it was a little presumptive for me to ask."

"I wouldn't' worry about it. I'm sure he wouldn't have offered if he hadn't wanted to."

It wasn't a half-hour before Chow-Ling came in. "A Mr. Bartley for Miss McMasters."

"Well!" Katherine said when she returned from taking the call. "Mr. Bartley was still very abrupt, but he informed me that his friend will pick me up at ten tomorrow morning for a tour of the waterfront. She stopped for a moment before she continued.

"I really find it extraordinarily difficult to appraise this Mr. Bartley but he certainly seems to get things done." The next morning, as they ate breakfast and read the paper, Katherine noticed a story on page three that General Alfredo Avalos, the commander-in-chief of the Argentinian army, had died.

"I wonder if Gloria and Otto will feel under increased pressure to return to Buenos Aires," she pondered as she finished her boiled egg and grapefruit. "They knew Avalos."

"Will they use his death as an excuse to apply more pressure to you?"

"I wouldn't be surprised. Otto is very skilled at twisting things around and getting the most out of whatever happens. I think he wants to get Gloria out of San Francisco anyway. This entire affair with Monique is too much for her." She stopped and looked at her watch. "Nevertheless," she continued, getting up and folding her napkin, "Brian Shaw is due to arrive in less than forty-five minutes and I'm not going to let a gold-digging femme entretenue or a crisis in the Argentinian Army put me off schedule. It seems they have one every week."

"First of all we'll drive the full length of the Embarcadero, from the Aquatic Park to the Third Street Channel at China Basin, to give you an overall picture," Brian said as they climbed into his car.

"I must thank you, Mr. Shaw, for taking the time to show me about," Katherine replied as they started down Lombard.

"Hey, call me Brian and don't mention it."

"Of course, then, Brian, I do appreciate it nevertheless. I'm afraid the closest I've been to the waterfront has been standing on my cousin's terrace, looking at the piers jutting out into the bay and I'm delighted to have the opportunity to have a closer investigation."

"I'm always happy to do a favor for Pat, especially if it's a pleasurable one."

"How long have you known Patrick?"

"Grew up in the same neighborhood in the Mission. He's a great guy, but don't tell him I said so."

They drove out on one of the piers to watch a McMasters cargo liner steaming along the waterfront towards her pier. "She's probably bringing in bulk sugar and pineapple from Hawaii, and then she'll load up with assorted dry goods for her westbound sailing."

"Did you work on ships like that?"

"All the time," Brian laughed. "It's hard work, believe me. My Dad was a longshoreman for over forty years before he retired and I worked the wharfs to get through law school."

At Pier 25 Brian pulled the car over to give Katherine a closer look.

"The ship owners and Merchant Tugboat Company own these old girls," Brian said pointing to a line of red stacked tugs.

"Why so many?" Katherine asked. "I noticed that sometimes the bay seems full of them. They are really rather intriguing in their own way."

"The tugs are a tremendously important part of the activity on the bay," Brian explained as they stood with the breeze blowing through their hair. "Just getting in and out of the Golden Gate can be a hazardous proposition for navigators. There are very strong tides out there because the whole bay, which contains over four hundred and fifty square miles of water, must drain through that narrow passage. Then the strong tides are often reinforced by currents from the rivers. That's why it's almost impossible for prisoners to escape from Alcatraz. A lot of good ships come to grief outside the Gate; they hit a sandy shelf at a place like Lime Point or get lost in the fog near the Farallons, and there's real trouble. Of course, sometimes they can be pulled off and repaired, but many times not. It makes for a good salvage business around here."

"And that over there?" Katherine questioned, pointing to a large ocean-going tug.

"That's just a bigger model. She's capable of towing barges up and down the coast to Puget Sound, or pulling log rafts down from Columbia. When you have an emergency, these big old girls come in pretty handy," Brian continued as they moved down the pier. "Of course, these smaller tugs are the ones that help incoming steamers alongside the wharfs and get them out into the stream along the waterfront when they are ready to sail. It may look like a big bay, and it is, but with the tides and currents the way they are, the management of a vessel at low speeds in a restricted area can be pretty difficult."

As they stood on the pier, several launches chugged by. "They're probably Immigration and Customs officials out to board that big transpacific liner which is just hove to there off Alcatraz."

"I believe we own a couple of liners like that," Katherine said, "I'd like to ride out and see how the Customs and Immigrations procedure operates sometime."

"That can be arranged, I think. You just let me know when," Brian said as they turned and walked back to his car.

Katherine was back in her office talking to Phillip Addison when Albert called.

"I just talked to Charlie Cahoun. The autopsy report is back."

Katherine braced herself. "Yes," she said tentatively.

"From what Charlie tells me, the report says your father died from pulmonary and cerebral edema due to congestive heart failure."

"Is that all?"

"That just about sums it up. The autopsy did mention that he had just given himself about 25 ius of insulin, but according to his doctor, it was the prescribed regimen for his diabetes and his sugar level was more or less normal."

"I see," Katherine said, noticing the concerned look on Addison's face. "Is there any conclusion as to what caused the heart attack?"

She could hear Albert thumbing through his note pad on the other end of the line.

"Not really. They evidently found the presence of some arterial sclerosis, but it was not particularly advanced. Not enough to be the sole cause of a fatal heart attack anyway. I guess they just figure that with the diabetes and the arterial sclerosis and maybe the exertion of the golf game—it was enough to bring on cardiac arrest."

"Well, that's a relief, I suppose," she said, not quite knowing what to feel or say about something basically so horrific.

"It certainly should be," Albert said, trying to place emphasis on the more positive aspects of the news which lay beyond the grim details of the post-mortem. "I think this should end any serious challenge by Monique Morales Monahan."

"Yes," Katherine said slowly, "I hope so."

Addison was visibly relieved when she told him the news. In fact, for someone who generally gave the impression of being firmly in control of his emotions, he seemed almost jubilant like a gambler who had just won a very large bet.

"Now there is nothing that can stand between you and your future happiness," he told her. "If Mrs. Monahan wants to file a claim on your father's estate, let her. She doesn't have a leg to stand on, and she thought she was going to make off with one of the largest fortunes in the city. The conniving little ..." He caught himself and stopped short, for he had noticed Katherine's astonishment at his uncharacteristic discomposure.

"Yes," she said, trying to interpret his behavior and at the same time not wanting to increase or accent his agitation. There was an awkward little pause and she added in an attempt to redirect the conversation, "Were you able to get any of the work my father had put in to the rewriting of his will?"

Addison suddenly became quite solemn. "Yes, I have some of the work. But I don't think it is of any consequence. I wouldn't bother with it, not now, anyway."

"Nevertheless, I would like to see it if you would."

"Yes of course. I'll send it over with Miss Tucker."

If Addison's reaction was one of relief and even joy at the news, Katherine found Horsley and Otto Brutmann rather unmoved. Indeed they hardly seemed to take note of the report, but instead redoubled their efforts to pressure her to consider selling her interest in McMasters now that it was "free and clear", as Otto put it.

And as Katherine had anticipated, their tactics had now changed in a final attempt to convince her to sell.

"We are required to make the reservation to fly back to Buenos Aires this Thursday," Otto informed her. "I suppose you know from the newspapers that General Avalos has died. This may make things even more uncertain for us. I think we will soon have to make a decision on how best to protect our capital. If you delay with our offer too long, we may have to find other means to invest our funds."

"Yes, of course, Uncle Otto," Katherine said, trying to sound at one both firm and sympathetic.

"The papers are full of news that should encourage you to sell," Horsley interjected. "If you read the Call Bulletin or this morning's Chronicle you would understand that."

"To just what are you referring, Mr. Horsley?" Katherine demanded, annoyed at his arrogance and insensitivity. "I have had my mind on other things. The report on my father's post-mortem came in today, in case you have forgotten."

"I'm referring to the expulsion of the International Longshoremen from the AF of L in St. Louis yesterday," Horsley pronounced with a condescending air. "And the charge against the I.L.U. was failure to purge their ranks of racketeers! Even a last-minute offer by their president to submit to an AF of L trusteeship was rejected."

"And what are you suggesting are the implications for me?" Katherine pressed.

"This only underlines the difficulty of running a steamship line," Horsley said, handing her the July reports from the Hawaiian Territorial Commission on Subversive Activities to provehis point.

"The nation's piers are lawless frontiers plagued by corruption, Communism, and racketeering," he continued, quoting a charge by Senator Tobey of the Senate Commerce Committee.

"You simply do not understand how rough it can get out there. But let me tell you, if Meany kicks out a union with over 6,000 members and a sixty-year tie with the AF of L, you know that things are getting pretty bad." He leaned forward and looked over the top rim of his glasses at Katherine in a threatening manner.

"This is a very competitive business," another member of the board advised. "Our overall volume of foreign trade has not shared equally with the absolute growth of the rest of the country in that trade."

Katherine did not understand the company's decline in inter-coastal and Pacific coast wide trade. Indeed, she was beginning to feel that she was not up to running a shipping line at all given the variables that seemed to be in operation, and she began to wonder why her father had left her in a position to make the decisions with which she was being faced. However, she had finished the 1950 Economic Analysis prepared by the Stanford Research Institute, and she decided to chance an opinion in the hope of showing the Board that she was not completely inept.

"I think, gentlemen, that although we enjoy a time and distance advantage over other U.S. ports in the case of Far Eastern traffic, we find we are at a disadvantage because consignees lack confidence in the stability of our management-labor relations."

"I see you've done a little homework," Horsley responded as the rest of the board exchanged astonished glances or diverted their eyes to their reports.

The rest of the meeting did not go much better. There were more discussions about the problems of labor relations in the country as a whole and a lengthy discussion on how McMasters should engage in a campaign and woo back lost markets to route their cargo via Pacific coast ports. Katherine again was made to feel ill at ease by Horsley, who took the opportunity of the general discussion to underline how little Katherine really knew about shipping. Finally, at the end of the meeting, the topic turned again to the offer on the table to purchase McMasters Shipping.

"I think this board deserves the courtesy of being given a date," Horsley pressed. "As you can see, long-term plans must be made if McMasters is going to remain competitive and we cannot do that as long as you delay making a decision."

"I don't know how much time I'll need. A week, two weeks, perhaps a month," she said, putting her pen down. "Frankly, gentlemen, you tread upon my patience. I'll let you know on the thirtieth of October!"

It was an arbitrary date and Katherine did not know why she picked it. All she knew was that she wanted to end this constant tension and get on with her life and business. Looking at her watch as a pretext, she closed up her Moroccan briefcase.

"Gentlemen, I'm afraid as far as I am concerned this board meeting is over," she said as she stood up. "Uncle Otto, I wish you a safe trip. We will be in touch."

Over a quiet dinner at Albert's apartment, Katherine related the vicissitudes of the day.

"I don't know anything about American businessmen," she commented as she discussed the offer with Albert. "I'm beginning to believe the negative stereotype of the Yankee Capitalist."

"In what way?" he asked, mentally sorting through the numerous images that came to mind.

"High pressured, boorish, arrogant, degoutant! Chambliss Horsley is the perfect example. I have made it quite clear on several occasions that I require some time to consider their offer, but he will not rest, even with all we have been through with Monique Monahan, the post-mortem, the will and all. He truly is a dreadful bore. And that reminds me," she said, getting up and crossing the room to take some papers out of her attaché case. "Here is the will Father was making when he died."

"What does it say?"

"I only had time to look at it briefly, but there doesn't seem to be much there. There are some sections dealing with the block of stock and properties given to Aunt Gloria and some sections on some of the smaller bequests and the right of partners to buy out my interest in some of the minor subsidiaries, but all in all, it seems more or less similar to the original will."

Albert took the documents and they both started to read and compare them to the completed will.

"You're right," Albert said after a half-hour. "There's nothing here that's dramatically different. A few more people mentioned and an update on a few assets, but nothing significant."

"Why then did Addison seem so elated, I wonder?"

"Elated? When?"

"When I told him about the post-mortem. He seemed over the moon about the whole thing, triumphant really. He said something about Monique thinking she was going to make off with father's estate. Started to call her a conniving something or other. It was all quite extraordinary. I'm beginning to think he's a bit unstable."

"Did he say anything else?"

"Oh, something about my future happiness being secured."

"There is nothing here to suggest that your future happiness would have been affected one way or another. But then ..."

"But then?"

"That just may be the point."

"What do you mean?"

"There is nothing here. What we have may not be everything. What might be significant is what is not here."

"But I asked Addison if these were all the relevant documents and he said they were. Why would he lie? What possible motive would he have?"

"I don't know and there is no way to find out, I suppose."

"I could go to the legal department and ask questions of the attorneys who worked with father."

"You could, but I doubt if that would prove very productive. In the first place, I doubt they would risk going against Addison in the event there has been an omission, and in the second place, I think that Addison would view such an investigation as a vote of no confidence, which would seem highly unwarranted."

"Yes, I suppose you are right there," Katherine concluded, thinking of her mother's piano and the loving devotion Phillip Addison had displayed since her arrival. "He seems to take the role of godfather very seriously. I find it all quite odd, really."

"What?"

"The attitude of most American man. There doesn't seem to be any cultural consistency in the way men and women relate to each other, the way there is in Argentina or in Europe."

"It's probably because we are a new country. We are still in our adolescent stage, so to speak, and we haven't quite decided on the rules."

"Ah, perhaps you are right. Take Mr. Horsley, for an example. He never misses an opportunity to make me feel inadequate. Today he even brought government reports, attempting to convince me how corrupt and dangerous the unions are."

"He's trying to convince you that owning a steamship company is such a Herculean task that you will cave in and sell just to be rid of the burden."

"I'm quite sure that's his game," Katherine smiled. "But I surprised him today if only for a moment."

"How?"

"Oh, I gave a short analysis of the effects of labor difficulties on our Pacific trade. I think I rather surprised the entire board."

"How did Chambliss handle that?"

"He made a sarcastic comment and then purposely tried to make me look incompetent. I just wish I knew more about relations between the Company and the unions."

"Why don't you ask Brian? He can probably tell you or set up a meeting with someone who has more current insights."

"Splendid idea," Katherine concluded after thinking about it for a minute. "I might gain some information if a meeting were arranged with the Port Authority. From what I've read, he is a central figure. His name popped up in several of the reports I've read."

"All I can tell you, Katherine, is that relations between the lines and the unions have never been good," Brian explained, attempting to be helpful when Katherine reached him later in the evening. "There's a long history of exploitation there from the workingman's perspective. The union has become pretty radicalized over the years. Unfortunately, there's a fair share of graft and exploitation there, too. Of course, I haven't been on the wharfs for over five years, but from what I hear, things have gotten a lot worse."

Katherine listened intently as Brian confirmed and expanded upon what she already knew.

"Tell me, Brian," she said at the conclusion of the conversation, "do you think it would be useful to arrange a meeting with the head of the Port Authority? I have after all just acquired a controlling interest in a major line and a meeting arranged under the pretext of courtesy call might …"

"I have to tell you, Katherine, "Brian interrupted, "that Richard Broderick, who is the Port Authority, is one of the most arbitrary and unscrupulous men in this city. I know from years of experience. I think it might be wise to consult your company attorneys before you arrange a meeting with Richard Broderick. You don't want to interject yourself if there are some sort of negotiations in progress. Dealing with Broderick can be a sensitive matter."

CHAPTER 21

*N*O SOONER HAD Katherine hung up from talking to Brian than the phone rang again. "Mister Bartley on phone for Miss Katherine," Chow-Ling announced, coming into the drawing room to give Hector an apricot.

"Patrick Bartley here, Katherine," he said as she took the call. "Sorry for calling this late, but I wanted to tell you that we have the wall out between the kitchen and the pantry. You have several choices about what you want to do with the added space and what materials you want for the counter tops. I have samples and rough blueprints for you to look at. When can I get them to you?"

I suppose sometime tomorrow," Katherine replied, trying to think about possible colors for the kitchen which, after all the events of the day seemed an insignificant consideration.

"Uh, let me see. I'm afraid I'm all tied up during the day but I could come by tomorrow evening any time after six."

"That would be fine," Katherine said looking at her calendar. "Why don't we say six-thirty then?"

"Fine. I'll bring the plans and samples by at six-thirty and then we can discuss them over dinner. You haven't been to Trader Vic's have you?"

"Well, no, I ..."

"Good. Then I'll see you tomorrow at say between six-thirty and seven."

"Between six-thirty and seven," Katherine repeated. She felt bewildered at being so easily maneuvered like a marionette pulled by unseen wires in a direction she did not want to go.

Before she could gather an excuse, Mr. Bartley said good-bye and hung up.

"My schedule is already overcrowded and I'm exhausted," she complained as she came back into the living room. "Mr. Bartley wanted to drop by some samples and plans for the kitchen and the next thing I know I am going out for dinner. He is truly too annoying for words!"

"Where is he taking you?" Albert asked.

"A place called Traders something or another. I can't remember."

"Trader Vic's?"

"Yes, that's the name."

"Ah, well, you'll enjoy that! The exotic South Pacific theme, tapa cloth walls, shrunken heads, sea shells and all that sort of thing. There's no place like it! All sorts of fun delicacies and outlandish drinks. I'll never forget the time Mother started off with something called 'A Missionary's Downfall'. She was three sheets to the wind after two. Dad had to take her home.

"It all sounds extraordinary, but I prefer to have gentlemen extend an invitation and then allow the lady a chance to accept or refuse. Mr. Bartley just presumes I will accept and presents a fait accomplis."

"Aw, shoot, you should go anyway," he encouraged her. "After all, McMasters will be here next week, despite what Horsley or Brutmann would have you believe. You might as well enjoy yourself a little when you are spending most of the day locked up with attorneys and accountants."

"I suppose I can take it as a business dinner," Katherine sighed reluctantly. "After all, I owe something to Mr. Bartley for introducing me to his friend Brian. And he is being very cooperative on the apartment."

The next evening when Katherine appeared dressed for dinner at six-fifteen, she looked absolutely ravishing and not at all like a woman who was reluctant about going out for dinner.

"Is this all right for Trader Dick's?" she asked, turning around to let Albert see the tortoise shell print silk dress that followed her long beautiful figure at every curve. "It's a de Givenchy."

"Great! It goes along with the theme. But it's Trader Vic's, not Trader Dick's."

They sat around waiting until 7:30 when Bartley finally arrived.

"I was tied up out in the Sunset," he said by way of apology. "I'm afraid we were due at the restaurant ten minutes ago. Why don't I leave the samples here and we can look at them later. I'll explain the different structural options for the kitchen over drinks."

Then awkwardly stepping forward, he diverted his eyes and handed Katherine a white box with forest green lettering.

"Here," he said quickly, "I picked this up on the way."

Slowly lifting the lid, Katherine found a lemon scented Catteleya with a deeply frilled lip making up most of the flower.

"How lovely," she commented, trying to disguise her surprise.

"We better be going then." He rushed as if not wanting to prolong the moment. "You can pin it on in the car."

"Perhaps I'll just carry it Latin Style. I can enjoy the fragrance that way."

After grabbing her coat, he yelled goodbye over his shoulder and they headed out the door.

"Have a good time," Albert called out after them. "Watch out for the Mai Tais!"

"Thanks, Al. We'll have Scorpions then."

"They're just as deadly!" he shot back. "Just as deadly."

The mention of scorpions brought back memories of the South Pacific during the war. Some beaches had been infested with scorpions and although Albert had never been stung, he had known guys who had … nasty business, very painful! He hated even the thought of arachnids and the image of their venomous tails crossed his mind, made him shudder and then for some reason, made him think of the syringe Stanley McMasters must have used to inject himself with insulin.

Albert had read the full autopsy report and part of it stilled bothered him. It had mentioned that after the initial heart attack, McMasters had suffered almost complete paralysis of the spinal cord and cranial nerves, which would normally indicate some sort of toxicity of the central nervous system. But the toxicology test had come up negative and there were no significant levels of any inorganic chemicals in any of the tissue samples. Specific tests for poisons like mercury, strychnine and arsenic had also been negative.

As they drove across town, Bartley was relaxed and talkative and Katherine was forced to admit to herself that she enjoyed hearing him describe the different possibilities for the kitchen. Entering the exotic world of the Trader, Katherine noticed something about Patrick Bartley that she had noticed at Vanessi's. People genuinely liked him. His forceful presence combined with an almost playful way of relating to people. He seemed to bring out in others something of his own expansive warmth. Yet at the same time, she felt that just under the surface was the quivering vitality of a Rugby forward. Occasionally it showed in a glance or in the way he asked her a question. She was no longer threatened by it. Now it intrigued her for she could not seem to put her finger on its source or its objective.

"How are things going with the shipping business?" Patrick asked after they settled into the Captain's Cabin. "I hope Brian was as helpful as you say he was."

"He was very helpful, an exceptional guide. I learned things about the waterfront I could never have picked up by staying in the office or listening to company managers."

"Sounds like you're getting matters pretty well under control."

"I wish that were the case, Mr. Bartley, but I'm afraid it's not. Confidentially, I am having my problems."

"With the company?"

"With some members of the Board. I have been presented with an offer by a group to purchase all or a large portion of my shares."

"So you would no longer be in control?"

"No."

"Are you interested?"

"I don't know. Maybe. I've hired independent counsel to help me evaluate the offer."

"Well, it's either worth it or it isn't. Don't be rushed into accepting their first offer. If they want it badly enough, they will go up."

"It's all a bit of a muddle because my father's sister and her husband are involved."

"They don't want you to sell?"

"No, they are members of the association that is making the offer."

"Do you trust them?"

"No, not really."

"You're getting a lot of pressure to make a deal?"

"To say the least. They all have spent the last few weeks trying to convince me that I have no business trying to run a shipping line."

"Have you asked yourself why they are in such a hurry?"

"Yes, but without arriving at a conclusive answer. They claim Peron is making changes that threaten their holdings. They say they need to move capital outside Argentina, but of course, that is difficult."

"And you don't accept that line of reasoning?"

"Not entirely. It is true that with nationalizations and land re-distribution they may feel uneasy but I'm not convinced that it's all that serious. It's more than that. My aunt is a very unusual person. Very jealous and unstable, really. She harbors tremendous animosity towards my mother's side of my family. She resents my having anything to do with the Devonshires."

Katherine paused for a moment and fingered the lip of the orchid she had carefully laid on the table. The thought crossed her mind that perhaps she was revealing too much. They were drinking something called a Samoan Fog Cutter and she remembered what her cousin had said about Aunt Victoria being potted after just two drinks.

"Excuse me for going on like this. I suppose the drinks have made me a little chatty," she said, trying to divert the conversation.

Bartley stopped for a moment and leaned back in the booth before continuing.

"I think you should move slowly. Give yourself a year. You just might like running a shipping line. You have a good head for business. I can tell."

The assured way in which he said this surprised her as much as the evaluation itself. He was, after all, supposed to be an excellent businessman and she wondered what basis he had for making such a judgment. And further, it seemed inconsistent with the way he had behaved towards her. He had given her the impression that he liked to think of himself in control, especially when it came to women.

"Thank you, Mr. Bartley," she said at last. "You're the first man other than my cousin to express any confidence in my abilities. I'm not sure why."

"Because I've watched you," he chuckled, looking her straight in the eyes. "You know what you want and have the right instincts to get it. You're not easily sidetracked. All you need is a little experience and you'll get that."

For some reason Katherine could not quite grasp, she suddenly felt exposed as if he had been playing a game with her to test her reactions.

"You need two things, Miss McMasters," he continued with an air of infallible authority.

"And what might those be?" Katherine asked with a slight note of sarcasm.

"You need to trust George Devonshire. I don't give a damn what this aunt of yours from Argentina has told you. For my money your Uncle George is the most honest guy I've ever done business with."

"Yes. I quite agree. I do trust Uncle George," Katherine responded in a much softer manner. "And what is the second thing, Mr. Bartley?"

"You need to get away from it all. I'm going up to my ranch this weekend. Why don't you come along? Bring your cousin if you like. A couple of days in the country and you'll come back with a different perspective. It's guaranteed."

"The country?" she thought aloud, enchanted with the idea before she caught herself. "Thank you, it's a lovely invitation, really, but I am afraid I can't accept. There are too many things that need my attention just now."

"Will you think about it? If you change your mind just let me know."

"Oh thank you, but I'm sure you will want to make other plans."

"No. No other plans. That's why I go to the country. It's the one place I don't have to have plans."

Albert was just getting into a new Steinbeck bestseller when Katherine brought Patrick Bartley back to look at his samples. They spent over an hour before Katherine decided. She would have coved red Formica counters and black and white speckled linoleum floors.

"I like the idea of a bright, bold kitchen," she stated, rejecting the more trendy colors like Shell Pink and Aquamarine. "I won't always have Chow-Ling to wake me up with morning coffee."

It wasn't until eleven that they finished and Bartley stood up to leave.

"Remember you have a standing invitation for the ranch this weekend," he said before turning to Albert. "I wish you would convince Katherine that she needs to get away. I wanted both of you to come up to the ranch this weekend. It's a great time of year for riding."

"That's an unrivaled plan!" Albert said. "Why not?"

"Because I must spend this weekend going over things, preparing for next week," Katherine insisted.

"Don't be ridiculous! To hell with those damned reports!" Albert shot back. "You need a rest and you'll love the Napa Valley. You'll see another side of California and feel like a million bucks when you get back. What the heck. You haven't even been over the Golden Gate or the Bay Bridge yet!"

"You can bring your reports up with you," Patrick continued where Albert left off. "You can go for a ride in the morning and then read them all afternoon in the cool veranda."

Katherine was dumbfounded. She was trapped for the weekend and she could not think of a way to get out of it. Yet at the same time the thought of again being on a horse was irresistible.

"It looks like I have little choice," she said trying to conceal her frustration.

"Good. Then it's settled," Bartley concluded. "Why don't we shoot for Friday noon. I'll see if I can put out some fires and we can get away early."

Albert could tell Katherine was angry about being railroaded and after Bartley left, he tried to smooth her feathers.

"You can get shell-shocked from the pressure and frantic pace," he argued, reaching for an analogy that seemed appropriate. "The success of any campaign is often determined by the strategic retreat. You need to regroup and believe me, there is no place better for regrouping than the Napa Valley. It's the South of France. I promise you, you won't be sorry."

"I suppose you're right, Albert, I could use a holiday," she concluded at last. "But I do object to being pressed and backed into a corner."

"I'm sorry. I suppose we did sort of stack the deck. If you really don't want to go, we can cancel."

"No," she said, getting up and giving him a good-night kiss on his forehead. "It will be good to get out into the country. I suppose if Mr. Bartley has a decent horse, I'll let him take me for a ride." She paused and turned back towards her cousin and smiled. "But after this, let me be the general when it comes to plans that affect my life."

CHAPTER 22

𝒯HE DRIVE UP to the Napa Valley was breathtaking. Patrick had done the unheard of by taking Friday off and leaving his partners with the business. The day was crisp and clean and as they approached the Bay Bridge, the rich aroma of coffee from the Hills Brothers plant filled the air as the waters of the bay lapped against the sides of liners and rusting old tramps.

"Amy quoted something by Gertrude Stein the other day when I asked her about Oakland, but I can't remember what it was," Katherine said as they pulled onto the great span that would take them across to Yerba Buena Island and then on to the East Bay.

"'There's no there there,'"Albert recounted. "San Franciscans love to be derogatory about Oakland."

"Why?"

"It's in their blood! They all maintain the East Bay is a cultural wasteland. Of course, there is the Port of Oakland. I've heard it's supposed to be a good deep-water port with excellent ware-house facilities."

"Get Brian to take you over there," Patrick agreed. "You should see the facilities at the Grove Street Terminal and the shipbuilding division of Bethlehem Steel in Alameda."

Katherine thought carefully for a few moments. "I don't think we ship into the Port of Oakland at all. I wonder why?"

"Politics," Patrick said caustically as he stepped on the gas of his Caddy to reach cruising speed.

They drove on across the bridge and headed up the east bay past Richmond, Kaiser's Permanente shipyards and Standard Oil's refinery. They came to the Carquinez Straights where a McMasters C-3 type freighter was lying alongside the bulk unloaders at the California-Hawaiian Sugar Company. Albert explained how Crockett was the great sugar port of the bay area, lying as it did on the straight between San Pablo and Sassoon Bays. "Further on up the river about fifty miles is the Port of Stockton." he continued, "It was just fully opened to ocean going steamers prior to World War II. It's the great grain port of the west, with modern wharves, bulk loading equipment and grain elevators."

Katherine began to understand how San Francisco Bay and its tributary rivers served to bind together the whole west central region of California into one cohesive economic unit. But she sighed when she thought of trying to master all the complicated rate structures and accessorial charges that she had been studying at the company offices.

After the Carquinez Straights they were quiet for a while. When they spoke again it was not about business but about horses.

"How well do you know the back country north of St. Helena, Albert?" Patrick asked finally breaking the silence.

"I'm not all that familiar with that end of the valley. I have friends in Rutherford and we ride a lot out of their ranch there."

"Ever taken the trails up to Calistoga?"

"Yes, a couple of times. I was out for three days in that country, but that was years ago."

As they talked, Albert could tell that Katherine was beginning to relax. She removed her wide-brimmed straw hat and let her long blonde hair blow free in the hot, dry wind. This was the kind of country she loved—the wide open spaces, ranch houses, horses, and the sweet smell of dried grass. She could always feel free in the country. It was her magic elixir and no matter where she lived, she could never remain in a city for more than a few weeks without escaping to the countryside for at least a picnic or a horseback ride. And she thought as they drove north, how the country always produced a similar effect on her. It contained a refreshing mystery deep down inside the earth, and as that mystery poured out into the each individual countryside, it produced its own peculiar sweet odor and its own strangely beautiful grasses and trees. It was always different, yet always the same. After thinking these things, her mind came back to the present. There she was in a great red American convertible, heading north into a valley thousands of miles from anything she had ever known. There was a sense of adventure about it all, and she felt an exhilarating kind of happiness like a child on a camping trip at the beginning of summer.

By two in the afternoon it was well over ninety degrees and Patrick pulled the Caddy into a roadside greasy spoon, which looked as if it had been built on the front of an old house. A big sign reading "EAT" with an arrow pointing downwards was anchored above the front door, and a hand-painted sign nailed to the front wall read, "JACK'S CAFÉ".

"Best hamburgers in Northern California," Patrick exclaimed as he held the door open. There were only two customers in the café. At the far end of the counter, a rancher sat over a piece of apple pie and his cup of coffee, while midway down the line of stools, a trucker was eating one of Jack's famous burgers. "This reminds me of the Captain's Cabin at Trader Vic's," Katherine quipped as she slid into the booth.

"Actually, Katherine," Patrick teased in a condescending manner, "Trader Vic's started with a little place just like this before he went Polynesian. But Jack gives you the real American, down-home, good old-fashioned country cooking. And that you can't beat anywhere."

"Gee, whiz!! Sounds irresistible!" Katherine said laughingly taking the red-and-white checked napkin and stuffing it into her blouse.

"Gee whiz?" Albert asked with surprise.

"Yes, gee whiz. If I'm going to live in the States, I think I better start speaking the language."

"Three deluxe Jack Burgers with a side order of fries," Patrick ordered as Jack's wife Shirley came around the counter. Katherine turned to Albert and there was a note of sarcasm in her voice. "This is the third time Mr. Bartley has taken me to dinner, and I have yet to be allowed to order anything, much less look at a menu."

"Gotta take care of your women," Patrick teased, winking at Albert, "say, what if I let her choose what she wants to drink?"

"Ah, hell, this is the country," Albert said, picking up Patrick's line, "women gotta learn their place."

"I hope you gentlemen are amusing yourselves with your preposterous chatter," Katherine said in the most condescending manner she could muster.

Soon Jack's Deluxe Jumbo Hamburger arrived, and it was just about the biggest thing Katherine had ever seen, despite the fact that she had been raised in Argentina, and was accustomed to large servings of beef. "I think probably one order would have been sufficient for all of us," she said, fingering the plastic ketchup container in an attempt to figure out how it worked.

"You have to squeeze it," Patrick said, reaching over to show her how.

Without understanding the direction of the container, Katherine did as he suggested, at which point a large blob of ketchup squirted across the table and hit Patrick's shirt. Their mouths fell open with the surprise delivery before they dissolved into unrestrained laughter. Katherine could not help but continue the assault. Reaching over, she carefully squeezed out a steady stream of ketchup, painting Patrick's chest with the outlines of a large face. He sat there half-stunned with her antics, as she painted in the eyes, nose and a squiggle of hair. When she came to the mouth, she thought for a minute, reached over and grabbed the mustard bottle, and proceeded to squirt out large blobs of mustard. At some point in the frantic play that followed, Katherine turned to Albert and for a moment their eyes met. They both knew then, although they had no opportunity to verbalize it, that Patrick had joined the club. Patrick retaliated by wiping the ketchup off his chest and smearing it on Katherine's blouse. Not to be outdone, Albert filled a spoon with pickle relish and catapulted it in Katherine's direction and then made a direct hit on Patrick. By this time Jack had come out from behind the counter, swearing like a trooper, "God-damned sons of bitches. Come up here and ruin my place! You'll pay for all this goddamned mess, Patrick Bartley. You goddamned son-of-a-bitch! You'll pay for this, or you'll never get another goddamned burger again for the rest of your goddamned life!"

"Settle down, Jack," Patrick said amiably. "What do you say I give you five bucks for the trouble of cleaning this place up?" Patrick reached into his pocket, pulled out his billfold, and handed Jack five dollars. Jack looked him in the eye, and began to laugh as he grabbed the bill from Patrick's hand. "For five bucks, you goddamned son-of-a-bitch, you can squirt the ketchup all day." Now eat your burgers and get out of here!"

They finished their burgers, left an additional two-dollar tip, and waved goodbye to Jack, who was laughing and swearing and telling them to come back. With a hose at the side of the building, they washed themselves off. It was refreshing in the heat of the afternoon and Patrick and Albert took off their shirts, and Katherine tied a knot at the bottom of her blouse, most of which had been spared from the ketchup and mustard by her table napkin. They drove up on the highway into St. Helena with the hot September sun beating on their shoulders, and the wind whistling through their hair.

Patrick's ranch outside St. Helena in the winding recesses of the Kahn Valley was in one of the most beautiful settings Katherine had ever seen. Over four hundred acres spread across the valley floor and up the gently sloping foothills. A stream, which at the end of the dry season, was little more than a trickle, gave the poplars and sycamores enough water to grow tall so that they provided great patches of shade around the ranch house in the late afternoon when the valley heat hovered around one hundred degrees.

The main house was a large, rambling structure built to surround an interior court, with one side open to the lawns, which ran down towards the stream. A deep veranda connected every wing from the outside, and provided a cooling effect for the interior. From the minute Katherine entered the house, she was in love with it. The stucco walls, tiled floors, and heavy beamed ceilings reminded her a little of Argentina.

"The living room was originally an old winery," Patrick explained as he showed them the floor plan. "I converted it into the living room. Used it as the core of the house. Then I built the south wing off there for myself and the North Wing for family or guest. I like the feeling of space and distance, with everything's in the same structure."

They sat down briefly for a glass of iced tea on the large oversized couches that formed a semi-circle around the baronial fireplace, which dominated the sixty-foot living room.

"The one thing I always wanted when I was a kid was a big fireplace. We had to do a lot of restructuring to put this baby in. It was worth it, though. It takes twenty logs when we get it going. We've had a lot of fun in this room on winter days during a storm."

"Have you ever spent Christmas here?" Albert asked, imagining the room filled with people.

"Always. Bring the whole family up. They all love it and it's great for the kids. This is my pride and joy," Patrick said, pointing out a beautifully crafted silver Mexican Prade saddle on display at one end of the fireplace.

By the time Rosa, the housekeeper, had helped them get settled, it was four p.m.

"How about a gin and tonic?" Patrick suggested as they joined him on the patio where he was playing with Echo the ranch Labrador retriever. "We can take it down by the stream or relax in the swings on the veranda."

"Capital idea," Albert said, with unmatched enthusiasm.

"Well, you can stay here and drink, Cousin Albert," Katherine said, "but I would like to see the horses, if Mr. Bartley would be so kind."

"Great," Patrick agreed. "I'll give you both a look at the stables. We can even go for a short ride."

"Thanks, but you two go ahead. I have my eye on one of those lounges under the sycamores along the stream," Albert said as he started across the lawn.

Patrick enjoyed showing Katherine the stables as much as he did his home, and she was particularly pleased to again be around horses. After taking the complete tour and introducing Katherine to each of his horses, Cody, the ranch foreman, saddle up two of his favorite thoroughbreds, and for the next hour, they rode around the rink and then over the back lawn to where they found Albert snoozing quietly in his lounge chair.

Patrick gave Katherine a high sign as they quietly walked their mounts over to where Albert lay dreaming about making love to Deirdre underneath a giant banyan on the banks of the River Ganges.

Patrick guided his horse, Seven, until it stood directly over Albert, and then very gently he let the reins drop until Seven's nose was within inches of their sleeping victim. Feeling the horse's hot breath, Albert slowly opened his eyes to find himself face-to-face with a large, dappled wet nose. "Ah, Beezie, I didn't know you had come along," he said drily.

When Katherine appeared for cocktails that night, she seemed to have gone through a transformation. She had pulled her hair back behind her head and tied it with a large piece of white lace ribbon. Her earrings were great loops of gold, a metal that she had repeated in her sandals. She wore a ruffled shirt of Irish linen and lace with a pair of ankle-length pants in pale turquoise. Albert had seen her up until this time in business suits, formal gowns and silk kimonos, but he never had seen anything of the gypsy in her before. Tonight, however, she reminded him a little of Deirdre, and it flashed through his mind that he might really be in love with her after all.

During a magnificent Mexican dinner of sopa and pepino frio, ensalado de chayote and carne asada, Patrick told them how he had acquired the ranch, and how he thought that the Napa Valley would someday turn almost completely into a wine-producing region. "My guess is that you'll continue to see land values around here go up through the fifties and beyond."

"Will you still be drinking beer with your meals?" Katherine asked teasingly.

"Probably will," said Patrick with an air of complacency. "When I come to the country, I always drink beer. Somehow wine just doesn't seem right up here."

That was the way Patrick Bartley was, Katherine was beginning to discover. He was a self-made man, and he did what he wanted to do on his own time, no matter how it might fly in the face of conventional norms. He was an ambitious, hard-working businessman, but he hadn't allowed success to change him much.

After dinner they continued to talk in the cool of the patio, listening to the night sounds coming up in a chorus from the stream. There is something eternally restful about the chirping of crickets, rather like an old grandfather clock whose ticking reminds one simultaneously of time and timelessness. And as they talked there settled over each of them that certain peace that one receives from being near Mother Earth.

They retired early and if Katherine had worried about Patrick making advances, she needn't have. He placed her along with Albert at the opposite end of the house from his quarters. Both their rooms were spacious, and contained a small fireplace around which comfortable chairs and old lamps had been placed to give each guest a reading area.

Albert's room was paneled in pine and contained a great old Victorian oak bed which he soon made use of, hoping to recapture his dream of Deirdre on the banks of the River Ganges. Katherine's room was more interesting, for it contained a rather splendid display of California Indian baskets, which had been attached to the stucco walls. She could not help but admire the great old oak bed that had been Patrick's parents, and the homemade patchwork quilt, which his mother had made from his old shirts. She undressed slowly and opened the windows on both sides of the room to let the gentle cross-breeze in during the night. Switching off the light, she climbed into bed naked and pulled the patchwork quilt up over her.

The next morning over a hearty breakfast of pork chops, eggs and fried mush, Patrick presented the different activities that they might use to fill up the day.

"I believe I'll elect to stay here," Albert said. "I'm reading 'East of Eden' and I can't put it down. I think it's one of Steinbeck's best."

"Well, that leaves the two of us then, Katherine," Patrick continued. "Would you like to go horseback riding, drive over and visit the old Christian Brothers Winery, or work on your papers?"

"A ride sounds lovely," she answered. "I don't even want to think about McMasters Shipping."

"I'll show you the lake back in the foothills. It's beautiful up there, although I'm afraid the water is a little low this time of year," Patrick said as they went out the kitchen door towards the barn, swinging the canteens they were taking along for the ride.

They saddled up their own horses and headed out towards the northeast. There had been a little rain during the night. It hadn't been much, but it had been just enough to settle the dust on the trail that led up through the dry brown hills. The sky was brilliant blue and the four-foot-high trellised vines in the vineyard were heavy with big clusters of ripe red Cabernet Sauvignon grapes that glistened in the morning sun. The world seemed fresh, clean and uncomplicated as they rode up the path past the adobe house where the ranch foreman lived. They began to climb the gently rolling foothills. The damp aroma of sage and coyote brush permeated the air and they could still hear a meadowlark singing somewhere across the valley.

Katherine felt exhilarated to be in the country and to be riding again. She could not help but admire Patrick's horsemanship. He seemed as natural on a horse as any gaucho she had known, and she wondered how he had become such an excellent rider in just the few short years he had had horses. At about eleven-thirty they had reached the lake tucked away in the foothills just a few hundred yards below the ridge. A small cabin sat at the far end of the dry grass, surrounded by branching California oaks. Pulling their horses up, they sat for a few minutes watching a red-tailed hawk making large free circles in the sky above the opposite shore.

"You know, Katherine," Patrick said quietly, "there's nothing more beautiful in all nature than a hawk on the wing. There's a freedom and power there."

The sun was hot and any moisture from the night before had long since evaporated. They rode their horses around the lake. Patrick dismounted and tied Seven to a large oak while Katherine sat admiring the little valley and watching the ducks feed in the shallows along the edge. He came over and secured her horse before reaching up to help her down. As he grasped her thin waist and lifted her free from the saddle, she felt the strength of his powerful arms and she could see his large, muscle-corded biceps fill the short sleeves of his red and black plaid shirt. He put his arm around her shoulder and they walked together to the lake's edge. The surface of the water was unruffled and reflected the clear blue sky and the few white cumulus clouds that floated slowly eastward. The heat of Indian summer hung over the hills, causing Katherine to sigh softly. She inclined her head to rest it on Patrick's chest. In the sunlight her luxurious hair was streaked with golden highlights and Patrick leaned over and slowly kissed the top of her head as if to smell the sweet scent of her hair. He moved his hands gently to caress her smooth shoulders and graceful neck, and as he did, Katherine felt a small charge of electricity flow through the mellow glow that filled her. She knew that she did not need the complications of a romantic encounter, but she didn't seem to care. With Patrick there didn't seem to be complications. He was too forthright and honest to indulge in the throwing of flowers, 'Eschar las flores', as the Latin playboys called it. His masculinity lacked the superficiality of a technique and this, although seemingly to be a contradiction, made her feel secure for the first time in her life.

He slowly placed both his hands on her shoulders and turned her around. Putting his hand under her chin, he slowly lifted her head up towards his face. She opened her translucent green eyes to find him looking down at her. For a moment out of time, they looked into each other's eyes without thought or movement. She felt his body close in upon her. Her lips opened to meet his and she felt her legs grow weak. His muscular arms encompassed her body, and his mouth ran across the soft skin of her neck before coming again to meet her seeking lips.

A stellar jay screeched mockingly from an oak, and for a second they stopped and half-smiled as if they had been discovered. Patrick turned and they walked the few short yards to the cabin and up the three creaky wooden steps. He did not bother to stop and open the door but put his boot against it and shoved it in. Her body twinged when he unbuttoned her blouse to caress her full, firm breasts with his rough hands. Slowly they moved to the floor. He buried his head in her white smooth stomach, and she felt her whole body convulse with a wave of desire. She grasped at his shirt and unbuttoned the first two buttons before his persistent caresses sent her body reeling back into uncontrollable ecstasy. She made a few feeble attempts to ritualistically resist. She found his ear in the rich mass of his sweaty black curls and sank her teeth into the lobe. He stopped and stretched his arms at length so he loomed over her and for a moment looked down into her anxious eyes. A curiously roguish grin crept across his face. She reached her hands up in a pretense of pushing him away, but they seemed so little and fragile against the rock-hard muscles of his thick chest. She heard his belt buckle hit the floor and felt him gently pulling off her panties. As he came back down, she made no attempt to resist. He was very gentle, slowly kissing her forehead, ears, and neck while gently kneading her bare breasts and firm nipples. She could feel his erection large and hard against the inside of her long, smooth, throbbing thigh and she opened herself up to receive him.

Katherine had never liked to feel dominated before, but with Patrick it was different. She gave herself to him completely and he filled her up, giving her every drop of passion his huge, taut body possessed. Her whole body shuddered as he entered her, but she could not remember anything more except an experience of a oneness she had never known. Beyond that transportation she remembered nothing.

When she awoke, Patrick lay asleep next to her with one arm draped across her body. She noticed for the first time the rough-hewn interior of the rustic cabin, a sturdy pine table, four battered chairs, and an old Navajo rug. All this was bathed in the soft warm glow of a yellow light that poured in on elongated shafts through the filmy windowpanes on both sides of the old blackened stone fireplace. Beyond the minute fibers of dust, which danced along the shafts of light, nothing seemed to move.

CHAPTER 23

*K*ATHERINE WAS BACK in her office early Monday morning, but she found it almost impossible to work. She attempted to go over the procedure for unloading cargo and learn more about the freight department, but the complexity of freight contracts, shipping permits, and bills of lading evaded her. Her mind was not on the bay, but back in the golden foothills of the Kahn Valley. She had learned in growing up to be cautious and self-reliant, and although she could be outwardly charming and at times even madcap, she always retained within herself at the core of her being an identity she fiercely guarded. It was that core sense of identity that allowed the outward Katherine to move so quickly through life without being significantly altered by events or other people. It was her strength. Now she found, as much as she resisted the notion, that she could no longer function as she always had. Patrick had not been her first lover, but he had taken from her something she had not been able to surrender before, and this made her feel at the odd moments confused and frightened. Without success she tried to force herself back into her work, but her mind would not follow her will.

She came home early Monday afternoon and took a nap, and did not awaken until well after five o'clock. She joined Albert in the drawing room at around six p.m., her eyes had a languid faraway look and she had to make an effort at conversation. Albert had been reasonably sure that she and Patrick had become lovers. He could always tell these things. He had noticed, among other small signs, that there had been a sensation of the sharp-edged humor. Indeed, the ride back to the city had been as quiet as a Quaker meeting, and Katherine seemed to glow as if caught in a far-off daydream.

A long finger of fog poured through the Golden Gate and across the bay as they listened to the distant whine of an electric locomotive and the banging of freight cars along the beltway.

"Have you heard from Pat," he asked, after a long interlude. He had never called him anything but Mr. Bartley or Patrick before. Curled up at the end of the Chesterfield studying the leaf monkey, Katherine turned her head and looked at her cousin and smiled knowingly.

The next morning she returned to her office and tried to work, but again without success. In the afternoon, she met with Roland Pike, the manager of the Traffic Department, to learn more about the different requirements for outbound and inbound cargo. It was not the most important part of McMasters Shipping, but it was a start and Katherine was determined to learn about her company from the ground up. Roland explained how cargos were booked and how the various shipping documents were issued. Towards three o'clock Roland left her in his office to go over some highly technical reports needed for the Customs House. Patrick had left a message that morning, but he was out at a construction site and she had not been able to reach him. Finding herself again unable to concentrate, she picked up the phone, intending to again call his office. Hearing a conversation in progress on the line, she started to hang up before she recognized Addison's familiar voice. "Roland, you tell the clerk in charge of clearance and the Wharf Supervisor that there won't be any problem. I just talked to Broderick and he'll see to it." Addison's voice sounded mechanical and she thought it odd that the president of the line would be talking to the traffic manager. Surely there were several levels of management between the president and the head of the traffic department.

"Yes, Mr. Addison," Roland was saying assuredly," I will see to it that the orchids are given special care, as always." The conversation did not last long and Addison concluded by stressing the fragile nature of rare orchids that were being shipped in from the Far East and Hawaii. "Just remember to use the special procedures," he said emphatically. "Special procedures for their handling are absolutely essential."

Addison hung up and Katherine waited a few seconds for a dial tone when Addison's secretary, came back on the line and placed a call to Richard Broderick. "Listen, Dick," Addison said when Broderick came on the line, "I took care of the details at this end. Roland will take care of everything as usual." Broderick's voice was hoarse and contentious. "All right," he snapped, "did you get anymore idea about whether she'll sell or not?" In the short pause that followed, Katherine felt an odd sense of puzzlement cross over her. "We don't know anything more today than we did a week ago. We'll just have to give it some time," Addison replied in a calm, matter-of-fact manner. "Listen, Addison! Goddamn it!" Broderick yelled. "I'm telling you, she has to sell. That's all there is to it. You get her to sell, goddamn it!" With these words he hung up the phone. Katherine sat for five minutes, dumbfounded at what she had heard. She could only assume that they were talking about her. For the first time since she came to San Francisco, she felt frightened. That evening she shared what she had heard with her cousin.

"Why would Addison be talking to the traffic manager about a specific piece of cargo?" she wondered aloud.

"More to the point, what is Addison's connection to Broderick?" Albert interjected. "That raises all sorts of questions in my mind."

"He has no right to talk about my concerns to anyone, especially someone who is reported to have such an unsavory reputation. He's the President of the Company. I should think I could expect some loyalty. I'm going to have a talk with him tomorrow."

"Wait a minute. I wouldn't jump so fast. There's obviously more here than meets the eye. If this Richard Broderick is somehow involved with the offer to purchase McMasters, you need to know why. No use tipping your hand."

"I suppose you're right," Katherine concluded. "But this changes everything."

"Maybe there's something here that explains his reaction to Monique Monahan." Albert pondered, "I mean, if he has some sort of reason that he wants the company sold, then … well, Mrs. Monahan would have threatened that move, wouldn't she?"

"And it could also explain why we were only given a part of the new will, if indeed that was the case."

"Precisely."

"I'd still like to talk to the company attorneys and try and ferret out if there were indeed additions we haven't seen."

"Too risky. Let me see what I can find out about Addison. It shouldn't be that difficult to get a run down on the President of McMasters Shipping by asking a few discreet questions around town.

The next morning Katherine had again scheduled a meeting with Roland Pike. "Tell, me, Mr. Pike, just what your duties are as Freight Traffic Manager," she asked as they started.

"Among other things, Miss McMasters, I am responsible for seeing that all ships' manifests and consular invoices reach the Customs House. I oversee the clearance clerks and wharf superintendents and it is their job to send these documents to the Customs House, along with a Notice of Arrival to the consignee so they will know when to settle their accounts. In a way you might say I am the middleman."

Katherine accepted his explanation and continued to review the procedures again and again, attempting to grasp the complexity of the operation in just this one small department of her company. But try as she would, she found it difficult to understand why Addison should involve himself in the minutiae of traffic operations. "Tell me, Mr. Pike, a little about Mr. Addison's management style," she said, again turning to Roland. "Does he ever reach down into the various departments to see how things are going?"

Roland looked at her and laughed, "Well, Miss McMasters, I'll tell you. Mr. Addison started in the company as the clearance clerk, and every now and again he still likes to get involved and follow a specific problem through. I guess you might say that shipping's in his blood."

Thursday morning Katherine met Patrick just off Union Square for breakfast at Sears, a plain, busy little restaurant crowded with people on their way to work. She had not seen him for three days, although he had called twice under the pretense of talking about her apartment. She had had a busy week, but even in the most hectic moment she had found herself waiting for his call, and each time she heard a telephone ring, her mind automatically jumped to the hope that it would be his voice on the other end. She could not know that Patrick was feeling a little confused about their relationship. He had not brought her to his ranch with the intention of seducing her, yet that was what had happened and there were moments when he felt guilty at having taken advantage of her. Yet, in the next moment he would find himself filled with desire when the thought of her body crossed his mind.

He had been working on his construction sites and he was dressed in an old blue work shirt, jeans, and construction boots. In contrast to the pasty Montgomery Street businessmen who crowded the restaurant, he looked particularly rugged and handsome. At first Katherine found herself feeling a bit awkward as she slid in beside him wearing a navy blue suit with a blue collar and her hair held neatly with an ivory comb to the back of her head. "I've been waiting for you for ten minutes, Miss McMasters," Patrick said, his face breaking into that broad, mischievous smile that she found so irresistible. "And I suppose you have ordered for me in that time," Katherine fired back, relieved that he had set a light playful tone to their encounter. "Of course," Patrick said, letting his smile break into a deep, rich chuckle. "We're having the crisp pecan waffles with a side order of bacon. Would you like some orange juice with that?"

Their breakfast together was brief because Patrick had a nine o'clock appointment out in the Sunset, which he could not afford to miss. Katherine wanted to tell him about her week and the phone conversations she had overhead, but somehow she couldn't bring the conversation around to business.

Patrick talked through most of the meal about the World Series.

"I have a hundred bucks on the Yankees. You should have heard the game! A seventh-inning homer by Collins and a three run rally in the eighth! We're one game up!"

Knowing nothing about baseball, Katherine nevertheless found his unrestrained enthusiasm contagiously appealing and she lost herself watching him try to explain the plays of Wednesday night's game. Before she knew it, the check had been paid and they were standing outside on the busy street. "Listen, Katherine," he said, turning to face her as an army of office workers and store clerks rushed hurriedly by on their way to work, "I almost forgot. I arranged to have your piano moved. You just name the date, and it will be in your apartment. Sort of a housewarming present from me." Appearing to be rather awkward about displaying his affections in public, he reached down and quickly kissed her on the forehead. "I'll call you tonight. We'll have dinner this weekend, O.K.?"

"Yes," Katherine said with surprised hesitation. "That would be lovely."

He turned, and Katherine watched him disappear down towards Post Street. She spent that morning aimlessly wandering through the shops around Union Square and along Maiden Lane. She did not think any more about the company and missed an appointment that afternoon with her accountants. Neither did the news that day that President Eisenhower had halted a walkout by 50,000 longshoremen in the East seem to interest her when that evening Albert attempted to explain the effects of the Taft-Hartley Act on labor relations. She seemed more than ever to be falling in love, and told her cousin in great detail about pecan waffles, baseball, and Patrick Bartley's offer to move her mother's piano. And when Albert tried to spark her interest by telling her about a party they were invited to in Sausalito the next evening, she was noncommittal, "I think I'm going to have dinner with Patrick," she said with a sigh before adding, "I guess there are some questions about the alterations that he wants me to go over."

CHAPTER 24

ALBERT AND KATHERINE slept late the next morning, as Katherine had decided not to go into the office. She wanted to stay at home and go over papers in the comfort and privacy of her own room. When she appeared for breakfast at nine-thirty, she looked searchingly at Chow-Ling. "Have there been any calls for me this morning?" she said, trying not to betray any anxiety. "No calls for Miss McMasters," Chow-Ling said as he shuffled off towards the kitchen to get the papaya and the strawberries from the icebox. Dejected and a little angry, Katherine hardly spoke during breakfast. She failed to be amused by a pithy comment in Herb Caen and she turned down an invitation to take Windsor on a morning walk up to the park. "I have to go over some papers," she said, walking off towards her bedroom. Halfway through the drawing room, she turned and came back to the doorway. "Didn't you say something about a party in Sausalito tonight?" "Yes," Albert said, looking up from the sports page, where he had been reading the account of Mickey Mantle's two-run homer in the eighth inning. "Good," she said, in a determined manner. "What time do we leave?"

"We can leave about two, drive over to Marine, see the sights and have an early dinner. Deirdre's parties never start or end at any particular time."

"Marvelous," she said, tossing her head back in a determined manner. "I'll be ready."

Albert knew Katherine's decision to join him was in a way calculated to take back the emotional independence she had relinquished to Patrick, who had not called as promised. He did not say anything, but he wondered if Bartley might not have been using her. Perhaps he wanted the social connection with the Devonshires? Or perhaps he saw the celebrated and beautiful Katherine McMasters as some sort of prize? If he wanted the former, he was not playing the game very well. If he wanted the latter, he may have already achieved his objective, and was now merely in the process of moving on towards a different conquest. Albert had had plenty of experience with obsequious social climbers and parvenues. The Episcopal Church, charities and the fringes of society were full of them. People willing to use other people to advance their own sense of self importance. Silly, small people caught inside their own limited egos, living without authenticity like children willing to cheat at Monopoly. Yet all in all, Patrick did not seem to fit into the mold. Perhaps his avoidance was due to some sense of guilt. This struck Albert as a possibility, for he knew that unlike Episcopalians, for whom the only sin was poor taste, Catholics had a more vivid idea of sin and its consequences. These speculations dominated Albert's walk with Windsor up to Pioneer Park. Returning he found that Patrick had called at last and invited Katherine to dinner Saturday night.

Thus it was with a much happier cousin that Albert headed out for Sausalito with the top down on his convertible. As odd as it seemed, Katherine had not yet been over the Golden Gate, and realizing this, Albert felt a keen sense of embarrassment. "Ah, the Golden Gate," he said in reverent tones. "The symbol of wealth and fortune. The Western Hemisphere's equivalent to the Golden Horn. There is not a bridge in the world that is more beautifully constructed or placed in a more dramatic setting." Katherine could feel his overwhelming sense of pride as they started across what he called "The Span of Gold". And she had to admit that for a city as diverse in architecture as in culture, this was its crowning achievement. The graceful lines of the single suspension span running between its two beautifully proportioned vermillion towers reached over seven hundred feet into the deep blue October sky.

On the other side he stopped the car at Vista Point, and for over an hour they gazed as if mesmerized back over the magic city that gleamed in the bright fall sun.

"It is a fabled city out of an old storybook," she said. "I can't recall a place in Europe that has a more beautiful panorama."

Beneath them tiny white sailboats crisscrossed and darted over the blue water as if playing hide and seek between Alcatraz, Treasure Island, and the large freighters riding at anchor.

"Do you know how the Bay was formed?" he asked, pointing down at the water rushing out the Gate past the towering cliffs of the Marin Headlands.

"No, how?"

"According to an old Indian legend the Sun God fell in love with the daughter of a great chief. In his attempt to carry the princess off into the heavens, he stumbled over Mount Diablo. The impression made by the impact of his fall created a large interior valley. Later in time, a great earthquake caused the earth to shudder and the mountains to part. The ocean rushed in, filled up the valley and made the bay.

"What happened to the Indian princess?" Katherine asked, enthralled with the story. "The Indian princess fell to her death and her profile can still be seen in the ridge of Mount Tamalpais, which lies a little farther north in Marin. They say that when the summer becomes too hot, the sun god allows the fog to come in so that he can wrap his beloved in a soft, cool blanket."

"Well, I'll have to remind Patrick to look out for Mount Diablo."

"Yes, I think that would be a good idea," he said, putting his hand gently around her shoulder. They stood there another few minutes, watching the bay and the city before they got back into the car. "You have just viewed Byzantium, and now we are going to go to Portofino," he jested as they wound down Alexander Avenue between the jagged cliffs that formed the entrance to Sausalito. "Since I arrived in California, I feel like I have been on a world tour," she said as she caught her first sight of Sausalito rising precariously up the steep hillside out of the blue waters of the bay. "You are absolutely right! This is reminiscent of the Riviera."

Albert drove up the winding street to his cottage on Buckley, but Deirdre was not home, and after showing Katherine around and introducing her to the cats, they decided to take a walk up into the hills.

"C'est charmant," she said, admiring the quaint cottages all tucked into the hillside among the native oaks. "This is absolutely charming! What is it like in the spring?"

"With the rhododendrons and wisteria in bloom! The gardens are full of color. Rose, pink, lavender."

Soon they turned around and headed down to catch glimpses of the yachts and sailboats out in the bay before walking down a flight of steps and across the street to Depot Park.

"Let's sit on the bench for a few minutes and enjoy the afternoon sun," she said wistfully. "This reminds me so of Italy. Those marvelous elephants on the base of the street lamps and the fountain! It is the Riviera!"

"It's all from the 1915 Panama Exposition," he explained.

They sat for a while enjoying the sun and watching the locals who make Depot Park their meeting place.

"Tell me, Albert. Tell me what you really think of Patrick," she asked out of the blue.

"You're in love with him, aren't you?" he said, reaching over and giving her hand a squeeze.

"Yes," she openly admitted for the first time. "I've never felt about a man the way I do about him."

"Is he in love with you?"

"I think so, but I'm not sure. Sometimes I think he is, but then there are times when he seems distracted. It's almost as if he wants to avoid acknowledging his emotions.

"I think he's a hell of a nice guy, Katherine," He's amiable, ambitious, and has an appealing sense of humor, and I'll have to say it's great fun to be with him. I guess my only advice would be to take it slow, kid."

Deirdre was still not in when they got back to the cottage and Albert guessed that she was on the Wire Man's houseboat getting ready for the party.

They had drinks on the deck of the Alta Mira overlooking the harbor before walking down to the Valhalla for dinner.

"In the 1880s this place used to be a beer garden," he explained after they were seated. "They ran pipes from a creek right down the hillside and into the building. During Prohibition it was the perfect setup. They just rolled the barrels into waiting ships."

"Who was that unusual lady that met us at the door?"

"Oh, That's Sally Stanford. In her day, she was the most famous madam in San Francisco. When she retired, she bought the place, brought in the Victorian furniture and Tiffany lamps and made an equally successful business as a restaurateur."

"Tell me about this party we are going to tonight," Katherine said, looking around the Valhalla in amazement. "Sausalito seems to be full of characters."

"You're right about that and you'll meet more of them tonight. The Wire Man and Miss Dhorgie always throw a great party."

"And just who is this Wire Man you have been referring to?"

"Oh, he's been of friend of Deirdre's and mine for years. He bends wire for a living. Makes all sorts of sculptures and little puzzles and sells them to shops and at fairs. He learned the craft wandering through India after the war."

"Is his wife Indian? The name Dhorgie sounds like it."

"No," he laughed, "Dhorgie is a yellow dog with a curved plume of a tail. He acquired her in Kashmir after making a pilgrimage to a Buddhist monastery in the Himalayas. She's his constant companion. The tourists all think he's crazy. He has long conversations with her when he sells his puzzles in Depot Park."

"He sounds a little off at that."

"Of course. He is crazy but so are all the other Bohemians and artists in Sausalito. They all live in little shacks hidden in the hills or on houseboats that float on the bay and pursue art or Truth or both."

"It sounds quite romantic in a way."

"Of course, although I suppose they don't think so. I'm sure they see themselves as post romantics. Anyway, the Wire Man came back from India with his Miss Dhorgie. He bought an old barge, constructed a squatter's shack and fished out the window. He named the boat after his dog and claims she is the owner."

"And this is where the party is going to be?" Katherine asked incredulously.

"Yes, but it's not a shack now. Over the years rooms have been added, torn down and reconstructed. In its present incarnation there are two stories. You'll have to see it to get the full picture. The whole place is made of materials salvaged from dumps and shipyards. It's very well done, really, especially the symmetrical iron scrap and oak strip paneling.

"And what, if I dare ask, is the occasion for tonight's affair," Katherine asked, her eyes flashing with amusement at his story.

"Ogden Wallraven's sixty-second birthday party. He's a retired professor of biochemistry from Cal Berkeley. Brilliant fellow. I heard he did a lot of top secret research for the government during the war. Something to do with germ warfare, I think. Whatever it was, he gave it all up, took up Eastern philosophy and settled in Sausalito. He's something of a sage to the locals. Although I must admit, I find his dire predictions for the future to be a little too plausible. I usually get quite drunk when I'm around him for very long."

By the time they walked down the rickety old pier it was growing dark and the party was well underway. They received the predictable two-bark welcome from Miss Dhorgie who ran to the edge of the boat to give her permission to board as each guest arrived. Suddenly Deirdre appeared out of the thirty or so guests.

"Deirdre, my cousin Katherine," Albert said by way of introduction.

"Yes," Deirdre said warmly. "You were predicted."

"Predicted?" Katherine puzzled.

"Yes, predicted. This is Ogden Wallraven's birthday. Come and see our sculpture."

"What does she mean I was predicted?" Katherine whispered as they ducked through the door into the large room that formed the first deck of the boat.

"I haven't the foggiest. That's just Deirdre."

"The Wire Man and I created this," Deirdre explained proudly pointing to an enormous steel spring upon the top of which they had welded the equation $E=MC^2$. "It represents the new god of the technological age."

"Should we genuflect or just bow?" Albert teased.

"We already have. This is the God that has enslaved mankind to the requirements of fixed schedules and unit time production."

"Of course," he agreed, "energy and matter in a never-ending spiral. But I think it's more Greek than Hindu."

"Whatever," Deirdre replied before wandering off.

"She is stranger than you described her," Katherine said.

"It takes a while," he assured her. "But she likes you. I can tell."

After pouring a mug of red wine, they moved over to where Ogden was seated in a barrel chair, enjoying his party and discussing how psychic reality was slowly beginning to change as man adopted the fragmented reality of flow technology. "What do you think of Superman, Albert?" he shouted without waiting to be introduced to Katherine.

"Superman?" he asked, "you mean as in Clark Kent?"

"Precisely!" Ogden said, pushing him to make a statement. "What do you think of Clark Kent as Superman?"

Albert did not quite understand where Ogden was leading, so he decided for the glib answer. "Gee, I suppose he can leap buildings in a single bound, and is faster than a speeding bullet," he said with a sheepish grin. "Yes, but how?" Ogden shouted, pounding his fist on a barrel top. "I'll tell you how! He has to go into a goddamned phone booth and put on a costume! He derives his strength from a goddamned costume in a goddamned phone booth. This is the great tragedy of the twentieth-century mind. We are so totally obsessed with outside reality that we have lost sight of the fact that the real strength comes from within." Ogden went on to explain that the dominant theme of Western civilization since the Renaissance had been an ever-increasing technification, which had brought on a neurotic preoccupation with the future.

Albert could tell Katherine was fascinated by Ogden and with his creatively flexible mind, bald head, and bushy gray eyebrows. They listened for over twenty minutes, occasionally being shot a question by Ogden, who always enjoyed bouncing off his audience. Somewhat to his astonishment, Katherine turned the tables after a while and asked Ogden if he thought there was an answer to the dilemma. "Celebrate the reality of the moment!" Ogden burst forth, obviously pleased at the question. "Technology is always concerned with abstract calculations. It can't experience the enjoyment of pure being. We have to discover who we are, not where we are going."

Katherine spent the better part of the evening sipping red wine and sitting on a pillow across from Ogden, who held court like a Mughal emperor, pontificated, and generally enjoyed himself.

Albert wandered off to talk with Rigg and Deirdre on the back deck, and then found the Wire Man, who was rapping on about the lack of meaning and content in modern advertising. They talked for a while before he rejoined Katherine and decided to investigate 'The Miss Dhorgies' newly-added second story.

They climbed the circular wooden stairwell, which had replaced the rope ladder of the year before, to find a large studio at the end of which the Wire Man had built an enormous wooden platform bed recessed into an alcove. The alcove was half hidden by an elaborately hand-carved teak screen and contained an excellent Tibetan Thangka the Wire Man had purchased the same day Miss Dhorgie had chosen him for her companion. The sweet pungent smell of burning peanuts that permeated the air signaled that opium had recently been smoked and as he moved towards the alcove to get a better look at the Thangka, Albert caught a glimpse of Kitty Bingsham reclining on the Japanese mats that covered the platform. She was talking softly to Sandy Peterson, a local Bohemian, with whom she had occasionally slept. Albert and Kitty's families knew each other, and although she was ten years his junior, Albert had recently seen her at various seasonal parties in the city and down at the Burlingame Country Club. "Kitty! Have we been indulging in the smoking pistol?" he asked sarcastically looking at the exquisitely carved bamboo pipe that lay on a small lacquer tray in front of them. "Oh, Albert," she said sleepily, her eyes glazed with the unmistakable dreamlike quality of an opium smoker, "come join us."

He smiled slowly as they stepped onto the platform and sat cross-legged on the other side of the tray, which also contained a cut-glass opium lamp and a small slipper orchid in a bright yellow Chinese porcelain vase. A small cup of water, slender wire pokers, and a sponge sat on another tray close by. Without saying a word, Kitty reached under a pillow and produced a tiny box made of buffalo horn as Sandy took the pipe and warmed it over the flame of the lamp. "I'll pass," Albert said, with an open gesture of his hand that was meant as a sign of thanks for the offer. Sandy smiled, took the wire poker and dipped it into the box, taking out as much opium as would adhere to the point. He proceeded to hold it over the flame until it swelled up to twenty times its original size and then rolled this larger ball over the flat surface of the earthenware bowl before again holding it over the flame. They watched him repeat this process several times before he worked the little opium ball around the wire and inserted it into the bowl in the pipe. Katherine followed Albert's lead and declined, but Kitty took the pipe's silver mounted mouthpiece and inhaled deeply until blue smoke poured back from her nose and mouth.

There was not much point attempting conversation as Kitty and Sandy slipped off into oblivion. They sat there for a few minutes admiring the Thangka they had come to see. Brahma the Creator sat on the lotus that sprung from the naval of Vishnu, who reclined on Ananta, the multi-headed serpent. And Brahma dreamed the universe. Below him, Kitty and Sandy dreamed their own dreams, and the slipper orchid seemed to sway ever so slightly on the end of its long spike that rose from the yellow Chinese bowl.

CHAPTER 25

"DO YOU THINK this will stir Mr. Bartley's Celtic blood?" Katherine asked, walking across the drawing room and twirling around to show off the Hardy Amies dress of blue English gingham with its daringly plunging back. "It ought to stir something," Albert said, putting down the almost-completed copy of East of Eden. "When does Prince Charming arrive?"

"In a few minutes," she said nervously looking at the clock.

Katherine's dinner with Patrick was one of those occasions in the course of a relationship between two people when things go a bit off the mark. Katherine had looked forward to a romantic dinner, remembering that it had just been a week before that they had been together at the ranch. She had returned early enough from Sausalito on Friday to have a good night's sleep and had spent the better part of Saturday at Elizabeth Arden's getting a facial and having her hair done. What she got for her efforts was not Prince Charming, but a rather out of sorts Patrick Bartley. The Dodgers had won the third game in the Series Friday and Patrick had gone out with some of his construction crew to have a few beers. A few beers had led to a lot of beers, straight shots, and a hell of a hangover Saturday. To add insult to injury, the Dodgers won the fourth game on Saturday, and the Series was tied two games each. Of course, there was no way for Katherine to understand the primitive passion the American native had for baseball, and Patrick's somber mood puzzled her from the outset. She could not imagine a sport being so important that a rational person would allow losing a game to ruin his entire day. Nor could she imagine that in baseball Patrick had found an escape from his need to address what was happening between them.

Albert was not much help. Being a Yankee fan too, he poured Patrick a stiff scotch and spent a good half-hour listening to his discouraged play-by-play review of the last two games, while Katherine pensively sat attempting to look interested. As they finished a second highball, the conversation turned away from baseball to Rocky Marciano's successful title defense and then to politics and Governor Warren's appointment to the Supreme Court. Rambling on, Albert thought how much he was beginning to like this Bartley fellow more and more. He was smart, unpretentious, and easy to talk to.

"We're going down to Burlingame tomorrow to spend the day with our great-aunt," he said on the spur of the moment as Patrick and Katherine finally got up to go. "Why don't you come along? We'll go for a swim and listen to the game around the pool."

Without even looking for a reaction from Katherine, Patrick accepted. "Gee, that sounds swell. What time do we leave?"

"Oh, about nine or ten. We'll give you a call in the morning. We can catch the first part of the game on the way down."

As Patrick turned to get his coat, Albert caught Katherine's eye. Her expression was one of anger and frustration mixed with bewilderment. She had been almost completely ignored since his arrival. Excluded from the conversation and the plans for the following day, she again felt manipulated. Yet she chose only to smile and ask, "Are you treating me to hot dogs or hamburgers tonight, Mr. Bartley?"

Patrick paused for a moment as if for the first time acknowledging her feelings, yet not wanting to admit he had ignored them. "Oh, I can get you a hamburger at Ernie's if you want. Just leave everything up to me."

"Do I have a choice?" she retorted.

Patrick did not respond. He chuckled a little, helped Katherine with her coat, said thanks for the drinks, and left, leaving Albert to finish reading.

Patrick was quiet on the way down to the restaurant, and Katherine, aside from the kidding, was still frustrated. She did not like to have decisions made for her without her consent. Otto and Gloria had done that to her all her life, and she had resented it. But by the time Patrick turned onto Montgomery, she began to relax and with new resolve, decided to make the best of the situation. She could not help but wonder if she had not miscalculated his interest in her. They had seen each other only once during the past week, and that was only for a quick breakfast at Sear's. It had been just a week since they had made love in the rustic cabin by the lake, and yet the man who sat next to her now bore little resemblance to the passionate lover of just seven days before. These Americans, she thought. So difficult to fathom. They certainly were not the same as the sophisticated Europeans she had known. She could, of course, not begin to comprehend the puritanical underpinnings that defined and restrained American morality and manners, especially in relations between the sexes.

Perhaps it was the memory of that weekend in St. Helena, along with Patrick's choice of a restaurant that helped her through the evening. She could not help but be impressed from the moment she entered Ernie's.

"This reminds me of Maxim's" Katherine commented as they were seated amid the opulent Victorian decor.

"Maxim's?"

"Maxim's in Paris. Very a la mode!"

"Well, I'll tell you what. How about it if I let you order tonight?"

"Ah, monsieur, you are too kind. What have I done to deserve such favor?"

"Golly, I figure your French is just a little better than mine. I'm O.K. with Italian, but that's about it."

"Then we'll start out with avocado a la Horcher's, the pate de Hormard Chaud and then La Pigeon en Chatiuse. And for dessert, perhaps Torte Tatin."

"You sure you wouldn't rather have a hamburger," he kidded staring for a moment at her across the table.

"Perhaps I would but they don't seem to have any catsup on the table."

Other than this light interchange the dinner conversationwas anything but romantic with Patrick talking on in great detail about his housing development and questioning her about McMasters Shipping.

"I don't think it sounds like this Addison is a very trustworthy character. I'd be very careful what you tell him if I were you," he advised after hearing about the conversation Katherine had overheard between Addison and Broderick. They've probably got some deal going to avoid paying customs."

"It's all rather odd, the more I think about it. On the one hand, he was so sentimental about my mother's piano and on the other—well, what can I say?"

When towards the end of the meal Katherine mentioned how much she enjoyed the ranch, Patrick diverted the conversation back to the alterations that he was making on her apartment. Sensing it might be a safe subject, she attempted several times to tell him about the party in Sausalito. He listened patiently to her description of the Wire Man's boat, and her conversation with Ogden Wallraven, but she could tell he was disinterested. She thought she might tell about the Vishnu Thangka and the opium smokers, but she hesitated. She wondered at her hesitancy. It worried her, for it told her she did not yet completely trust him. Yet even more distressing was an image that somehow intruded itself from the evening before. She remembered the small orchid in the Chinese vase next to the opium lamp. It seemed to sway in front of her like some sort of beautiful but deadly form of life. As Patrick talked on about the apartment, she remembered the orchid that had been next to her mother's picture. It was the same variety, a slipper orchid. She was sure. It was only a coincidence, she thought, but it bothered her, nonetheless.

Before she knew it, the evening was over and she was back at the apartment. Chow-Ling had retired and Albert was out at a late movie watching Gary Cooper as a beachcomber in "Return to Paradise".

"Would you like a brandy perhaps?" Katherine offered as they walked into the living room.

"I want to get a good night's sleep if we are heading down to see your Aunt tomorrow," he said as he bent over and barely kissed her goodnight. "Gee, I certainly hope Albert is right about being able to listen to the game."

"Yes, well, tomorrow then," she said as they walked back towards the front door.

She turned on the light over the Rousseau and sank into an armchair. The evening had certainly not been what she had anticipated. On the surface it had been pleasant enough, but that was about all, and she had to admit she felt disappointed. Again she wondered about his intentions. She hardly knew this man, yet she had thought she was in love with him. Now she was not sure. Perhaps she was moving too quickly, and he felt threatened. Perhaps asking him to Treehaven had been a mistake. Would he get on with Aunt Louisa, or find her to be a stuffy old bore? How would Aunt Louisa like him? She tortured herself with questions and could not satisfactorily answer any of them. Was he perhaps using her to advance his business interests? After all, her uncle was his banker and he was undoubtedly an ambitious man. Yet he was not the deceptive sort, or at least he did not seem to be. He certainly lacked the savoir-faire of knowing how to treat a woman. But then she thought, how does a woman want to be treated? She smiled to herself and sighed.

CHAPTER 26

𝓘F AT TIMES in the course of a relationship things miss the mark, there are other times when events, despite all expectations, work out even better than one had hoped. It is not usually until after the fact that we learn to appreciate where events have led. This was exactly what happened to Katherine the following day when they took Patrick to meet Aunt Louisa.

No doubt in the back of her mind Katherine wanted to have Aunt Louisa's opinion of Patrick, but on the other hand, she worried in the event that the opinion might be unfavorable. She was also worried a little about Patrick's feeling comfortable at Treehaven. Her great-aunt lived in a very grand manner, and was a little eccentric at times, and she thought Patrick might feel slightly out of place with Prentice and Bridget popping in and out and the dogs constantly yapping underfoot. The more she thought about her aunt and Patrick, the more she worried, and she confessed to Albert over breakfast that she was not sure it had been such a good idea to invite Patrick without having more fully consulted Aunt Louisa. "Don't be silly," he said, thinking of all the eclectic parties and eccentric people Treehaven had seen over the years. "Patrick will get on famously, I have no doubt of that." He could tell from the look on her face that she was not convinced, and her concern was only to intensify over the next several hours.

The fifth game of the World Series had just started when they picked up Patrick, and they listened to the first two innings all the way down to Burlingame. Even though San Francisco did not have a major-league team, most San Franciscans loved the Yankees since the DiMaggio brothers went to New York in the 1930s, and Joe DiMaggio, the Yankee Clipper, set a world record getting a hit in fifty-six consecutive games. Patrick was a true San Franciscan but he was more than just a fan, he was a fanatic. And when it came to the Yankees in the World Series, everything else was secondary.

"I've placed another two hundred bucks on the Yankees," he said climbing in the front seat.

As they motored south along the bay, Katherine made several unsuccessful attempts to change the conversation from baseball to Aunt Louisa as a way of preparing Patrick for the afternoon. Each attempt, however, was soon interrupted by the game and Patrick's equally unsuccessful attempt to explain the intricacies of a particular pitch or play. All this served to unnerve Katherine. She became more and more frustrated with the intrusion of a sport, that she did not understand, into what she wanted to be a pleasant and memorable afternoon. "Don't worry," Albert said as they passed through the village, "you'll be able to listen to the rest of the game. Aunt Louisa has been a Yankee fan for longer than any of us can remember." His assurance did not seem to allay Katherine's fears. She continued to picture an afternoon in which Patrick, absorbed in his baseball, avoided making conversation and indulging in the social graces, which she associated with her great-aunt.

The second inning was just about over as they drove into Treehaven and Patrick hesitated in the car to hear the last out. Prentice, who took his time getting to the door, informed them that Aunt Louisa was out in the garden pavilion. The third inning was underway as they crossed through the maze garden and heard the faltering, sharp, cracked voice of the commentator calling the plays. Albert could not help but be a little amused at the look on Katherine's face as they entered the pavilion to find Aunt Louisa, Ivy and Andrew huddled around the Magnavox radio, eating pretzels. "Did you hear the first two innings?" Aunt Louisa asked without looking up. "Find a chair, we have a man on first." For a moment

Katherine stood, half-stunned by the reception. By the time she recovered and attempted to make a formal introduction, Patrick had opened a bottle of Pabst Blue-Ribbon and had pulled up a chair. Another hit put a second man on base for the Yankees, and Aunt Louisa slapped her knee and turned to Patrick, "You're a Yankee fan, I hope," she said, looking at him for the first time. "You bet, Ma'am. Have been all my life." Aunt Louisa did not respond, but turned her full attention back to the game. "That's another one on!" Aunt Louisa screamed as the Yankees got another hit. "Mantle's up next. Grab a beer, Mr. ...?"

"Bartley, Pat Bartley," Pat answered sharply. "Thanks, I have one already."

"Aunt Louisa," Katherine started, sensing an awkwardness in the situation that was not there, "Mr. Bartley is a friend of Uncle George's. We met him at the dinner—"

"Sshhh!" Aunt Louisa said impatiently, waving her hand. "Mantle's coming up and the bases are loaded."

Feeling reject, Katherine sat back, unable to comprehend her aunt's behavior. Surely in a game, which lasted for several hours, there should be at least a few moments afforded to welcome a guest and exchange a few pleasantries. "That's it!" Patrick yelled, jumping up and throwing a punch into the air.

"That's it! Grand slam home run!" Aunt Louisa echoed, throwing her head back and again slapping her knee in undignified excitement. "Just like the second game where Old Mickey drove them in!"

By the time the excitement subsided, Katherine felt even more confused. She had never seen anything quite like the American reaction to baseball and slowly she began to see a side of the American character that seemed incongruous with what she had previously observed. Her great-aunt, who had so graciously received her into her home, and who had so grandly held court at the opening night of the opera, was reduced to behaving like a fishmonger by something called a home run. And what she found even more peculiar, as the game progressed, was the intimate camaraderie Aunt Louisa and Patrick seemed to share, despite the fact that they had not even been formally introduced.

Soon, however, Katherine gave up trying to understand or predict what was happening. Slowly she began to relax and observe the unfolding drama reported in a jargon she could not comprehend.

At the seventh inning stretch Prentice and Bridget brought in a steamer filled with hot dogs and sour kraut and a large silver tray with bowls of chopped onions, bottles of ketchup and mustard. What Katherine had anticipated as a formal lunch beneath the Gobelins tapestry in the Venetian-paneled dining room had turned out to be a picnic in the garden pavilion, and Albert caught her smiling at Patrick when she took hold of the ketchup bottle. He smiled back, and for the first time that day, they seemed to make contact with each other beyond the superficial level.

The Yankees went on to win 11-7, yet not even after the end of the game did the talk of baseball cease. Plays were reviewed and speculation on the next game gave way only slowly to normal conversation, through which Albert could observe Aunt Louisa assessing Patrick more closely.

"Let's go for a swim," Albert suggested about three o'clock with the afternoon temperature in the mid-seventies.

"Great idea!" Patrick exclaimed. "I could stand cooling off. Gee, I can't believe Mantle. A grand slam homer! How about you, Katherine? You coming?"

"Perhaps I'll join you later. I think I'll stay here and have a visit with Aunt Louisa."

"Don't stay here with me. Go for a swim. It'll do you some good!" Aunt Louisa barked.

"Perhaps later. I thought you might let me have a look at your greenhouses. Aunt Victoria says they are really very interesting."

"Yes, of course, dear," Aunt Louisa said with all the subtlety of her innate charm restored. "We shall have a tour of the greenhouses and a chat."

As the men disappeared across the lawn towards the pool, Aunt Louisa and Katherine went out the west door of the pavilion and headed down the hedged path that connected the greenhouses and the formal gardens. There had been very little hint of fall in the air, and the summer plantings were still in full bloom. For a while they moseyed along the paths, stopping every few yards at an intersection for Aunt Louisa to explain the history of the garden, or for Katherine to admire its masses of color.

As they entered the first and largest of the greenhouses, the conversation changed to orchids, "They still present the greatest challenge to me," Aunt Louisa said as they stepped into the long, whitewashed glass structure and beheld the long tables filled with exotic plants. "Of course, the mistake most people make is thinking that orchids are fragile. They have survived for over one hundred million years, and can be found in every climate from the jungles of Southeast Asia to the high Andes. Like humans, they're really quite hardy. The trick, Katherine, is good air circulation. You can smother an orchid by packing it too tightly around the roots. It has to breathe and be allowed to move on the air currents." Aunt Louisa went on to explain in rather lengthy detail about the best possible growing conditions for different varieties of orchids, and how the English in the 1840s had failed to raise them in greenhouses that were overheated and over humidified.

Katherine listened patiently, but her mind was on Patrick. "What do you think of Mr. Bartley, Aunt Louisa?" she asked at last, attempting to casually introduce the topic.

Aunt Louisa paused and smiled patiently. "It's just as I was saying," she continued slowly. "People, like orchids, must be allowed to breathe. They can't be packed down too tightly. As for your Mr. Bartley, I could tell right off that he was definitely F.C.C."

"F.C.C.?" Katherine asked, uncertain of what the initials meant.

"First Class Certificate," Aunt Louisa said, looking her great-niece squarely in the eyes. "F.C.C. is the highest award an orchid can get and your Mr. Bartley is definitely F.C.C. He reminds me of my father,

Michael Patrick Fitzhubert; I suppose it's the Irish in them that makes them so irresistibly attractive."

Katherine felt herself blush. Her aunt had instinctively sensed that Patrick was more than just an acquaintance and she marveled at Aunt Louisa's insight. "He's the kind of man who will hold you without smothering you," Aunt Louisa continued with her orchid analogy. "You would be wise to do the same with him. A strong, independent man like your Mr. Bartley will never last long with an insecure woman who wants to tie him down and smother him with a lot of silly domesticity. He is the kind of man that has to be allowed to have a certain amount of freedom."

Katherine listened intently. Aunt Louisa, in a few short sentences, had been able to summarize Patrick in a way that allowed Katherine to break through her emotions and see him more clearly. They were both strong, independent people and more than anything else she realized that she had to respect his strength and independence if she didn't want to lose him.

"I rather think your Mr. Bartley is like this Dendrobium Speciosum," Aunt Louisa laughed as she pointed to a leathery-leafed orchid, sending up an amazing flower spike bearing a profusion of white blossoms. "It's a wild, hearty Australian orchid that will take the full sun without wilting."

Katherine smiled reassured and with great affection for this wise old sage of an aunt. "What kind of orchid am I?" she asked impishly picking up on Aunt Louisa's metaphor.

"You, my dear?" Aunt Louisa pondered, her bright eyes flashing at the possibilities. "I suppose you are a Ipidenchum Ibaguense. When they are raised in a cool, light-filled environment like San Francisco, they produce the most absolutely marvelous orange and scarlet flowers. Truly quite spectacular."

"Cool light-filled environment like San Francisco!" Katherine said, emphasizing the not-too-subtle message Aunt Louisa was giving her.

"Yes Katherine, like San Francisco," Aunt Louisa said emphatically.

"Well, if I take a cool environment like San Francisco, and Mr. Bartley survives best in the hot Australian sun, I think we have a botanical dilemma," Katherine said, seeing an opportunity to play with her aunt at her own game.

Aunt Louisa turned from where she was fingering moss back into a wire basket and looked Katherine mischievously in the eye. "The most interesting orchids are bigeneric hybrids," she said with a note of triumph in her voice. "Cross two different genus and you'll get something truly spectacular."

For the most part, Aunt Louisa was a concrete person of unusual directness and force. She was not given much to philosophy, but in the rich, warm air of the greenhouse and among her exotic orchids, she became a sort of high priestess of her own unique mythological system. There was a primary quality to that atmosphere that made Katherine listen intently to each word her aunt spoke as she talked on about orchids and life. For Aunt Louisa, each orchid displayed certain qualities of character, from those who grew upright to those, which grew sideways. The flamboyant, the flat, the symmetrical, the extravagant, the small and delicate, the sweet or repugnant, all conveyed a quality whether hanging in the air, or emerging from rotten compost. They were icons through which Aunt Louisa served as a guide into a reality that otherwise might not have been achieved. By the time Katherine emerged from the greenhouse, she had experienced a great sense of calm, as if the events of September had all been packed into perspective.

CHAPTER 27

ONDAY AFTERNOON PATRICK called Albert just after the Yankees clinched the Series in the last of the ninth inning. "We're all going out to celebrate," he said excitedly. "I got Katherine at the office. My brother Mike and his wife Sally are coming along, and my partner, Dick Fleherty. I have a reservation at the Papagay Room for seven. I can't believe that game—the bottom of the ninth and Billy Martin drives in the winning run."

"All right, Patrick," Albert said, amused by the overwhelming enthusiasm. "It sounds like fun. Should I bring Beezie along as a date? She can be great sport if we are all going to get crazy."

By four o'clock Katherine was home for a short nap before changing into a two-piece Shantung dress by Emilio in bright yellow, green, and red stripes that complimented her luxurious hair and made her wildly beautiful. For once Albert thought Beezie might be outdone, but of course, such thoughts were the occupation of the foolish. He had not recalled mentioning the Papagay Room, but evidently he had, for Beezie swept down the staircase of her parents' house dressed ready for the running of the bulls in Pamplona. A great shawl dangling with purple balls was draped mantilla-style from her head and shoulders, and she wore a white Macromere dress that was at least two sizes two small, judging by the way her breasts jiggled precariously in view.

By the time they arrived at the Papagay Room and ordered their drinks, everyone was in a mood to celebrate. "Gee, I can't believe those

Yanks," Patrick said, making a toast, "fifth straight year in a row to win the Series. Ol' Casey Stengel must be putting a few back tonight. He broke all past records for consecutive world championships."

"Could you believe Billy Martin?" Dick Fleherty added, reliving the game. "In the last of the ninth, he drove in the winning run. He got twelve hits. That's more than any other player in a six game Series, and he's only twenty-five. With baseball like that, Charlie Dresden might as well give up altogether."

"Oh, dear, you should tell him to read Norman Vincent Peale if he feels like that," Beezie declared to a table that fell silent in disbelief.

After the Papagay Room, Patrick suggested they all go down to the Buena Vista. "The Irish can't celebrate properly without topping off the evening with a couple of Irish coffees," he said as he helped Katherine on with her coat.

The Buena Vista was packed to standing room only when they arrived. "There's an old house rule here," Patrick explained to Katherine, "that a gentleman cannot buy a drink for a lady with whom he did not enter the premises. It's a great place. When I first moved to Russian Hill, I used to take the Hyde Street cable car down and have dinner here almost every night. There's nothing like good honest pub food and a little Irish whiskey to keep a man in order."

"You know, Patrick," Albert reminisced as they finally got a table and started a second round of drinks. "San Francisco is not the way it used to be before the war. Those were the days. We used to dance to all the big bands like Guy Lombardo, Artie Shaw, Lawrence Welk and Benny Goodman. Every hotel had a big dance floor. There was the Peacock Court at the Mark, the Palace's Rose Room Bowl, and the Drake's Persian Room."

"Golly, what about Griff Williams, Skinny Innes and Paul Whitman?" Patrick recalled. "We used to dance the shag, the dipsy doodle, and the Big Apple until they closed the place down. You'd buy your girl a gardenia or maybe an orchid, if she was really special, and swing all night."

"We were damned lucky to get in on the end of a fantastic era, Pat. Of course, for most of it I was underage, but we usually could sneak in anyway."

"Oh, I was too young for any of that," Beezie said as she wistfully spooned the whipped cream off the top of her glass and placed it seductively on her tongue.

"Ah, that's too bad," Albert sympathized, reaching over and patting her hand, "I can't imagine anyone who could have done the dipsy doodle better than you."

As they finished their second drink, Albert saw Rigg at the far end of the bar. He caught Rigg's eye and motioned for him to come over. "I'll have the usual Tequila Sangrita. Save the Irish coffee for winter," Rigg said as he joined them.

"Oohhh—I'd like to try one of those, too!" Beezie giggled as she eyed Rigg and fingered the purple balls on her shawl.

"Anything my little snookums requires," said Albert, "after all, it's one of the house specialties."

By the time the waitress arrived with another round of drinks, Beezie was explaining to an awestruck Rigg that the purple balls on her shawl were designed to resemble the edible berries of the Madonna tree. Rigg couldn't have cared less about purple balls or edible berries, but he listened patiently, his eyes fixed on Beezie's incredible cleavage and a lurid grin across his big mouth.

"Gee, what is this?" Beezie squealed as the waitress placed the two-glass drink in front of her.

"This one's straight tequila," Albert explained patiently. "The other glass is a mixture of red wine, orange juice, grenadine, Tabasco, onion and salt. Now the object is to sip first from one glass, and then the other. You watch old Rigg here. He'll show you how." Out of the corner of his eye, he caught Rigg's expression which roughly translated to "Where the hell did you get this dame?", but it was too late, and Beezie, with all the charm she could muster, attempted to follow Rigg sip for sip.

"That's right, you're getting the hang of it," Albert encouraged after they had downed their first round. "With a couple more of those, you'll be an old B.V. expert and then you can show old Rigg here how you do the dipsy doodle. My God, what Xavier Cougat would have done with you in the 1930s!"

Albert could tell that Rigg had been in an unfavorable mood when he arrived, and he could only guessed that it was somehow related to the dock strike. Fortunately, he knew Rigg had a keen sense of humor, and was capable of appreciating the existential absurdity of Beezie. With only a little encouragement, Rigg took up the challenge of teaching her to drink tequila sangritas. After several more rounds, Beezie began plucking the Madonna berries off her shawl, and with a zany laugh, tried tossing them into the drinks. "I know," she said, interrupting a discussion Katherine had started to have with Rigg about the waterfront. "Let's ride the cable car up Hyde. I can always get the conductor to let me ring his bell."

$\mathcal{T}$HE TWO WEEKS that intervened between the World Series and Aunt Louisa's party were crowded for Katherine. Most of her days were spent with company business. She read reports in her office, met with executives and investigated the wharfs. A couple of evenings she had dinner with Patrick, who remained somewhat distant; always managing to keep the conversation focused on a topic of exterior concern, like his development project or the alterations on her apartment. But usually she came back to Albert's apartment on Telegraph Hill, too exhausted to do much more than have a quiet evening and early bed. Chow-Ling, as always, rose to the occasion and made Katherine do Tai Chi to relax and filled her with soups and herb teas to give her strength. There was no doubt that Chow-Ling had adopted Katherine into the family. In many small, almost imperceptible ways, he began to incorporate her well-being into his own.

With his extensive network of connections throughout the city, Albert had compiled a profile of Phillip Addison, and much to Katherine's relief, there was nothing in his background that would suggest anything sinister. Indeed, quite to the contrary, he seemed to have lived an exemplary life.

Born 1898: Westport, Connecticut.

Graduated Annapolis 1914: with degree in Biochemistry.

Married 1915: Elizabeth Fletcher, who, along with a baby girl, died in childbirth in 1916.

Navy career:

1914–1918. Served on the battleship Texas

1918–1921: Staff of the Secretary of the Navy, Washington, D.C.

1921–1925: Naval Attaché to France

1942–1945: Naval Liaison to the U.S. Army Medical Research
and Development Command Fort Detrick, Maryland.

1925–1941: McMasters Shipping

1945–1953: McMasters Shipping

Katherine spent the better part of Tuesday with the company attorneys attempting to understand the issues involved in the strike, which had threatened to paralyze the entire east coast with 50,000 workers out. The issues were complex, but essentially they boiled down to disputes between the International Longshoremen's Association and the new AF of L groups over who would represent the dockworkers. In addition, the ILA was also at odds with the New York and New Jersey Commissions and the New York Shipping Association. "The problems of hiring and racketeering on the east coast are incredible," the attorney had explained. "What really hurts the shipping industry is that there isn't any protection against outlaw strikes. It makes doing business pretty difficult if you can't depend on having your cargos unloaded on schedule. The damned unions will destroy us if they are given half a chance. Your father fought hard to keep their power limited."

"Thank God Eisenhower has enough guts to ask for an injunction," another attorney said. "It's going to be an interesting couple of weeks, because the federal judge only gave a ten-day temporary restraining order."

Aside from studying labor relations, Katherine spent a few hours towards the end of the day reviewing what she had learned the week before in the Traffic Department. Patrick's friend Brian had arranged for her to review Customs procedures the following day. There was a McMasters freighter due in from the islands, but to avoid suspicion, Brian had arranged to board a liner owned by another company and follow its cargo and passengers through the various procedures.

"I can't believe how complicated all this is," Katherine told Patrick that evening when he called. "I'm going to bed early tonight so I can have a clear head for tomorrow. Brian insists we get an early start to ensure catching a launch."

On Wednesday, Katherine was out of bed at five a.m. By the time they were down on the Embarcadero the early morning traffic was beginning to roll. Trucks and drays rumbled along in front of the ferry building and a switching engine shunted railroad cars along the beltline, carrying their cargos to and from the docks. There was something vital and exciting for Katherine with all the noise and activity in the early morning hours. White-capped longshoremen congregated in the cafés between Market and Mission Streets, talking about the World Series, the dock strikes, or the night before.

They boarded the company launch along with representatives of the railroads, airlines, and travel agencies. It was cold and choppy out on the bay, and Katherine was glad Brian had insisted that she wear a heavy coat. She pulled up the hood of her bulky Bainin tweed jacket, as the low white craft cleared the quiet water offered by the protective pier and headed out into the bay, bucking a headwind and flood tide. Alcatraz appeared off the port bow looking sullen and cold in the morning light. A freighter silhouetted against the coal gray sky slowly inched its way past the Marin exchange lookout station, attracting a screaming cloud of seagulls swirling around its mast. It took about twenty minutes to reach the Nola, which towered above them, glistening white in the few shafts of sunlight that filtered through the morning fog. Soon they pulled alongside the liner and jumped from their swaying craft through one of the ship's big cargo doors on the port side. Katherine followed Brian past the engine room and crew quarters up to the lobby on B deck, where she was introduced to the Customs officials and ship's purser.

"The cargo of a vessel entering from a foreign port is discharged under the supervision of the Customs authorities which operate with the highly technical Customs Code," Brian explained as they watched the various clerks begin to go over the forms. "The government requires the importer to present a bill of lading, a consular invoice, and other documents, depending on the type of cargo and its point of origin. Then the master of the vessel is required to present copies of all consular invoices conveying the cargo to be unloaded. The exporter must have prepared an official invoice containing a complete list of all items shipped to the U.S., how they are packed and marked, and their quantity price per unit, etc."

Brian could see that Katherine was becoming a little overwhelmed with all the details. "All these procedures and requirements can be so complicated that most firms like McMasters hire a Customs House broker to take care of the paperwork," he explained sympathetically.

After reviewing the procedures on B deck, Katherine and Brian walked up to the promenade deck to watch the Nola come in alongside the pier. The crisp bright fall sun had broken through the early morning overcast and Coit Tower stood majestically above the tiny wooden houses and modern apartments that clung to the rocky ridges of Telegraph Hill.

Back on the wharf, they headed towards the Customs House to observe the operations. A few blocks down the Embarcadero they stopped in briefly at the pier where a McMasters freighter just in from Hawaii, had tied up. As they walked down the pier towards the ship, Brian pointed out a large, heavyset man with enormous jowls and thick bushy eyebrows. "That's Richard Broderick of the Port Authority. He was the fellow you were thinking about making an appointment with, the one with the unsavory reputation for being a real S.O.B., if you'll pardon the expression."

Katherine observed the man from a distance. A half-smoked cigar dangled from his large thick lips, and his fleshy face and bulbous nose looked beet red as he waved his arms and yelled orders at a small Chinese delivery boy who had backed his truck into the loading area. Katherine remembered the name. This was the man that she had heard on the phone pressuring Addison. He looked both sinister and repulsive at the same time like a Sicilian butcher about to attack a side of beef. With so much else to fill her thoughts, Katherine had quite forgotten to pursue a meeting with this Mr. Broderick and now that she had seen him, she felt glad she hadn't. Even from a distance, there seemed to be something unsavory about him.

"Let's go on to the Customs House," Brian said, "I don't think we have enough time before lunch to see much here."

They toured the Customs House, observing the brokers, pursers and clerks processing documents. But as Brian explained the function of arrival notices, Katherine's mind wandered back to Broderick and then to Phillip Addison. "What about cargo that is just being sent in from the islands?" she asked as Brian had paused to give her a little space to think.

"Oh, that comes under a completely different set of rules involving bills of lading, manifests, shipping permits, and arrival notices, but that cargo does not go through customs. It all comes under the Freight Traffic Department."

"Would there be any reason to have the president of a company check on specific cargos?" "No, the president probably doesn't even know what ship is in port," he said, shrugging his shoulders. "That may be an overstatement, but I'm sure someone like Phillip Addison is far more concerned with things like cost overruns on new ships, long-term interest rates, labor relations, and the opening of new trade routes."

By the time they had seen enough for Katherine to at least grasp a general idea of how things operated, they headed for Tadich's Grill on California Street to meet Patrick for lunch. "This is a San Francisco institution," Brian explained as he entered their name for a table at the cash register. "If you like fish, this is the place to come. Nothing fancy, but the chefs really know how to cook! Everything from Abalone to swordfish is great. They squeeze us in here like sardines in a can, but believe me, it's worth the wait."

It wasn't long before Patrick joined them and in twenty minutes, they had a booth well to the back. After they had ordered Brian excused himself to the restroom. When he rejoined the table he chuckled, "You'll never guess who just walked in. Richard Broderick, the fellow I pointed out on the pier."

"That's the fellow I overheard talking to Addison," Katherine confided as she craned her neck around the high wooden booth. "Remember Patrick? I told you about the conversation I overheard on the phone last week."

Suddenly she pulled her head back. Her expression was perplexed and her face very pale. "I think he's with Chambliss Horsley," she said very slowly. "I wonder what—?" She did not finish, but sat looking searchingly into Patrick's eyes.

The next day Katherine continued her investigation into the waterfront, but this time with Rigg. They walked for miles over the piers, talked with longshoremen and watched cargoes loaded and unloaded. There was something honest and open in the faces of the dockworkers that Katherine liked. They swaggered and swore, but she sensed that underneath their cocky devil-may-care attitude, they were good, hardworking men. She was also learning to enjoy being on the waterfront with all its different smells and sounds. There was the whining of the winches, the smell of oil and salt and paint. Water sloshing against creaking old piers and the clatter along the beltline blended with the whistle of ships.

Rigg knew a lot, not only about the workings of the waterfront, but about the history of labor's struggle for a fair wage and better working conditions.

"My father was a good friend of Andrew Furuseth, the union leader. He fought to get the Thirteenth Amendment to cover sailors," he explained as they walked along pier 38.

"What is the Thirteenth Amendment?"

"The Thirteenth Amendment to the Constitution. It abolished slavery. Involuntary servitude they called it. People don't realize how bad conditions were back then, or how repressive the government was.

"And he was successful?"

"Hell, yes. He got together with progressives like Senator LaFollett and they got legislation passed. To this day seamen look on Furuseth as the great emancipator. So do longshoremen."

As they walked along, Rigg told Katherine about the 1934 general strike. "The company was hiring scabs. My father was on strike. One Thursday, they came down here to prevent the scabs from coming on the piers to unload. When they got here, they were met by a line of mounted police. The cops wanted to shove them back away from the pier and protect the goddamned scabs. They resisted, and the cops used tear gas. Dad and his friends started tossing cobblestones and the whole goddamned thing erupted into a bloody Donnybrook. In the end two strikers were killed and labor called a general strike. They shut down the whole goddamned town. My dad knew Harry Bridges pretty well, too. He's a tough S.O.B., but you have to be if you're going to protect your ass."

There was a pause as Rigg seemed to relive the intensity of past struggles. "I guess my father was one of the S.O.B.'s on the other side," Katherine reflected.

"Yeah, I guess he was," Rigg said, sensing her offer to bridge the difference in their backgrounds.

"Well, that's one thing I'll never be called," Katherine smiled. "If they call me anything, they'll have to call me a D.O.B."

At noon the siren on the ferry building blew and was joined by a chorus of sirens, horns and factory whistles all along the Embarcadero. "Come on," said Rigg, "I think it's time for a break." He had not been overly anxious to show Katherine around, but he had been impressed by her honesty, willingness to learn, and down-to-earth manner. They walked a few blocks north on the Embarcadero to the Eagle Café on the corner of Powell.

"Hey, Steamer. Whalebone. How's it going, man?" Rigg said, greeting a couple of longshoremen at the long wood bar.

"Rigg! Where you been hiding? You been shacking up in Sausalito again?" a fellow named Spar shouted.

Rigg guided Katherine to a table on the side of the large square white-walled café.

"What do you recommend Rigg?" Katherine asked as she looked over the menu.

"I'm going to have the corned beef hash and a mug of beer."

"Sounds good. I think I'll have the same."

About the time they were finishing, an old man approached the table. He was unshaven, and his old, baggy clothes were well-worn, but his long gray hair was neatly combed and his walk, though a little unsteady, had a certain air of authority. "Good morning, Admiral," Rigg said, standing up and giving the old salt a snappy salute. "It's a fair day for the fleet to be in port."

"Carry on, Captain," said the old man as he returned the salute and sat down to join them.

Katherine, I want you to meet Admiral Donovan, Commander of the Pacific Fleet."

"Ma'am," the old fellow saluted.

There was nothing patronizing about Rigg's manner, but Katherine could see that the old man was a little daft. "Dropped anchor off Mare Island and put some of the cruisers and destroyers in for repair," the Admiral explained, looking at Rigg for sympathy. "I sure could use an anti-fogmatic. It's been a long tour, Captain."

Rigg ordered a bumper of raw rum for the Admiral, explaining to Katherine that an anti-fogmatic was always useful when taken in exact proportion to the thickness of the fog. "The Admiral here has one of the most distinguished careers in the Navy. He was a veteran of Manila Bay. Isn't that right, Admiral?"

"Damn sure. Served on the revenue cutter Hugh McCullough in Dewey's squadron," said the Admiral as he took a swig of rum. "Beat the hell out of those Spaniards, too. I was a young man in my twenties in those days. Had been at sea for years. Started out as a cabin boy on the old square riggers. Signed on by Mike Connor outside the Old Chain Locker Saloon down at Bryant and Main and sailed around the Horn in 1888." The Admiral went on for nearly an hour with yarns of his seagoing career. At times his tales were somewhat contradictory and departed from historical fact, especially after several more anti-fogmatics, but Katherine was fascinated nonetheless and Rigg's admiration for her was considerably enhanced by her interest and enjoyment of the old character. She seemed to naturally possess that typically San Franciscan quality which prizes originality no matter how eccentric.

They left the café around two p.m. and walked back down the Embarcadero.

"Tell me what you know about Richard Broderick," Katherine said after a block. "From what I have heard he has a rather unpleasant reputation."

"Unpleasant isn't the word, Lady!" Rigg snorted. "If you take my advice, you'll stay clear of the likes of Richard Broderick."

"That might be a bit difficult when I am in the shipping business," Katherine replied stiffly, half resenting the tone of Rigg's emphatic warning.

"Then let someone in your company deal with him, your attorneys or someone. He's a parasitic son-of-a-bitch and he's protected well enough to be dangerous."

"What do you mean by 'protected'?"

"I mean he's got connections and power in this city. Political connections and union connections. I wouldn't mess with him to save my life. I can't give you details, but you just ask anyone who has worked the piers. They'll tell you. They say he's had men rubbed out."

"Rubbed out?" Katherine asked, not understanding the slang.

"Killed," Rigg said bluntly.

A sense of the ominous encompassed Katherine's thoughts as they continued south along the Embarcadero amid the creaking rattle of winches unloading cargo. The crude, sinister image of Broderick would not leave her mind. What was he doing having lunch with Horsley? And an even more threatening question interjected itself. What was his relationship to Addison? She mentally recounted the phone conversation she had overheard some ten days earlier and the threatening nature of Broderick's demands. She knew too much to pass everything off as mere coincidence, but she did not know enough to formulate a theory. She was left grasping at the possibilities, all of which seemed shadowy and circumstantial.

CHAPTER 29

*T*HE WEEK HAD been a long one, filled with company business and days on the waterfront and Katherine had not seen Patrick since leaving the Buena Vista on Monday. He too had been busy, although he had called twice in the evenings to ask her about the Jones Street apartment.

"Would you like to have dinner Saturday?" he asked at the conclusion of their conversation Thursday. "It'll give us an opportunity to tie up all the loose ends." He sounded like the idea had just occurred to him.

"On the apartment, you mean?" Katherine asked caustically.

If he noticed the note of irony in her voice he chose to ignore it. "I'll make reservations for eight and pick you up around seven."

The day with Aunt Louisa at Treehaven and the dinner at the Papagaya Room had done much to dispel the dreary memory of the previous Saturday at Ernie's, yet Katherine was still ambiguous about Patrick's feelings. There was not an hour of the day that she did not find herself thinking of him, but he had always seemed so matter-of-fact when he called that she was beginning to wonder if he was not trying to distance himself in the relationship. Perhaps she had misinterpreted what they had shared in St. Helena. Aunt Louisa's warning in the greenhouse echoed in her ears: "A strong independent man like Mr. Bartley will never last long with an insecure woman who wants to tie him down. He's the kind of man who has to be allowed a certain amount of freedom."

Nevertheless, she found herself again building a fantasy around his invitation and she was angry that she was allowing herself to become so emotionally obsessive. There was too much to do, too many decisions to make to allow her to be distracted. And the more she thought about her relationship with Patrick, the more she was determined to wait and see.

What she could not guess was that Patrick was becoming equally obsessed with her and was far more annoyed and frightened by the prospect than she was. He had dated many women but he had never fallen in love and had been too busy to ever consider marriage. Usually, he dated Irish girls from good families, but he never slept with them. They were the nice Catholic girls, self-sacrificing and maternalistic; the kind that he might consider marrying if he were ready to settle down and raise a family. Occasionally he picked up girls after a few drinks in a bar, enjoyed their company for a night or two and then dropped them. The cabaret type excited him, but he could never consider becoming emotionally involved beyond the purely physical level. For him there were only two kinds of women, those you screwed and those you married and with this tidy view of the opposite sex he was assured of always remaining in control.

Katherine, however, had destroyed all his expectations about women and this was frightening. For the first time he found himself emotionally defenseless. She was so exquisitely beautiful, the most beautiful woman he had ever known. The thought of touching her sent unexpected charges of passion through the pit of his stomach, making him feel inexcusably weak. The smell of her hair, her long graceful legs, and the way she had responded to his caress obsessed him. Yet these feelings somehow did not diminish her for she remained too intelligent and sophisticated for him to reduce to a mere object of lust. There was a strength of character there, an adventurous self-reliance combined with spontaneous warmth and humor that he had never known. He was at once enthralled and challenged as much with her mind as with her body. Never before had a woman captured both his respect and his desire and this threatened not only his composure but his sense of mastery.

His answer to the dilemma had been to ignore it, to push his feelings aside. He poured himself into his business, spent his passion on the Yankees and supervised the apartment alterations. And when his feelings crept back in upon him, he redoubled his efforts. He covered his fear by putting on a mask of certitude or indifference. By a sheer act of will, he impressed upon others and himself the image of a man in control.

Saturday had been hot with the temperature in the high seventies, and the October sun flooded the city with strong Mediterranean light. At dusk the city took on a timeless quality as it hovered between two lives. The air was warm and still and not even the slightest breeze rustled the eucalyptus trees around Coit Tower. For a few moments, her life seemed dreamlike as Katherine stood watching the reflection of a thousand lights against the pond like waters of the bay. She drew into her being the still calm, as if it were enough simply to be alive for that moment.

When Patrick arrived, breaking her meditation, he seemed his usual good-natured self. Albert joined them on the terrace for a bottle of champagne and the last traces of light in the western sky. There are so few warm evenings in the city that the native counts them as treasures to be enjoyed. Patrick, however, did not seem to notice. He questioned Katherine about her trip with Brian, rambled on about his development and joked about Beezie drinking Tequila Sangritas with Rigg. Finally, in an attempt to bring him into the present, Albert got up to top off his glass and in doing so, said as he turned towards the bay. "We don't get too many evenings in the year like this except in the fall."

"No," Patrick said slowly after giving the statement consideration. "That's why I like to be at the ranch on the weekends. The valley has nights warmer than this half the year."

Then without seeming to think about what he was saying, he turned to Katherine. "I wish you would come up to the ranch in the winter sometime. It's beautiful when the hills are all green and wet from the rain."

The way he said this struck her. For a moment he seemed almost like a little boy making a Christmas wish.

"It sounds very lovely," she replied, holding herself back from making any commitment.

This was the first time he had made reference to the ranch in the two weeks that they had been back and it came in an invitation to return, but not until the winter. Katherine could not help but feel amused by his shy boyish manner. It was at one both endearing and rather silly.

"We'd better go," he said, diverting his attention to his watch.

"But it's not winter yet," Katherine said, reaching over and touching the inner part of his thigh above the knee.

In the awkward moment that followed Patrick felt himself unable to move. His mind raced forwards but he could not follow his mind. Then he was on his feet. He had felt embarrassed by her outward display of affection and even more so by his response to it.

"We're going to the Blue Fox," he said emphatically. "The reservation is for 8:30. Did Albert tell you it's across the street from the morgue?"

"Oh, it sounds lovely, too!" she said, mimicking her reply to his other invitation.

He stood there for a moment with the most ridiculous and sheepish grin on his face. As they drove downtown he was very quiet and it wasn't until they were settled at their table that he again began to take charge. "I think we should have the lamb Verdi and a good white chardonnay."

"Perhaps," Katherine said, "but maybe just a little Vitello Tomato and a Belgian endive and watercress salad. I am not that hungry."

By the time they had decided, Patrick had had two double martinis and was again rambling on about the waterfront, his friendship with Brian and the apartment's alterations. Katherine listened for a while, making the appropriate comments to keep the conversation moving. Finally she became frustrated.

"Tell me, Patrick," she said, reaching across the table and touching his hand, "tell me why haven't you ever married?"

"I suppose because until I met you, all my relationships with women have been superficial."

The directness and honesty of the reply caught her completely off guard. Her question, aided by the Beefeater's, had opened the door to his emotion and once opened, he found it surprisingly easy to pour out the complex feelings he had repressed since he had first laid eyes on her a month earlier.

"I wouldn't lie to you by saying there haven't been women in my life. My mother is always after me to find a nice Catholic girl from a good family and settle down."

Katherine, who had resolved to protect her own feelings, listened intently. She followed his words, wanting to believe him, wanting to understand him.

"Why haven't you?"

"Ah well, I don't know. I suppose I haven't had time. Most of my relationships have been pretty uncomplicated. I suppose that's the easiest thing to do when you're trying to build a business." He stopped for a moment as if trying to reflect on his life. "I suppose too, it's also a matter of not wanting to give up my freedom. I have struggled all my life to get to where I am. Only recently have I been able to make enough money to give my family the security and comfort they deserve. Having discharged that obligation, I guess I haven't been anxious to add any new ones."

"And now?" she prodded gently in a sympathetic whisper.

"And now I don't know. From the first time I met you at the Devonshires I knew I wanted you, but I was afraid of the reasons. At first, I thought it was just the physical attraction, but then there was something more, something I have never known before." He paused, looking down at his drink and twirling the olive at the end of the toothpick through the cold dry gin. "I suppose it's that you're so damned much fun to be with." He smiled. "I guess it doesn't sound very romantic, but it's true. You're different than other women. You don't want something. You're free." Again he paused, slowly lifting his eyes until they met hers. "You remind me of a hawk, like the one we saw at the ranch up near our cabin. That's what you remind me of, a beautiful hawk making beautiful free circles in the sky."

A strange warm feeling came over her. She believed what he was telling her, but at the same time, she realized he was a little drunk and she was half afraid that he would say things he might regret the next morning. She didn't want him to be sorry. He seemed so vulnerable.

"Why, Mr. Bartley," she said warmly, "are you telling me that I remind you of a bird of prey?"

Patrick stopped for a moment and began to laugh. "Yeah, I guess you do at that, Miss McMasters. You've torn the heart clean out of this Irishman, all right."

As they talked quietly on through dinner, Katherine began to put his behavior into perspective. She could see that for the first time in his life, he was emotionally involved with a woman and that he found that difficult to handle. Here was a man who had met every other adversity and challenge with firm resolve, but now was unsure of how to meet the challenge of his own feelings. Yet she had to admit as she thought about it, that she found his honesty and openness very attractive. It was as if he were laying his deepest fears before the monster that was their source and that this made him seem both fragile and heroic.

The evening was still warm as they left the restaurant and drove west up Union.

"Would you like to stop by and see how your apartment is coming along?" he asked, trying to decide what to do next.

"I suppose so, although I've never seen your house," she said wistfully.

"Perhaps we would be more comfortable there," he concluded, not quite sure just what she had intended by the remark.

Within a few minutes they had turned onto Chestnut and parked the car. Patrick's house was not quite what Katherine had anticipated. They entered at the second story level into a spacious hall. The hall led to two bedrooms and a large deck which encompassed the north and east sides, providing a magnificent view of the bay from the Golden Gate around to Coit Tower. An open staircase descended to the living and dining rooms below where indirect lighting softly illuminated the rich redwood paneled walls. On the lower level, the rooms were sparsely furnished providing a feeling of uncluttered space. A large brown leather davenport stretched before a simple stone fireplace under the stressed rafters of the ceiling.

In the dining room a fine English west country sideboard displayed a collection of American and English pewter.

"I'll light the fire," Patrick said as Katherine admired a unique collection of antique craftsman's tools.

"These are beautiful," she said, running the tips of her fingers along the smooth hard surface of an old axe.

"Most of those date from the sixteenth or seventeenth century. I don't know much about antiques, except when it comes to tools. That's a seventeenth-century French side axe. The plane just to the left is a Spanish rebate plane. About 1650. Old tools have a lot of character. You wonder about the men who worked with them."

They sat for a while as Patrick explained how he had designed the house to make the best of the difficult grade and take advantage of the view. He seemed more relaxed now then he had been during dinner. His attention was again focused on one of his accomplishments and Katherine for the first time in the evening began to release the guards she had placed around her heart. She fingered the soft cashmere blanket that was thrown across the back of the davenport. Once having disclosed his feelings his calm, easygoing nature had returned and Katherine could not resist leaning her head against his shoulder while he gently caressed her neck with his large powerful fingers. Then she felt herself grow weak with desire as he enfolded her in his protective arms. She wanted him more than she had ever wanted a man before, and she knew he wanted her. She felt his muscular body throb with excitement as he lifted her slowly and looked down on her with his dark determined eyes. A small black curl hung across his broad forehead, softening his rugged features. As he began to enfold her again, she momentarily lost consciousness, her body quivering with delight.

"Katherine," she could hear him whisper, "Katherine. I want you."

But from somewhere deep within her soul she knew that she must somehow refuse him. She did not know why. Everything seemed so unclear. Yet, she knew instinctively that on some level there was an unconscious battle for control and that if she wanted to keep him, she would have to win. She would have to resist him and her own desires with every fiber of her being. By a sheer act of will, she made her body say no to his touch. She detached her mind and found the floor with her feet. Sensing the change, he pushed harder against her. Running the tip of his tongue along her smooth neck, she could feel the virile tensing of his body. She began to feel her body giving in and she summoned all the concentration she could find.

"Mr. Bartley," she heard herself saying in a slow, firm voice that did not seem to come from her, but from somewhere else.

"What's the matter?" he asked gently.

"I think perhaps it's time for me to go home." Her voice was soft but decisive.

"All right," was his only reply.

He seemed sullen and a little hurt as he drove her back over to Telegraph Hill. He was used to winning and although it had not been her conscious intention, she had conquered him both physically and spiritually. He had poured out his true feelings. He had let down his defenses and now he felt confused and rejected. The driving strength and determination that made him so attractive had not been enough. Now she would see how he handled defeat. Now she would really know him.

Edward J. Dumke

Once inside the apartment, he put his hand around her shoulders and drew her to his side. Her body did not resist and she felt a still sense of completeness. She turned so they faced each other.

"I'm in love with you, Katherine," his voice held a note of resignation as if he had finally accepted a loss.

She did not speak. She rested her head against his shoulder as he held her tightly. For a long time they stood there without moving, listening to the rhythmic beatings of their hearts against the hushed sounds of a sleeping city.

CHAPTER 30

IN ADDITION TO company business and the developing relationship with Patrick, one issue needed to be resolved before either Katherine's Aunt Victoria or her Aunt Louisa could rest. It was the problem of the Dress. What would Katherine wear to the ball given in her honor given at Treehaven? Victoria thought pink and offered her diamonds. Aunt Louisa thought blue and offered her sapphire necklace and diamond tiara. Nothing was to be done but to go to Herschell, whose advice on these matters was invaluable for the select clientele who enjoyed his services.

With everything else in her life, Katherine least of all wanted to think of clothes. She was striking enough to look splendid in just about anything, and she would have been perfectly happy to go to a store on Union Square and select a dress by one of her favorite designers.

"Oh, but you must go to Herschell," Victoria insisted. "He absolutely does the most divine gowns."

It was one of those very rare occasions when Aunt Louisa agreed. "Victoria is right, Katherine," she insisted. "Herschell does a gown for everyone in San Francisco at least once. Usually when they make their debut but you weren't presented, so now's your chance."

There was nothing for Katherine to do but accept their advice and cancel business appointments for Monday afternoon. In the end, she was trapped for the entire day, for Victoria quietly arranged lunch in the Mural Room of the St. Francis.

"Oh, this is lovely," Victoria had said. "We'll have an absolutely divine day."

"I am looking forward to the luncheon with your mother," Katherine confessed to Albert Sunday night. "It will give me another opportunity to get to know her a little better. I've been so busy I feel I've neglected seeing her."

"I'm afraid if you're looking for a chance to have an intimate visit, you are going to be disappointed. Monday lunch at the St. Francis is not what one would call a private affair."

"Je ne vois pas."

"It's a social ritual, an old time-honored tradition among those considered to be San Francisco's social leaders or would-be socialites. The implication years ago, was, that if you were rich enough you could go out on Wash Day. You left the laundry to the maid and went to lunch with friends," Albert explained.

"I see."

"It's all really rather stuffy, but Mother enjoys it. Aunt Louisa used to go from time to time, but not much anymore. Columnists from the press are always there and the ladies have lunch, gossip, watch each other, have a fashion show and then go home. Mother will probably have two or three of her close friends."

"It sounds rather frightful," Katherine said in a half sigh

"That's the spirit," Albert said. "You'll do just fine. They will all want to meet you, the mysterious Katherine McMasters. They'll look you over again, but you'll be a sensation, just like you were at the opera. Oh, by the way, the headwaiter is Swiss. Ernest Gloor. He's bound to like you. I had quite forgotten about old Ernest until just this moment."

"Ernest Gloor?"

"San Francisco is a funny town. It's very competitive. I suppose it has something to do with our frontier heritage. Anyway, since no one can decide who is socially more prominent, they let old Ernest decide. He's been the headwaiter in the Mural Room for centuries and is said to decide social importance by where he seats people. If Aunt

Louisa was going, you'd have the best table in the house. Anyway, you'll be on either side of the center aisle, which is considered very 'in'. It's all a very complex sort of an outlandish way of arbitration. Ernest is rather like a witch doctor or high priest."

"Somehow your description reminds me of Trixie Metcalf's portrayal of Boston," said Katherine, half teasing.

"I rather think it might," Albert laughed.

It was not without trepidation that Katherine left her cousin's apartment at 9:30 Monday morning, safely in the care of Thomas whom her aunt had sent to collect her. The possibility of being dressed in some frumpy gown annoyed her despite Albert's assurances that everything would be okay. Only after Chow-Ling applied his thumb to pressure points in the palm of her hand did Katherine relax for a few minutes after breakfast.

"We always have white spiders, don't we, Victoria?" Dolores Whitney commented as they were seated by Ernest.

"Yes, they are very nice," Victoria replied, looking carefully across the aisle to see who was there. "We always have two white spiders."

Katherine looked around the room, which was rapidly filling up with smartly-dressed women in hats and gloves. She had met at least ten or more of her aunt's friends in the lobby and now more were stopping by to say hello. Fortunately, the table, which included Dolores Whitney, Gertrude Waters and Mildred Klassen, gave her some sense of insulation, and the presence of Amy Mackie proved a sympathetic relief from the ongoing chatter and endless introductions.

"If I haven't told you for the hundredth time, Gertrude, the decorations for opening night were too marvelous. Even Edwin commented on them."

"Mildred, you're too cute to say so. Did you notice Marilyn Weaver? I haven't seen her forever. You remember Marilyn. They moved out to Marin several years ago and everyone just sort of forgot about them. You know her daughter married a cowboy up in Reno and she was simply undone. Of course, I can't say that I blame her."

Thinking of her first husband, Amy turned to Katherine. "I bet they talked about me for a couple of years after I married the ski instructor."

It was just as well the ladies did not hear her comment. Their attention was focused on a new arrival. A bleached blonde lady in her mid-thirties was being seated well away from the door towards the back of the room. She was wearing a stylish Norfolk pink tweed jacket balanced by a narrow wool jersey skirt that looked like a Balenciaga and Katherine sighed, thinking of what she might be forced to wear to Aunt Louisa's ball.

Attempting to include Katherine, Dolores lowered her voice to a whisper that was both confidential and condescending. "I'm afraid she is one of those women who makes a career out of marriage. Absolutely no background. She moved here from Los Angeles or Sacramento or some dreadful place and within a year, she married Randy Miller. He's old enough to be her father. She came with an introduction and, well, that was that. Randy's first wife was a darling. She was my second cousin. She had only been dead for three years, and well ... you understand."

"All too well!" Katherine exclaimed with a relish that seemed to titillate all the ladies except her Aunt Victoria, who nervously fiddled with her gloves.

"Yes, Monique!" Gertrude commented with just the right mixture of sympathy and sarcasm. "What a frightful person she is. It's simply dreadful, all that unpleasantness you've had to endure. Men are such silly creatures, really."

"Oh, Dolores, she's not all that dreadful. I've met her at a couple of dinner parties. She's halfway acceptable, even if she is from Hollywood," Victoria said in an attempt to be pleasant and divert the conversation.

"Who, Randy's blond or Monique?"

"April Miller, of course," Victoria said, perturbed that her little ploy had backfired.

"That's right, she is from Hollywood," Dolores continued, disdainfully sipping her white spider. "She is one of those Los Angeles people, a starlet or something. Randy bought her a diamond choker and you wouldn't believe it, but I've heard that she wears it for breakfast! I saw her at a benefit luncheon, and there she was at Filoli, in the garden, with diamonds around her throat and a mink stole, in the broad light of day!"

At the mention of Los Angeles and starlets the table fell silent as if Dolores had mentioned a disfiguring disease.

"N.O.C.D." Amy whispered with her jaw held rigid, mimicking Beezie.

"N.O.C.D.?" Katherine asked.

"Not Our Class, Dearie," Amy continued lifting one eyebrow in a mocking manner. "It's one thing to have a Madame in your family tree, but not, Heaven forbid, an actress!"

"Have you been to Los Angeles?"

"Yes, many times. It's really not that bad. The beaches are lovely down on the south coast. I'm afraid though when it comes to Los Angeles, that San Franciscans are just terrible snobs."

Victoria, who did not want to give the wrong impression, again tried to save the conversation by adding, "There really are some lovely people in Los Angeles. George and I have friends in Pasadena."

"But they are not movie people are they?" Dolores interjected.

"No," Victoria said thoughtfully, fingering her pearls. "They were originally from San Francisco, but the doctor said they had to have a warm dry climate for her emphysema."

"Well, I suppose if one has to live in Southern California for health reasons, one must learn to bear one's cross. My mother always said 'when life gives you lemons, learn to make lemonade!' But really, it is such a wasteland. You can't really consider Los Angeles a city. It's just a collection of orange groves and nondescript towns all spread out without rhyme or reason. And the people! Mercy! I think I would choose exile in Arizona. Anyway, I've been told the air is going quite foul. It isn't what it used to be. Smog, I think they call it."

The fashion show was soon underway. The look was new, away from the nipped and pinched feeling that had been in style through the forties. Loose fitting suits made of rough lightweight tweed and unfitted jackets provided an unfenced feeling and Katherine, in a dark green Hardy Amies, felt very much in style.

Through lunch Amy gave Katherine a running commentary on the ladies she had met and most of the descriptions involved who and how they were related to everyone else. "Everyone seems somehow related, at least by marriage," Katherine commented. "I suppose it gives a certain solidarity to society.

"A generation or two ago, our ancestors were shooting at each other in the goldfields and on the streets. It takes about three generations to round off the frontier edges and age the money."

"Or, buy a title?"

"Oh, yes. I've known mothers to drag their poor daughters off to Europe in search of some penniless count or baron in the hopes that they can arrange a marriage."

As luncheon drew to an end and the ladies started to filter out through the lobby into the din of Union Square. Suddenly an imposing lady in a rather ordinary gray suit came up to the table. She had been sitting just across the aisle and Katherine had observed her earlier.

"I'm Jennie McVeagh," she said in an imposing manner. "Your Aunt Louisa has been a friend of mine since the flood. Where is she hiding out today?"

Katherine attempted to be polite but she was caught a little off guard by the tenor of the question.

"I believe she had other obligations," she answered rather coolly.

"Other obligations! You tell your aunt that Jennie McVeagh was looking for her. You'll come over someday soon. Bring Louisa. We'll have some whiskey and I'll tell you stories about your Auntie." Then looking directly at Katherine, she continued, a deadpan expression on her face, "There isn't anything your Aunt and I haven't done, from fighting wars to breeding horses. Tell her to fire up the pool for next Saturday night and we'll all go for a swim in the raw."

"That sounds delightful," Katherine shot back as she reached out to grasp the hand that had suddenly been thrust towards her. "Perhaps we can arrange to have a few violins for the event."

"Marvelous! Couldn't be better!" Jennie McVeagh laughed. She abruptly turned and left with a nod of acknowledgement to the rest of the table.

"Who was that?" Katherine asked, searching for an explanation from Amy.

"Old Jennie McVeagh is considered along with your great Auntie to be the last of a breed. Between them they have done more for this city than time would permit telling. When they throw themselves behind a project, it gets done whether it's a new museum or one of a dozen charities. She has an enormous home up on Washington. She throws the most fabulous parties for everyone from the Queen of Holland to our GI's. She used to make all the debs in town show up to entertain the fellows before they shipped out to the Pacific. 'Let the boys know what they're fighting for' were her only marching instructions."

"I like her," Katherine said thoughtfully.

"I'd say she likes you, which is probably more to the point," concluded Mildred Klassen.

"Yes," said Victoria, nervously looking at her watch. "Jennie is a dear soul, but I think we had better think of going. We have an appointment with Herschell, you know."

The pensive Katherine who had left that morning was not the Katherine who retreated back up Telegraph Hill at 4:30 loaded with packages and aglow with enthusiasm.

"How did it go?" Albert asked as Chow-Ling helped Thomas in with a small mountain of boxes.

"C'etait fantistique."

"And?" he said, waiting for the critical moment.

"And, Herschell is too divine for words," she said laughing in a way that reminded him of a sixteen-year-old girl.

"The first word out of his mouth was 'Aqua'. He's designing the most absolutely elegant light aqua sells moire evening gown with a straight fitted front and slight train. He absolutely insists that it be off the shoulders with small poof sleeves and dyed shoes to match. And of course, long white kid gloves."

Her enthusiasm seemed for a few moments uncontained as well as out of character.

"Herschell must be a bloody wizard," Albert said, pouring himself a scotch to calm the effects of so much fashion.

"Ah, but here is the piece de resistance."

She reached into her purse and removed the unmistakable silver box that meant Shrives. Her hands seemed to tremble ever so slightly as she opened the box and lifted out a fabulous aquamarine and diamond necklace.

"Herschell said aquamarines and diamonds and I ..." she did not finish but held the jewels up to her neck and smiled.

CHAPTER 31

TREEHAVEN WAS IDEALLY designed for grand parties and it had seen some of the most dazzling events in California since the turn of the century. Over the decades many of these occasions were family celebrations and so for Aunt Louisa, her ball for Katherine was more than just a way of resurrecting the grandeur of the past. It was the vehicle by which she would formally introduce her niece to San Francisco. It was another chapter in the family history, a gift of continuity, a rite of passage.

The preparations, which had been underway for several weeks, reached a fevered pitch the week before the event. The staff from Pebble Beach was brought up to help. Floors were buffed, chandeliers cleaned, and extra silver was taken from the vault. Madame Ng was called daily for consultations, even though she had been down twice the week before to finalize the plans. Katherine and Albert had little to do with the preparations, although Aunt Louisa managed to call at least once a day under the pretext of asking their opinion on various details. "She's as excited as an overheated Spaniel," Albert joked. Towards the middle of the week she had decided to open all of Treehaven. Over three hundred and fifty people had accepted with only a handful of regrets. Several friends were known to have postponed trips abroad and Katie Butler was cutting short a stay on the Riviera to fly in from Paris.

"I'm opening the sitting room on the second floor and all the bedrooms will have fires laid," she had said as the acceptances piled up. "If it's cold, people can take breaks and wander off and have a brandy. If it's a warm night, we'll have lights on the Italian Garden and everyone can stroll out to the pavilion."

Katherine and Albert left for the topsy-turvy world of Treehaven late Friday afternoon. It had been a long week with the continued exigencies of company business and they were glad to leave the city behind.

"Did you talk with Auntie today?" Katherine asked after they stopped on the way to pick up her gown.

"She called at least three times. She was debating having a second orchestra in the pavilion. At last report, the plan has been scotched."

"I hope she isn't exhausting herself," Katherine said, concerned that Aunt Louisa might be overdoing.

"Hardly! It's all great fun. She hasn't thrown a truly big bash since 1945 when San Francisco hosted the Charter conference for the U.N.!"

"She gave a reception for the United Nations?"

"Everyone from Russian commissars and Arab sheiks to Nelson Rockefeller and Lady Halifax. She loved it! Politics and champagne!"

"What was it like before?"

"Before what?"

"Before the war. What were the parties like when my mother was alive?"

"Well, your mother would have remembered the early years. There were very grand costume balls and from what Mother tells me, everyone wore very elaborate costumes and waltzed the night away until the wee hours of the morning."

"And what are your first memories?"

"The Jazz Age! My formative years were the 20s. The waltzing was replaced by the Charleston and the dancing went on until after gin fizzes and breakfast at sunrise. Aunt Louisa never recognized Prohibition or teetotalers. Treehaven was never dry."

"You must have enjoyed that," she teased.

"I was a little young, but I was allowed to watch from the balcony. Occasionally I would sneak down the back stairs and slip into the conservatory unnoticed but I had to be very clever to outwit Miss Ward. The parties, of course, continued through the thirties when I was liberated. Aunt Louisa felt that social observation was an intricate part of my education and I was required to report my adventures in great detail the next day."

"And did you always report everything?"

"Yes, everything, even Mrs. Greenrouse."

"And what was there to report about Mrs. Greenrouse?"

"A great deal! It was, if I recall, 'A Night on Olympus' and all the guests were dressed as Greek gods. I was Pan. Aunt Louisa had just acquired that sixteenth-century bronze of Amphitrite and The Dolphins. The one off the conservatory. She rigged it so Amphitrites' breasts squirted martinis! What a riot! Cold delicate arches of icy gin!"

"It sounds most extraordinary, but what about Mrs. Greenrouse?"

"Mrs. Greenrouse had gone to the fountain once too often! Drunk as a skunk! When she went back for her fifth or sixth martini, she cornered me and asked if I didn't think she had a better bust than Amphitrite."

"And did she?"

"Jeez! Talk about lollapaloozas!"

"What did she say when you told her?"

"Well, I didn't actually tell her. I was only about ten at the time and as far as I knew, Mrs. Greenrouse had the only bust in San Francisco, let alone the biggest. When I hesitated, she pulled apart her toga and showed them to me. 'I don't give a tinker's damn what the fashion is,' she said, 'I still have the most beautiful breasts in the city!'"

"And what did Aunt Louisa say when she heard that story?"

"Oh, she just laughed. She said that Mrs. Greenrouse had netted three husbands with her bazooms. Anyway, it all left a lasting impression on me. I spent the rest of my adolescence making comparisons."

"And did you reach a conclusion after this scholarly pursuit?"

"Yes."

"And that was?"

"That Mrs. Greenrouse was right and that she undoubtedly deserved all three husbands."

"It all sounds rather decadent."

"Not really. Pamela Greenrouse is always getting plastered and pulling out those boobs of hers. Everyone has seen them."

"Will we have a display tomorrow night?"

"One can only hope," he laughed. "Anyway, the war put an end to the parties for a while. We've never been able to fully recapture the innocence and gaiety of the 20s and 30s. So many of the old characters are dying off and the new generation is rather less self-assured. We have so many new people making their way to California now. You know, the corporate manager types. Very dull. They buy tickets to charity events and sort of quietly infuse themselves around the edges. Dreadful bores, really."

Arriving at Treehaven they found Aunt Louisa sitting in the conservatory giving orders to her army of domestics. The great iron and glass structure had been added in 1923. Designed to open off both the main hall and the ballroom, it was ideal for large parties allowing guests to retire from the dance floor into an indoor tropical garden.

"How does it look?" Aunt Louisa asked sharply as she surveyed the progress being made by her gardeners who were busy unloading wheelbarrows full of potted flowers and maiden hair fern.

"Lovely, Aunt Louisa!" Katherine said, kissing her on the cheek. "It's all very lovely."

"How many more dozen do you have in the greenhouse, Francis?" Aunt Louisa demanded, looking at the raised fountains down the center of the conservatory.

"About seven dozen of the yellow mums and six of the spider."

"Good. Bank more spider mums and ferns around the center fountain. I want the maximum effect there. Use the yellow behind the white along the walls. Then eight more palms and four more banana plants. I want height at the end around the doors but mind the catteleyas."

"I think we'll go upstairs and have a rest before dinner," Albert interrupted.

"Good for you!" Aunt Louisa exclaimed. "But first take a peek at the tea house. Francis had over five-dozen gardenias still in bloom and I covered the floor and steps. That will be the place to take your Mr. Bartley, Katherine," she said with a wink before returning to her command. As Katherine and Albert left, Aunt Louisa was calling Andrew on the intercom to come over from the garage and adjust the gargoyles, which spit a continuous stream of water into the fountains.

"You know, Katherine," Albert said as they took the elevator up to their rooms. "I never enter that conservatory without feeling a smile bubbling somewhere just under the surface. The education I received hiding behind banana palms!"

By Saturday noon all the flowers were in place and Treehaven was given a final review by Prentice, who marched through the halls much like a general reviewing his troops.

The library and game room reserved for the men on such occasions passed inspections, as did the drawing room, which was festooned with large displays of cut snapdragons and stock. In the ballroom, arching spikes of yellow and white Vanda orchids mixed with hundreds of Japanese hydrangea and tiger lilies were set in strands at intervals along the walls.

"You look smashing," Albert told Katherine when she joined him in the drawing room a little after seven. "We have about an hour before the guests start to arrive. Would you like a cocktail?"

"No, Prentice just informed me there would be a family photograph in twenty minutes. I think I'll wait. Your parents should be arriving shortly."

"In that case I'll have a double," he joked, trying to bring some humor to what he thought was a rather downhearted expression on Katherine's face.

Katherine did not respond, but sat down and quietly folded her hands as if waiting for a dentist appointment.

"What time did Patrick say he was going to get here?" Albert asked in a further attempt to draw a response.

"I don't know. He didn't say. He was supposed to call today but I haven't talked with him since Wednesday."

"What did he say then?"

"He called to cancel dinner. He said he had to work late Thursday. For all I know, he may not even come."

"Why would you say that?"

"Oh, I don't know. I think perhaps he is retreating emotionally. He was very honest about his feelings at the Blue Fox. Now he may be feeling a little embarrassed or vulnerable. It's difficult to say."

At 7:45 the family assembled for a photograph and then promptly adjourned to the entrance hall where they took up their places before walls of green, white and pink cymbidiums banked in maiden hair and asparagus ferns.

Aunt Louisa, looking majestic in her sapphires and a dark blue taffeta gown, was seated in her Gainsborough chair with Ivy stationed just behind to help her with names in case old Prentice had difficulty. Katherine came next with Albert to her left, followed by Victoria and George Devonshire. This strategy of reception gave Aunt Louisa, as matriarch of the family, the honor of formally introducing her great niece. Albert would be next to Katherine to lend support and comments when there was a pause between arrivals and introductions.

Promptly at eight, cars started slowly pulling into the center court and depositing guests. Every vault in San Francisco had been opened for the second time that season and the bosoms of the older generation heaved under a blaze of jewels. Mrs. Greenrouse, now well into her seventies and still claiming the best chest in San Francisco, arrived wearing a low cut red chiffon dress with a great ten-karat ruby at her throat set off by a grid of diamonds around her neck.

"You see what I was faced with at such a tender age?" Albert whispered. "But you have to admit they are magnificent."

"The ruby? C'est magnifique, Albert. I'll grant you that!"

After introductions, guests proceeded down the great hallway for champagne in the ballroom where small gilded tables, covered with yellow linen, had been arranged around the edges.

At precisely nine o'clock Aunt Louisa stood up and the family followed her down the hall. When they entered the ballroom the Orchestra struck up "San Francisco Open Your Golden Gate" and as the assembled guests applauded, Katherine proceeded to dance the first dance with Uncle George. Albert then danced with Katherine and George with Victoria before others took to the floor midway through the second number.

Patrick had not arrived and Katherine, although she tried not to show it, was disheartened with the thought that he might not come at all. It wasn't until the fourth dance that she noticed him standing alone, watching her from the end of the room. Their eyes met and her smile conveyed her delight. When the music ended she crossed the room without looking to either side where guests were positioned to engage her in conversation. She didn't notice them but half the room watched her to see the object of her attention. She came up, stopped short to kiss him on the cheek. It was a quick greeting, but there was something very sensual and intimate about the way it was executed.

"I was worried, Patrick," she said, looking up into his eyes.

"About what?"

"I'm so glad you came. I wanted you here tonight."

There was a sincerity in the half-pleading way she said this and Patrick felt a little self-conscious.

"I think you must be mistaken, Miss McMasters," he said laughingly. "I don't even dance."

"You will before the evening's out," Katherine shot back. "But first we'll get you a drink."

As the orchestra started a fox trot Katherine left the room, taking Patrick into the conservatory where, finding two wrought iron chairs they sat for a while, holding hands and listening to the music.

Soon however, Albert was sent to interrupt them and pull Katherine back to the ballroom, where Aunt Louisa wanted to get underway with late introductions.

"I've been tracked down by Beezie," he explained as he rejoined Patrick. "After two foxtrots and a tango I need a scotch. Let's make a strategic retreat to the library."

One scotch led to another as Fenton Norris and Albert reminisced about the summer's play at the Bohemian Grove. They had both had minor parts in "A Romany Legend" and old Fenton was trying his best to convince Albert to go it again.

"What the hell. I was going to skip next year, too, but what the hell. With Fred Harris as director!"

Old Fenton just about had Albert convinced to be one of Robin Hood's merry Men when his wife found them and pulled him away.

"What the hell!" was his parting shot, "You were a fool in the forest a couple of years ago. You can be Robin Hood next year!"

After Fenton left, Albert tried to make conversation over a third scotch but Patrick seemed preoccupied. All of a sudden he stood up. "This is a bunch of crap," he said. "How many more goddamned people does she have to meet, anyway?"

He was genuinely annoyed and not the least bit apologetic about being so.

"She'll be trapped forever if you don't rescue her," Albert said lightheartedly.

From the expression on Patrick's face it looked as if he had taken Albert quite literally and without saying another word, went off in the direction of the music. Finding Katherine dancing with Doug Mackie he unceremoniously cut in.

"Where the hell have you been?" he asked, awkwardly taking her hand and attempting to make his feet follow the incomprehensible pattern on the floor.

"If you would pardon me, Mr. Bartley, I could well ask you the same question," she snapped.

The music stopped briefly, and taking her hand, he led her from the floor and back into the conservatory.

"I don't dance," was his only explanation.

The conservatory was filled with couples drinking champagne, bragging about their duck season and telling each other how divine they looked in their dresses. Without stopping, Patrick walked straight through the French glass doors into the rose garden, which, with the conservatory ran at a perpendicular angle to the ballroom. The rose garden, laid out in formal boxwood paths, ran the length of 80 feet to where it ended in the lathe work tea house. It was down these paths and into the recesses of the tea house that Patrick led Katherine in unhesitating flight.

Once in the tea house and comfortably concealed on the wicker settee, she turned to him.

"What's the matter," she asked, half out of breath and perplexed by his abrupt behavior.

"Nothing. I just wanted to be with you for a while."

Then quite unexpectedly he reached over and grasped her hand in his. She could tell he was agitated as well as being rather drunk.

"I can't just leave," she objected as she felt the power of his big hand slowly squeezing hers. The notes of Pee Wee King's "You Belong to Me" floated out of the ballroom and across the garden wall.

"I really should go back. I can't just—"

"Sure you can," he said, cutting her off in mid-sentence. She looked at him, somewhat annoyed. His eyes, which had been fixed on hers, looked glazed and a silly grin seemed permanently fixed on his rugged face.

Again she started to protest but gave up. The evening air was refreshing in the relative quiet of the garden. It couldn't hurt to stay for a few minutes, she thought. She looked out over the clean uncomplicated pattern of the garden, conscious only of Patrick's hand on hers. Several minutes passed as a feeling of indescribable bliss settled over her. She sighed finally and leaned her head back against his shoulder.

Another moment passed before she could hear his voice. "Katherine," he said slowly, "will you marry me?"

"Of course," she heard herself saying. The words came automatically as if flowing out of some unfathomable primal impulse.

She had not considered a marriage proposal a possibility but when it arrived at this unexpected juncture, she surprised herself and accepted without consideration.

A moment later she found they were both laughing, sensing in each other that undeniable urge that coursed between them. It had broken down their mutual defenses and rendered them helpless. At the deepest level of their beings, they had long before surrendered to the inevitable. Now in the tea house at the end of the rose garden, they became conscious of that surrender. All tensions were resolved, all doubts forgotten.

Patrick took her in his arms and pressed his lips to her mouth. For a long while they sat holding each other, their minds full of thoughts.

Then there were the unmistakable quick steps crunching across the gravel path and Ivy's thin voice calling Katherine's name. She stopped just at the edge of the tea house and peered into the shadows.

"Mrs. Harte has been looking for you, Katherine," she said nervously. "I'm sorry to interrupt, but she sent me to find you over half an hour ago and I've been everywhere. Do you know where Albert is? I'm supposed to find him, too."

Without waiting for an answer, Ivy turned and started back across the path.

"It seems I have been summoned," Katherine sighed.

About the time of Patrick's proposal, Albert had escaped to the pantry where he was trying to explain Dada to an attractive maid who was doing something in connection with midnight supper. When Ivy finally ferreted him out he was ready for a change of scene, but not wanting to return to the ballroom, he artfully detoured through the drawing room, into the library, to have a cigar with Judge McGwin and Horace O'Keefe. One of the double oak doors connecting to the great hall was opened and from where he stood he could see into the sixth alcove across from the Han Dragon. Phillip Addison was sitting alone in the alcove and Albert thought at the time that he looked peculiarly pensive, as if absorbed in some problem. The next time he noticed Addison he had been joined by Madame Ng. This did not strike Albert at first as being particularly unusual, for Madame Ng always received an invitation to the parties she did and used the occasions to circulate, making discreet contact with as many guests as possible. Yet what did strike him as odd, as he observed their conversations, was the way in which Madame Ng seemed to be lecturing Addison. She sat forward in the chair, her back ramrod straight, her face stern, and her eyes intense. She was talking rapidly, making short emphatic jabs into the air with her index finger as if to underscore the importance of what she was saying. Perhaps, Albert thought, she was discussing business but the expression in Addison's face contradicted this theory, for he looked unusually distressed. Nor could Albert comprehend what, if anything, Madame Ng could possibly have to say to Addison. But too many spirits and conversations had dulled his powers of speculation. Then suddenly Beezie was there. He had at last been caught and was forced to dismiss the observation from his mind.

Back in the ballroom the orchestra was playing a slow romantic piece. Katherine, after fulfilling social obligations had persuaded Patrick to dance. Slowly he turned her around the floor in an awkward box step. The room was filled with a soft radiant yellow glow, which sparked down from the chandeliers and reflected on the gilt edged mirrors. She felt Patrick's arm around her waist and her body seemed to melt into his slow turning movements. Her mind wandered back to the rustic cabin, recalling what it had been like to hold him deep inside her and to awaken with him asleep next to her. She remembered how still it had been, how she had watched dust fibers dance on elongated shafts of light. It seemed, she thought, to be the same soft yellow light through which they now danced in Treehaven's gilded ballroom.

CHAPTER 32

SIDE FROM THE hours they spent working, Patrick and Katherine were inseparable the week following Aunt Louisa's ball. The crew of carpenter and painters had worked overtime to finish Katherine's apartment and with her Aunt Victoria's help she began the process of decorating and moving in. Patrick had insisted upon refurbishing the entire place and Victoria, armed with interior decorators, had supervised much of the operation. It made her feel a part of Katherine's life and Katherine was grateful to relinquish the time-consuming task. Patrick supplied a company truck and two movers and slowly, Katherine began trying various pieces of her father's furniture that she thought she might use. Patrick came by several times to take her out to lunch and he left work early every day so he could be with her in the afternoon. In the evenings they dined out and Patrick took great delight in continuing to introduce her to San Francisco's finest restaurants. At Omar Khayyam's, Schroeders, and Alfred's, they finalized their wedding plans, choosing to have a small family wedding November 7th at Treehaven.

On Wednesday Patrick picked her up at the office for a late lunch at Sears. It was a romantic gesture and Katherine enjoyed making Patrick order for her, as well as teasing him about not going back to Schroeders, which had a men-only rule for lunch.

"Now that you've decided on where and what we will eat, I want your decision on something else," she kidded.

"And what might that be?"

"Aunt Victoria has located an exceptional Persian Serapi carpet. It's over a hundred years old, but in excellent condition and will fit the dimensions of our drawing room perfectly."

"Good. We'll have a look at it after lunch," he said agreeably.

Patrick liked the carpet, bought it on the spot and had it delivered.

"Let's go to Emilio's tonight to celebrate," he said as they left the shop. "I'll reserve a table in one of the shadowy corners and propose to you all over again."

"And if I don't accept the second time?"

"We'll have to see about that, won't we?"

After dinner they rode back up Nob Hill on the Powell Street Cable Car, had a nightcap at the Top of the Mark, and walked home past the bronze curtain that protected the palatial brownstone Pacific Union Club. They strolled hand in hand through the park, and then up Sacramento between the unfinished cathedral and the charming little apartments with their French wrought-iron balconies and Beaux art decorations. It was still warm at eleven o'clock and the city was almost dreamlike in the lazy autumn air. No foghorn interrupted the stillness and there was only the rhythmic click and hum of the cables running through the slots beneath California, Powell and Hyde. Patrick opened the door to the apartment. They crossed through the entrance hall and stood for a moment at the drawing room entrance admiring the rich patterns of their new carpet as it stretched into the shadows.

Katherine caught Patrick's hand as he reached for the light switch and guided it away. Aware of his surprise, she smiled and diverted her eyes to where a shaft of moonlight streamed through the drapeless bay windows at the side of the room. She removed her jacket, placed it carefully on a packing crate and walked into the empty room, stopping just short so the moonlight backlit her tall graceful body. Slowly she turned and stood for a moment looking at him. Then reaching behind her, she unfastened a snap and let her skirt drop to the floor. Carefully she unbuttoned her silk blouse, never once looking away from where Patrick stood transfixed in a terrifying sort of reverence. When she reached to undo her brassiere he found himself unbuckling his belt. They removed all their clothing and stood naked at opposite ends of the empty room.

He could see each smooth gracious curve of her body silhouetted against the thin silver white light and he was consumed with the desire to reach out and touch her. He wanted to have her, to hold her, to possess her, to smother her neck and breast with kisses and then dominate her and feel himself deep inside her, but he could not move. When she finally reached out and called to him with uplifted arms he found himself standing in front of her. The momentum of his thoughts vibrated between two dispositions. His hunger raged against his sense of adoration. She was the object of his lust and the intent of his devotion. Caught in this confusion he again could not resolve an action until she reached out and took hold of him. Only then could he begin to cover and caress her body as he slowly sank to his knees, her fingers running through his thick dark hair.

They made love in the living room on the new Persian carpet and slept the rest of the night entangled in each other's arms amid unpacked boxes and fabric samples. They awoke early in the morning with the sun streaming through the drapeless windows and made love again. Those were the last peaceful moments they would have together for over a week.

The next afternoon Katherine had a meeting with Phillip Addison, who told her that he had been authorized to increase the offer for McMasters Shipping by three million dollars. "To tell you the truth, Katherine, this is a very excellent offer. I think they are offering you well over the actual value of the company, and I would seriously consider it. I can't tell you what to do, but I can tell you that this offer will not be extended indefinitely." Phillip did not seem to be high-pressuring her. His manner was very calm, almost subdued. And beyond advising her that the offer was a good one, he did not go into much detail. Again she thought there was something sad in Addison's manner that she could not quite understand. He seemed too noble to be involved in anything underhanded and she had become quite convinced that he was devoted to her, despite the unsettling evidence of the conversation she had overhead.

That evening Patrick had promised to take her to Oris' for a little Tuscan cooking and was to pick her up at about five o'clock. When he had not arrived by six, Katherine became concerned and called Albert to see if he had heard anything. It wasn't until six-thirty that Patrick finally called. He was extremely short and sounded like he was under a great deal of pressure. "Look, something important has come up. I won't be able to make it out there for at least another hour or so. I'll meet you at Albert's at around seven p.m."

"Is there a problem?"

"It's too long to go into now. I'll tell you later."

It wasn't until after eight that they saw him. Katherine and Albert were more concerned than annoyed by the hour, and when Patrick walked in the room, they could tell something had happened. He looked very tired.

"It's the Sunset project."

"You're behind schedule?" Albert asked as he mixed a stiff drink.

"I wish that was it. Dick Fleherty's loan came due and the bank is refusing to refinance. They're threatening to foreclose on other properties he used for collateral."

"You can't refinance with another bank?"

"There's not enough time. We're all overextended, anyway. Everything is already mortgaged up to the hilt!"

"How bad is it?" Katherine asked, observing the pinched, worried look in his eyes.

"It could be disastrous. We're in a critical period. We're not far enough along. We won't start to see a reversal in the cash flow until April or May."

"That's six or seven months from now!"

"I don't know what we are going to do. I may have to sell both the ranch and the apartments to save the Sunset project from going under. I don't even know if we can meet next week's payroll. We're all stretched so thin that there isn't any extra source of capital to fall back on."

"What bank is recalling Fleherty's loan?" Albert asked thoughtfully, stirring the olive in his martini.

"Dick does business with Western Empire," Patrick answered. "He says he has done business with them for years, and has never had any trouble."

"Your friend Chambliss Horsley is President of that bank," Albert said, turning to Katherine. "I think I smell a rat. They must really want McMasters Shipping very badly if I'm right."

"What are you driving at?" Patrick asked

"Well, it's only a guess," Albert continued, attempting to sort out his suspicions. "They probably think that your engagement will distract Katherine from business and make her more willing to sell the company. As an added inducement, they arranged to put your finances in a precarious position by calling in your partner's loans. They must know how thinly your spread. At the same time they up the offer a couple of million for the company, it's the old carrot and stick routine." Albert noticed he was a little ahead of them, and he continued to develop his conspiratorial theory at Oris' over his cannelloni. "I think there isn't much doubt about it. This is just the sort of move I would expect from Horsley. And of course …" He stopped as if not wanting to jump too far ahead and expose what he knew was only an intuitive perception.

"And of course what?" Patrick pressed, anxious to follow Albert's thoughts.

"Oh, nothing really. I just keep thinking that it is odd that both Phillip Addison and Chambliss Horsley were with Katherine's father when he died. I'm not conspiratorial by nature, but I keep wondering. Perhaps something was said on the golf course. You know how golf games are. They might have been putting pressure on McMasters."

"What kind of pressure?" Katherine asked.

"I don't know. Pressure. Pressure. Business pressure, pressure not to marry this Monique Monahan, some kind of pressure, any kind of pressure."

"And you think it caused him to have the heart attack?"

"I don't know, could have. It's happened before. Out of shape, high-pressured businessmen get on the golf course and well … a coronary is not that unreasonable. Anyway, it's a sure thing that these guys want the company pretty badly now and will go to almost any lengths to get it."

By the time they were having coffee and chestnut flambé, Albert had devised a solution. "Just have your partners go to Dad. I'm sure old George will help them out with a loan. After all, you're going to be family, and if there is one thing that Dad holds dearer than his money, it's family."

Patrick was grateful for Albert's suggestion, but he was a little embarrassed by it, too. "I think that would put your father in a difficult position, and I don't want to do that," he said slowly. Instinctively Katherine could tell that Patrick did not want to rely on her family only days after they had become engaged, but Albert continued to press the plan, citing practical considerations. "Look at it this way," he advised, "you are bringing Dad business from one of his competitors, and I'm sure he will be happy to extend a loan."

They talked late into the night about their options. For the first time Katherine seemed to be seriously considering accepting the offer for McMasters Shipping. "I think Addison is probably right. For all I can tell from studying the company's financial position and discussing it with the attorney's, it's a fairly generous offer. And one thing's for sure, I don't know much about running a steamship line. I'd probably be better off just washing my hands of the whole thing."

"You're not saying that because you think I am in financial straits, I hope?" Patrick asked, making sure she was not being motivated solely out of a desire to help.

"I don't know," she said. "The money might be better invested in real estate development, which you know something about, rather than a shipping line that I know very little about. What I don't like is the way they keep pressuring me. Addison says the offer is only good until the end of the month, and that's less than ten days off."

"I'm still curious about where all this money is coming from," Albert said pursuing his conspiratorial theory. "Surely Otto and Gloria don't have that kind of liquid capital unless they are using gold from the Third Reich. Horsley is of course loaded, but it would surprise me if he had anywhere near the millions they are offering. Maybe there are silent partners we know nothing about. Of course, I would like to see you keep the line for purely sentimental family reasons, but those are not the ones that should really be considered in a business decision."

"I wonder if Broderick is involved financially?" Katherine wondered, remembering his conversation with Addison.

As they talked on, Katherine and Albert continued to insist that Patrick and his partner Dick Fleherty, at least go see George Devonshire. "He trusts you anyway, Patrick," Albert argued. "And I think he should be given the opportunity to become involved. He might even want to become an investor. It sounds like you are all spread a little thin, anyway. Maybe the solution is to bring in another partner." In the end Patrick reluctantly agreed at least to talk the matter over with Albert's father, while Katherine played for more time at McMasters. "I can't help but think they will be willing to extend the offer if they are really interested in the company," Patrick concluded, "And I just hate like hell to knuckle under to some god-damned banker who thinks he can come around the back door and put pressure on me through you and ruin nice guys like Dick Fleherty and Don Higgins, to boot."

CHAPTER 33

*A*UNT LOUISA HAD arranged to have "A Family Day at Treehaven". It was to be the only opportunity for Patrick's family and Katherine's family to meet before the wedding, which was now but two weeks away.

Saturday morning as Albert finished his second cup of coffee, he had to admit that he was not particularly looking forward to the day ahead. "Family gatherings can be tedious," he confided to Chow Ling. "The more I think about my parents and the Bartley family all trying to make polite conversation, the more I dread the prospect."

Patrick and Katherine had been a little edgy because of his business problems and Albert felt their relationship might be showing the strain. The added commotion of family dynamics was not something they needed.

"You not looking for good day?" Chow-Ling queried, noticing his pensive mood.

"No, not very much," Albert replied, lighting a cigarette and resting my head on the back of the chair. "Too much family."

"How Mrs. Devonshire like idea of wedding?" he continued, moving towards what he sensed might be a source of difficulty.

"She's a little reserved. I think she feels Katherine should wait until the spring, but she hasn't said so in so many words."

"She doesn't like Mr. Patrick?"

"Oh, no, it's nothing like that. I think the rapid succession of events has thrown her off pace. You know Mother. She likes things to move slowly. Katherine's reunion with the family has been exhilarating but also an emotional drain on her. Brought back a lot of memories. You know."

"And your father?"

"Father," he laughed, "he couldn't be happier. He thinks Patrick Bartley is the cat's pajamas! He embodies all the virtues Father holds dear. I think he sees something of himself in Patrick's aggressive business acumen. Hopes it will rub off on me."

"You think parents like Mr. Patrick family?"

"Oh, I think so. They're not exactly 'our kind of people' as Mother might wish, but I think they will see them as the good, stable, hard-working sort. They obviously have a keen sense of family and that should help. Of course, they are Catholics, but then so are half our friends. As long as they are not fanatics I think we'll survive."

As Albert said these words he felt a wave of anxiety. Patrick had mentioned half-jokingly that his mother was displeased that he was not being married in the Catholic Church. Would she at some point in the afternoon, after a couple of drinks, openly object to the plans for a Protestant wedding at Treehaven? The thought of some sort of religious strife touched off visions of an Irish fistfight in the drawing room. Perhaps Mrs. Bartley was even now lighting candles to some martyred saint, praying for strength and the Catholic cause.

Of course, knowing the Irish as he did, Albert was also a little concerned that Katherine might find her mother-in-law a force with which to be reckoned. Patrick, her first born, was her partner in raising his brothers and sister. He was undoubtedly the light of her life. He had become a success and had provided her with all the comforts. In her eyes, Patrick probably could do no wrong. She might feel any girl should consider herself blessed by the saints to be lucky enough to marry him. The oldest daughter of nine children, six boys and three girls she had raised two families, taking much of the respon-sibility for her younger brothers and sisters before she was married to Patrick's father at the age of nineteen. Seven of her brothers and sisters were still living. One was a priest, and her youngest sister was a nun with the Mercy sisters. When she was widowed at forty, she picked up the pieces and raised her five children through love-laced discipline, prayer and the example of hard work. Such a mother-in-law, although admirable, might prove an unpleasant distraction. Albert knew that Katherine possessed a strong will and determined spirit but he wondered if she fully understood the strong emotional ties that existed between an Irish mother and her sons.

In order to make their first meeting a little less formal, Albert decided to meet Patrick's family at the door with old Prentice.

When the Bartley clan arrived to meet their future in-laws, Patrick's mother looked very proud in a new soft shell pink suit with box jacket and big pearl buttons. She was a small wiry woman in her late fifties whose appearance and manner expressed a patient strength of character. Her face was wrinkled and set with large dark eyes that appeared all the darker underneath her white hair, which was neatly pinned on top of her head with a silver clasp. Supported by her daughter Mary Colleen and surrounded by her hulking sons, she walked through the massive oak door and into the great hall with assured dignity. From the moment they shook hands, Albert took an immediate liking to Helen Bartley and felt less worried about both the afternoon and Katherine's future.

The Bartley brothers looked a little like they had landed on another planet. Along with Albert they followed old Prentice down the hall past the art-filled alcoves towards the drawing room where the rest of the family had gathered. They eyed their surroundings in silent amazement, except for Shawn, whose attempt at a wisecrack was quickly stifled by a quick snap of his mother's fingers.

As Prentice announced the Bartleys, Albert identified a very brief sense of panic pass through the room. He had noticed an almost imperceptible stiffening in Katherine and his mother, as if they needed to draw up a defensive posture against some unimaginable catastrophe.

"I am Louisa Fitzhubert Harte," Aunt Louisa's voice rang out in a clear, strong statement of fact. "Welcome to Treehaven."

Faced with what seemed a very grand room full of people she did not know, Helen Bartley paused for a moment, not understanding quite which way to direct herself. Then she followed the voice and moved to where Aunt Louisa was enthroned in her favorite Gainsborough armchair.

"I'm Helen Bartley, Patrick's mother. I'm pleased to meet you," came Helen's voice in clear sweet tones.

"So you're Patrick's mother," said Aunt Louisa, drawing herself up and looking critically back at poor Helen Bartley. "Well, all I have to say to you, Mrs. Bartley, is that if I were fifty years younger, I'd give your son Patrick a good chase. He's the best-looking man I've seen in 23 years."

With this remark, Aunt Louisa rolled her eyes and laughed as if she were recalling a romantic escapade from her past. She grasped Helen's hand and shook it vigorously.

"Well, Helen Bartley," she continued, "welcome to our family. What would you like to drink?"

Whatever tension there was in the room seemed to dissolve in the wake of Aunt Louisa's irrepressible charm and wit. Of course, Victoria pursed her lips a little bit, but that was to be expected.

"Prentice, get these Bartleys a drink!" Aunt Louisa bellowed.

If the Bartley brothers had felt the least bit defensive about the afternoon, they were instantly disarmed by Aunt Louisa, who flirted and kidded with each one in turn.

"You're almost as handsome as your brother Pat," she told Dan. "How about a date?"

Mike Bartley's two children, Sally and Kevin, who had been largely ignored until now, soon became the center of attention as Aunt Louisa called over each of the dogs to introduce them. Sally was a little afraid of the wolfhound, but Aunt Louisa had Fergus shake hands and all was well.

Likes and dislikes are always very personal and tell a great deal about the people that hold them. And if Aunt Louisa was wild about Patrick it was mostly because he reminded her of her father. Not only did they have the same first name, but ,there was that Irishness about them, that certain robust humor and sense of poetic blarney that delighted her. Patrick Fitzhubert, like Patrick Bartley, had been a shrewd, hard living, self-made man who had fallen in love with a socially prominent San Franciscan. Aunt Louisa was a product of that union. She saw in the forthcoming marriage the marriage of her own father and mother over eighty years before. So, in characteristic style, she was determined to have the afternoon as well as the wedding turn out to be a splendid success. From the time of their arrival until the next morning, she artfully orchestrated the gathering pulling from each of the players in the scene a moment of glory on center stage so that each came away with a feeling of importance. It was one of Aunt Louisa's best performances.

After all the introductions and a drink, Aunt Louisa selected a pause in the conversation to turn to Kevin and Sally.

"Come on, you two. I'll show you the swimming pool."

"We're going to have a good, old-fashioned California barbecue. These are the golden days. Absolutely the best time of year!" she said pushing herself out of her chair and starting out the French doors.

The party filed out behind her, not quite knowing where they were going. Turning on the terrace, she took Helen Bartley's hand for support and proceeded to tell her about the gardens as they walked along. The children, excited by the adventure, ran ahead with Maggie and Jigs yipping behind them. They ran ahead, ran back and ran ahead again with ever-increasing excitement.

About fifteen minutes later, when Aunt Louisa reached the sundial in the rose garden from which one can go off in any of eight directions, she turned around and waited for the party that had straggled along the paths behind her.

"Albert," she announced, "I am going to show Mrs. Bartley and her daughter the medieval knot garden. You take the boys through the maze down to the pool. You can all have a swim before lunch. There are plenty of suits and towels for everyone. If these Bartley boys can't find one to fit, go skinny dipping."

"Oh, Aunt Louisa!" Victoria gasped somewhere amid the Tropicana roses. There were noticeable sounds of amusement from Shawn and Dan and a quick wink of glee from Aunt Louisa to Helen.

"You have a fine bunch of boys there, Mrs. Bartley," and then with a sigh she added, "You must be very proud of them."

Aunt Louisa continued to pour on the charm as she walked the gardens with the Bartley women, Katherine and Victoria. Albert and Patrick took the men and children over to the pool, which was situated on the half-acre of lawn between the formal and the late eighteenth-century gardens.

In their mother's presence, the Bartley boys had been as docile as teddy bears, but once out of her sight, they were a rough and tumble bunch of hooligans. They flipped towels in the changing rooms, played tackle on the lawns and tried to drown each other in the pool. By the time the women arrived, everyone was engaged in a cutthroat game of rag tag until Shawn inhaled some water and Albert had to drag him out of the pool.

They had an informal lunch in the pool house with barbecued steak, potato salads and Peach Melba Grand Marnier for desert.

Katherine and Patrick were unusually quiet during lunch. They had come down the night before to rest and get away from the city, but they had argued on the drive down over business difficulties. In his world a man was supposed to be the provider and the fact that Katherine had money, power and connections continued to bother him. Katherine considered his concerns trivial and obsessive. In her world where marriages were frequently mergers between family fortunes, it was simply assumed a woman would have her own money.

"I cannot see why you are being so bullheaded" she had remarked when he had questioned the propriety of seeing her uncle. "He's not only your banker but, a family member and couldn't possibly—" He had cut her off abruptly.

"That's the point, isn't it."

"The point?"

"I don't want anyone saying I married you for your money."

"My God! You Irish and your dreadfully bloody dark moods" she had flared. "I truly do find them a bit tiresome." They had ridden the rest of the way down in silence.

Neither had slept very well. In the morning after breakfast, they had had a long talk in the library and by the time the rest arrived, they had come to a common mind. Patrick would see George Devonshire and Katherine would not consider selling her company until after their honeymoon. The decision made, they seemed to flow along through the afternoon without a care in the world. Always together they appeared to enjoy the day from a psychological distance. They were at that wonderful point which comes after battle when in utter exhaustion one feels victorious just to have survived.

During the course of the lunch, Albert assessed Patrick and Katherine and came to the conclusion that this was the appropriate moment to give them their wedding gift. Aunt Louisa had already given them a Stubbs painting and his mother and father had presented them with a twelve-piece setting of eighteenth-century Staffordshire porcelain. After a great deal of thought and with the help of Chow-Ling, Albert had decided to give them an extraordinarily rare tricolored Ming vase. The choice operated symbolically on several levels. The vase was decorated with two intertwined yet opposing dragons pursuing the precious jewel amid clouds and flames in leaf green, yellow and aubergine on an apple green background. It had been Katherine's mother's christening gift to him back in 1921. He excused himself during desert and returned to the house to collect the gift. By the time he returned, trays of champagne were being served from the pool house kitchen and toasts were in order.

Albert's father went first, as Aunt Louisa had instructed. In a simple dignified manner he welcomed Patrick to the family.

"I would remind you all that I introduced this young couple, so I feel much of the credit for their happiness belongs to me."

The manner in which he exerted the claim provided that patriarchal approval that every young couple seeks when they marry.

Albert noticed Patrick during the toast and he looked very grati-
fied if just a little uneasy. Mike Bartley followed George Devonshire.
He spoke a bit formally and seemed a tad hesitant as he recited the
toast he had rehearsed for his wife all morning. At the end, however,
he departed from the memorized text and spoke from the heart.
The effect was much better and he ended by thanking Aunt Louisa
and saying that if he were not married, he would most certainly take
her on a date.

Albert could see that his time had come and after a few sips of
champagne, he arose and the tables fell silent.

"Katherine and Patrick, I want to take this opportunity not only
to offer you a toast but to give you a wedding gift. I do this because
my gift is my wish for you as it was Katherine's mother's wish for me
over thirty years ago. It is the wish that you will evermore pursue the
precious pearl of happiness as you entwine your lives together. The
pearl may be at times hidden from view, but you must never give up
the search. The Dragon of power and happiness must always search
for the pearl. In this there is a great irony. For it is the search, the
struggle, and the pursuit, which makes the dragon both powerful and
happy. It is then the journey, which becomes for us an end in itself.
You are twin dragons wrapped in fire. So for you both I wish power
and happiness on your journey. May you never give up your opposing
identities, but may there always be harmony in your union."

Katherine became a bit undone when she opened the box Chow-
Ling had so carefully wrapped. It was as if at that moment she realized
that all life was a web of interrelationships forming a mystical pattern
through time. She looked at the vase carefully as one would a relic,
an amulet from the past for the future and she began to weep.

The rest of the afternoon was spent swimming and playing
badminton and Patrick and Katherine became more animated with
the exercise. The warm dry day was fragrant. The scent of native bay
and eucalyptus combined with the smell of the grass. Beyond the
formal gardens there was only the occasional rustle as a light breeze
moved through the brittle leaves of ancient oaks. It was a splendid

day, calling up images of Eden. Aunt Louisa and the women retreated to the main house after a while and had tea.

"Why don't you send your mother and sister and the kids home with Andrew?" Albert suggested when Katherine reappeared to tell the Bartley brothers that the ladies were ready to leave. "You can stay into the evening. It's going to be a warm night. Great for a swim!"

Patrick looked at Katherine and thought for a moment. "Frankly, I would like a few more hours. I'd like to have a talk with Mike and fill him in on a few things."

"It sounds very nice," Katherine agreed. "I'll tell Aunt Louisa and then take a siesta."

"Great! Katherine can have a nap, Patrick can have a talk with Mike and I'll take Shawn and Dan up to the folly," Albert concluded, slipping on his shirt.

Patrick was particularly close to his next-eldest brother. Mike had been his confidant and lieutenant from an early age and they had learned through rough times to depend on each other. Now, Patrick wanted his brother to know about his business difficulties and what lay ahead. So Albert took Dan, Shawn and a couple of bottles of champagne up through the yew-lined alley which lead after half mile of gradual ascent, to the top of a knoll at the west side of the estate. At the end of this long avenue of Irish yews, Patrick Fitzhubert, Louisa's father, had built a Roman Temple, which was seldom used because of its distance from the house. Yet the view of the woodlands and bay was spectacular and the spot was a great place to have a drink in the late afternoon. Unfortunately, the two bottles of champagne finished off poor Shawn, who had been drinking heavily since lunch and it was with some effort that Dan and Albert got him back to the house and upstairs, where he passed out in one of the guest bedrooms. He had only been back a few months from Korea and Albert realized he was going through that difficult period of adjustment. "War changes a man's view of reality and never allows him to see things in quite the same light again," he told Dan. "The realization that life is very transitory either makes one bitter or appreciative. Shawn is still bitter. I would guess he has recently seen death on the face of his friends."

"You'll stay for dinner," Aunt Louisa said as they came downstairs. "Then we'll have a poker game. You boys do play poker, don't you?"

"Yes Ma'am, we do," Dan said, looking at Mike, "but we—"

"Fine, then I'll have Prentice put out the chips."

Undoubtedly the Bartley boys thought they had been trapped into playing a friendly game to amuse an old lady, but they soon found out differently, as Aunt Louisa out-bluffed them time and again. She presented quite a sight sitting in the walnut-paneled card room, puffing on her small meerschaum pipe, a green visor smashed unceremoniously down over her forehead. As far as she was concerned, poker was poker and she was not interested in idle chatter. She was only interested in winning.

"Golly, your Aunt Louisa's a real sport!" Dan said as they went to bed. "I've played poker with the best of them, but that old girl tops 'em all!"

CHAPTER 34

*T*HE MONDAY MORNING newspapers served Katherine with the sharp reminder that her life was involved with difficult business decisions as well as family and fiancée. On Sunday, while they swam at Treehaven, George Meany had announced that 9,000 New York dockworkers had quit the International Longshoremen's Association to join the AF of L. She sighed as she put down the paper. "Labor problems! Just another reason to accept the offer and let Horsley and Otto, or even Addison, worry about labor, restructuring rates and competing with the airlines."

Patrick looked up, annoyed at the suggestion. "I thought we decided to stall the offer and continue with the refinance strategy we agreed upon," he snapped.

A little bit shocked by his tone, Katherine shot back, "Watch the tone, Mr. Bartley. I don't tolerate unpleasant people at the breakfast table."

Patrick was irritated with her condescending manner. "I'm just pointing out that once you devise a business plan, you stick with the program, and don't go revising your strategy because of some damned headlines."

Katherine carefully put down her cup and looked directly across the table at him. He sat there, reading the sports page, and pouting like a little boy. He caught her eye and smiled sheepishly and she smiled too. They did not finish their breakfast, but retired back into the bedroom to make love. A long finger of fog was thrusting its way through the Golden Gate and the waters of the bay were rough and dotted with whitecaps as the currents and tides ebbed and flowed beneath the infinite thin blue sky.

That afternoon Patrick met with George Devonshire. Katherine had wanted to come along, but Patrick had insisted that it would place her uncle in an awkward position. "It's best that we keep business business and not mix it with family."

Nevertheless, Patrick did feel a little awkward as he arrived at the bank, for he knew that his conversation with his banker was no longer purely a business meeting. He need not have worried, however, for George Devonshire was more than glad to help, not only with a loan, but with a financial strategy that would ensure the project's survival. His father did what Albert had predicted, but with a twist that he had not anticipated

"The project has significant prospects of a handsome profit," he concluded after spending several hours reviewing the entire financial situation. "All you need is more capital. Would you consider taking in another partner?"

"I don't see that we have much choice if I read the figures right," Fleherty said.

"It's O.K. by me," Higgins agreed.

"What I would suggest is that you make Albert a silent partner," George continued, looking at his son. "It's a sound investment and I think he might find it interesting as well as profitable."

"Look," Patrick interrupted, "I appreciate your suggestion, but I don't want to put the squeeze on Albert unless he's really interested."

"As a matter of fact, I am interested," said Albert. "If Dad thinks it's a good investment, I'm game!"

"I hope you're being honest when you said you weren't being pressured," Patrick said as they left the office.

"Of course. It sounds like a winner and dear old Dad obviously feels you will be a good influence on me. He's been trying to stimulate my appreciation for the marketplace for years. You've made his day.

Just don't expect me to supervise the building. I'm strictly in as a silent partner."

"Oh, no, not at all," Patrick kidded. "We want you out there with hammer and nails every morning."

"Right!" Albert laughed, "You can depend on that, but if I'm not there, just feel free to start without me."

Katherine was pleased, too. Having Patrick and her cousin as partners gave her a sense of security. It helped cement her position and the relationships she had so quickly forged over the past two months. To celebrate, they walked down Lombard to North Beach where they enjoyed a new Joe's Special. On a lark after dinner, they took in part of the Parisian Revue at Finocchio's, ending up the evening drinking cappuccino and brandy and listening to Beniamino Gigli and Lucia Albanese on the jukebox in the Tosca Café. The next three days were spent drawing up the necessary legal documents and making the financial arrangements for the refinancing of the Sunset project. Patrick's partners were happy to have saved their skins, and eagerly went along with his strategy for reorganizing They had all been altar boys together at St. Kevin's in the Mission, and there was a bond of trust between them that went beyond the legal requirements of a written contract. But even with the road cleared of time-consuming negotiations, the financial documents were not ready until eleven a.m. on Thursday morning.

"Sit down," George Devonshire said as Patrick, Dick Fleherty, Dan Higgins and Albert met in his father's office to sign the necessary agreements. "Before we get underway here, I have something you will be interested in knowing."

"Yes?" Patrick said with concern. "Is there a problem?"

"Not with our arrangement, but I just received a report about an hour ago. I ordered some investigatory work done and it appears we've uncovered a series of very complex financial transactions on the part of Horsley and his Western Empire Bank. Some of the moves seem directly linked to a purely hostile attempt to jeopardize your development."

"And how would that be to his advantage?"

"Conceivably he could have his eye on taking over the project but that seems highly unlikely. He needs all the capital he can get to back up his part of the offer for McMasters Shipping, which appears to be his main interest at the moment."

"So why would they attempt to undermine Patrick?" Albert asked, knowing full well what the answer would be.

"To put pressure on Katherine through Patrick!" His father shouted, showing a sudden spark of uncharacteristic temper. "It's the most unethical and underhanded tactic I've ever come across."

Then with an air of triumph he added, "We've outmaneuvered the bastards. Let's sign these papers and make it official!"

"Now we can go ahead full steam, get those roofs on before the rains and keep the whole bloody project on schedule," Patrick said as he toasted their deal over the French-fried eggplant at Jack's. "And here's to Albert, our new partner, and his father, whose advice, help, and counsel has been invaluable over the past few days."

That evening, Patrick joined George and Albert for the Thursday evening show at the Bohemian Club, where they met in the Cartoon Room and again toasted their success. About half an hour after they arrived, Patrick noticed a strange, rather fateful smile come across Albert's face. "Chambliss Horsley just came in with Phillip Addison," he said, looking directly at his father.

"Remember Albert, weaving spiders," his father warned, reminding him of the club's motto, which forbade any business intrigue within its walls.

"Yes, Father, weaving spiders come not here," he said, completing the saying. "Don't worry, I wouldn't tip the bucket anyway. The less they know, the better for us."

Horsley avoided them all evening, but Addison came over and extended a rather strained greeting as they went in for dinner.

On Thursday when Patrick, Albert and his father were occupied with business, Katherine had lunch with her Aunt Victoria under the stained glass dome of the garden court at the Palace Hotel, and went shopping with Amy Mackie. It was one of those October days when sunbathers still attempt to soak up a few rays on the grassy banks of Union Square beneath the Dewey monument, while elderly matrons in their mink stoles, hats and gloves, wandered through the City of Paris or browsed in the shops along the once-infamous Maiden Lane. "This is typical of San Francisco in October," Amy explained. "We always have a week or so of spring before the rains come in November."

Katherine loved Union Square and the sidewalk flower stands always reminded her a little of Paris. They walked down to Brooks Brothers, where Katherine bought a tie for Patrick, and then back up Post, browsing through Shreve's, Gump's and Dunhill before heading over to the St. Francis to have a cup of coffee and rest their feet. As they walked along a smiling heavyset man dressed in an outrageous costume approached them. "Hello, my beautiful lady!" he said, politely tipping his star-studded top hat in a courtly manner. At first Katherine thought he was a clown of some sort and slowed her pace to observe his performance. But Amy, with an amused giggle, reached into her purse and handed the man a quarter whereupon he blew a little bird whistle that hung around his neck and deposited the quarter with great ceremony into a toy cash register. "That's Tiny Armstrong, the Bird Whistle Man," she explained as they continued on towards the St. Francis. "He's one of our favorite characters. Nobody knows where he came from, but he's such fun, everybody seems to enjoy supporting him. From what Douglas tells me, he eats free in a lot of the restaurants around here."

"That's the sort of business to be in, I should think," Katherine said after a half a block.

"What business?"

"Mr. Armstrong's. He doesn't look like he has people trying to drive him under or buy him out!"

The following day, Friday October 30th, Patrick Bartley and his partners were able to meet the payroll and the news of their survival spread quickly from office to office among those who had had a vested interest in either their success or failure. The news reached Chambliss Horsley at the same time in the late afternoon that Katherine delivered yet another refusal to sell her line.

Phillip Addison was stoic and philosophical about her decision, yet Katherine still detected a certain wariness beneath his kindly manner and dark blue suit. She could not guess how Horsley or Otto or Gloria would take her decision, but by the time she left the office, she could not have even bothered. She had not been with Patrick since Monday, and he was taking her back to Trader Vic's where she had first admitted to herself how attractive he was. Again they sat in the Captain's Cabin, ate Oysters Hamburg and shared a bottle of Pinot Chardonnay. Despite their intensely busy week, they did not talk excessively about business, preferring the silence of each other's company. Nor did they linger for Kafe-LaTe, or Chinese gooseberry surprise, but hurried back up Nob Hill. As the front door of her apartment shut behind them, Patrick began to unbutton Katherine's blouse and gently caress her neck as he guided her down the hall towards the bedroom. He could feel the uncontrollable heat of passion rise through his body and fill him with desire. It was all he could do to hold back as he gently undressed her and slowly pulled from her body the desire to match his own. The intensity of his passion always surprised Katherine as he moved suddenly from a posture of cool control to the demonstration of an all-consuming love. Yet with her surprise, Katherine always felt the reassurance of his devotion and she could tell from the way he touched her that he was at once her master and her slave.

CHAPTER 35

*A*LBERT'S ANNUAL HALLOWEEN party in 1953 was in Sausalito. Chow-Ling had put his foot down after the 1950 bash and had banned any further Halloween celebrations at the Telegraph Hill apartment.

"Too much damage," he had announced. "You have complaints from neighbors. You have in Sausalito next year." It was not a request but a command and Albert knew he had no choice but to comply.

"What time does the party begin?" Katherine asked before he left in the morning.

"I don't know. Whenever the first person comes. Why don't you and Patrick come over about seven or eight. Things ought to be really cooking by then."

"And we are supposed to come dressed as famous people?"

"Yep, famous, infamous, real, fictional, whatever you like. I thought of King Farouk, but haven't have had time to do anything about it so I borrowed Greg's mountain climbing gear. I'll be Edmund Hilary."

"You don't seem very certain about any of the details."

"I never am. I don't even know how my Halloween parties get their themes, but somehow they always do. I think Deirdre decides the year before and tells everybody at the party and they somehow remember. I don't even send out invitations. Everyone just comes. All I have to do is haul out some tiki torches, fill them with fluid and stick 'em in the garden. Then Saturday I'll get a bag of apples, some cheese and liquor and we'll be set."

Everything went as unplanned and the party started about four in the afternoon when Rigg stopped by and started drinking bourbon on the porch swing. It didn't end until around noon the next day when he finally sobered up enough to walk back to his boat.

A couple of hours after Rigg appeared the first costumed guests arrived. It was difficult to tell at first just who the Wire Man and Miss Dhorgie were trying to portray, but Deirdre finally guessed Ike and Mamie Eisenhower.

"Far out, man! Was it the stars on the hat?"

"No," Deirdre replied, "It's the pink bow between Dhorgie's ears."

Not long after Ike and Mamie the party started to gather steam. Doug and Amy came dressed as Sid Caesar and Imogene Coca along with Beezie who, in red espadrilles and a frilly white skirt over black corduroy pants, looked more like a Spanish bullfighter than she did Rita Hayworth. Of course, social and political statements were made. Ogden Wallraven was Senator Joseph McCarthy and Hal and Ellen had the delightfully gruesome taste to come as an electrocuted Julius and Ethel Rosenberg, with their hair pasted out in spikes from their head and an upside-down picture of the Statue of Liberty hung around their necks. Gary and Bruce appeared as Christine Jorgensen and Tallulah Bankhead and never stepped out of character the entire evening.

Albert had told Katherine that costumes were optional, but Patrick bought a pith helmet and safari outfit and arrived as Robert Stack's character from his recent 3-D African adventure, Bwana Devil. Katherine of course was the Bwana Devil, wearing a Hubert de Givenchy glazed cotton dress with an exotic fur design, and a long ostrich boa for a mane.

At one point, Rigg fell off the porch into the oleanders. He was completely bagged and suddenly realizing he was out of costume, started apologizing.

"Hey man, we thought you were Zorba," Albert said as they hauled him back up the steps.

"Zorba, Zorba," he slurred. "I will dance!" Then, lurching away, he attempted to take the first steps before falling again over the rail back into the oleanders

Not long after Rigg fell off the porch, a fellow named Vance stumbled into the party arm-in-arm with a waitress from Valhalla. They were both pretty well gone when they joined a conversation Ogden Wallraven was having. Evidently Wallraven's portrayal of Joe McCarthy sent Vance off in a long diatribe about the recent five-year sentences handed down to five Communists in Seattle.

"The whole fucking country is like gripped in this Red Scare. Like I mean, man, they never roust the big shucksters. You see that complaint against Tough Tony and Anastasia for coercion in New York. Shit, man, the heat ain't gonna mess with those cats. Like, I mean it's the same here. I've worked the wharf for years. You think they are going to mess with some cat like Broderick? They never going to hassle the big connection."

Albert had been on the periphery of this conversation, but with the mention of Broderick's name, he became interested.

"Like what is Broderick into?" he asked, reaching over and pouring Vance some more bourbon.

"There ain't nothing that man doesn't have his fat fingers into," Vance slurred, happy to have someone to show some interest in what he was saying.

"Man, you've got over 12 miles of waterfront, 42 piers, 18 miles of berthing space. You think the man who controls all that doesn't get in on the action? Believe me, there's a lot of bread made that no one ever knows about. Hell, he picks the goddamned wharfs, supervises the unloading, and schedules the boats to meet the ships. Shit he can do anything."

Albert attempted to sound Vance out even further, but by now he was too drunk to make much sense, and he soon shifted his conversation to the threat of nuclear war.

"What the hell, we can blow the whole goddamned world apart and who the fuck cares? The goddamned government? Shit!"

"Atomic weapons! They're not as ominous as the stuff they're developing in biological research," Ogden said, assuming a professorial tone. "One drop of some of the toxins they have would kill a whole herd of sheep if it could be distributed. They work as depolarizing agents on nerve junctions, causing almost instantaneous paralysis. Makes them ideal for military application. They only need a few molecules to do their work."

"No shit!" Vance kept saying as he swayed back and forth, attempting to follow what was becoming a technical lecture on biological warfare, while all around him the party became increasingly more bizarre.

Jimmy Durante, Willie Shoemaker, Eva Peron, Rocky Marciano and a trio dressed as Kukla, Fran and Ollie made appearances. In the course of the night almost a hundred people came and went or came and stayed. The party picked up around eleven with conga drummers who started pounding out neo-African rhythms in the garden. It wasn't long before Lyric began to dance. She danced on the porch and down into the garden. She arched and writhed more violently as the tempo increased.

"Is this the pagan rites of All Hallows Eve?" Patrick kidded as he and Katherine joined Albert and Deirdre.

"I certainly hope so," Albert replied, "that's what the party's for!"

Wicks, a friend of Rigg's, stripped off his shirt and shoes and wearing only blue jeans, began to dance around Lyric in a primitive fashion. Back to back, front to front, side to side, he matched her moves, becoming ever more provocative. They danced in the yellow light that fell on the garden from the porch. Tiki torches flamed in the background and everyone began chanting: "Go! Go! Go!" Locked in a hedonistic fury, Lyric tore at herself, tore at her breasts and thighs and hair. Wick's torso, gleaming with sweat, twisted and flexed as he weaved around her. Gradually Lyric sank to her knees and arched back. Wicks arched over her. Still in time to the beat, and without touching, they imitated copulation. The entire dance had taken a good 20 minutes and when they were finally finished they fell back, exhausted, against the porch steps.

CHAPTER 36

WITH THEIR WEDDING but several days away, Katherine and Patrick spent the first week of November wrapping up loose ends. Patrick had a lot of work to do with his company after its reorganization, and he confessed to his partners that he felt guilty about leaving them with the development not yet half completed. "Don't be a jerk," Fleherty said Monday morning following the restructuring. "You saved our asses last week. Go on, get out of here!"

"You haven't taken a vacation since you were six years old," Higgins kidded. "I think we can handle things around here for a couple of weeks without the likes of a Patrick Bartley."

While Patrick worked ten to twelve hours a day, Katherine put her desk in order at McMasters and gave her new private secretary, Joan Bywater, what she hoped were the necessary instructions.

"Sometimes I think we are absolutely crazy to try to go off to Hawaii with all that there is going on here," she confessed to Albert over creamed spinach at Townsend after the final fitting of her wedding dress.

"Don't worry," he advised, "if George Hampton tells you it's all right to go, then it's all right. You have faith in Joan, and you know there isn't a hell of a lot you can do here anyway. Think of it this way: since you're sailing on your own liner, you can consider the honeymoon a business trip any time you start feeling guilty, which I hope won't be at all."

Katherine smiled. She knew her cousin was right. There wasn't much she could do in San Francisco. She had firmly held her ground against increased pressure to sell and she had learned more about the shipping business in the last two months than she had ever thought possible. She trusted her attorney's judgment and knew she could rely on the honesty and efficiency of Joan Bywater in taking care of her office and personal affairs. But beyond these reassurances, she knew she needed to get away from all the madness and be with the man she loved. They needed uninterrupted time together and they could never have that if they tried to honeymoon in California.

The actual plans for the wedding were not much trouble. Aunt Louisa, fully recovered from the triumph of her magnificent ball, had plunged herself headlong into planning the event. She called Katherine at least twice a day to ask her preference on various details, and then often ended up doing something completely different. The wedding was moved from the ballroom, to the conservatory, to the drawing room, and then back to the ballroom in the course of two days. The menu and the flowers changed almost as frequently as the place, and by the middle of the week, Aunt Louisa had driven Victoria into the distraction of ever-increasing amounts of sherry.

Through all the excitement and turmoil surrounding the wedding, Katherine maintained a remarkable degree of serenity.

"I don't care very much what Aunt Louisa arranges," she confided to her cousin. "I know it will be lovely. All I care about is that you will all be there when we exchange vows."

Albert helped her achieve the correct perspective. "Aunt Louisa is her own art form," he advised. "It's best to detach yourself and observe from a distance. Detachment from the Treehaven dynamic and daily spinal adjustments from Chow-Ling will produce a harmonious wedding,"

On Wednesday evening Albert gave a pre-wedding dinner at Julius' Castle on the peak of Telegraph Hill. They met early for drinks to watch the panoramic view as a fiery sun started to slip towards the Golden Gate, turning the waters of the bay into a shimmering sparkle of pinks and blues. Among the guests, he had invited the Mackies, Patrick's brothers and sister, and his partners and their wives. Of course, Albert had also included Beezie, who came wearing a taut torso dress that clung to her shapely body like poured wax. "You better be careful, Beezie," he said as she sat down. "If you swallow the olive in your martini, it's going to show."

The waiters popped champagne and toasts were made as millions of lights began to twinkle and glow in the twilight and spread over the hills that ring the bay to the north and east. Soon a pale white moon rose out of those same hills, bouncing long beams of light on the dark waters beneath them. For a few breathless moments, time seemed to stand still, and they all moved towards the windows in reverential silence. As the last blush of light faded from the far western sky, Katherine could feel Patrick reach down and take her hand, as if to comfort her in the fragile beauty of a dying day. Moments later it was all gone, and they went back to their champagne toasts and laughter. Two months earlier Katherine might have wondered at the spontaneous silence, but not now. She had come to know what every true San Franciscan knows by nature. There are moments of such incredible beauty over the ever-changing city that they can only be properly met in silent contemplation.

"Didn't the Golden Gate look like a perfect postcard tonight?" Beezie exclaimed to Dick Fleherty and his wife.

"I suppose it did," Dick replied with a degree of wonderment.

"That's my Beezie!" Albert interjected in order to save Dick the agony of engaging Beezie in absurd conversation. "Beezie always compares whatever she sees to a postcard image she carries in her mind. It is a most extraordinarily intellectual process."

"Gee, am I really an extraordinarily intellectual process?" Beezie asked, obviously pleased to be the center of attention.

"Most assuredly you are, my little sweet pea, most assuredly you are," he reassured her while trying to control an uncontrollable need to laugh.

"Well, I do remember when I first saw the Eiffel Tower," she continued, without any sense of self-awareness. "I remember commenting to my friend Phoebe that it looked just like one James Hollingsworth sent me the summer before."

During a long pause in which her end of the table waited for her next comment, Patrick leaned forward and asked Katherine in an audible, but somewhat secretive tone, "What do you think the picture of the Eiffel Tower looked like, that Hollingsworth sent her?"

Katherine gave Patrick a condescending glance, "You know, Patrick, the standard American postcard shot. Straightforward and erect."

"Yep, you're absolutely right," Patrick replied, "that's the kind I always send. Straightforward, erect, and very tall."

With this remark, they all burst into laughter and there were hoots and hollers from the Bartley brothers and Don and Dick alike. "How do you know so much about post cards?" puzzled Beezie when the laughter had subsided. "I didn't know that you had even been to Europe."

"I've been around the world, Beezie," Patrick said, giving the faint touch of an Irish brogue to his story. Albert found he could no longer refrain from the verbal melee. "Wasn't that on an anthropological expedition to study the pubescent rituals of the cannibalistic Tar Tua tribe as they compare to the coming-out rituals of the American debutante?" he asked in a most scholarly manner.

"Yes, yes, quite so!" Patrick confirmed, taking a serious frown to his forehead. "That was just the expedition!"

"Oh," sighed Beezie, "I didn't know you studied native tribes."

As the dinner progressed, the stories and jokes became more ribald and the toasts more immodest as the wine flowed and everyone relaxed and enjoyed the humor.

"Hey, let's go down to Bimbo's and see the girl in the fishbowl," Mike Bartley suggested after several rounds of brandy.

Within minutes Albert had paid the bill, and they were on their way. When they reached the street, they found the night had become cold and mysterious under a damp gray blanket. A silent stream of fog had twisted its way through the Gate into the streets of North Beach and up along the ridges of Telegraph Hill. They could no longer see the orange lights of the Bay Bridge mirrored in the inky waters, or the searchlight from Alcatraz. Only muffled foghorns somewhere out in the bay seemed to break through the isolation, calling a warning of unsuspected perils in the night.

They walked the short distance to where Patrick's car was parked on Montgomery near Alta.

"You know, Patrick, Beezie was the original lady in the fishbowl at Bimbo's" Albert remarked as they climbed in. They started laughing hysterically as Beezie misinterpreted the remark and for some unknown reason, started an imitation that escaped interpretation. Patrick started the car, turned onto Union and headed down the east side of Telegraph Hill. At the top of Union, he attempted to slow the car. His foot pressed the pedal to the floor without result. He pumped the brakes again, trying to produce some response, but again they wouldn't grab. Katherine could feel the car gaining speed as again and again he tried to slow its progress. He pulled the emergency brake. It was loose and came out in his hand. From where she was sitting in the back seat, Beezie was oblivious to what was happening and continued her improvisation, but Albert could feel his whole body tense as the car began to careen towards the intersection of Kearny.

"Patrick!" Katherine gasped as she fought her instinct to grab hold of him.

"Hold on! Goddammit, we're out of control!" Patrick shouted as they nearly missed hitting a car coming south on Kearny.

Suddenly realizing the danger, Beezie screamed, "Oh, God! We'll all be killed!" She gasped, screamed again, and threw her arms around Albert's neck.

The car headed towards Grant Avenue as Patrick yelled, "Hang on!" He tried to slow the car several times by glancing it off the side of parked cars. The rest happened too quickly to recall, but from the reports of witnesses, they lurched through the intersection of Grant and crashed into a pole.

In the back seat, there were hysterical screams and sobs as Beezie buried her head in Albert's chest. Patrick's forehead was bleeding, and Katherine held a badly bruised left arm, which had been thrown into the dashboard on impact. Minutes of silence passed as they sat in shock, not quite believing they were alive. Finally, Albert realized what had happened. "When you get back from your honeymoon, I'll treat you to a roller coaster ride out at the beach," he said, before pouring his shock into uncontrollable laughter.

The next minute, Patrick's brothers, Mike and Dan, were helping them out of the car. They had turned onto Union immediately behind the ill-fated car, and had witnessed the entire horrifying ride. "I couldn't get the brakes to grab," Patrick said over and over again. "The emergency brake just came off in my hand."

A police car arrived. Mike knew the cop from five years before, when they had both worked out of Ingleside station together. "You take the girls home," he said to his brother. "Dan can give you a lift, and Joe can drop me off later. You'd better take care of that cut, too."

"Capital," Albert agreed, realizing how badly shaken they all were. "We'll go to my apartment. It's only four or five blocks around the other side of the hill. We'll have Chow-Ling look at the cut, and you can have Joe drop you."

It was eleven o'clock by the time they reached the apartment and woke Chow-Ling. Half an hour later, Mike and Joe were there, and Mike pulled Patrick aside. "It looks like your brakes were cut," he told his brother. "I don't like the looks of it. I'd say someone was deliberately out to—" He did not need to finish the sentence. He could see the possibilities were already racing through Patrick's mind.

Patrick and Katherine decided to spend the night with Albert. Dan took Beezie home. The next day they agreed Albert should drive Katherine down to Treehaven, where she would stay until the wedding. "If someone is out to get one of us, you'll be much safer down the Peninsula with your aunt," Patrick insisted. "I have things I have to get done, including a few things I want to check out with Mike regarding the accident." Katherine reluctantly agreed to go, but there was no reason for her to stay in the city. Her dress would be sent down, and any odds and ends could be wrapped up by Joan Bywater.

They left early and were at Treehaven by nine o'clock, where Aunt Louisa greeted them amid the confusion of yapping dogs and wedding preparations.

CHAPTER 37

THURSDAY, KATHERINE AND Albert had their meals brought up on trays, staying in their suites until dinner. Only once did Albert venture downstairs into the madness of wedding preparations, where Aunt Louisa had the staff worked into a frenzy. She had popped in during breakfast to inform him that her doctor was coming out at eleven a.m. to look them over and that she had scotched the conservatory, deciding to have the wedding in the ballroom.

By the time they appeared for a light super in the library, Aunt Louisa was triumphant. Dr. Leighton had pronounced Katherine unharmed and Madame Ng had delivered thirty-six Coelogyne Cristala orchids with a profusion of spikes in full bloom. And as Aunt Louisa took great pains to remind everyone, "finding Cristala orchids in bloom in November is an unmatched coup. They usually don't spike until midwinter."

"This is going to be an interminable day," Albert told Katherine before lunch on Friday. "The staff from Pebble Beach has arrived to swell the ranks and generally add to the confusion. Mrs. Lindler is in such a foul mood that she has banned everyone from her kitchen except Prentice. This morning she harassed Bridget so unmercifully that the poor girl was reduced to tears. Everything is in turmoil downstairs, my back is out and I have a splitting headache. I suppose it's delayed shock from the accident and all. I saw a lot of that in the war. Men would think they were fine after a battle and then suddenly ... well ..."

"Mir gets auch nicht gut." Katherine complained. "I have a headache too and I think my shoulder is worse today than it was yesterday."

"In that case, I think I'll get Chow-Ling down here. It'll take some doing, but the conspiracy might take our minds off everything else."

Not wanting to chance going through Prentice, Albert called down to the garage and arranged to have Andrew leave for San Francisco immediately. Chow-Ling arrived at 3:30, and somehow with Andrew's aid was able to get up to Albert's rooms without being detected. As always, Albert slipped five dollars to Andrew and no one was the wiser until the next morning, when Chow-Ling emerged from his suite and with the air of a Ming Emperor, descended the main staircase. He marched through the hall and into the kitchen, where with excruciating formality, he informed an awestruck Mrs. Lindler that he would prepare herbal tea for the bride.

"As you know, Chow-Ling does not get along at all well with Aunt Louisa," Albert explained before he arrived. "Each time I ensconce him in my suite I evoke her wrath."

"Is she really that adamant?"

"She claims his presence spooks the servants and intimidates Ivy. We'll have to fortify ourselves in our rooms but since I have the sleeping porch off my suite it won't prove very difficult to conceal his presence."

By four-thirty, after a series of successful spinal manipulations, their tension and aches had been dispelled. With harmony restored they enjoyed a late tea with Aunt Louisa and viewed the resplendence of the ballroom. Patrick was having an early dinner with his family and would not arrive until two hours before the wedding. This arrangement gave Katherine a quiet evening to go over the script for the next day, which Ivy had typed from Aunt Louisa's often contradictory instructions.

8:00 a.m. Messrs. Patrick and Michael Bartley Arrive
• Dress in the Constable bedroom (att. Albert)

8:45 a.m. Mr. and Mrs. George Devonshire arrive.
- To morning room (att. Prentice, Bridget)

9:00 a.m. Mrs. P. Bartley, Mother of groom and Miss Bartley, sister of the groom arrive
- To morning room (att. Prentice, Bridget)

9:15 a.m. The Rev. Jonathan Williard and St. Matthew's Boy's Choir arrive
- To Ballroom (att. Andrew)

9:15 a.m. Mr. and Mrs. Douglas Mackie arrive
- Mrs. Mackie to Regency Bedroom (att. Ivy)
- Mr. Mackie to Ballroom (att. Daniels)

9:30 a.m. Guests arrive
- Seated in Ballroom (att. Prentice, Andrew, Daniels)

For the second floor, another military strategy had been designed by Aunt Louisa to ensure the smooth control of events. Katherine and Albert would receive their trays at 7:30. At 8:35, Katherine was to be taken by Aunt Louisa to the Regency bedroom, where Bridget and Ivy would dress her before the same great gilded Regency mirror Aunt Louisa had used on her own wedding day. Albert's assignment was to be downstairs fully dressed in morning suit by 8:00 a.m. and look after Patrick and his brothers until just before the ceremony. At 9:35, he was to report to the Regency room and await the news that Mary Bartley and his parents had been seated. He would then seat Aunt Louisa and return to bring Patrick and Mike down.

"Now don't be late," Aunt Louisa admonished as they sat discussing the game plan she had devised.

"No, I'll be awake by 10:00 o'clock, in time to meet Patrick," Albert teased, trying to lighten the marshalled spirit imposed by the script.

"You'll be awake by seven or I'll send in Fergus and Ginger," Aunt Louisa laughed, referring to her favorite prank of sending the dogs to attack late sleepers with nuzzles and licks. Ginger the golden retriever had been especially trained as a morning router and since she always took a morning walk with the gardener, her coat and muzzle were unusually wet and cold when thrust into an armpit or neck of an unsuspecting guest.

"I'll be up by six, then," Albert surrendered with a mocking tone.

It had always been to Aunt Louisa's great credit that she could enjoy a party once she had formulated the event and instructed the principles in their various duties. She was able to assume a serene composure, transcend details, and relish the drama that played across her stage. Being a grand master at this technique, she gave her guests the impression that she was concerned for little beyond the moment. And when the unforeseen happened, she possessed the flexibility of a truly great general. She improvised!

Aunt Louisa retired early, leaving Katherine and Albert to sit by the library fire. Katherine, seeming to be alternately reflective and nervous, had not eaten her dinner. Her life had been topsy turvy for over two months and the events and decisions of the days and weeks accumulated in her mind and made her a bit fragile as she faced her wedding day. They talked quietly for over two hours, recounting all that had happened as if to place events and personalities safely into perspective. They both knew that the next day would formalize the future and consolidate the past. It was one of those turning points in life when one is compelled to reflect on the quality and meaning one derives from living.

At ten o'clock as they concluded their conversation and walked down the hall, Katherine turned and stopped.

"You'll always be there for me, Albert," she said, taking his hand and looking half-searching into his eyes in a way that reminded him of a small child on her first day of school.

"Yes, Katherine, always," he said, carefully bending forward to give her a reassuring embrace. "I think we can count on both of us being here for each other." He gave her a kiss on the forehead and they went upstairs.

The morning of the wedding went smoothly. Sun broke through and filled the air at Treehaven with the warm wet smells of autumn.

Chow-Ling supervised Albert's morning bath, applied pressure to points along his head and neck, and helped him dress. Patrick and Mike arrived promptly at 8:00 a.m., albeit with hangovers they had acquired at Bimbo's the night before. "Come on, I'll steady your nerves with a Bloody Mary," Albert said while they watched the cars pulling up in the courtyard below.

Albert was called downstairs only briefly to go over last-minute details with a rather distracted Reverend Willard, who nervously glanced back and forth between the assembling choir and the peach and green savonnerie carpet where the ceremony was to take place.

The morning sun fell through the tall east windows, bathing the ballroom in shafts of thin light. The elongated spikes of snowy white Cristala orchids splashed with golden yellow at the lip were banked among ferns and palms to a height of ten feet. Twenty-four Hepplewhite mahogany chairs were set along an aisle created by garlands of lemon leaves strung between mahogany pedestals decorated with yellow, apricot and white chrysanthemums. A viola, two violins and a cello waited alongside the harpsichord, which filled the room with a pattern of pleasant notes. Everything was in place and seemed caught in a moment of anticipation.

Upstairs Katherine was the vision of elegance in a Pierre Balmain ivory satin gown edged with white mink. A family heirloom of Belgian lace was held in place by Aunt Louisa's diamond tiara.

"It's almost time," Albert said. "Everything downstairs is ready!"

She carefully picked up her simple bouquet of Phalaenopsis. "Oui, je suis prete," she replied.

The next thing Albert recalled, he was seating his mother and then Aunt Louisa, who carried on her shoulder a gigantic pinky-lavender Cattelya with a deeply frilled lavender lip and a yellow center. The orchid, a good five inches across, seemed to assume a personality of its own as it bobbed and swayed along down the aisle. The choir was singing Bach's "Jesu, Joy of Man's Desiring" when he returned and escorted Patrick to his place.

At the top of the great staircase, Katherine stopped and waited until the voices died. Then with a nod from Prentice, the strains of Mendelssohn's Wedding March could be heard. Katherine looked at her Uncle George. He smiled and patted her hand, trying to be reassuring. They paused for a moment and then Katherine and her uncle preceded by Amy in an empire-waisted yellow chiffon, began their long measured descent.

As they turned into the ballroom and started down the aisle, Albert could not help but notice Patrick waiting beside him. For the first and only time during the day he looked vulnerable, like a patient with a fever waiting for his doctor. He shifted his large frame nervously from side to side, and unconsciously opened and clenched his hands. Small beads of perspiration appeared on his forehead, and his eyes, which were fixed on Katherine, seemed almost childlike in wonderment.

As the ritual began, Albert could feel the gathering of past and future into the present moment, and in that gathering was the presence of his ancestors—the adventurers, John Milton Harte and Howard Samuel Templeton, who had come to San Francisco to make their fortunes; the notorious Lily Martin and the well-bred Phyllis Livingston Butler of the Philadelphia mainline; Jose Aquirre, who had come six generations before, and the legendary beauty Emma Nickels Templeton, who had married the passionate Anglo Greek, Nicholas George, and Elizabeth, the tragically enchanting Elizabeth, Katherine's mother and his aunt. They were all there somehow to witness this next union. And now a Bartley and the tapestry would have another texture and San Francisco a new name.

Reverend Willard intoned the brief service with Gothic reverence in contrast to the vows, which were exchanged in quiet simplicity. The Lord's Prayer was recited, the benediction supplied and the Patrick Bartleys arose for the nuptial kiss, then turned and recessed down the aisle to Wagner's "Lohengrin." Victoria had managed to cry through the entire ceremony, along with Dolores Whitney while Aunt Louisa discreetly dabbed her eyes, unencumbered by excessive sentimentality.

After pictures in the drawing room, they proceeded into the dining room, where from 11 to 12:30 a breakfast of sautéed frog legs, jellied pheasant and boned squab was served.

At first Aunt Louisa had thought to have three tables of eight, but in the end, she had opted to place everyone at the long table, which she had set with Staffordshire porcelain and a profusion of small Miltonia orchids brought in from Hawaii.

The bride and groom, flanked by their attendants, were seated in the middle of the table on the east side of the room with the Gobelins tapestry as a backdrop. Aunt Louisa and Albert sat directly across from them on the west side, providing a sort of social counterpoint, while George Devonshire and Helen Bartley were seated respectively at the north and south ends of the table. This of course left Victoria in a rather awkward position, but Aunt Louisa solved this problem by giving Victoria the honor of sitting next to the Reverend Jonathan Willard. "They can bore each other," Aunt Louisa had commented the night before.

Compared with the reception that was to follow, the wedding breakfast provided an oasis of settled serenity. Bach and Handel patterned the air and played off the Venetian renaissance paneling, the string quartet having been discreetly moved into the hall and out of view. A splendid Bienvenie-Batard-Montrachet complemented the conversation, which was subdued and almost reverential, as if the breakfast was a continuation of the wedding ceremony itself.

Katherine and Patrick were particularly private, talking to each other in long smooth sentences. Aunt Louisa, who usually sparked conversations in every direction, seemed content to quietly hold court, watch Katherine and make the occasional comment in Albert's direction. She had ordered that no toasts be made until the wedding cake, thus allowing everyone to enjoy the meal uninterrupted by a lot of senseless babbling. Only poor Douglas Mackie was caught. He had made the fatal mistake of trying to explain the plot of *A Midsummer Night's Dream* to Beezie.

"But why did the Queen of the Fairies fall in love with a weaver wearing an Ass's head?" she giggled, sensing something spicy.

"Because Puck, the King's page, put the juice of 'Love's Idleness' into her eyes while she was sleeping," Doug tried to explain for the tenth time.

"But why would he do that?" Beezie puzzled.

"Because Shakespeare modeled the character of Puck on Albert," he said in a confidential sort of way.

"Oh," said Beezie, thinking for a moment, "I didn't know Shakespeare wrote the Wedding March."

Albert had overheard enough of the conversation to know that old Douggie had scored a point, but his lack of proximity prevented his getting into the game. Quite by chance, Albert happened to be looking in the direction of Phillip Addison when Doug began his explaining the effects of "Love's Idleness" to an enraptured Beezie.

"No, no, Beezie, just a drop of 'Love's Idleness' is enough to make all the lovers in the play switch their affections and fall for the most unlikely creatures and on the whole behave in a totally irresponsible manner."

"Ooh!" squealed Beezie, "That sounds like fun!"

"Yes, I thought you might think so. Anyway, you of all people can imagine the effect when the king's page put a drop into the queen's eyes."

For a reason Albert could not have explained, Addison had captured his full attention and he stared transfixed for an inordinate length of time at the godfather and President of McMasters Shipping until he felt the firm tug on his arm of an insistent Aunt Louisa. Awakening from his preoccupation, he fond half the table staring at him.

"Albert, are you quite all right?" Aunt Louisa was asking.

He turned and looked at her and she could tell she had drawn him back from another plane.

"What? Yes, quite. Just a drop would be enough," he answered, trying to focus simultaneously on what he had missed and on what it had been that had apprehended his attention so completely. But it had been lost in the moment.

It wasn't until the wedding cake was brought in that Albert again noticed Phillip Addison. He looked strained and Albert noticed a small twitch at the corner of his right eye. Albert wondered if he would make a toast. He elected not to, but sat fidgeting with his fork, an uneasy smile fixed across his face. Mike Bartley made the first toast, followed by George Devonshire and then Albert. Imbued with Aunt Louisa's rule, they kept them short. The cake, an ethereal three-tiered Gateau au Citron, was a triumph for Cook, who could now rest her tyrannical control over the kitchen.

Breakfast ran a little late, leaving Patrick and Katherine only half an hour to change while everybody else enjoyed a glass of champagne in the drawing room or wandered into the main hall and listened to the Bach. At precisely 1:14 Prentice informed Aunt Louisa that the bridge and groom were ready and the party filed out into the center court where the staff was lined up at attention to say their good-byes. Not much fuss was made. A few more strains of Mendelssohn, a little rice and Katherine and Patrick were safely away in the back seat of Aunt Louisa's car. Then Aunt Louisa and Albert climbed into her old Packard and, driven by an off-duty policeman, raced for the city.

Andrew had been instructed to drive slowly, thus allowing the guests at Treehaven the opportunity to arrive at the pier before the bride and groom.

Aunt Louisa passed Katherine and Patrick shortly after getting on the Bayshore but she prodded her poor officer to "break the damned speed limit and get there." She was successful and they arrived with a good five minutes to spare after taking their place on a slightly raised platform in the reception room.

CHAPTER 38

HE FESTIVITIES SURROUNDING the sailing were in marked contrast to the quiet family wedding at Treehaven. Over five hundred friends, politicians and employees wearing orchid leis awaited Katherine and Patrick's arrival in the luxuriously appointed McMasters Aloha Lounge, which had recently been redone in vivid reds, yellows and greens to resemble a tropical paradise. Palms and large stands of Anthurium were placed along the walls to add to the effect and Madame Ng had created a grotto at the end of the room with overarching trees and sprays of Cattleya orchids. It was all rather corny, but at the same time, great fun. A Mai Tai fountain had been constructed in the center of the room surrounding a statue of a Hawaiian maiden from whose voluptuous breasts a steady stream of Mai Tais poured forth, delighting Aunt Louisa and scandalizing Victoria.

As the wedding party arrived, the band struck up yet more Mendelssohn, and loud applause and cheers greeted Katherine and Patrick as they entered the room. Katherine had changed into a bright pink silk Dior suit, which she complimented with a white orchid lei and a big leghorn cartwheel hat with yards of pink satin streamers. She looked radiant beside Patrick, who wore a lightweight tropical suit.

"We'll never get out of here if we start a receiving line," Patrick said, looking out over the crowd. "I think we just better cut the cake."

"It looks like it was baked by the National Geographic Society," Albert remarked to Amy as they surveyed an enormous sheet cake decorated with the Hawaiian islands in relief.

"That chocolate cone shape which looks like it's erupting raspberry icing must be Kalauea. And look at the sugar model of the Princess Hena entering the Kawai channel. I've never seen anything so divinely bizarre in my life," she laughed.

Toasts were made, a soprano from the San Francisco Opera sang a rather structured rendition of the Hawaiian Wedding Song, and there were personal good-byes to family and close friends before boarding.

"All right, Mr. Bartley, you watch your okole now," Aunt Louisa teased.

"My what?"

"Your okole."

"I'm afraid I don't know what that is, Aunt Louisa," he confessed.

"Jeepers! You're in big trouble," Albert interjected, catching Katherine's puzzled expression. "You've married a man who doesn't know where to find his okole!"

"We'll work on that during the honeymoon," she said with a wink. "If he doesn't know in three or four days, I'll have the captain throw him overboard."

As everyone wished their alohas the bride and groom left the lounge and the band struck up "Aloha Oe." The entire party, many with tears in their eyes, either from romantic sentiment or too many Mai-Tais, joined in the chorus. From their private balcony above the promenade deck, Katherine and Patrick soon appeared to wave their own alohas of good-bye and throw streamers and confetti out to the host of well-wishers who accompanied the orchestra by singing "Sweet Leilani, Heavenly Flower". Katherine caught Albert's eye and threw a kiss.

"Aloha! Aloha no!" he yelled through a tumultuous noise.

It had been a fantastic day, a great week, and a splendid fall. But in a sense, Albert was glad to see Katherine and Patrick sail happily away. They all needed to rest, a space to put their lives back into perspective, a few moments uncrowded with decisions. Now that they were off to Hawaii, he thought perhaps he would go down to

Pebble Beach, or even the desert, or at least spend a week in Sausalito with Deirdre.

At exactly four p.m., with a blast from the ship's whistle, everyone again broke into a chorus of "Aloha." A chill of excitement mixed with joy and sadness ran through Katherine as the great white-hulled Princess Hena backed into steam away from the disappearing faces on the pier.

"I love you, Patrick Bartley," she said as he put his arm around her, gently giving her a reassuring hug and tender kiss. All along the waterfront, whistles gave the traditional three loud blasts, the wish for a good sailing, as the Princess Hena slowly headed out towards the Gate. The November air was sharp and clear and the dark blue of the white-capped bay lay in sharp contrast to the then clear-blue sky that stretched overhead into infinity. Telegraph Hill, the apartment, North Beach, Pacific Heights and the Presidio all slid slowly before them. With the sun now well into its westward retreat, the skyscrapers and mansions that ran over the hills and filled up the valleys turned pink and gold and gleaming. San Francisco seemed like Oz, Athens and Byzantium all rolled into one.

They sailed beyond the majestic Golden Gate and the rugged beauty of the Marin Headlands into the deep swells of the Pacific, where small fishing boats bobbed and chugged against the current. They passed the lonely Farallons inhabited only by egrets, gulls and cormorants and then sailed on into the glow of the setting sun. When the sun finally outdistanced the ship to disappear behind the rim of the Pacific, Katherine and Patrick also disappeared into their staterooms. At last they were alone beyond the reach of business problems and family complications. Katherine slipped into a cream silk peignoir as Patrick loosened his tie and popped the cork on a bottle of Mumm's champagne. As they lay together that first night, listening to the quiet creaking of the ship cutting through the water, they felt more at one than ever before.

For the first two days, Katherine and Patrick did not leave their rooms, preferring to take their meals alone and make love and sleep for long hours. They wrapped themselves in the luxurious security of each other's arms, preferring the silence of their own company to the gay parties that continually ran through the lounges and ballrooms on the lower decks. Only for brief intervals did they venture onto their private deck to take the ocean air. The days were cool and overcast, and the sea always seemed the same dull slate gray. By contrast, their newly decorated suite was done in warm shades of coral, lime-green and off-white, with large comfortable couches and chairs. In the sitting room, the hand-painted French wallpaper displayed an island landscape of palm, Kakui and Plumeria trees with extraordinarily plumed birds among ti leaves. Live tropical plants and delicate sprays of orchids were creatively arranged to extend the effect of a secluded tropical garden.

Yet as isolated and comfortable as Katherine and Patrick were, they could not entirely lock out the recent past. The accident continually loomed in their minds, as did Patrick's financial difficulties and Chambliss Horsley's malicious manipulations. "Other than that cock-and-bull story your aunt and uncle are feeding you about conditions in Argentina, I can't see why the others seem so desperate to get you to sell," Patrick said as they lay in bed together, staring up at the ceiling.

"It's Addison that keeps running through my mind," Katherine said. "That conversation he had with Broderick and then seeing Horsley and Broderick having lunch, I keep wondering about Broderick, too. I'm beginning to feel Aunt Louisa was right," she continued. "They're all a bunch of crooks." She paused for a moment and then added, "Except Addison. I think he is somewhat embarrassed, or trapped, or something. I just can't put my finger on it. He looked so sad at the wedding. There were tears in his eyes when he kissed me after the ceremony. She paused again and snuggled her head up closer under Patrick's arm. "Do you think there are some hidden assets that are not showing up on the books which would make the company worth more than the reports show?"

"I don't know. It sure sounds like it could be something like that," Patrick said, smiling to himself as he remembered how he had kicked the hell out of Horsley in his attempt to drive him under.

The Princess Hena had been converted from wartime use in 1949 at a cost of over twenty-one million dollars. Containing two royal stateroom suites, four hundred and ninety-two first class staterooms, and two hundred and thirty-four cabin class rooms, it was the pride of the McMasters fleet. For passenger comfort, Sperry Gyrofin stabilizers had been added to reduce the vessel's roll by over eighty percent. The outdoor swimming pool was surrounded by recreational verandas for shuffleboard, Ping-Pong and moonlight dances. The best naval architects had been employed to draw up plans for a ship with a streamlined profile that offered all the latest in modern design and speed.

On the third day out, they emerged from their cabin for an afternoon dip in the pool and in the evening, joined the captain for dinner in the King Liholiho Dining Room. The weather was growing warmer as they steamed into the lower latitudes and they spent more time reading on their private deck and taking midnight strolls around the ship.

On the fourth night, Captain Halversen gave a cocktail party in their honor. "I wonder if the officers call you Madame Admiral?" Patrick had teased.

After a number of rather stiff introduction a lady, whom Katherine had noticed the evening before, excused herself from a conversation and purposefully crossed the room to meet them.

"Katherine, I'm Lydia Holt," she said extending her hand. "I've been trying to find an opportunity to congratulate you on your marriage since we left San Francisco."

"How very kind," Katherine replied as she noted the lady's unusually striking appearance.

"My husband Zeke is an old friend of your uncle, George Devonshire. It seems they were at Stanford together and all. As a matter of fact, we just had dinner with Victoria and George about a week ago. And you are of course Patrick," Lydia continued, turning and again introducing herself. "I suppose you know George Devonshire is very fond of you."

"Gee, thanks," Patrick said, feeling a little embarrassed. "I'm very fond of them, too."

"Are you going to Hawaii for a holiday?" Katherine asked, trying to pick up the conversation.

"No, we live in Hawaii. My husband is a rancher. We usually try to get over to the mainland once a year."

"Your husband's a rancher?" Patrick interrupted, pleased at the prospect of finding a kindred spirit.

"Yes, we raise cattle on the Big Island. I'll go pull him away. I'm sure he would like to meet you."

Both Katherine and Patrick took an immediate liking to the Holts. Zeke Holt was a descendent of the early missionary families who had come from Boston in the early nineteenth century. He was a tall, dignified man with a full head of thick snow white hair; his face was brown and wrinkled from the sun and his eyes were patient and kind. Lydia Holt was similarly striking, tall and dignified. She pulled her salt-and-pepper hair onto the back of her head and fastened it there with a beautifully carved whalebone comb. Her full face and high cheekbones ensured an aristocratic beauty, while her slow graceful movement gave to her presence a rare Hawaiian charm. Like Zeke, Lydia was also a descendent from one of the first missionary families, but she also was one-eighth Hawaiian, a descendent from one of the great chiefs of the royal Hawaiian family.

But more than her appearance, Katherine sensed that Lydia possessed a beautiful soul, which seemed close to the surface of her world like a bee just within a flower.

They were up early the next morning to catch the first glimpse of the islands.

"I sailed once through the Greek islands, but this is very different," Katherine said as the Princess Hena steamed into the Kawai Channel between Molokai and Oahu.

"How do they compare?" Patrick asked, putting his arm around her shoulders as they watched an orange sun explode over the horizon and shoot the deep azure blue sky with warm light.

"I suppose they seem less stark and more mysterious somehow. In the Aegean, the islands stand out in rugged contrast to the sea, but here they seem to rise out of the ocean like great mounds covered in blue and green velvet."

Zeke and Lydia joined them in their suite for coffee and after stepped out on the deck to watch Diamond Head come into view. "According to legend those deep vertical ridges on the side of the volcano are the long canoes of raiding warriors," Lydia explained. "The warriors angered the fire goddess Pele when they put their canoes up to rest on her side. In a rage she erupted, causing their canoes to be sealed in lava forever."

"I hope not all Hawaiian women take after Pele," Patrick remarked.

"From my experience, just about all women do," Zeke said in a low confidential tone. "They're all capable of quick anger and fiery eruptions."

"I suppose that should be a lesson. Be careful where you park your canoe," Katherine said.

As they rounded Diamond Head, hundreds of small pleasure craft came out to meet them. Motorboats darted in and out among the outriggers and sailboats moved in long, feminine sweeps covering the sea with their graceful white sails. Dark-brown-skinned divers plunged off their canoes after coins thrown overboard by excited passengers. Retrieving their tribute between their grinning white teeth, they bobbed carefree in the swells, calling for the game to continue. Beautiful girls and plump older women wearing flowers in their hair laughed and waved welcome up at the haoles on their great white ship.

"What is that great pink palace among the palms?" Katherine asked as she looked down the long beach of Waikiki.

"The Royal," Lydia replied. "Isn't that where you said you were staying?"

Soon hula girls came on board, presented leis to the passengers and performed their graceful dances conveying a combination of innocence and sexuality. To everyone's delight, one girl pulled a middle-aged passenger from the crowd and tried to teach him the dance as his wife and friends howled in amusement at his awkward gesturing.

They came in gingerly and docked under the spire of the Aloha Tower. On the pier, more dancers awaited with leis and warm greetings of "aloha" while a tall Hawaiian dressed as King Kamehameha in a red and gold feathered cape, made an official greeting, presenting Katherine with a Pikaki lei, symbolizing royalty.

CHAPTER 39

*F*OR THE FIRST few days, Katherine and Patrick continued their honeymoon, preferring to remain in the luxurious seclusion of their suite until noon when they would emerge for a few hours to swim and walk the beach. Most of the tourists were gone, and Waikiki was beautiful as it stretched away from the stately charm of the Royal Hawaiian towards Diamond Head in the east. The beach was quiet, except for the tumble of the surf as it ran up the sand and retreated again into the sea. There was a clarity to the sea and sky that Katherine had never known. One evening in the twilight the Hawaiians call Molehu they walked down the beach and watched a fisherman standing motionless on a reef, ready to throw his net out to catch the akule or aholehole. He was in perfect harmony with his surroundings, and in the gathering darkness, seemed to blend into the sea and the mountains. There was magic in the tropical air that soothed away care. The sun was warm and the sea was like silk and nothing pressed for their attention but the love they had for each other. In that peace Katherine learned again that Patrick was an excellent lover. At times he was tender and romantic, while at other times he could be demanding and strong-willed. Each move excited and pleased her appetite for diversity. Yet he was never calculating or manipulative nor did he seem to pride himself in his performance. There were moments during these days when she wished that Patrick had been her first love. But these moments were infrequent. Most of the time she thought of him as the first, for he had truly been the first love to possess her completely, and she worshiped him with her soul as well as her body.

Unfortunately not all their time was free from business and on the third day they visited the McMasters branch office in downtown Honolulu where Preston Dexter, the branch manager, showed them around. He reminded Katherine of a squirrel as he hurried this way and that, his bright eyes popping nervously from his head.

"It seems that there is a need to simplify our overall rate structures," she commented to one of their agents who was a member of the New York Produce Exchange.

"That is one of our major obstacles, Mrs. Bartley," the agent commented.

"The problem of attracting more trade is a little more complicated than that," Dexter interrupted.

"I'm sure it is," replied Katherine, a little annoyed at his rudeness, "but I think you will agree that complex problems often need to be analyzed in part before one can arrive at a comprehensive solution."

"Yes, of course, Mrs. Bartley," he said, half apologetically. "I didn't mean to suggest otherwise."

"What do you think about the possibility of McMasters establishing an airline from the mainland?" she asked, attempting to get on with a more serious topic.

"It hasn't even been considered."

"Why not?"

"It was never considered to be profitable."

As she continued to ask questions she noticed that her branch manager seemed reluctant to discuss matters in much detail. In many ways, Katherine felt she was being put off in much the same way that she had been put off by Horsley. And when she asked to have a tour of the wharf, Dexter was particularly evasive. Katherine began to feel that he had been programmed by the home office to impress upon her the difficulty of running the line. "In 1949 the stevedore strike almost brought the entire economy of the islands to a standstill," he said as they ate lunch. "We lost 2,509 vessel days in that year alone, and last year we lost over 900 vessel days because of labor difficulties. The union has organized the sugar and pineapple industries as well as the longshoreman and warehouse workers. If they want to, they can withhold services in three interrelated areas."

Growing somewhat tired of the lecture, Patrick tried to shift the conversation back to the possibility of seeing the wharves, but Dexter would not be dissuaded. "Last June a Federal jury in Honolulu convicted seven Hawaiian Communist labor leaders of conspiracy. It was a seven month trial and Jack Hall, who is the regional director of the International Longshoremen's Union, was one of them. Over 2,000 ILWU dockworkers and about 22,000 ILWU sugar and pineapple plantation workers walked out. That was a hell of a tie-up. The unions wouldn't even load our ships headed for Korea with military supplies."

Over dinner that evening Katherine and Patrick talked about their impressions of Dexter. "He doesn't treat me with much more respect than Horsley," Katherine said. "I am tired of people trying to impress upon me how difficult it is to run a steamship line. I'm convinced it is a hard business, but they seem to want to pound it in."

"Didn't you tell me several weeks ago that your father had considered the possibility of starting an airline from the mainland?" Patrick asked, trying to recall the conversation.

"Yes, I found that very strange. When I asked Dexter about the airline he seemed emphatic that the idea had never been considered. Yet, I know Father started to investigate the possibility in the late forties. If he knows so much about the big strike in 1949, he must have known about the airline."

"How's that?"

"The project wasn't dropped until 1949 when they failed to gain approval from the Civil Aeronautics Board."

"Well, whatever Mr. Dexter's game is, I think it will have to wait," Patrick said as the lights dimmed and Hawaii's beloved Hilo Hattie appeared on stage in her outlandish muumuu to sing, "Cockeyed Mayor of Kaunakakai."

"Aloha, Kakahiaka," their guide Kana said when he picked them up the next morning. "You friend Zeke and Lydia. Today we go to Pali, No?"

"Yes, that's great!" Patrick said, shaking the old man's hand. "Zeke said we should go up and see the view. He says you're the best guide in Honolulu."

Kana laughed, causing his dark eyes to disappear under his slightly protruding brow ridge and white hair.

"Lokomaikaioe," he said. "We have good day. You bring swimsuit. We stop in Hanauma Bay."

As they drove around Diamond Head, Kana explained his connection to the Holts.

"I am a Kaamaaina. That mean half-Hawaiian and half-haole."

"What is a haole?" Katherine asked.

"You Haole. My father Haole ... Come to Hawaii as ship captain. He retire and live in Hawaiian way with my mother. He good friend to Zeke father. I know Zeke when he just Keiki. Zeke and I hoopile, good friends."

Kana showed them many delights. The multi-colored tropical fish in Hanauma bay, Koko Crater, the legendary vagina of Pele's sister and the Hibiscus, Oxora and Pentas that filled the countryside with their intense color. His English was understandable most of the time, but without a conscious effort, he lapsed into pigeon, which made his stories all the more interesting, if harder to follow. He was a crusty old fellow with bronzed leathery skin, white hair and a quick smile.

The view from the Pali was spectacular. The jagged Koolua cliffs profiled against the sky fell thousands of feet down to the verdant, gently rolling lands of the coastal shelf. They could see from Makapuu Point to the end of Kaneohe Bay. Clouds drifted below and moved up over the valley walls, dumping their moisture onto the steep cliffs. From the heights, the contrasts in the ocean was even more spectacular. Purples, greens, and ambers blended out into a depth of royal blue.

"Over this cliff Kamehameha drove enemies in 1795, when he conquer island of Oahu," Kana explained with the high winds gusting around them.

On the way back down, Kana stopped at Queen Emma's summer palace, built by King Kamehameha and his wife in 1843. "When Kamehameha the First unified islands, the role of women strictly regulated. Even most powerful of King's wives forbidden by Kapus to eat with men. There many Kapus in those days. Everything in life subject to the Kapus."

"What is this kapus?" Katherine asked, trying to grasp the story.

"Kapus like taboo. Kapus is law. Tell who have more power."

"And the women weren't allowed to eat with their husbands?"

"Women inferior to men. Common people could not mingle with great chiefs. Even to look upon highest chief was to have instant death from guards. High chief full of mana. Then in days of King Liholiho, son of Kamehameha, everything change. Liholiho weak. His mother, Keapuolani, joined with Kaahumanu, favorite wife of Kamehameha. They hold big feast of forbidden food. They force Liholiho to eat with them. When earth not tremble, old ways died. Women become more equal to men."

"I hope you're taking all this down, Mr. Bartley!" Katherine teased as Kana finished his history.

"He said more equal to men, not equal," Patrick replied giving Kana a friendly nudge.

Kana laughed. "Auwenohoie! Auwenohoie! I make trouble. You be careful. You no want to make wahine angry. She your ipo."

Old Kana told them many stories about the Hawaiian gods, Kani the Supreme God represented by the sun, and Lono, who was responsible for the fertility of the earth and Ku, the god of power and force. "There are thousands of gods and spirits. Each type rain has own god, and winds, lagoons, valleys, mountains. In old days, only the Alii, the high priest, talk with great gods."

That night Katherine was filled with dreams. Terrifying gods haunted the shadows of the valley rain forest. Alone and afraid, she tried to hide beneath a towering palm. She covered herself with ti leaves, but she could hear the pounding of drums as warriors of Ku searched for her, coming closer up the valley towards her hiding place. She reached up to pull more leaves over her, and in doing so, dislodged a white orchid, which fell on her head. She could feel her heart beating faster. It seemed to out beat the drums that came up through the valley. Her veins coursed with fire and the ti leaves dropped away. Suddenly she became Madame Pele, her red hair flowing wildly in the winds over the Pali. She could feel herself growing at will up through the towering forest until she was above the highest palm. Below she could see the frenzied warriors on the forest floor. She became enraged and they vanished.

Early in the morning of their sixth day they flew off to the big island of Hawaii on one of the company's small twin-engine planes. Brad Garrick, the pilot, had been born in Hawaii of Mormon missionary parents. He was a clean-cut sandy haired young man with a quick smile and a can-do attitude. Taking off from Honolulu, Brad flew past the island of Molokai where the Belgian priest, Father Damien spent his life with the lepers. They flew over the island of Maui, with its quaint nineteenth-century whaling village of Lahaina and the large dormant volcano, Haleakala, which rose ten thousand feet above the ocean. "The Hawaiians believe that the god Maui hid in the rain forests for many years until the sun came out. When it did, he lassoed it and tied it down so it could not move and he would not let it go until the sun promised to move slowly across the sky. That is why we live in the eternal summer," Brad explained as he dipped the plane to give them a better view.

Landing in Hilo they were met by the company representative, Jack Dunston; a thin, bald-headed man in his mid-fifties who wore a white straw hat, light blue denim suit and a conservative black tie. It was raining heavily when they arrived and Dunston gave them each an umbrella to keep off the "liquid sunshine". They settled into their hotel overlooking Hilo Bay and Coconut Island, had lunch with Mr. Dunston, and then drove out to visit the pier where they watched a large McMasters C-3 type freighter being loaded with raw sugar. "This is the fastest of the sixteen freighters in the fleet," Dunston explained. "These freighters have been in service for about five years now. They have cut the sailing time between the islands and Los Angeles by about thirty percent. It used to take a good six to seven days, but now they can make it in five and a half."

As they stood on the wharf, Katherine remembered Lydia Holt talking about an orchid nursery near Hilo that was worth seeing. Reaching into her purse, she pulled out a notepad and found the name, Lehua Nursery. "Do you know the Lehua Nursery?" she asked after Dunston finished explaining about the freighters and sailing time. For a moment a puzzled look came over his face and he seemed hesitant. "Yes," he said finally. "It is only a few miles out of town."

"It was recommended to us by friends," Katherine continued. "If it isn't too much trouble, I'd think we'd like to have a look."

The rain had stopped, the sun was making his scheduled appearance, and the air smelled moist and clean as they drove north of town to the Lehua Commercial Gardens. Acres of orchids greeted them on their tour. Beds of white, pink, mauve, magenta and chartreuse bandaceous orchids delighted Katherine before they moved into the thermostatically controlled greenhouses where more delicate specimens were raised. Emerging from the last greenhouse, their guide showed them the cloth covered sheds where hardier breeds were grown.

"In this shed we raise the Paphiopedilum, or slipper orchids," she said as she opened the door to allow Patrick and Katherine to step forward. Within the cloth shed, Katherine found herself confronted with thousands of the strange little orchids that she had come to know only too well. This was the same orchid Addison had kept beside her mother's picture on the piano, it was the orchid by the dragon in the sixth alcove of Treehaven, and it had been the orchid beside the opium pipe on the houseboat in Sausalito. "What a strange, awful little plant," Katherine said to Patrick. "They look like so many little cobras ready to strike."

As their guide trailed off into a lengthy explanation of how orchids were classified into sub-tribes, genera and species, Katherine noticed a strange feeling come over her that she did not quite understand, and thus dismissed without further thought. But she did remember her conversation with Aunt Louisa about orchids having a quality of character, and she knew she had somewhere deep within her an unexplainable aversion to this hooded little plant with terrestrial habits.

"The habitat of the slipper orchid ranges from the Himalayas through Southeast Asia to New Guinea, but most are found in Thailand and Burma," the guide explained as they walked down the narrow aisles of the cloth shed. "This is a favorite orchid of the nursery's owner, and we have tripled our growing area for this species in the last few years. The name Lady Slipper, or slipper orchid, is derived from the pouch which is formed by the two petals joining together at the front of the flower."

"Who is the owner?" Patrick asked, attempting to change the conversation.

"The owner of Lehua Nursery is a Margaret Ng. She lives in San Francisco and runs one of the finest florists on the West Coast. Perhaps you have heard of her?"

For a moment Patrick and Katherine looked at each other in utter amazement. They could not believe the coincidence. How strange it was that no one had thought to mention the nursery before they sailed. "Surely Aunt Louisa or Aunt Victoria would have mentioned something," Katherine said as they moved across the lawns towards the shipping department.

"Did they know we were flying over to the big island?" Patrick asked, searching for a possible explanation.

"Yes, I'm sure that Joan Bywater sent our itinerary at least a week before the wedding. Perhaps they just didn't read it closely or forgot it in all the confusion."

Still amazed at the coincidence, they toured the potting sheds and shipping departments.

"Here we place our orchids in a specially prepared mixture of perlag and perlite," their guide explained as Patrick reached down to feel the thermally processed volcanic rock. "We also use charcoal, fern bark and sand to give our orchids just the right amount of material upon which to grow."

In another small building, Chinese and Filipino workers pressed tree fern fiber into small figure totems which were used to support the heavier orchid plants. In the last building orchids were being carefully placed into boxes and packed in rice husks for shipment to the mainland.

With the tour of Lehua Nursery over, they thanked their guide, and rejoined Dunston, who waited in the car. Turning out of the long driveway, which led to the gardens, Patrick noticed a small sign posted on a gate just across the road. "Broderick Ranch. Private Property. No Trespassing."

"Look Katherine," he said, pointing to the gate. "There's another coincidence for you. I wonder if the rancher is related to our San Francisco Broderick?"

Dunston did not seem to know anything about the ranch or its owner. "I'm not sure exactly who Mr. Broderick is," he said before changing the subject back to the scenery.

That night Katherine dreamed about her wedding. She could see the orchids covering the mantles and tables at Treehaven and Madame Ng arranging them the day before. Then Hilo Hattie joined the wedding, but her dance was not friendly. The movement of her hands had an ominous quality about them, as if she were casting a spell. As she danced, the hibiscus in her hair became a cluster of three slipper orchids and her grass skirt a black silk sheath embroidered with a fierce dragon. It was Ng, not Hilo Hattie, who danced through Aunt Louisa's conservatory among the viper-like orchids that hung from the ceiling. Addison appeared standing at a doorway. Looking much like a ghost, caught between the dance and the hallway beyond he was unable to move. His face was sober and gray like death. Standing just behind him was a woman shimmering and gossamer and transparent like the winter sun through stained glass. Katherine could not make out who she was.

The following morning they drove from Hilo to Wainea along the high Hamakua coast. There was a gentle rain as they made their way north past the sugar plantations and the rich exotic plant life. Bamboo groves, fern forests, and orchids crowded the road. In the old plantation town of Paauilo they stopped for gas and macadamia nuts. After Honakaa, they started to climb up the Waimea Plateau, leaving the lush vegetation of the rain-drenched coast behind.

"In many ways this reminds me a little bit of Napa," Patrick commented as the dense foliage gave way to grasslands dotted with eucalyptus trees.

To the north the Kohalo mountains and to the south, the steep slopes of Mauna Kea provided dramatic relief.

About two o'clock in the afternoon, Patrick turned off the main road onto the Holt's Mauka Ranch. Lydia was waiting on the broad veranda of the great white rambling Victorian ranch house. "Hele Mai! Nou Ka Lale!" ("Come in—the house is yours") she said as she greeted them with plumeria leis. For a while they sat on the lanai sipping a fruit concoction, relating their day with Kana and enjoying the cool of the deep veranda, set as it was under the flowering branches of Jacaranda and Plumeria trees.

The main house was a unique combination of the New England and the native. From its outward appearance, it could have easily been placed anywhere on Cape Cod, but the interior contained beautifully crafted koa wood paneling and museum quality artifacts, which coexisted in a harmony with other large Victorian pieces. Sharkskin drums were used as tables and native bowls held fresh flowers. The library contained a splendid display of Hawaiian art, with a large collection of carved household gods standing around the room on tables and shelves.

"These were the royal capes made from the neck plumage of Hawaiian birds," Lydia explained showing Katherine and Patrick the two life size statues of old warriors that stood by the door. "Unfortunately the birds are now extinct," she continued as Patrick examined the helmets and carved weapons that adorned the two ancient guardians.

"Why? Were they all killed off?" Katherine asked, feeling the loss of such beauty.

"Yes. I'm afraid they were unable to compete with species that arrived with the white man. Much of what was old Hawaii is gone forever."

Lydia Holt took special pride in her display of Hawaiian anklets and necklaces, made from corals, bones and shells, and she took time to explain how each piece was made and its particular significance. There was something in her manner that inspired a sort of awe in Katherine. Perhaps, she thought, it was the strange combination of a family who had mixed the European virtues of industry and ethics with the Hawaiian appreciation for poetry and time. It was a beautiful combination, but Katherine wondered if perhaps it might only survive when nurtured in the very rare environment of the islands.

Zeke joined them, and for the next several hours, along with Lydia, he gave them a horseback tour over part of the 1,000,000-acre ranch. His new prize was a Santa Gertrude's bull, a cross between a shorthorn and a Brahman. "This type of cattle has all the heat-resistant hardiness of a Brahman, and the high beef production of the shorthorn," he explained. "They're doing amazing things with breeding nowadays which will make ranching in the tropics much less risky. There is even a new cow, a cross between the Red Sindhi and a Jersey. It is supposed to be a great milk producer for tropical areas."

"Will that significantly change the value of ranch land in Hawaii?" Patrick asked, unable to contain his instinct for the possibility of a good real estate deal.

"Oh, it might," said Zeke. "But there are so many other factors that will probably inflate prices over the next several decades, the increased dairy and beef production is probably not much of a long-range factor. Pineapple and sugar production, along with tourism, are probably more important for our long-range economic growth."

"Do you know the Broderick who owns some land out by the Lehua Nursery?" Patrick asked, recalling the sign he had noticed the day before.

"I don't know him personally, but rather by reputation. He has been buying up land near Hilo for several years now, and I have heard he's acquired a few small coffee plantations on the Kona coast. He's supposedly from San Francisco and from what I've heard, not the most savory person to deal with."

Katherine caught Patrick's eye for a brief moment, but she did not want to say anything, which might interrupt Zeke Holt's train of thought.

"How do you mean?" Patrick questioned.

"In the first place, he is a partner of a Madame Ng, who owns the Lehua Nursery, and that alone is enough to ward me off."

Without much further prodding, Zeke and Lydia revealed their distaste for Madame Ng. They accused her of bringing in slave labor from Hong Kong and corrupting both the Chinese and Filipino workers she employed. "Some Hawaiians say she sells her workers opium to keep them living under subsistent conditions. Understand, we have never met the lady in question," Zeke concluded, "but word gets around."

Patrick pulled his horse to a stop and turned in the saddle to look Zeke squarely in the eyes. "You probably have met her and didn't even know it," he said, watching Zeke's expression. "She did the flowers for our wedding and was at the lounge for the reception," Katherine added, feeling again the strange, almost threatening force of the woman who had always made her feel a bit uneasy.

"She is a close friend of both Aunt Victoria's and Aunt Louisa's," Katherine continued. "I don't think they ever give a large party without engaging her."

"Oh, I'm sorry," Lydia apologized, "we didn't know—"

"That's all right," Patrick explained, waving his hand to discount Lydia's need for an apology.

"I knew there was something about that woman that I didn't trust," Katherine interjected. "And she is in partnership with Broderick, you say? I wonder—" she paused, deep in thought.

For a moment everything seemed connected. Yet she could not place those connections into an overriding pattern. She had instinctively disliked both and to have a confirmed connection between them alarmed her.

Lydia could see the troubled expression in Katherine's face, and again tried to apologize for the unpleasant subject, but Katherine explained that it was on the contrary, very fortunate to have gathered such information. "It's strange," she said, "that our Hilo representative, Jack Dunston, didn't know anything about the Broderick that owned the ranch."

"Oh, I'm sure he does," Zeke interrupted. "This may be a big island, but with so few people, word gets around. He would know about Ng and the Lehua Nursery, too. From what I've heard, the two of them have been trying to sell a lot of their holdings over the last two months."

By the time they returned to the ranch house, it was close to six o'clock. While Katherine changed into a pair of Givenchy high-waisted pants and a fluffy blouse, Patrick recalled their conversation and wrote a brief memorandum.

"I don't like it," Patrick confessed as Katherine sat down to brush her hair. "Ng and Broderick in cahoots! I think we are up against something much bigger than we thought. The fact that Jack Dunston covered for Broderick means there's a pretty big organization out there. With the accident and all, I just don't like it."

"I know. It frightens me, too. I don't feel I trust anyone anymore."

"I wonder if there are hidden assets in Hawaii?" he puzzled as he fastened the clasp on a strand of pearls and kissed her behind the ear.

"I don't know," Katherine sighed, content with his show of affection. "I thought we came to Hawaii to have a honeymoon, and here we are, discussing business."

"You're right," Patrick said, slamming closed his notebook and putting it back into the suitcase. "We'll kick this around some other day. They'll wait."

After dinner Patrick and Zeke retired back to the lanai to share an after dinner brandy. Katherine and Lydia strolled across the manicured lawns to where a large Hawaiian woman sat under a Breadfruit tree, softly humming a simple melody and watching a little girl who played at her feet. Judging from her white hair, she was well beyond childbearing years, and Katherine assumed the little girl was her granddaughter. Lydia greeted the woman, whose name was Ewa, and then in a pigeon English that was barely understandable, introduced Katherine. Ewa looked up slowly with eyes that smiled from a full, round dark face. "Aloha ahiahi," she said, opening her hand as a sign of greeting.

"Aloha," Katherine smiled. "How old is your granddaughter?"

"This my daughter," Ewa said with great pride as she looked at the little girl sitting naked in the fading light and playing with a coconut which had been carved with an fanciful face.

As they walked back to the main house, Katherine laughed. "I think we lost something in translation. How do you say 'grandchild' in Hawaiian?"

Lydia smiled, understanding Katherine's confusion. "Moopuna is Hawaiian for grandchild, but that was not the woman's grandchild. She thinks of her as her own daughter, although she didn't actually give birth to her. The little girl was born to her daughter, Momi."

"So that would make her a granddaughter," Katherine insisted.

"Well, not really, because Momi was not really her daughter, either, but her hanai daughter. She was her brother's daughter, and Ewa asked for her at birth and raised her as her own daughter. It's all very complicated for a non-Hawaiian to understand. Hawaiians have a very broad inclusive sense of family, and they often give their children to be raised by another family member. They call these children 'hanai' children. When the Haole tries to understand using our genealogical system, they become completely confused." She paused for an instant before going on. "You know, come to think of it, I don't even think her brother, Hale is really her brother." She looked as if she were trying to pull memories out of the distant past. "I think her real brother's name was Kome. He moved down to Kawachae years ago, but as far as I can remember, I never heard her speak of him. I don't think they knew each other particularly well. She never knew her father, either, but her hanai father was very dear to her."

"She never had any children, then?" Katherine asked, feeling sorry for the old lady whose fate it seemed, was always to raise other people's children.

"Oh, heavens, yes! She had eight altogether. But she only raised five. One died, and the others she gave to her sister."

For a while they were quiet as they turned to watch the sun plunge beyond the horizon. Katherine wondered about the culture she found so foreign in so many ways. It seemed to run on an entirely different set of rules and relationships. Yet on reflection, she realized her own life had been one of a hanai child who really did not know her mother or father. It seemed to ease the little bit of guilt she harbored for not mourning more over her father's death. She thought also of Aunt Gloria and the large Hawaiian woman who sat under the bread fruit tree and she thought how lucky the little girl was that sat in the dusk playing with her coconut.

"My ancestors came here as missionaries to civilize the natives," Lydia said as they climbed the steps of the main house. In many ways, I suppose they succeeded splendidly. In other ways, I often think the natives ended up civilizing us. Their values are often closer to what God intended than the values imposed by our missionary forebears. Sometimes it amuses me. The idea, that is, that missionaries tried so diligently to bring paradise to paradise."

The next morning Katherine and Patrick were up early. After a light breakfast of papaya and toast, they said their alohas to Lydia and Zeke and drove down to Kawaihae on the Kona coast. At Kawaihae they turned south towards Kailua, where Zeke had arranged a chartered boat for deep-sea fishing. The Kona coast, protected as it is from the trade winds by the great Mauna Loa volcano, was a sharp contrast to the lush eastern side of the island. This was the home of Pele, the fire goddess, who still occasionally breathed fire from the active volcanos and appeared to travelers along windy roads. Broad stretches of desolate lava covered the land, but the sand beaches were exquisite and the coral reefs teeming with tropical fish, had made this coast a favorite playground for Hawaiian royalty.

"There's supposed to be a temple built by King Kamehamiha in 1791 somewhere along this road," Katherine said, as she read a book she had borrowed from Lydia. "We just passed Kawaihue, didn't we?"

"About two miles back," Patrick grunted.

"Evidently Kamehameha built the temple in obedience to a prophecy that it would help him gain victory over rival islands. It says that he helped fulfill the prophecy by slaying one of his chief enemies at the dedication."

"Ah," said Patrick as he continued along the road. "I think we'll skip the temple. I'm going marlin fishing, in case you don't remember."

"Yes, I do remember, Mr. Bartley. Thank you very much," Katherine snapped, annoyed at his tone.

"I'm sorry," he said, "but we can't do everything and I've had enough of Kamehameha to last a lifetime."

They rode on in silence for a while, and by mid-morning they were on the wharf at Kailua. The fishing was everything Zeke Holt had said it was. They trolled for a while in the warm sun, eating sandwiches, drinking beer, and admiring the beauty of the great island mountains that rose out of the sea and looked blue and serene in the distance. Soon the afternoon clouds came over to shield them from the hot sun. Katherine found herself nodding off to sleep, slowly rocked by the gentle sea. Suddenly she was startled out of her dreamy state by excited voices.

"Au wenohoie!! Kaohinaioe!!" The Hawaiians yelled as they strapped Patrick into a chair at the stern.

"I have a strike!" he yelled as he watched a big Pacific blue marlin leaping between the waves before exploding out hundreds of yards in a run for life. The battle, which raged on for over two hours, was exhilarating. Patrick's rod arched and shuddered with the strength of the fighting marlin. Katherine could see the intense pleasure in his eyes. There was something very sensual about the fight between man and fish, and Katherine retired to observe the long struggle from a distance. Patrick's clothes were soaked with sweat, as he played his fish and Katherine watched his muscular body strain and pull as the engagement reached its climatic stage. When the battle was over, Patrick had landed a 450-pound marlin, and with it, the unmatchable primitive peace that comes to the hunter when he has succeeded in gaining the object of his quest. Patrick leaned back against the side of the boat, sipped a beer and admired his prize under the screams of gulls and boobies that darted overhead. Katherine sat down beside him, put her arm around his neck and rested her cheek on the top of his curly dark hair. Neither of them spoke. The marlin, the sea and the beauty of the island, was enough.

As the boat pulled alongside the pier, there was great excitement as the Hawaiians gathered around to watch the great trophy hung by its tail for pictures. It was the end of the fishing day, and several smaller boats were already in with the scad, manini, and parrot fish. Large, round-faced women in their loosely-fitting muumuus laughed and talked as they divided the catch, ignoring the men who had supplied the bounty. Most of the women were not even related to the fishermen. This was the Hawaiian way. The sea was generous and supplied enough for everyone, and they all shared in the gifts, because they were all related to the sea. At the end of the pier, an enormous, fuzzy-haired grandfather sat cross-legged, mending his nets, his thick arms working skillfully around his extended stomach. He looked up and grinned warmly as a woman laid a fish at his feet.

That evening a great luau was given in their honor. Early in the morning villagers had split open a pig, filled it with hot bricks, and wrapped it in taro leaves before burying it to cook through the day. Yams, pineapples, and shredded salmon mixed with onion, were spread out on tapa cloth, as saronged women with hibiscus in their hair, served rum punch in hollowed bamboo sections. With the soft notes of the ukulele the sun went down through the line of coconut and houla palms into a fiery black satin sea. Katherine and Patrick strolled along the beach late that night and in the quiet rhythm of the surf, they could imagine the ghosts of old Hawaiian warriors marching across the lava beds, their spears and brown bodies gleaming in the moonlight. They could see the chiefs wearing gold feathered capes, and they could hear the ancient chants accompanying the distant beat of drums. It was as if they were caught out of time. The islands had finally won. Their need for order and abstract reference surrendered to the uncluttered gentle poetry of the native mind.

The next morning Brad was waiting with the plane when they arrived at the small airport nine miles out of town and they flew the two hundred and fifty miles northwest to the garden island of Kauai.

"You'll be here for only one day and one night, so I'm flying you around the entire island," Brad said, dipping his wings. "That's the Napali coast down there."

"Look at that, Patrick!" Katherine exclaimed peering down at the roaring surf that gathered in great swells and came charging at the shore in a boiling crash of white swirling foam.

"Those cliffs are two thousand seven hundred feet up," Brad explained, obviously delighted at the thrill he was giving his passengers. He turned the plane south and flew down the length of the 3,600-foot Waimea Canyon, with its amethyst and greens and browns ever changing in the changing light. To the east, Mount Waialelae rose over 5,000 feet, lost in the dark clouds which surrounded the top. A rainbow appeared and disappeared and reappeared again in yet another place, as if the gods were playing jump rope.

"We'll be touching down near Lihue in a few minutes," Brad told them as he brought the plane in over Port Allen where a freighter was unloading cargo and taking on pineapples for the West Coast.

"After our experience in Honolulu and Hawaii, I'm glad we told your company representatives to take a hike," Patrick said as they left the airport and drove north towards the Cocoa Palms. "What we need to do is find a local guide."

"Someone like Kana," Katherine added.

As fate or the gods would have it, they found an old Hawaiian named Ekewaka not far from the hotel. He had been resting beneath a plumeria tree when they stopped to view the Wailua River and Patrick had struck up a conversation. He was a toothless, wrinkled old man, but there was a wise ageless dignity about him, which held Katherine's attention. The more he talked, the more entrancing he seemed to be.

"You need guide, so you see island," he said, looking at Katherine through hauntingly soft eyes, which possessed a warm life-giving quality like sunshine on a deep forest pool.

Before they knew it, they had engaged his services. "Aloha nui kakou, a big welcome to you," he said when they met after lunch in the hotel lobby. "Come, I show you my garden."

They drove about ten minutes and turned up a dirt path that took them to a small house about two hundred yards off the main road. "Come, I show you my garden," Ekewaka said, getting out of the car. The garden, which surrounded a simple one-room shack, provided an extraordinary, display of exotic plants that seemed almost surrealistic in size and intensity of color. Ekewaka moved through his garden with great care and reverence and Katherine felt as though he was bestowing a special honor by bringing them there. "How perfectly lovely," Katherine said as she stopped in admiration.

"You must spend a lot of time working in your garden, to get such wonderful results."

Ekewaka smiled knowingly. "Not much time. This is Lono's garden."

"Lono?" Katherine asked, wondering if perhaps the old man had a wife.

"Lono is god of growing things," Ekewaka said very simply. "This is a favorite garden of Lono. Everything grows here." He went on to explain how everything that was created had mana, the impersonal force, which flows through the world. "Some people and places have more mana, just as some clouds carry more rain than other clouds. My grandfather was a great priest, a Kahuna of the old way. He lived here, as did his father before. This is a sacred spot, full of power." He paused for a moment, as if to ponder the very words he had spoken. Then quite unexpectedly he looked at Patrick in a strange sort of way. "You want to have children with your wife?" he asked. The question surprised Patrick and made him feel a little self-conscious.

"We were just married a few weeks ago," he said nervously.

At this Ekewaka smiled warmly. "Come. I show you Pohaku-Ho-O-Hanau."

After a short drive they reached a sacred spot where royal Hawaiian women came to give birth to their children. Climbing to the top of a hill, they reached the bell stone, which had been used in the old days to announce the birth of royal children "Come," Ekewaka said, reaching out and taking Katherine's hand. "You touch stone." His manner was so kind and unassuming that Katherine felt quite comfortable as the old man guided her hand to the stone. "Come," he said to Patrick. "You touch stone."

Patrick hesitated, not quite understanding what this eccentric old man wanted. But Ekewaka motioned and Patrick complied with the wish and laid his hand on the stone beside Katherine's. For a moment he thought he saw Ekewaka's lips moving. Then Ekewaka smiled. "Now you have many children," he said with a note of reassurance. "Come. I show you more Kauai."

They spent the rest of the afternoon touring the old temple refuge where Hawaiians who had broken a taboo could find safety. They listened to Ekewaka tell about the different Hawaiian gods and the Menehune, the little people who were responsible for events that could not be explained. They went up the Wailua River to a fern grotto and ended the day with a swim on a beach that was not far from their hotel. Ekewaka accompanied them and sat for a while under a palm, while Patrick and Katherine played in the surf. But when they had finished their swim and came back up the beach, Ekewaka was gone. He seemed to have vanished into thin air, and they could not find him anywhere, nor did they see him again. "What an odd little man," Katherine said as they walked back to the Cocoa Palms. I'm not sure why, but I found him utterly charming."

As evening came on, conch shells were sounded towards the cool mountains that stood silhouetted against the improbable purple twilight, and as drums began to beat the ceremonial lighting of torches commenced. Young Hawaiian men dressed in sarongs ran out through the swaying palm grove carrying fire into the soft darkness.

Patrick made love to Katherine that night. He came to her again and again, awaking their passion anew each time he touched her. Having achieved the moment when their souls and bodies became one, they fell into a twilight of dreams. The god Lono appeared to them in an unknown garden and spread a tapa cloth before their feet and bid them to lay down beneath green palms that swayed in gentle contemplation of an overarching sky.

CHAPTER 40

As the Princess Hena had backed into steam and Katherine and Patrick had faded out of sight on their way to Hawaii, the farewell reception broke up. Andrew drove Aunt Louisa and Ivy home to Treehaven, Thomas drove the Devonshires home to the Devons, and Albert caught a cab with Chow-Ling up to Telegraph Hill. By the time he walked into the apartment, the Princess Hena was just under the Golden Gate. He felt tired and a little sad as he watched his beloved cousin disappearing in the gathering twilight. They had been so close and through so much in the last months. But beyond the sadness there was a deeper joy that she was happy and safe with Patrick. He knew Katherine needed Patrick's strength and he smiled to himself as he thought how Hawaii would encompass and soothe their souls with its incomprehensible beauty.

Albert woke the next Monday to a drippy, cold November day. It had rained a little in the night, and the bay was gray under a low, dark sky. He could hear the scream of the seagulls as they swirled around the apartment and down over the wharf. He thought of Deirdre and a fire in the cottage in Sausalito, and the garden with the fresh smell of eucalyptus and pine after the rain.

"I think I'm going to stay for a couple of days," he said when he walked in and found Deirdre painting in the kitchen by the small pot-bellied stove.

"Good," she said, looking up and smiling. "It was predicted."

"I thought it might have been. I'll change into cords and my old Pendleton and then go down and get some groceries. Do you need anything?"

"Coffee, firewood, food for the cat. If you don't find it, I'll give him a rat!"

By the time Albert came down through the back garden, it had begun to rain again. Deirdre lay on a rug by the fireplace, her shoulders propped up against an overstuffed pillow. Her dark devouring eyes watched him carefully as he slowly placed each piece of wood in the fireplace.

It was good to be back with Deirdre. Sometimes he did not realize how much he missed her. After he had placed the last log she reached up and pulled him down, kissing him fully on the mouth. Albert smiled and as the wood began to crackle Deirdre unbuttoned his shirt and ran her fingers up his back until he gave way and lay face down on the floor. Gently, very gently, she began to massage his body; her artistic hands treating his flesh like sculpting clay. With the end of the summer's tanning oil she massaged his taut back and sinewy thighs. He moaned now and then as she pulled the tension from him.

As the logs began to split in the leaping delight of the flames, she coaxed him over. There was just enough oil left and she warmed it in her hands before smoothing it on his chest and arms. Then climbing on top she slowly surrounded him; and imitating the consuming fire, burned out his desire.

"You make love like Doris Day," he teased as they moved towards the bedroom.

Deirdre smiled and crawled under the goose down comforter and held out her arms. Albert accepted the invitation and pulled the comforter up around them.

For several days Albert stayed in the cottage, resting, enjoying the warmth of the fire, and reading a new biography of Caruso. But throughout these days he found his concentration broken by the haunting theme of Mendelssohn. Unsolicited it sprang up from his subconscious and he would catch himself humming the tune at the most inopportune moments. At first he did not think about it, then he put it off to the happy memory of the wedding, but after a few days it began to annoy him like an unwanted guest who stays too long. When he found the melody invading his dreams, he became irritated. The sun finally broke through, casting rays of reflected light upon the dark surface of the bay. He emerged from his hibernation, hoping that fresh air and sunlight would exorcise the music from his soul. In mid-afternoon, when the streets were half dry, he walked along Buckley to the corner of Harrison and found the great granite bench dedicated to Daniel O'Connell, the unofficial poet laureate of Sausalito. O'Connell's Bench was filled with fond memories of childhood. On numerous occasions, he had accompanied his grandfather there to see the splendid view of the bay with the Chaparral slopes of Angel Island in the distance. A few brave sailboats tacked in and out of the dark shadows caused by the interplay of the last rain clouds and the cold rays of the November sun. He sat for a long time bundled warmly in his old wool Navy jacket, enjoying the cool crisp freshness of the air. The events of the preceding week came into mind and they seemed more detached from time now that he had come away from them.

The next morning the Princess Hena would be coming around Diamond Head, and Albert wondered if Katherine and Patrick were able to put aside all the problems that had crowded in on them before the wedding. The accident made him cringe. How close they had all come to being killed. An uneasy feeling settled over him like the dark clouds that shifted over the city. "My mind is troubled, like a fountain stir'd, and I myself see not the bottom of it," he thought to himself, remembering a quote from "Troilus and Cressida". The accident haunted him. The treachery of Horsley was obvious, but was he the kind to involve himself in attempted murder? That did not seem likely. Neither did Addison seem a possible candidate, but why had he seemed so shaky at the wedding? Why had he acted so strangely to the news of the autopsy and what had Madam Ng been lecturing him about in the hall at Treehaven? And there was Addison's conversation with Broderick, and Broderick's meeting with Horsley at Tadich's. There were many connections to consider, and Broderick seemed always to be lurking somewhere on the fringe.

By the time he arrived back at the cottage, Albert had decided to try and locate Rigg and Ogden. They might be able to help him sort through the perplexing labyrinth of interconnecting relationships. Unfortunately, Ogden was not anywhere to be found and after searching for the better part of the afternoon, Albert was told by locals that Ogden had probably gone off to either Arizona or Mexico for the sun.

Rigg, however, was in Sausalito living on a yacht he was restoring for a Sunday sailor from St. Francis Woods. Albert went over that evening with a bottle of wine and found Rigg depressed and very drunk.

"What's the matter, man?" he asked, examining the empty bottles on the table.

"Deep within the first dead lies London's daughter.
  Robed in the long friends,
  The grains beyond age, the dark veins of her mother
  Secret by the unmourning waters
  Of the riding Thames
  After the first death, there is no other,"

Rigg quoted in majestic melancholy as he poured a water glass full of vodka and pushed it towards Albert.

"Yeah, I know," said Albert. "Dylan Thomas."

"Died Monday. Fuckin' brain hemorrhage!"

"How long you been drinking?"

"Who gives a fuck?"

It took Albert several drinks to place himself somewhere near Rigg's frame of reference. He too, mourned Dylan Thomas and he aided Rigg's mourning by reciting several lines of "Do Not Go Gentle Into That Good Night". When he had finished, there was a long pause, and Rigg reached into his sea bag and pulled out an opium pipe.

"Where do you get that shit, anyway?" Albert asked, refusing the offer.

"That depends on who you are," Rigg smiled. "I get it from people I know. There's a hell of a lot more morphine and opium coming into San Francisco than they think. People have friends around the wharf. It's easy. Of course, there are other sources for the highfalutin' bourgeoisie like your friend Beezie, Christ, what a tremendous screw."

"I should have known," Albert said with an irrepressible smile. "What happened?"

"She called me after we all met at the Buena Vista. She came on with this line about how interesting it was learning to drink tequila sangrita and how she had always been fascinated by the sea. I knew she wanted to screw, so I asked her over to see the boat. She's a tiger in the bunk, but God, she's a dumb broad. I had a hell of a time getting her out of here the next morning."

"What do you mean, sources of opium for people like Beezie?" Albert asked, flashing back to Kitty Bingham's habit.

"I don't mean Beezie necessarily, although I wouldn't be surprised. I mean if you want the shit, and want the maximum amount of discretion, there are sources who will take care of you. I knew this one chick in Pacific Heights who used to have the "O" delivered by Chinese who worked at some big florist downtown. She gave these incredible scenes at her daddy's pad when he was off fucking the Europeans on some goddamned business deal. She'd have them deliver the shit right in the plants. One time she pulled a ball of "O" right out of the flower of some goddamned orchid."

Albert's mind raced. "What florist?" he demanded.

"I don't know, man. That big florist in San Francisco."

"Ng's Florist?" he pushed.

"Yeah, that's the one. You know."

His mind now raced so quickly that he could barely think. He saw Madame Ng sitting with Addison. He thought about the piano Addison had saved and the orchid that Katherine had observed next to her mother's picture. He felt an acid fear in the back of his throat as he thought of Madame Ng's position in the city. She knew everyone.

He could see her talking to Aunt Louisa and coordinating countless parties with his parents.

It took another fifteen minutes to grill Rigg on what he knew or could remember about how the opium was delivered. "I don't know. I told you. I get my shit on the wharf. Like I only balled this chick a couple of times. It was years ago."

Realizing Rigg had little more to contribute, Albert left. "I have to split now, man. Like I've gotta make it over to San Francisco now."

Rigg argued to have him stay, but was too drunk to care much one way or the other. Albert went back to the cottage and gave a brief explanation to Deirdre in the hopes that she might add to Rigg's story. "Yeah, I've heard of the orchid delivery," Deirdre confirmed dispassionately. "It's just the sort of thing a decadent chick would do to get her kicks."

The roadway on the bridge was wet and gleamed from the orange lights shining down through the heavy mist. Beyond the city lights were blurred into a melted glow under a thick low sky.

Chow-Ling had gone to bed by the time Albert reached the apartment, and it was too late to call Aunt Louisa. He went to bed, but he could not sleep. For hours he lay fitfully, listening to the irregular blast of foghorns out on the bay. So many questions raced through his mind, and Madame Ng was at the center of every one.

The next morning Albert greeted Chow-Ling with an uncustomary verbal exchange. "Chow-Ling, I want to ask you something," he said, stirring under the covers. Chow-Ling did not alter his pattern, but merely said, "Be in kitchen."

Halfway through his second cup of coffee Albert was awake enough to continue. "How much do you know about Madame Ng?" The ordinarily impassive countenance of Chow-Ling's face changed and an expression of disapproval and concern appeared. "She is very powerful lady. I tell your mother years ago. She is evil, but she never listens. She think I don't like her because she comes from different Tong. She right, but she still not understand."

"What doesn't she understand?"

"White people never understand Chinese. They read about white man rob bank and they remember. They read about Chinese gangster in the morning paper, they no remember when they leave house. To your mother, Chi, Chow and Ching all sound same."

Albert knew Chow-Ling was right. To those outside Chinatown, all the names like the language itself, seemed the same, and the Chinese, with their great capacity to withdraw into themselves, seldom wasted time making useless explanations to Caucasians.

"Why haven't you ever said anything to me about Madame Ng?" he asked, half-knowing the reason why. Chow-Ling shrugged, "No important."

"It is important, Chow-Ling," he contradicted in frustration. "I want you to tell me about Maggie Ng. Why is she no good?"

"She no good. She come from very powerful family. Her grandfather head of Chee Tong. He flee china. Bring Chinese girls to San Francisco. You know, what you call sing-song girl. He leave China after General Gordon put down revolt against Manchu."

Albert was sufficiently versed in Chinese history to remember the Tai Ping Rebellion that had rocked China in the last century, but he knew nothing of the role of the Chee Kung Tong. Over the next two or so hours, Chow-Ling told him about the group of monks from Fookien Province, who had defended the ruling Manchu emperor from a rebellion of barbarian tribes. Worried about the monks' motives, the Emperor betrayed their loyalty and sent Tartar soldiers to kill them. Only a few monks survived. Legend had it that they received signs from heaven to form a movement aimed at replacing the Manchus with a descendent from the ancient Chinese dynasty. This had been the noble beginning of the Chee Kung Tong. In later years the band of rebels had become like so many other revolutionaries, a mere band of cutthroats, involved in everything from gambling and prostitution to blackmail and assassination.

"Grandfather bring sing song girl. Father also. He use hatchet boys. Get tribute each week from owners of new slave girl."

As Chow-Ling continued with his saga, Albert began to get the picture.

The Chee Tong eventually came to control the notorious gambling clubs and opium dens and then made killing for consideration a way of life as they fended off the white man's legal system by bribing police and hiring attorneys. Even attempts by respectable

Chinese merchants, under the leadership of the Six Companies, were unsuccessful in their attempts to curb their influence, which eventually reached into all fraternal guilds and touched even the benevolent associations. They were parasites, feeding upon thousands of innocent Chinese who had come to California to work on the railroads and in the mining camps.

"Father shot in barber shop," Chow-Ling concluded. "Big funeral."

"In the barber shop?"

"Go in. Have queue replaited. He shot by hatchet boy."

"What happened to Madame Ng?" Albert asked impatiently, trying to bring Chow-Ling around to the present.

"She raised by grandparents. Grandfather just die last year. Ran business through grandmother. She a great dragon. Much feared. I think she raise Maggie Ng. Maggie Ng's mother very beautiful woman from good family in northern China, but she have no say against mother-in-law."

Beyond this rather frightening background, Chow-Ling seemed unwilling or unable to move. "I don't know. I ask cousin Sammy. He big gambler. He knows what go on today. I lose too much on Tsi Mei. I no gamble."

"What about opium? Is Madame Ng? Does she deal in opium?"

Chow-Ling shrugged again. "I ask Sammy."

The next day, Friday the 13th of November, Albert sent a reluctant Chow-Ling off to visit his cousin. Although he was anxious to go along, Albert knew that his presence would only block the exchange of information. He gave Chow-Ling four hundred dollars in fifty dollar bills and a bottle of Chevis Regal to use as an inducement for his cousin's cooperation. By late afternoon, Chow-Ling was back. He came in quietly and laid two hundred dollars on the table and Albert knew that he had been, as always, both thrifty and clever.

From the information Chow-Ling had gathered, Maggie Ng was still a controlling factor in the Chinese underworld. According to Cousin Sam, she had become far more sophisticated than either her father or her grandmother, and she ran her illegal activities well hidden behind the screen of respectability. Gone were the days when the sing-song girls cried out to their customers from the cribs down darkened alleys but still, for a good price, a client could experience a beautiful young woman and be assured of complete discretion. Madame Ng knew people and she had people introduced, but she was never directly involved. She did not run her nefarious operations from her office at the florist, but from an old three-story building that once was a family home and store. Jade and pearls could be obtained and for soldiers hooked on morphine in Korea, she would see to it that they found a supply for their habit. Her florist business must have been very profitable in itself, but Albert could see how she used it as a front. Through consultations with her clientele and by arranging social gatherings, she could observe the needs of people from every conceivable corner of San Francisco society. For several hours his mind was stunned by the possibilities. How was she connected to Katherine? Had she supplied his Aunt Elizabeth with the drugs that had contributed to her death? What had she done for Aunt Louisa? Had the rare pieces of jade in Aunt Louisa's collection been smuggled illegally into the country? There was no evidence to firmly link her with McMasters Shipping, but he felt there must be a connection somewhere. What it was he could only guess. He thought about Katherine and Patrick. They had been in Hawaii now for only two days, and the thought of calling them entered his mind. He hesitated, not wanting to pull them back and disrupt the time together they so desperately needed. There was nothing concrete to tell them, anyway. He had only discovered that Madame Ng was involved in criminal activity, and that only on the word of Cousin Sam the gambler. There was always the possibility that Chow-Ling's cousin had exaggerated his tale out of an old hatred. Perhaps he had lost money, or there was an old family feud. Albert decided to wait. It was not until he retired for the night still restless with thought, that a concrete plan formed in his mind.

The next morning he left early for Treehaven to spend the day with Aunt Louisa. It took all the skill he could muster not to reveal what he had learned. Normally he would have shared such information with Aunt Louisa, but he feared that she might become overly upset and he did not want her to do anything that might tip his hand. They talked mostly about the wedding, and it was only after several hours that he turned the conversation to Ng's floral displays that had graced the reception.

"Can you imagine the luck of having four dozen Christalas in November!" Aunt Louisa remarked, as she admired the still fresh spray of white flowers that had been moved into the conservatory. "I don't know how Margaret Ng got them to spike so early."

"I would imagine Madame Ng can get all sorts of things. She's a very resourceful woman," said Albert.

"She certainly is that," Aunt Louisa laughed. "Any species of plant on the face of God's earth."

"Only plants?" he pushed, attempting to lead the conversation.

"I've done business with Margaret Ng for more years than I care to remember. She's truly quite extraordinary. I purchased the Han dragon from her in the late twenties—always can find a treasure! Pearls, lapis, porcelain. You pay half what you would at Gump's or Shreve's!"

Arriving back in town on Sunday, Albert asked Chow-Ling if he could find out if there were particular hours Madame Ng kept in her Chinatown office. Again Chow-Ling went to see cousin Sam using the pretext of wanting to buy some pearls for his employer. This time the information was purchased for a mere hundred dollars.

"Cousin Sam say Ng in old family house Wednesday. House over store. Store run by cousin who care for aged mother. No one suspicious when Ng come and go."

Since Albert had to wait a day before going to see Madame Ng, he decided to pursue another avenue. He could not get the picture of Madame Ng and Addison's discussion out of his mind. The expression on Addison's face haunted him.

On Tuesday morning Albert called Charlie Cahoun at the *Examiner*.

"Charlie, I need a good private eye. You know of any?"

"Yeah. Nigel Sayer's your man. Best P.I. in town."

On Charlie's advice Albert called Sayers and was able to get an appointment for Thursday morning.

CHAPTER 41

THE NG HOME was reported to be halfway down a narrow alley off Grant Street between Washington and Clay, only about ten or so blocks from Albert's apartment. Wednesday had turned out to be a beautiful day. The rains had disappeared and the city was fresh and clean under a bright blue sky. After lunch and Windsor's afternoon walk, Chow-Ling and Albert started out. They walked a block down Lombard and turned left on Grant and began walking south through Little Italy along the bottom of Telegraph Hill, passing through the intersection of Grant and Union where Patrick's car had crashed just two weeks before. Within a few more blocks they were in the heart of Chinatown and the smell of garlic was replaced with that of straw matting, nut oil and burning incense.

Chinatown had always held a fascination for Albert since childhood, when he would beg to accompany Chow-Ling on his daily errands. At the obligatory bakery stop, Chow-Ling would spoil him with a nut star cookie or a cake stuffed with sesame seeds and bits of pork. Then there were sugared strips of coconut and dried litchi nuts at the corner market, and the wonderful smell of spare ribs and prawns, and the sight of dried ducks hanging bloated and glazed in the windows.

"I remember the first time I witnessed death, Chow-Ling. It was in a poultry shop just like this," he confessed, looking into the store where tier after tier of chickens and ducks squawked noisily from their bamboo cages. "The proprietor took a chicken out of a cage and wrung its neck for a waiting customer. I was horrified."

Chow-Ling laughed. "No good talk about death. You go in shop. You like see bowl of rooster comb and chicken feet. I buy. Great delicacy but we never tell Mother."

Chinatown had slowly changed, however and most of the old Chinese with their braided queues and blue denim jackets had disappeared. Albert could remember them in Portsmouth Square, where he played in the winter sun as Chow-Ling would visit for a few minutes with his friends. But old Chinese ladies still tottered up Grant Avenue on their tortured little feet that had been bound at birth. And there were still the wonderful shops, each with their own special memories— the herbalist with walls of calligraphy-covered wooden drawers containing everything from ginseng and dried beetles to tiger balm and powdered deer horn, everything for health, happiness, long life, and vitality. The candle shop with the festival candles carved into dragon and pagodas. The corner grocer's stacked with merchandise piled high above the narrow aisles. The auntie behind the counter skillfully working her abacus keeping track of business. She would give a little boy she knew a small bag of melon seeds for a treat, and in later years she would provide him with illegal firecrackers for the Fourth of July.

Within a few blocks they turned off Grant to Washington, only to turn again a few steps later into a narrow alley lined with old brick buildings, and overhung with wooden balconies. Empty crates and boxes of garbage made the alley seem even more confining. An open door revealed a dingy sweat shop crowded with noisy sewing machines and racks of quickly-made garments. Just past the middle of the block they came to the address Chow-Ling had obtained from his cousin. The storefront read: "Ng Furniture Company."

At the front door Chow-Ling turned. "Remember, Albert, fine words and insinuating appearance are seldom associated with virtue."

These were familiar words, one of Chow-Ling's favorite among the countless Confucian sayings Albert had heard from infancy. With the utmost respect for Chow-Ling's role as teacher, Albert looked away and replied, "The man of virtue makes the difficulty to be overcome his first business, and success only a subsequent consideration." With this interchange they were prepared to proceed, and Albert turned the knob on the old wooden door and entered. The shop was filled with tables and intricately carved teakwood chests piled with smaller chests and ivory carvings. Bells on the door had announced their entrance, but it was at least a minute or so before a bamboo curtain parted and a squat middle-aged man appeared. He was dressed in a simple black suit that appeared two sizes too big and a stiffly starched white shirt with a narrow black tie. Chow-Ling spoke in Chinese, informing the man that they had come on business and wished to see Madame Ng. The man asked their names and then without a word, disappeared behind the bamboo curtain at the rear of the shop, leaving them waiting among the piles of furniture. Over five minutes passed before he returned. They seemed like fifty. Albert thought he could hear a voice or perhaps voices from somewhere in the back of the building, but he was not sure. When the little man returned, he beckoned them to follow. They did his bidding and found themselves in a long corridor, which led to what appeared to be a packing room that was filled with more boxes and furniture. At the back of this room a sturdy-looking Chinese in his mid-twenties sat at a desk to the side of a door. Chow-Ling eyed the young man carefully, for he seemed somewhat out of place behind the desk. He had the feeling by the sullen look in the man's eyes that the fellow was a man of physical, rather than mental force. The old man led them past the desk and opened the door, revealing a flight of very steep stairs. As they started to climb the dimly lit stairwell, the door closed behind them and Albert wondered if it had been locked. They passed another door on a landing and turned to ascend yet another flight of steps to what seemed to be the third floor. At the top of these steps, another door was opened and, judging from the effort of their guide, it was quite heavy. Noticing a small observation hole and the great thickness of the door, Albert speculated it might have been constructed to withstand the axe blows of the police, who had occasionally raided gambling and prostitution dens in the old days. Once through this door they found themselves in yet another hallway that turned several times as they followed it. Old ropes were strung along this last hallway connecting the heavy door with each of the various rooms and Albert guessed they were part of some elaborate warning system and he wondered how many of the rooms had secret panels which could provide a means of quick escape.

Finally they found themselves at the end of the hall. Albert was not sure of his sense of direction after going through the labyrinth of winding corridors, stairs and connecting doors, but he felt they might be towards the front of the building over the alley. Reaching the last door in the middle of the hallway, their guide stopped, reached up and pulled a rope hung by the side panel. The door opened and their guide stepped aside and gestured them to enter what appeared to be a small waiting room. Another middle-aged Chinese sat behind a teakwood table upon which rested a small pile of papers and a telephone. The room was without windows, but it was comfortably furnished and an oblique glass skylight admitted a little light.

"You sit," the man behind the table said motioning to a carved ebony bench.

Chow-Ling and Albert did not speak to each other, but waited patiently as the man went back to his papers. The room was exceptionally quiet. Noise did not seem to penetrate from either the street below or the rest of the building. A narrow well-crafted wooden door stood opposite the one they had entered and after about ten minutes, the door opened and Madame Ng suddenly materialized. Although she had been the object of their journey, her appearance was somehow unexpected. She seemed to have gained an element of surprise, and for a moment Albert was unable to speak. He had known Madame Ng his whole life, but he had never known her in these surroundings, and he felt like a traveler in a foreign land confronted by a local magistrate. She was wearing a black brocade silk sheath over a pair of butter yellow trousers revealing her still sleek well-formed figure. Her black hair was pulled to the back of her head, making her pale skin appear to be tightly drawn over her high cheekbones and narrow face. She did not seem surprised to see them.

"Follow me," she said with an air of haughty confidence.

Madame Ng's office was sumptuously furnished in marked contrast to the rest of the building. The walls were covered in perfectly fitted teakwood panels and a large table with chairs stood in front of delicately carved wood screens that let in light. Albert thought that the entrance to the building must be just below and that the screens, if pushed aside, would reveal the balcony they had observed upon entering. On the far end wall stood a splendid seventeenth-century Huanghuali cabinet inlaid with jade and semi-precious stones.

Madame Ng moved to the other side of the table and motioned them to sit opposite her. She seemed to be waiting for them to begin the conversation, her disarming eyes calculating and cool. "I am not one who was born in the possession of knowledge," Albert began, quoting Confucius, "but I am one who is fond of antiquity, and earnest in seeking it there."

Madame Ng smiled as if to acknowledge the source of the quote. "I have been given to understand from certain acquaintances," he continued in a steady tone, "that I might come to you for guidance in certain matters." Madame Ng still said nothing, but nodded her head slightly, indicating that he should go on. "I have for some time, perhaps due to the good influence of Mr. Chow, been interested in the history of Chinese philosophy and scholarship, and consequently in the collection of Chinese table screens, much like this one," he said, pointing to a small apple-green and enamel jade screen that sat between them on the table. "If I am correct, this particular one symbolizes longevity by depicting a pine tree." Madame Ng nodded again and added, "You are quite right, Albert. This particular screen is from the Ming Dynasty. They were placed on scholars' desks to give them something beautiful to contemplate when they were deep in study."

He completed a careful examination of the screen before continuing. "And I believe the scholars also used them as screens to conceal their works from the prying eyes of a visitor."

There was silence as Madame Ng looked impassively into his eyes, which met hers with an equally inscrutable expression. "Quite so!" she commented thoughtfully, giving no sign of recognition to his obscure double meaning.

"I have been told that you sometimes sell screens from your collection, or know people who might have screens for sale. And that this is discreetly handled, as a perfectly private transaction between friends."

Madame Ng smiled. "And what type of screen are you interested in obtaining, Albert? As you know, since the Nationalists were expelled to Taiwan, such objects are increasingly difficult to come by."

"That is precisely why I came to you," he said, pretending to be just a little eager. "I have been told that you were somewhat of an expert at finding things that are difficult to obtain, and that you are willing to help friends and clients who express a certain interest in, well, shall I say, the more exotic Oriental art forms? Indeed I have been told you supply many rare commodities for the enjoyment of those willing to pay for them."

Again Madame Ng's expression gave no indication of understanding an implied double meaning, but her words, although also obtuse, implied she had penetrated beyond the surface of the conversation. "It seems you have been told a great many things Albert," she said in a tone of parental admonishment. "There is an old Chinese saying of the philosopher Lao Tzu. 'To know what you do not know is the best; to pretend to know what you do not know is a disease.'"

It was now Albert's turn to pretend to ignore the double meaning, which on one level might have been taken as a warning, or even a threat. After a short pause in which he politely pretended to think about Madame Ng's quote, he abruptly stood up and moved to a black lacquer opium table which contained a collection of jade figures. He reached over and picked up a figure. It was an extraordinary piece of vermillion streaked white jade portraying two dragons pursuing the pearl of wisdom. "I have always admired the mythological Chinese dragon and his relentless pursuit of wisdom," he said, turning the statue over several times and examining the excellent quality of the craftsmanship and the splendid way in which the artist had used the rather detailed vermillion streaking to the best advantage.

"There is, I believe a Confucian saying which maintains that when a man's knowledge is sufficient, but his virtue lacking, he will lose everything he has gained." As he finished these words, Madame Ng arose and came around the table. "You have memorized many sayings, Albert. You and Mr. Chow are to be congratulated. I will see if I know anyone who wants to sell such a table screen as you mentioned. Then I will let you know."

Albert placed the dragon figure carefully back on the lacquered table and moved slowly towards the door. Then with the utmost formality, he turned to thank her. "I knew you would be of help. You who have been the source of so many exotic plants for the pleasures of your clients." They did not shake hands, but slightly inclined their heads as a gesture of recognition, and Chow-Ling and Albert left, following their guide back down the windy halls and narrow stairs to the front shop and out into the street.

Once out on the alley, they breathed a sigh of relief and for the first time since entering the labyrinth, Albert looked at Chow-Ling. Chow-Ling looked back, his eyes filled with concern. "I told you she an old dragon," he said, shaking his head from side to side as they retreated down the alley towards Clay Street. "She more dangerous than the Emperor Dowager Tz'u Hsi."

Nothing had been said directly about opium or prostitution, but Albert knew that Madame Ng knew that he was onto something. He had undoubtedly caused a good deal of suspicion by his surprise arrival at her secret offices, and his veiled references to exotic Oriental art forms and plants, along with the contrived quotations would have been more than enough to cause alarm. His hope was that he had served a warning. Perhaps she would act more cautiously in the future, knowing that he might be willing to expose her if she did not.

"She might want to reconsider whatever plans she has been entertaining," Albert theorized as they walked back up Grant. "She may not know what we know, but she knows we know something, and that ought to at least give the old cow pause to think."

Of course he knew he had taken a calculated risk by alerting Madame Ng to danger, and that by representing that danger to her, he had placed himself in a rather precarious position. Nevertheless, he hoped that her instinct for preservation would moderate her activities. If she was in any way connected to the attempt on their lives, or was planning to use his family she might think twice before trying again.

That evening he tried to call Katherine and Patrick in Honolulu, only to find that they had flown off to the big island and would not return for several days. Frustrated with having missed them, he poured a stiff Scotch and water and lit the light over the Rousseau in the drawing room. I'm tired of dragons and pearls and Oriental opium intrigues, he thought to himself as he sat there in the fading twilight, contemplating the apes devouring their bright pieces of fruit. Perhaps he thought Rousseau had captured that pre-symbolic reality, that reality that had not yet dissected the orange into categories. His mind shifted back to the funeral at Grace Cathedral, and he wondered if Stanley McMasters had been devoured by the dragon or empowered by it. He didn't know why but he kept thinking about McMasters' death. Charlie Cahoun had interviewed Joey Chang and had given Albert a full account of what had happened in the locker room that day. He had read the autopsy and had witnessed the mourning of Monique Morales Monahan. He could not tell why or what but something seemed amiss.

"Heaven and earth are not humane; they regard all things as straw dogs," he thought, remembering a quote from Lao Tzu he had not remembered for a long time. Again he thought of the car accident, and then he thought again of the dragon in the sixth alcove at Treehaven, and Madame Ng's earnest conversation with Addison. His mind doubled the number six and he contemplated the number twelve, the months of the year, the signs of the zodiac, the cycles of the Chinese calendar. It was too much for him to think about, but he promised himself he would think about it all in the morning. What he needed now was a spinal readjustment, and some time alone with Windsor and Hector and these Rousseau apes.

Restless midnight revels filled his disconnected dreams as strange creatures cavorted through deep woodlands playing pranks across forest floors covered in purple flowers. He chased unknown phantoms, which disappeared at his waking and he heard from beyond it all the chords of the Wedding March breaking through. None of it made any sense! "Hermia must marry Demetrius or be put to death," he said suddenly at breakfast, but could not understand why he should make such a reference.

On Thursday morning he was up by eight o'clock and ready for Nigel Sayers, who arrived on time for their ten a.m. appointment. Nigel turned out to be just the sort one would want for the sensitive business of a private investigation. He certainly looked the part and reminded Albert a bit of Sherlock Holmes, with his worn tweed suit, horn-rimmed glasses, and well-trimmed mustache. He seemed to be the trustworthy sort with impeccable credentials, which included service in the Royal Canadian Mounted Police and eighteen years as a private eye in San Francisco. Albert wasted little time filling him in on all the relevant details.

At the end of two hours they had agreed to an arrangement.

"I'll launch an investigation of Phillip Addison and Chambliss Horsley," Nigel concluded. "But given the amount of time we have, I think it would prove fruitless to go after this Margaret Ng. Investigating the Chinese is the most difficult thing to do in my business. You have to have very good contacts, and you obviously have those already. I doubt if I could find out much more about her than you already have. I think trying to put a tail on her would prove very dicey."

That evening Albert again tried to reach Katherine and Patrick, but without result. They had left Hilo and were not expected to arrive on the Kona coast until the following evening. Since he was not exactly sure of their itinerary and did not want to unduly alarm them by leaving a series of messages, he decided to drop the effort. He began to think it was perhaps wise to let the whole matter rest until they were back in San Francisco. There was really nothing they could do based on the information he had, and as long as he felt they were safe, he saw no need to alert them and perhaps throw a damper on their honeymoon. He could not have known that they were making parallel discoveries that would eventually prove fateful.

CHAPTER 42

ALBERT MET THE Princess Hena when it docked in San Francisco after the five-day passage. It was a cold, rainy late November day and the bay was dark and choppy. As he waited at the pier, he noticed Phillip Addison a little distance off, and when he caught his eye, he went over and said hello. He felt a little awkward, since he had Addison under investigation but within minutes Patrick and Katherine were down the gangplank.

"Aloha!" Albert greeted them. "How was the crossing?"

"Schrecklich!" said Katherine, leaning on Patrick's arm for support. "The first two days out were smooth, but then the Pacific went rough. I've been sick for three days."

Nothing seemed to help," added Patrick who looked tanned and rested. "All she could do was stay in bed. I've spent the last three days reading. Finished Michener's new book, 'The Bridge at Toko Ri', but she didn't even want me to read to her."

"All I want to do is go home and lie down without all that dreadful motion," Katherine moaned as Patrick helped her into the waiting limousine. "Call us this evening," They drove off down the pier through the misty morning. Katherine bundled up in Patrick's arms against the cold. The difference between San Francisco and Hawaii was striking. The cold gray of the city in late November seemed like a black and white movie compared to the intensity of the tropical colors to which they had so quickly become accustomed. When they arrived back at their Jones Street apartment, Katherine took tea and crackers and then went to bed, while Patrick unpacked, called his partners, made a few appointments, and began to open the mail.

Around noon the phone rang. "This is Phillip Addison calling. I wonder if I might have a word with Katherine." He sounded hesitant.

"She's asleep right now, Phillip. As you know, she had a pretty bad case of seasickness," Patrick explained. "Let me have her call you later."

Addison called back again at two, and by this time, Katherine was awake. He sounded anxious.

"I am so sorry about your feeling ill. I didn't want to bother you, but I thought I should catch you up on a few things."

"It's all right, Phillip. I feel much better now than I did a few hours ago, but I'm still a bit queasy."

"That should go away in a day or so. It usually does. If you don't feel up to it, I'll call back, it's just that I thought …"

"It really is quite all right, Phillip. What is it you want to tell me?"

"You might try a few drops of Dramamine to relieve the symptoms. It can make you a bit sleepy, but other than that there are minimal side effects. I used it when I was in the navy. It works wonders. I'll have some sent over if you like."

"Oh, that's very kind, Phillip, but I shouldn't want to trouble you. I'll be all right, no trouble at all."

"I suppose you know your aunt and uncle flew up from Buenos Aires?"

"No I did not."

"They would have been there to meet you, but your aunt said she had not been feeling well after the long flight. They asked me to apologize for them."

"I see," Katherine said, slowly trying to anticipate what Addison was leading to. When she did not continue, he stumbled.

"I suppose you will—I hope you—that you and your husband had a pleasant time—that you enjoyed the Islands."

"Yes, it was all very beautiful. The Princess Hena was delightful, very well run, I must say."

"Good! Good! I'm so pleased to hear that. Did you find everything all right with the Honolulu office? Did Mr. Dunston and Mr. Dexter meet with you?"

"Yes, everything went very well. Thank you," she replied, sensing that Addison might be fishing for information.

"Good! Fine!"

"I suppose you really didn't spend much time considering the offer to sell?" he said, sounding more than a little embarrassed at bringing up the topic.

"No actually, I didn't think about it at all," Katherine replied, feeling annoyed that Addison would bring up the subject when she had been back only a few hours. "I can tell you right now and you can tell Otto and Gloria that I will not have any decision on the matter until the end of the week."

"Yes, well, I see. Perhaps you will, that is, I would like to talk with you, that is, about the Islands."

"Yes Phillip, of course," Katherine said coolly before ending the conversation. "We'll have a meeting later this week."

After meeting them at the wharf Albert had returned home, a bit disappointed that Katherine's illness and Addison's presence had prevented him from saying anything. Nevertheless, he gave them the day to recuperate and waited until late afternoon to call. "Aloha, Alberto," Katherine said in a voice that sounded a lot more sturdy than the one he had heard that morning.

"Aloha, Katrina," he replied, happy to hear her sounding so chipper. "So sorry you had a bad crossing, but it can be that way sometimes."

"I feel much better now, thank you. Phillip Addison sent over something called Dramamine. He prescribed just a few drops and it did provide some relief. I don't know why, I didn't think to get something from the chemist before we sailed."

She told him about how much she had enjoyed the islands. "They truly are, as you said, an enchanting paradise. We hated it when we had to sail. We threw our leis off into the water and made a wish.

The Hawaiians say that if they float to shore you will return." She characterized the different islands the way a jeweler might compare priceless gems, each one so rare and different. After a few minutes of describing the grandeur of Hawaii, the beauty of Kawai, and the excitement of Oahu, she realized that Albert was not listening. She paused to allow him to pick up the conversation, but there was only an awkward silence from the other end of the phone. "Albert?"

"Oh, yes, all quite spectacular," he said hesitantly. There was another pause before he continued. "What did you say about Phillip Addison prescribing Dramamine?"

"I said he sent over some Dramamine and it seems to be very helpful. He had used it when he was in the Navy. He said just a few drops was all that was necessary. Why do you ask?"

"Oh nothing, nothing. I just …" he fumbled to remember what he had wanted to say. He resisted bringing up Madame Ng because he sensed that Katherine needed one day free to adjust to being home. The faster pace of the west coast was always a shock after the slow pace of the Islands. But at the end of their conversation Katherine mentioned the tour of the Lehua Nursery.

"We were very surprised, really. No one mentioned that Madame Ng ran such a large operation in the Islands. I would have thought that Aunt Louisa or Aunt Victoria might have mentioned it. But more to the point, we discovered something quite extraordinary. It would seem that our Madame Ng and Richard Broderick own a great deal of property over there. We were told that they both have very unsavory reputations.

"As far as we could tell, there was something fishy going on with the company, too," Patrick interjected, having picked up the extension.

There was a long pause as Albert slowly absorbed what they were telling him. We'd better talk," he said finally, with an unmistakable note of urgency in his voice. "I'm coming over right now."

It was raining pretty hard and Albert decided to take a taxi, rather than bother with the car. It only took him a half an hour to get ready, and he was at their apartment with Chow-Ling by five p.m. Patrick and Katherine were surprised when Chow-Ling, following Albert, carried in a great wicker picnic basket filled with sandwiches, champagne, and fresh fruit. "I knew you wouldn't have any food, and Chow-Ling was good enough to make up a basket," Albert said. Then looking Patrick straight in the eyes, he added, "we'll need his advice before the evening's out."

For the next four hours Albert explained how he had discovered Madame Ng's criminal involvement in a network of illegal operations, how she had come from a notorious Chinese Tong, and how her father and grandfather had exploited the Chinese community. "They've been into everything from prostitution and gambling to opium smuggling. I'm afraid over the years they've even obtained illicit goods for Aunt Louisa."

Patrick and Katherine were astounded. In their turn, they related meeting the Holts and how they had learned about the close relationship between Margaret Ng and Broderick.

"I'm very suspicious about their real estate partnership," Patrick concluded. "It may be the means of hiding funds they made from drug smuggling, although who knows? The whole thing sounds extraordinary. I just wonder if she is using your line to bring things in."

"I wouldn't doubt it."

"If the opium comes from the Orient, I wonder how she gets it past customs. Unless …?" Albert paused, "… unless Broderick somehow arranges for her to slide the stuff past?" His mind was crowded with all the new possibilities Broderick's involvement presented, and as they reviewed the implications, they filled each other in with additional pieces of the puzzle. The more they talked the more complicated and interrelated everything seemed to be.

Finally Albert told them about his decision to hire Nigel Sayers to investigate Horsley and Addison. "I hope you don't think I was too forward in putting a private eye on the president of your company, but the more I thought about Addison and Ng talking at Treehaven, the more I felt he was compromised somehow. And the more I thought about that S.O.B. Horsley trying to ruin you, the more I felt we needed to get the goods on him as well."

Katherine closed her eyes and massaged her temples with her fingertips. "No, Albert, you did the right thing. I just find it difficult to believe that Addison could be involved with anyone so corrupt, even though the evidence seems incontrovertible."

Albert looked at Patrick to gauge his reaction. He sat quietly chuckling and turning his head from side to side. "I don't mind at all, old sport. As a matter of fact, I asked my brother to do a little probing on the same two people before we left for Hawaii."

"You know, I keep thinking," Albert continued, aware of the suggestive nature of what he was about to say. "Both Phillip Addison and Chambliss Horsley were in the foursome with your father when he died. If he had become aware of illegal activities, perhaps they were ..." he did not finish the thought but added: "According to the police report, the locker room boy, Joey Chang, was the one who stored your father's insulin in the club refrigerator. If they had wanted to get him out of the way, well ...!"

"But there was no evidence of any poison in the autopsy," Patrick insisted.

"Yes, I know," Albert thoughtfully concurred. "Nothing appeared in the toxicology report."

Early the next morning, Katherine called her secretary at home.

"I'm sorry to call you so early on a Sunday, Joan, but I was curious to find out how everything went along while I was gone."

"Very smoothly," Joan replied, "with the exception of a rather unfortunate difficulty with your aunt. She came into the office Friday morning and insisted upon looking through your father's desk for what she said were personal letters. When I told her that I didn't have the authority to allow anyone to go into the office, she became quite irritated, and insisted that as his sister, she had every right to look through his letters." As Joan told the story she began to sound a little shaky, and Katherine could visualize Gloria in one of her rages, trying to intimidate her poor secretary. "Thank you,

Joan," Katherine said reassuringly. "You were quite right to refuse. Everything in that office is mine, whether it is the personal or business effects of my father."

"Imagine the bitch!" Katherine said when Albert joined them later in the morning to drive down to Treehaven for a family homecoming party. "I wonder what she was up to, trying to go through Father's papers." They talked more about the intriguing scenarios given the facts they had uncovered and began to chart a course for the next few days.

"We need to find out as much as we can about the real estate in Hawaii," Patrick insisted, "who owns it, how it was acquired and how much there is."

"What are you getting at?" Albert asked, lighting a cigarette.

"I'll bet you dollars to donuts there's some scam in which these clowns are in cahoots and have been secretly diverting company funds to build a secret little real estate empire directed by Ng and Broderick."

Passing the little village of Brisbane tucked into the folds of the San Bruno Mountains, Albert suddenly hit upon a plan.

"I'll call Ross and see what he can do for us. He must know how to get hold of someone who can do a quick title search at the Recorder's office in Hilo."

"That's a great idea!" Patrick agreed.

"It looks like you're the point man all the way around, Albert. First you go smell out Madame Ng in her den, and now you're onto Broderick."

As Patrick and Albert talked about how they would engineer the scheme, Katherine was silent. She was thinking about the orchids. "I think I'll call Brian Shaw tomorrow and see if he can find out any more about just how they ship these orchids in from the islands."

The afternoon with the family was pleasant. For a few hours they put away the plots and intrigues which had again crowded in on their lives and Katherine and Patrick were able to relax and tell Aunt Louisa all about the cruise and the Islands.

CHAPTER 43

ARLY MONDAY MORNING, they started to work. Albert called Ross Paige to see what he could learn about the property Ng and Broderick had up for sale. "I want to find out how much they are selling, and for what price."

"That won't be difficult," Ross said.

"If you can find out about other properties they might own, that would be even more helpful."

"I'll see what I can do, Al. It may cost a little, but I'll have someone into those records before this afternoon. Is there anything else?"

"We're particularly interested in getting a picture of how much money they've invested over the last seven or eight years and before, if possible."

"That we can calculate from tax stamps if we can find all the pieces. Searching out all the grantees in an area can take some time, but then there can't have been much activity on the Big Island. It's pretty remote."

After getting Ross on the track, Albert made an excuse about another possible lead. He slipped out of the apartment and drove across the Golden Gate. He had heard from Deirdre that Ogden Wallraven was back from Mexico and Ogden was the only person he thought might be able to answer one question that had troubled him since the wedding.

When he left for Sausalito, Patrick was on the phone with Brian Shaw to see what additional information he could find out about

Broderick. "We may be on to something big here, so try and keep a low-profile. It could be a large smuggling ring. We're just not sure yet."

"You've got it, Patrick!"

"Specifically, we need to know how the Lehua Nursery in Hilo ships their orchids, how they are handled on the wharf, and what special procedures or arrangements there might be. See what you can come up with." Patrick gave Brian a complete run-down on all his suspicions. They talked as old friends using a shorthand evolved out of years together in Catholic schools and the old neighborhood.

"Broderick is corrupt, no doubt about it. He's an S.O.B. I told Katherine that on the wharf. Don't worry pal. I'll see what I can do. He's had a reputation for years. It shouldn't be hard to find out why." Brian concluded.

Patrick put the phone down and looked at Katherine across the table. She looked so lovely with her beautiful gold hair against the yellow and green wallpaper that had been hung in the breakfast room while they had been away. "Brian's on the job, so that's taken care of," he said with reassurance. He could tell she was pensive, and he knew the rest and relaxation of the islands was slowly slipping away as their problems seemed to grow. Katherine sighed as she put her coffee cup down. "I suppose I really must call Gloria. I dread the thought of having to endure one of her unpleasant moods, but I suppose there's no way around it."

"Then you better call and get it over with. If she starts to pressure you, just hang up."

"She'll be furious about the wedding."

"Why? Because it thwarted her plans to have you return to Argentina?"

"Yes, that's part of it, but she'll be incensed that I was married at Treehaven. She'll consider that the ultimate betrayal."

"Better to get it over with than to let it worry you all day."

"I don't know," she said, half-pleading. "I just don't feel like dealing with Aunt Gloria."

"Look, why don't you just call her? Tell her you're sick, or you have the Aole Aole flu, or something? If you don't want to talk to her, don't. But you have to at least call her and there's no use putting it off."

Katherine usually would have come back at Patrick for being so directive, but she was too distracted to even notice. "You're right," she said with a deep sigh of resignation. Then with a puzzled expression, she added, "What is the Aole Aole flu? Doesn't Aole mean 'no' in Hawaiian?"

"Yeah," Patrick grinned, "the no-no flu! No, you can't talk to her, and no, you're not interested in selling the company. She won't know the difference."

"It's such a ridiculous deception," she laughed. "It's just absurd enough to work."

Katherine's call to her aunt was not what she had expected. Gloria was rigidly cold in an eerie sort of way, but there were no recriminations or wild accusations. There was only a deadly distance, as if she had retreated to the dark side of the moon. Gloria did not make an attempt to congratulate Katherine on her wedding, and it was Gloria who suggested they hang up when Katherine mentioned that she had the flu. All Katherine could remember after the conversation was that her aunt had informed her that they had come back to San Francisco to wrap up business affairs and would return to Buenos Aires as soon as possible.

"She didn't even mention selling the company," Katherine explained. "I have seen her before when she was angry and refused to speak for days, but this was different."

Then quite suddenly Katherine remembered her conversation with Joan Bywater the morning before. How very peculiar, she thought, that while she was talking to her aunt, she had forgotten all about Gloria's demand to go through her father's desk. Was this some sort of final symbolic gesture on Gloria's part? A final act of severing family relationships? As she attempted to analyze Gloria's mood, the telephone rang. It was Joan Bywater and she sounded frantic. "Oh, Miss McMasters, I mean, Mrs. Bartley, I have been trying to reach you. The office, when I came in this morning, was—was, had been—broken into." She sounded very upset and it took Katherine a few minutes to calm her down and get the story straight. Upon arriving at work that morning, Joan had noticed that the papers on Katherine's desk had been moved. "They weren't scattered around, or anything like that," she explained, "but they had just been moved. I always know exactly how I leave an employer's desk. Then I noticed one of the file cabinets was open, and the files inside, I am quite sure, had been tampered with. I can't be absolutely certain, but there was also a desk drawer open and the smell of cigarettes. It couldn't have been the janitorial service, because it was Sunday night."

Katherine and Patrick dressed quickly.

"I don't want you to go alone," he said. "What with the accident and all, it pays to be cautious."

"I haven't even asked you about your own business," she remarked as they drove downtown.

"I talked with both Dick and Dan this morning. They both said everything was O.K. In fact, Dan said that the company ran better with me in Hawaii. He said I should have stayed the hell away for another two weeks."

Katherine purposely did not inform anyone of her arrival. She went immediately to her office unnoticed except for the doorman and the few clerks she encountered in the hall. Joan Bywater was at her desk and was relieved to see them. The idea that someone had broken into her office made her feel violated, for she was the kind of secretary that lived for her work, and her office was an extension of her psyche. She showed them how she had found everything, and explained again how she prided herself on always leaving her employer's desk in a very precise manner. "Who has keys to your office?" Patrick asked, trying to figure out the possible suspects.

"I don't really know," said Katherine after thinking for a moment. I suppose night security, and beyond that, I couldn't guess."

"Would Addison, or any of the company executives?" he pressed.

"I suppose someone must, but I can't say. I never asked," Katherine said as she sank into her chair. "Is Mr. Addison in his office this morning?"

"Yes, he called about nine-thirty and asked if you were in," Joan replied. "When I told him you weren't in yet, he asked that I have you call him. I thought he sounded a little funny. I can't say exactly how, but he sounded very distracted."

After talking it over, Katherine and Patrick decided a meeting with Addison would be a strategic move. If Gloria and Otto had obtained keys for the office, it might well have been through Addison. Further, Addison was their best means of finding out what was going on with the company and offer. "If your aunt is not talking to you, it might be fair to assume that they're going to try to continue through Addison. If he's the front man, then we'd better find out what they are proposing," Patrick advised.

Addison arrived within ten minutes of her call, and they were both shocked at his appearance. His face was thin and pale, and his eyes were very tired. His normally calm, gentlemanly manner had been replaced by a nervousness that manifested itself in a strange undirected twitching of his right hand. But most disturbing was his failure to hold eye contact. When they spoke, his eyes seemed to fall and focus on some unseen spot on the floor. "I want to apologize for disturbing you when you had just arrived home," Addison began as he sat down.

"That's perfectly all right," Katherine assured him. "But we were tired and as I said, a little bit queasy the first day back." As Joan served coffee, Addison inquired about their trip, but his questions seemed disconnected, as if he were not really listening to what they were saying. After a while Katherine changed the subject, bringing the focus back to the company. "Now tell us what has gone on in the last few weeks," she began.

Addison seemed hesitant at first, but finally came around.

"The offer for the line will not be extended beyond Friday," he said.

He spoke without betraying any prejudice, as if he were merely reporting a fact that did not involve himself, and for which he could offer no opinion.

"What do you think, Phillip?" Katherine asked in an attempt to draw him out.

There was a long pause, and Addison looked as if he had not quite heard the question.

"Do you think we should sell?" Katherine asked, restating the question in a more precise manner.

Again there was a pause, and Addison continued to stare, his eyes cast down towards the floor. "I don't know," he said at last, shaking his head from side to side as if the question posed too big a weight for him to bear.

Katherine could tell from his manner of speaking that he was deeply disturbed about something. "To be very honest," Addison continued unexpectedly, "I really can't tell you what you should do. It is a fair, even a generous offer, but—" He did not complete the sentence.

"But what?" Patrick interjected a little impatiently.

Addison seemed startled by Patrick's intrusion, as if he had forgotten that Patrick's opinion counted. "I just want you to know that whatever happens, I want the best for you, Katherine. I want you to believe that." Again, the manner in which he said this conveyed a deep concern, which conflicted with the fact that he was involved with Broderick. It was this conflict that led Katherine to her next question. "We have reason to believe, Phillip, that someone went through my office last night. Do you know who that might be, or who might have the keys?"

Addison looked up nervously. His body seemed to stiffen and his hand twitched more than ever.

"I have a key, and I'm sure your father's secretary, Mrs. Tucker, still has one, and perhaps there's one at his home with Mr. Deng."

"Do you know of anyone who might have wanted to go through the files or desk for any reason?" Katherine asked.

Addison seemed to hedge for a moment, but his eyes did not leave hers. "Your aunt asked me the day she arrived if I knew where your father's private papers were, but I don't recall her asking for keys to his office."

"What did you tell her?" Patrick pressed.

"I told her I didn't know. That I assumed they were either in his office at home, or here. Where else would they be?"

Katherine pulled herself forward and leaned across the desk. "What about my aunt?" she asked.

Again Addison became nervous, looking away and sinking back into his chair. "I don't know, Katherine. I just want you to believe that I want the best for you. That's all. I don't want to interject myself into ..." he hesitated.

"Has Gloria been pressuring you to pressure me?" Katherine asked instinctively.

"To say the least!" he answered in an ironic tone.

Beyond this point, Addison seemed unwilling to go, and Patrick and Katherine sensed that further questions might only serve to inform Addison about their suspicions. As Addison left, Katherine took him by the hand and walked him to the door. "I'll be around here for a few hours today, if there's anything that needs my attention. And I'll be in tomorrow." Then quite unexpectedly, Addison bent forward and kissed Katherine on the cheek. "Be careful, Katherine. The shipping industry is a rough business." He turned and looked at Patrick in an almost pleading manner. "Take good care of her," he said before turning and walking slowly back through Joan Bywater's office towards the outer door.

Katherine and Patrick spent the next half hour attempting to analyze Addison's behavior, but he remained an enigma. His allegiances were so unclear. On the one hand, they had evidence of his involvement with Broderick and Ng, and they knew he was a partner in the offer with Gloria, Otto and Horsley. Yet on the other hand, they sensed a sincerity and deep devotion towards Katherine's welfare. They spent several more hours in the office quickly going through the stacks of mail Joan Bywater had so neatly organized. Then Patrick drove Katherine back to their apartment and went on to his own office. "Why don't you call Albert and ask him to come over?" he said as he kissed her good-bye. "I don't like leaving you alone."

Albert had a late afternoon meeting with Ross Paige and was unable to see Katherine until four p.m. By that time Patrick was home, and at Albert's suggestion they went down to Yamamoto's for a quiet dinner. Katherine had never had Japanese food before and she was enchanted by the formality and presentation.

"I have found out some interesting information about the Hawaiian properties," Albert commented over the first order of sushi. "Evidently Ng has been acquiring real estate on the big island for years. Most of the real estate is near Hilo and is related to her orchid industry, but just a couple of years after the war, she started buying up other pieces, and for some of those she had Broderick as a partner. But now, get this! Two pieces of real estate on the Kona coast were owned by Ng, Broderick and a third partner, and in one case, a fourth." he paused briefly, allowing them to prepare for what was to come.

"Who are—?" Patrick asked, annoyed at the suspense.

"In two of the properties, Chambliss Blackman Horsley is a third partner, but there is a coffee plantation south of Kailua on the Kona coast, in which Horsley and your father were also partners," he said, pausing to sip his sake. "But in no way was the company involved in acquiring any of the land. It was all done as a separate transaction. Further, the land for sale does not include the small plantation. The only way we found out about your father's interest was because Ross Paige has damned good contacts!"

Katherine and Patrick looked at each other and then at Albert. "I don't remember any Hawaiian properties in my father's will," Katherine said, trying to recall the odd pieces of real estate in his estate. "Maybe that was something he left to Gloria. But why wouldn't it …?" she paused, trying to make sense out of what they had just uncovered. "Why wouldn't it be for sale?"

416

"They don't want to attract attention to the fact that your father owned it," Patrick answered without hesitation.

"And that implicates Father, doesn't it?" Katherine concluded.

"I'm afraid it does," Patrick said, reaching over and taking her hand.

"So if Father was a partner with Broderick, Horsley, and Ng, that more or less scotches the theory that they would want to …"

"Get him out of the way? Yes, I suppose it does. That is unless he wanted out, but that seems a very remote possibility," Albert concluded.

"Why would you draw that conclusion?" Patrick asked.

"Because according to Ross, Katherine's father along with Mr. Horsley, Mr. Broderick and Madame Ng were negotiating to acquire additional properties not only on the Big Island, but in Maui and Oahu. They set up a separate company undoubtedly designed to hide their involvement, but here again Ross's contacts are superb."

"Sounds like they have someone on the inside," Patrick interjected.

"Probably, but then in Hawaii you can always buy information if you know where to go for it."

Katherine took a long, deep breath. "I suppose I'm not surprised, really. I don't know why, but I'm not really surprised. I think I expected something like this would turn up." For some reason the news was not all that depressing. Perhaps after all the intrigue concerning her father, adding an extra piece to the puzzle was almost a relief.

They sat quietly for a while, listening to the patterns made by the individual notes of a Japanese shimasen, slowly sipping tiny cups of warm sake and contemplating all the interconnecting patterns that formed the web of their lives. After some time Albert reached over and gingerly picked up a piece of sushi, which he held carefully at the end of his chopsticks. Then, as if half to amuse and half to instruct, he painstakingly inspected the delicately wrapped piece of raw snapper, attentive to its color and form.

"You know, in Japan the greatest delicacy is the sushi made from the puffer fish," he said with a slight note of irony. "There is a gland in this fish which contains an extremely deadly toxin. When the gland is removed and the fish properly prepared—it is the Japanese equivalent of Beluga caviar. But even the slightest amount of the rodotoxin from the fish and it's … Sayonara!" At this he discreetly placed the sushi into his mouth and with calculated effect slowly chewed it as if half expecting to be poisoned himself.

"You can eat your sushi, but I'll stick to the tempura," Patrick laughed.

"Ah, so," Albert mocked, inclining his head, "That is your intent."

The following morning, Patrick went out to inspect his construction projects, promising to be back by one p.m. so he could escort Katherine to her office. Albert arrived unexpectedly at noon, just as Katherine was about to get dressed. "Where's Patrick?" he asked, excitedly bursting past her into the foyer of the apartment.

"He's out, but he'll be back within an hour or so. What's wrong?" she exclaimed, pulling her green silk robe around her waist.

"I just talked to Nigel Sayers. You'd better come in and sit down to hear all this," he said, moving towards the living room. "His men have got some stuff on Horsley. He's evidently notorious for hiring prostitutes and from what they gather he has them up to the hotel rooms which are never registered under his name. What's more, he has some strange perversion where he likes to watch teenage boys warm the girls up before he gets involved."

Katherine was contemptuous. She sat quietly, shaking her head from side to side. "I felt there was something dreadfully uncouth about that man from the very first time I met him. There is a German word, 'furchtbar', that describes Chambliss Horsley."

"The point is, Katherine, from the information Nigel gathered, it seems probable that Madame Ng's organization is supplying the women and the boys. And that, along with their real estate venture in Hawaii, puts him right in the middle of Ng's web."

For the first time since being back in the city, Katherine began to feel frightened. "I don't know," she said as they talked about Horsley, "with each new revelation, things become more and more sordid."

Within a few minutes, Patrick returned and Albert explained the news. "I've heard remarks over the years that the S.O.B. was a randy old buzzard. I guess they were true," he said, laughing at the thought of Chambliss Horsley, the president of Empire Bank and the grandson of the famous judge, Louis Blackman Horsley, frequenting hotel rooms supplied by Madame Ng.

After they had absorbed the information about Horsley, Albert turned to Katherine, "Nigel gave me another strange piece of information. He put a tail on Phillip Addison, and within the last week or so, Phillip Addison has gone out to Cypress Lawn several times to visit your mother's grave. Evidently he always leaves a bouquet of orchids and spends about ten to fifteen minutes there."

Albert could see the blood drain from Katherine's face as the thought of Addison at her mother's grave ran through her mind, alongside the image of the back bedroom, where he had enshrined her mother's piano.

"I keep thinking about the slipper orchid on Mother's piano," she said after thinking for a few moments. "If there is, as your friend Rigg suggests, such a thing as the 'orchid delivery', perhaps Ng supplied my mother's habit in just that way."

"And if she was in cahoots with your father, well, then ..."

"Speaking of orchids," Patrick interrupted, "Brian says that there are regular shipments of orchids from Asia through the Lehua Nursery to San Francisco. The boxes are never inspected in San Francisco, because they have already been cleared in Hawaii. He says it is all a bit irregular, but things like this can be arranged."

"So the conversation I overheard between Addison and Broderick was really a ..."

Just then, the telephone rang and Patrick crossed the room to answer it. He spoke briefly in a hushed voice and then came back to where Katherine was sitting. "It's Phillip Addison on the phone. He says he must talk to you. He sounds upset."

For a moment Katherine was confused, but she pulled herself together. "I'll take it." She felt her hand trembling as she picked up the receiver and heard Addison's voice. "I have to see you, Katherine. I have to see you today!" he said, without even saying hello.

"Why? What's the matter?" she inquired, not knowing what to expect.

"I can't, I don't want to talk about it on the phone. I can't now. I'm, I'm at the P.U. Club. When can I see you?"

Katherine felt an element of desperation in his voice, but she was instinctively cautious. "I can't see you this afternoon," she stalled, attempting to buy a little time.

"This evening, then," Addison insisted.

After checking with Patrick, Katherine agreed to a six o'clock meeting in Addison's apartment. For some reason, he wanted her to come there rather than meet at the offices. "I have some documents and letters I think you need to see." Then suddenly he changed the tone of the conversation. "Katherine," he said just before he hung up. "Be sure that Patrick comes with you and—" His voice faltered for a moment. "Be careful."

Katherine put the phone down and walked across the room. She felt numb by the overload of unanswered questions. And for the next hour they pondered the possibilities in the penthouse. Outside the day was cold and crisp. A bright December sun and great cumulus clouds contended with each other, making the bay a patchwork of shifting shadows.

At around two p.m. the telephone rang, and Patrick again answered it. He returned shortly to the terrace where they had been having a cigarette.

"It's your father, Albert."

The moment Albert heard his father's voice he could tell something extraordinary had happened.

"I've just witnessed the most tremendous row at the club," he said in an unusually agitated manner. "I was playing dominoes before lunch and Phillip Addison and Chambliss Horsley started quite a fracas. Raised voices, accusations and threats, I'm afraid. It all ended with Addison storming out. Didn't even finish his drink. Quite off the mark, I'm afraid."

The time between George Devonshire's call and their departure for Addison's apartment seemed like an eternity. Whatever it was Addison had to relate must be of tremendous importance. Perhaps it was all important. More than anyone else, Phillip knew both the company and the family and all the interrelations between the two for almost 30 years.

"I fell like everything is about to be resolved," Katherine said nervously.

"It sounds to me like Addison is about to crack," Albert suggested as he tried to speculate on what it was Addison had to relate. "For my money, I'd bet he's making a lot of people rather uneasy right now. If he's going to expose Chambliss Horsley for the S.O.B. he is, that would be enough to rock a few foundations around town. But I'd bet it's more than that. He's going to expose something about this syndicate."

"It might not have anything to do with the company," Katherine interrupted. "I mean, why is Phillip Addison visiting my mother's grave? There is obviously some connection there that we can't see. It could even involve ..." She paused, as if not wanting to contemplate the conclusion. "It could even involve Mother's death."

"Or your father's," Albert added.

Around 2:30 Katherine called Joan Bywater to see if there were any messages. In addition to the ones Katherine already knew about, two calls had come in from Gloria, who was looking for Addison.

"How did she sound?" Katherine asked in an attempt to get a reading on Gloria's emotional state.

"She was really quite short, I'm afraid to say. She was, to be honest, exceptionally excitable. Towards the end of the second call she started screaming into the phone before slamming down the receiver."

In addition to Gloria, Mr. Horsley's secretary had called, trying to track down Addison. When Joan had suggested she try Addison's office she had hung up rather abruptly. "I checked with Thelma at our switchboard and with Mrs. Burns," Joan continued, "and from what I can piece together, several other people seem desperate to find him."

"Thank you, Joan," Katherine said as her mind locked upon the deadly distance she had heard in her aunt's voice. "Let me know if there are any other calls for Mr. Addison in the next hour and a half. In fact, if there are any calls for me, you might tell them that I have gone," she paused, trying to think of a possible place in order to cover where she was. "Tell them I've gone to Sausalito for dinner," she said as she looked out across the dark bay to Marin.

The growing suspense had made them all a little nervous and Phillip's phrase "Be careful" seemed more and more like an ominous warning. There was no point in letting anyone know their whereabouts. The next several hours dragged by. They were becoming a little jumpy as their minds seemed to run in separate but overlapping circles.

At one point, Patrick, who had been considering the possible dangers they might face, turned to Albert when Katherine was out of the room. "The whole thing could be some sort of a set up," he confessed. "I think if Addison wants to see her, he should come here."

Albert readily saw his point. "You suggest it and I'll back you up."

At twenty minutes to six Katherine, who thought the idea more than sensible, called Addison's apartment. She let the phone ring nine or ten times, but there was no answer. "He's not there yet," she hung up. "Should we give him another few minutes and try it again?" They waited another five minutes, but still there was no answer.

For a few seconds, she looked searchingly at Patrick after putting down the receiver. "Let's just go," she said, looking for agreement.

"Yeah, O.K., let's go," Patrick. "I think we can take care of ourselves."

CHAPTER 44

A LIGHT RAIN had begun to fall and since Phillip's apartment was only a few blocks away, Albert suggested it would be better to take a cab than worry about parking along California Street. As Katherine called the doorman to summon the cab, Patrick excused himself under a pretext of getting a raincoat. He didn't want to alarm Katherine but he had decided several hours before to take a gun and he needed a couple of minutes to quickly load it and put on his shoulder holster under his coat.

Their cabbie was waiting when they reached the lobby. Nothing was said as they rode the three blocks down Jones towards California. As they passed the Gothic majesty of Grace Cathedral the thought of her father's funeral crossed Katherine's mind. He had only been dead a little over three months. It seemed like three years. Was she now on the verge of discovering something about her father that would complete a cycle in her life? Albert noticed the faraway pensive expression on her face as she gazed at the looming walls of Grace as they rose from the peak of Nob Hill. Stanley McMasters funeral, an old Chinese map of San Francisco, and the head of the dragon shot in disconnected segments through his mind. The power of place mingled with a feeling of finality.

California Street was busy as cars came home bringing their occupants from a hard day on Montgomery Street or frenzied Christmas shopping in Union Square. Cable cars filled with tired San Franciscans and happy tourists clanged their way along their slots, their grip men ringing their bells as if they were performing for the symphony. Taxis pulled in and out over the sparkling wet black pavement, making their evening runs to and from the Fairmont and Mark Hopkins.

Within a block they pulled up in front of Addison's apartment building. As Patrick paid the taxi, Albert climbed out. Turning around to hold an umbrella for Katherine, he noticed an unusually tall Chinese delivery boy come down the steps. He darted across the sidewalk, jumped into a truck and pulled sharply out into the traffic causing an oncoming cab to swerve and honk in loud protest. The logo on the truck read "Ng's Florists". A chill shot the length of his entire body and he could feel his heart pounding. There was no time for words.

Katherine and Patrick climbed out and hurried across the sidewalk and up the front steps into the portico of the building. There appeared to be no doorman on duty, but Katherine, remembering an earlier visit, tried the door. It was open and they pushed their way in. The lobby was deserted. They waited for the elevator for what seemed to be an eternity. Finally it took them up to the landing that served as the outer foyer to Addison's fourth-floor apartment.

Patrick stepped across to the front door. He rang the bell with his left hand as he reached under his coat and felt the comforting cold of his revolver.

"Stand over there," he said, directing Katherine to the side as he stepped over to the railing and looked up and down the stairwell.

He thought he heard some movement in the apartment but he wasn't sure. He waited and then rang again. There was no answer. A third time still produced no response. "What do you think?" he said over his shoulder. "Try it again," Albert insisted, reaching forward and giving the buzzer three firm rings. "He has to be in. Maybe he's in the john."

To break the tension, Katherine sat down on one of the small gilded armchairs that flanked the Italian marble hall table. Albert turned to see if she was all right, and in doing so noticed a large orchid plant. The interior pot had been slightly dislocated from the cardboard container that surrounded its base and it tilted awkwardly at a peculiar angle to the side. It was an unusual orchid, one he did not immediately recognize. A long branching spike produced white flowers with violet blotches. The sepals and petals were unusually twisted in upon themselves. From behind, the elevator suddenly lurched, causing Katherine to jump.

"Come on, let's get out of here," Patrick said impatiently jabbing the doorbell in several more futile attempts. "We'll go across to the Mark."

The elevator had been called up to the fifth or sixth floor, and not wanting to ride down with other people, they decided to take the stairs. On the second floor landing, the elevator clanged past, but by the time they reached the ground floor the lobby was deserted.

It was not raining very hard but the wind blew what moisture there was at an almost horizontal angle across the broad top of Nob Hill. They crossed Mason Street and the brick courtyard of the Mark Hopkins.

"My Dad remembers the day when Prohibition ended in 1933 and George Smith rolled a barrel of beer across the courtyard through the lobby and right in here," Albert commented, trying to break the tension as they found a table at the Lower Bar.

Katherine smiled and looked at her watch. "You always have something under your hat," she said nervously. "It's six-fifteen."

"Order me a scotch and soda," Patrick said as he lit a cigarette. "I'm going to try the telephone." By the time he came back to the table drinks had arrived. "There's still no answer," he said as he took a large swallow of scotch. "We'll wait for another ten minutes and try again."

He was only gone a few minutes on his second attempt when he hurried back to the table. "Come on. Let's go. I got a busy signal this time."

He threw a couple of bills on the table and they left. As they waited for the light to change before starting across Mason, Katherine noticed a large heavyset man in a trench coat emerge from the portico of

Addison's apartment building and cross California. "That's Richard Broderick," she said, giving Patrick a nudge with her elbow. "I'm sure that's who it is."

"I think you're right," Patrick agreed, noticing Broderick hurriedly disappearing down the street as a cable car clanged past, interrupting their view.

For an instant Patrick thought of following him, but just as quickly decided against it. "Come on," he said, increasing their pace. This time they reached the lobby door only to find it firmly shut. Albert leaned on the buzzer as Patrick rapped loudly through the ironwork that protected the beveled glass. After several long minutes, the doorman, looking annoyed at being aroused, emerged from a room at the back of the lobby. "Sorry sir, I was just tending the furnace," he mumbled as he pulled the door open. His eyes were dull and bloodshot and from his slurred speech they could tell he was drunk. Patrick pushed passed him and opened the door to the elevator.

Again the elevator climbed slowly up to the fourth floor and deposited them in the outer hall.

"Stay here for a second," Patrick commanded as he stepped out and cased the stairwell before ringing the apartment bell.

Albert stepped out after him as Katherine held the elevator's metal gate. They waited for a few seconds before Patrick impatiently rang again.

"The door's ajar," Albert said, reaching forward, catching the latch and pushing the door open a crack.

Patrick and Albert looked at each other for a second before Patrick instinctively pushed the bell in a series of quick jabs. Opening the door slightly, Albert hesitantly called out Addison's name. There was no response

"What do you think?" he asked, over his shoulder.

"I don't like it," Patrick whispered, analyzing the busy phone and the open door. The images of Broderick retreating down the street and the delivery truck's hurried departure flashed through Albert's mind. Katherine remained motionless just behind them.

Albert pushed the door further open and called repeatedly. Still nothing. He leaned into the entry hall and called again before stepping in. Patrick followed behind him, his right hand on his gun.

The only sound in the apartment was the distant clang of the cable cars and the honking of cabs coming up from the street into the living room at the far side of the hall. Across from them the library door stood half open, revealing a large mahogany desk strewn with piles of disheveled papers, a few of which had dropped to the floor in front.

"Mr. Addison?" Albert called quietly as he walked to the door and looked into the room.

Phillip Addison lay face down in a pool of dark blood, his eyes glazed and fixed on the blood-soaked pattern of the Oriental carpet. The muscles of his face had clasped and Albert knew he was dead. He froze for a moment at the horror of Addison's lifeless expression and Patrick could tell from his rigid posture that he had seen something dreadful. Patrick stepped past and looked in. He knew immediately that Addison was dead. Katherine had moved into the entry hall. "What is it?" she murmured. Patrick turned back and caught her terrified expression. "Don't," he said as she stepped forward. He moved towards her. Every part of her body was trembling as he caught her in his arms.

"What is it?"

"It's Addison. He's dead."

For a few long seconds, Katherine ceased to tremble as her mind flashed with images: the car crash, Broderick's bestial face, Horsley's eyes, veiled threats and the note of desperation in Addison's voice. Then the most terrifying thought of all—was he dead because of her? Patrick could feel her convulse in long, heaving sobs. He guided her down the hall into the living room and found his way to a Chesterfield.

"I'll call the police," Albert said as he followed them into the room. He reached for a telephone on an end table only to find there was no dial tone. He returned to the library and found the receiver had been dropped among the disheveled papers on the desk. Without thinking, he placed the received back on the phone and returned to the living room to make the call. Within five minutes they could hear the sirens as they climbed up Mason Street to the top of Nob Hill. "Take care of Katherine," Patrick said as he loosened his embrace and got up. "I am going to try to get Mike."

Patrick was still trying to reach his brother when the police arrived at the open door.

"In there," Albert said, coming into the hall and motioning towards the library before going back to Katherine. Seeing Addison's body, one officer went into the library while the other followed Albert.

As he came across the living room, Patrick concluded a message to his sister-in-law. "Sally, tell Mike to get over here. I have to go. The police just came in."

"I was just calling my brother, Mike Bartley," Patrick explained, thinking he recognized the officer who introduced himself as Chris Curley. His partner was Shawn McGillacut.

Everything was a blur. Katherine sat in a state of near shock as Patrick and Albert started to answer questions. Afraid Katherine would faint, Albert crossed the room and started to pour a drink from a Waterford decanter.

"Don't touch that, Mr. Devonshire!" Officer Curley barked. "Don't touch anything before the lab gets here."

An ambulance was summoned and two homicide inspectors arrived from the Hall of Justice to take charge. Inspector Key secured the scene while Inspector Crompton started to take statements. A photographer and a fingerprint expert were summoned from the Crime Lab and the coroner was called. They could hear the voices of men as they came and went over the next several hours. At one point Inspector Key questioned Albert separately in the dining room while Crompton questioned Patrick and Katherine. Time and again they went over the incidents of the day in ever-increasing detail as the inspectors tried to reconstruct all the events leading to the discovery of the body. Patrick told them he was carrying a gun and handed it over. Explaining his motive for carrying the weapon, he told them about his brakes being cut and Addison's warning.

Albert described how he had observed the delivery boy running out the door and speeding off in his truck.

"That was the first time we came in, but as I told you, no one answered the bell."

"Was the door ajar then," Key queried for what seemed to be the hundredth time.

"I don't think it was. It could have been. I can't say positively that it wasn't."

"And then you went across the street to the Lower Bar at the Mark?"

"Yes, we took the stairs down. We lost the elevator and we thought it would be faster just to walk down. It went up and we didn't want to ride down with anyone else."

"Why not?" Crompton pressed.

"Gee, I don't know, we were kind of jumpy, I guess. We just wanted to get down as fast as we could."

"Were you with Mr. Bartley when he made the first call at the Mark?"

"No, I told you I stayed in the bar with Katherine."

"How long was he gone?"

"Not more than 5 minutes."

"Time enough to run across the street and up four flights of stairs?" Crompton asked, looking at Patrick.

"No, not that long."

"Now look!" Patrick angrily flared. "I told you we went across the street. I made the call and nobody answered. We had a drink. I called again, and the line was busy. Then we left."

"All right, don't get excited," Crompton said, trying to put a lid on Patrick's temper. "I'm sorry, but we have to ask these questions."

As they continued, Patrick related how they had seen Broderick coming out of the apartment.

"He was wearing a trench coat. He came bolting out into the sidewalk, crossed California and went down Mason just along the east side of the Pacific Union Club. If you ask me, you need to talk with Richard Broderick."

"Don't worry, we'll be sure and do that," Crompton assured.

Katherine related the best she could Addison's urgent call and his plea for her to meet him at his apartment.

"He sounded very strange, desperate, even," she said, beginning to cry. "I knew from his voice that something was very wrong." With Patrick's help, she outlined her relationship to Addison and the attempts to purchase the company. Helping to fill out the picture, Albert reported the angry exchange his father had witnessed between Addison and Horsley earlier that afternoon.

"Addison was the middle man," Katherine explained. "He was in on the offer but he didn't seem much to care what we decided, at least not after we returned from Hawaii."

Partly because they were still somewhat in a state of shock and partly because they instinctively sought to protect themselves, they did not offer information about Addison's visit to Katherine's mother's grave or the details of all that had been learned in Hawaii.

Albert made an attempt to explain his suspicions of Madame Ng, but the inspectors were not particularly interested past a certain point. Perhaps they thought he was trying to divert attention. He was not sure. Perhaps they were only anxious to conclude the investigation at the apartment and get on to the examination of other suspects. At any rate, he never mentioned opium or what had led him to engage Nigel Sawyers.

The body was not removed until 10:45. Then for over a half-hour Patrick and Albert demonstrated each step they had taken since entering the apartment.

Walking Inspector Crompton through the sequence, Albert showed how he had first discovered the body and then followed Patrick and Katherine into the living room. As he entered the room, recreating the scene, he saw something that he had not noticed before. On the piano was a most unusual orchid. It was an Oncidium, he thought, but the twisted petals of the flower were white with a violet purple blotching, unlike the typical yellow and brown color of the species. It crossed his mind that he had seen this orchid recently but where he had seen it did not seem important at the time.

Finally at 11:45 Crompton and Key were ready to wind things up.

"I don't see any reason to have you come down to the Hall tonight," Crompton said in a way that seemed to imply that they were not completely above suspicion. "But we will want to talk to you tomorrow." It was midnight when they took the elevator down to the lobby and made a dash past a crowd of reporters into Mike's waiting car.

Patrick was the first to speak. "Do you think they suspect us?" he asked his brother pointedly.

"No, don't worry," said Mike. "They just have to examine all the possibilities, that's all."

As they walked into their apartment, Katherine began to cry. The tension of the last twelve hours needed to be released, and feeling the safety of her own home triggered tears.

"I think we all need a double brandy and a few hours of sleep," Albert suggested as Patrick and Katherine went into the den and collapsed into the red leather armchairs. "Behind the panel to the left of the fireplace," Patrick agreed. "I think there's a bottle of Cognac."

They sat for over an hour, as if in a trance, too exhausted to feel much of anything. The effect of the Cognac along with the fire was relaxing. Katherine moved to the sofa and curled up under a satin comforter. Patrick tucked it around her feet and kissed her on the forehead as he refilled her glass. Then he settled down on the floor beside her and slowly stroked her hair.

Somehow they made it to bed before two and slept until 7:30, when Albert's father called. Addison's murder was headline news and the front pages were dominated by pictures of the three of them leaving his apartment building. Although there was nothing in the copy that implicated them, George Devonshire was nevertheless in a state of panic. He was livid to find out that Albert had not immediately phoned George Hampton and he insisted his son get hold of him before he talked to anyone else about anything. "Goddamn it, Albert! I don't

want you to tell the time of day without George telling you it's O.K.!
This is a murder case!"

Albert tried to assure his father that they were above suspicion
and that Patrick's brother Mike had been there throughout the entire
questioning. "Furthermore, Father, we were the ones who found the
body and called the police."

"None of that makes any damn bit of difference. I'm telling you
Albert, I'm calling Hampton right now," he yelled.

"All right, Father," he agreed. "I'll call him right away."

Without coffee and with very little sleep, Albert's mind was unable
to coordinate very well and his conversation with his father seemed
even more disorienting after he put down the receiver. Yet he knew
through the fog that his father was right and he felt a knot in the pit
of his stomach at the thought of needing a lawyer in a murder case.

Stumbling to the kitchen he spied the happy Arab on a can of Hills
Brothers. The aroma alone was enough to suggest that there might
be hope in the world. He could not find a coffee pot, so he poured
the grounds into a sauce pan and added water. Patrick joined him
momentarily. "Dad insists I call George Hampton," Albert said as he
removed the boiling coffee from the stove and added a shot of cold
water to settle the grounds.

Patrick thought for a minute, bewildered at his attempt to make
the brew. "I think he's right. We should call an attorney. We probably
should have last night.

Before they finished their second cup, George Hampton was on
the line. Albert's father had reached him at home, and Hampton had
interrupted his breakfast to call the partner in his firm most familiar
with criminal law.

"Mr. Martinez will meet you at the Bartley's apartment at ten," he
informed Albert with the authority that comes from being the head
of the most prestigious law firm in the city. "And I would advise you
not to talk or make statements to anyone until you meet with him. I
don't want to alarm you because I am sure there is nothing to worry
about, but it's always wise to be on the safe side."

For the next several hours the telephone did not stop ringing. Everyone from the newspapers to Beezie called. Albert talked again to his father and then Aunt Louisa, who had kept Ivy busy trying to get them for over an hour. She wanted to know every detail of what had happened and it took Albert's greatest skill and diplomacy to finally get her off the line. At Albert's suggestion, Amy Mackie arrived a little after nine to answer the phone and screen calls. They all agreed that after their meeting with the attorneys, they should get out of the apartment and go down to Treehaven. "My apartment will be just as flooded with calls and I don't want to go over to the Devons and have to put up with Mother and Father. They're absolutely undone," Albert said.

Their meeting with Mr. Martinez lasted a little over two hours. They reviewed all the salient facts and answered another barrage of questions before finally grabbing a few clothes and leaving. As they closed the door, the phone was ringing but they did not bother to answer it. "Here's the list of calls over the last several hours," Amy said as they rode down in the elevator. "We'll take care of them when we get down the peninsula," Patrick said, thanking her and placing the folded paper in his shirt pocket. A few reporters waited outside the apartment but Albert let them off with a simple "No comment, fellows."

Aunt Louisa had insisted upon sending Andrew and the quiet comfort of the limo was a welcomed relief. The streets were still wet after the night's rain and the pale blue of the sky competed with billowing white clouds that blew eastward high above the city.

CHAPTER 45

ANDREW TURNED THE limousine through the iron gates of Treehaven a little after one and drove up the long drive. The old estate seemed so quiet as they stepped out of the car into the courtyard.

"Katherine! Albert! Patrick!" Aunt Louisa exclaimed as they came into the library where she was sitting by a crackling fire. "Thank goodness you're here! You're all right! What has happened since I talked to you? What did the attorney say?" A flood of questions followed, but Aunt Louisa did not wait for any of them to be answered. Beyond all the questions, there was the overriding concern for their safety and she was too relieved to have them safe at Treehaven to pay much attention to anything else.

They each greeted her with a kiss and as Katherine bent over and felt her Aunt's old hands grasp hers, she began to cry. The ordeal of the last few days had left her emotions very close to the surface.

Prentice and Bridget rolled in the tea cart containing sandwiches and a tureen of hot clam chowder. As they devoured the informal lunch Albert again tried to relate the events of the last twenty-four hours as best he could. After they finished, Aunt Louisa looked at Katherine. "You look exhausted. Wouldn't you like to go up to your room and have a rest?"

Without hesitation, Katherine agreed. She felt very tired and the warm soup and fire made sleep seem an attractive possibility.

Albert also felt sleepy, but he knew there was no possibility of taking a nap before he had exhausted Aunt Louisa's curiosity. For the next two hours, Patrick and Albert filled Aunt Louisa in. Not only did they relate all the circumstances immediately surrounding the murder, but the information they had gathered on Madame Ng, Broderick, Horsley and Addison.

Slowly sipping on iceless scotch and water, Aunt Louisa sat intently listening to each episode. She did not ask many questions. As her nephew related his meeting with Madame Ng, he could tell his Aunt was deeply shocked. Her old friend, who for years had supplied her greenhouses with orchids, was also guilty of supplying San Franciscans with everything from opium and prostitutes to illegally imported jade and pearls.

"It would seem that our Madame Ng is somewhat of a racketeering old dragon," Albert offered, trying to help Aunt Louisa formulate the information into a conclusion.

"A hooligan in silk," Aunt Louisa snapped, shaking her head from side to side. "She certainly knows how to manipulate. I'll give that to her. Imagine, for all those years she played both sides of the fence."

It said something for her resiliency that beyond being shocked, Aunt Louisa was intrigued. Of course, her mind returned to the past and her beloved Elizabeth.

"I wouldn't be surprised if Margaret Ng was responsible for introducing Elizabeth to opium?" she wondered. "If Ng was involved with Stanley McMasters, it's a pretty sure bet."

"Did Aunt Elizabeth know Madame Ng that well?"

"Of course, we all did."

"Katherine said that when Addison showed here her mother's piano, there was a slipper orchid on it."

"So?"

"Was that genus a particular favorite of Aunt Elizabeth's?"

Aunt Louisa thought for a minute, trying to pull from the past some recollection that would help her answer his question.

"I suppose it might have been," she said at last. "It seems to me that she often had one in her living room, but I don't recall her ever saying much about it one way or the other. Why, is it important?"

"It might be," he said. "Your Margaret Ng seems to have specialized in delivering all sorts of exotic things to her clients."

"To think that beautiful strand of baroque pearls I gave your mother could be contraband," Aunt Louisa said with a twinkle finally returning to her keen blue eyes. "She'll probably never wear them again."

As Albert explained all the intrigue surrounding Madame Ng, Patrick sat quietly analyzing all the interconnection between the various people. Dovetailing into what Albert had explained, he told how they had discovered the partnership between Ng and Broderick in Hawaii and how Horsley and Katherine's father were also involved in the ownership of some of the same real estate.

Aunt Louisa listened to Patrick with equal intensity, her mind swiftly placing each detail of information into the overall picture. But it wasn't until Patrick started reviewing the events in the hours just preceding the discovery of Addison's body that she became particularly animated and questioned both of them at length about the telephone calls and what they had seen.

At four o'clock, Prentice brought tea and they paused for a few moments as Aunt Louisa arose for the ceremonial pouring. When they had settled back again with their tea and scones, Albert began to tell how maddening the morning had been with the attorneys and telephone calls. Suddenly Patrick remembered the list in his coat pocket that Amy had given him as he left the apartment.

"Gee, I forgot about these calls," he said with a note of concern as he read the names. "Inspector Key, Joan Bywater, Mike—I think I better get on the phone."

At the same moment, Patrick and Albert realized that they had not thought to inform the police that they were leaving the city. It was simply an oversight, but they both instinctively knew that it did not look good.

Patrick reached a very angry Inspector Crompton at The Hall of Justice and he insisted they drive back to the city immediately. "We've been trying to get hold of you all day," Crompton shouted. "They're a lot of questions we need answered. You can't just drive off after a murder and not tell us where you're going!"

Patrick apologized, but resented Crompton's demand that they return to town. "We've been through enough in the last twenty-four hours. If you want to talk with us, you're welcome to come down here." Crompton did not like the idea, but Patrick held firm. "My wife is not feeling well and and I'm not going to subject her to a trip." After a few minutes of an intense interchange, Crompton finally gave in and agreed to meet them at Treehaven at seven o'clock that evening.

Patrick followed up the conversation with Inspector Crompton with calls to Greg Martinez and Patrick's brother Mike. Both agreed to come down to Burlingame. He put off calling Joan Bywater until 4:45, hoping Katherine would awaken from her nap.

"I'm going to go ahead and call her," Patrick finally said, looking at his watch. He got Joan just moments before she was going to leave the office and she was very relieved to hear his voice. What she told Patrick dramatically changed the perspective on the murder.

"Mr. Horsley and Mr. Brutmann came into the offices about five o'clock yesterday," she reported. "They spent over three hours in the board room going through company files. They kept Mrs. Burns here until well after six o'clock," Joan explained, relating how she called Addison's office before she had gone home.

"Has anyone been there today?" Patrick asked.

"The press and the inspectors. The police sealed off Mr. Addison's office and began questioning several of the company's employees. I'm afraid Inspector Key was not very happy with me. I refused to provide him with answers. I thought it would be best to forestall him as long as possible until I had a chance to talk to Mrs. Bartley."

"Very wise," Patrick said reassuringly. "They will be down here at seven o'clock this evening to grill us again. Let me get back to you before then. I'll probably have Mr. Martinez, our attorney call you in the next hour or so at either the office or your home."

Patrick knew from the information Joan had supplied that Horsley and Brutmann now had excellent alibis and that Crompton and Key knew of their whereabouts during the murder. There of course remained in Patrick's mind the possibility that Horsley or Brutmann could have murdered Phillip earlier in the afternoon, but Patrick knew this was probably a very remote possibility. His brother had told him that from the initial lab reps, the police were estimating the time of death sometime between six and six-thirty p.m., exactly the time Albert and Patrick had reported their arrival at Addison's apartment.

"No wonder Crompton is anxious to interview us this evening," Albert said as they discussed Horsley and Brutmann. "They have two less suspects and we're probably looking better to them all the time."

"I better give Martinez a ring and tell him about all this. He'll probably want to speak with Joan as soon as possible," Patrick said before going upstairs to awaken Katherine.

Martinez and Mike arrived half an hour early while Crompton and Key were half an hour late, having gotten somewhat lost in the winding streets of Hillsborough.

For another three hours, Albert, Patrick and Katherine answered the questions put to them by the inspectors but rather than ask about the actual events immediately surrounding the murder, the questions were more concerned with Addison's role in the company.

Katherine explained how Addison had always served as her father's right-hand man, and how she had always found him to be the perfect gentleman.

"But he seemed to be under a great deal of pressure over the last few months," she explained. "Increased pressure, I should say. Especially after we returned from the Islands. His personality changed."

"Do you know what the source of this increased pressure might have been?" Crompton asked.

"Yes."

"Well?"

"You see, Inspector, there has been since my father's death, a group of people who have wanted to buy out my interest in McMasters. A few of them appear to be rather desperate. They will obviously go to any lengths to see that an agreement is concluded."

"Desperate enough to commit murder?"

"Obviously so," Albert interjected without waiting for Katherine to answer. "Our brakes were cut on the car, weren't they?"

Katherine and Patrick continued to explain the strange business interconnections they had uncovered in San Francisco and Hawaii. Albert supported their story by again relating what he had learned about the nefarious activities of Madame Ng. At first the two inspectors were a bit incredulous, but they began to place the events surrounding the murder within the broader context of a struggle for control of McMasters Shipping. Broderick had been their chief suspect, but although he admitted to going to the apartment at around 6:30 to see Addison, he claimed Addison had not been at home. A subsequent search of his office netted a revolver but it had not recently been fired and it did not match the ballistics information supplied by the lab. Nor were there any fingerprints to indicate that he had been in the apartment. Nevertheless, Crompton had brought him down to the Hall for questioning, but they could not hold him without any hard evidence.

For a considerable while, Key questioned Katherine about company and family matters. They wanted the names of all directors and chief executives, and they seemed particularly curious to find out just how Addison's functioned as President of McMasters Shipping.

It wasn't until 10:30 that Crompton and Key finally finished their evening's work.

"You look exhausted," Katherine said as she served them another cup of coffee before they left.

Everyone stayed up and talked for another two hours after the inspectors finally departed. Greg Martinez and Mike were encouraged by the general direction of the questioning.

"They're looking for motives tonight, and they didn't find any related to you," Mike told Patrick as they analyzed the questioning.

"I still think Broderick is a likely suspect," Patrick maintained. "Just because he had a gun that didn't match the ballistics information is no reason to think he didn't do it. He could have damned well had another one and ditched it in the bay. That kind of guy can always get a heater. He could have been out with Addison having a drink, followed him home and shot him while we were at the Mark. At that time of night, no one would probably notice a gun shot."

"Perhaps he just came home with Addison and shot him in cold blood after they opened the door to the apartment," Albert speculated, helping Patrick reconstruct the possible scenario.

"But what was the motive?" Mike asked, coming back to what had seemed to be the central question of the evening.

"To cover up his involvement with Ng and her smuggling operations," Patrick suggested. "He 's obviously involved somehow. Perhaps Ng told him Addison was about to spill the beans. For all we know, Horsley and Otto Brutmann are in it up to their necks, too. Any one of them could have tipped Broderick off."

"Or have shot Addison Themselves," Albert added, temporarily forgetting the time of death excluded both Horsley and Brutmann as suspects.

"Not if he died when the coroner said he did," Patrick reminded him, "and anyway, I don't read Horsley as the violent type. Violence fits Broderick's M.O. much better than Horsley's."

"Even given the fight at the PU Club and his attempt to ruin your development project?" Albert challenged.

"It doesn't matter, Albert," Patrick insisted, a little annoyed at his persistence. "He was in Addison's office at the time of the murder, and so was Brutmann."

More and more Broderick seemed a possibility and Katherine recalled the strained conversation she had overheard between Broderick and Addison as well as the meeting they had observed between Broderick and Horsley at Tadich's. But although Albert admitted Broderick remained a likely suspect, he was not willing to give up his suspicion of Madame Ng.

"Crompton and Key will undoubtedly check her out tomorrow, after what we've told them tonight," he said, wondering how much of their story the inspectors believed. "Perhaps I should have had Nigel Sayers down to give his report," he pondered, half asking Martinez for his legal advice.

Martinez looked up and waved his hand in a discounting manner. "No, Albert," he said. "Let's let Inspector Crompton and Inspector Key do some of the work. We don't need to tell them everything until we see where they're going with their investigation. I don't want you to know too much about smuggling operations if Katherine owns the line they're using."

Both the image of the delivery boy dashing out of Addison's building and the memory of Addison and Ng talking in the sixth alcove at Aunt Louisa's ball crossed Albert's mind again. "I'll still bet anyone here dollars to donuts that old Madame Ng did in Addison or had him done in," he said. "If she was using the McMasters line and Addison found out about it, he might have threatened to expose her. Of course, she wouldn't do it herself, I suppose. She'd have a hatchet man do the dirty work. She'll have an alibi."

Towards one o'clock in the morning, Martinez and Mike left to drive back to the city and for a few minutes while Patrick walked his brother to the car, Katherine sat with Albert by the fire.

"You know, I wonder about the funeral," she said. "It's strange, isn't it, that I don't even know if Addison has any relatives. I think he said something about a sister in Connecticut, but I'm really not sure. It's very sad somehow. I mean, his life. He was successful but in the end he had nothing."

"Yes, I suppose so," Albert puzzled. "But for Addison I think his life was over 33 years ago."

"You mean with Mother's death."

"Yes, it would seem so. Why else would he go out to her grave with such regularity?"

"And he worked all those years for Father, a man he must have despised. It doesn't make sense."

"It does if he wanted to protect the company for the one person who meant something to him, the daughter of the woman he loved."

"Yes," Katherine said, drawing a deep reflective breath. "Such loyalty is in rare supply these days. I suppose it is possible."

After a while Katherine and Patrick went off to bed but although Albert felt tired, he wanted to think. He collapsed into an armchair and looked at the dying embers of the fire. The great house was quiet now, and as he sat in the library he felt he was in the presence of an old friend. Treehaven was filled with many memories and his mind wandered back towards his childhood. He remembered the grand parties, the Christmas Eves and games of hide and seek in the conservatory, and soon he found himself wandering through the rooms attempting to recapture in their presence the security and strength they had to offer. He wandered down the long hall now only dimly lit. At the sixth alcove he stopped and looked towards the great jade and quartz dragon. The body was only faintly outlined in the dark recesses of the alcove, but the fierce head stood out in clear relief, having caught a few rays from the light above the conservatory door. He stood for a moment, looking into the eyes of the dragon as if trying to decipher some hidden mystery. Then without thinking, he walked into the alcove and stroked the jade head. It was surprisingly cool to the touch.

In the conservatory the damp air felt refreshing. He found the light panel and turned on a few backlights, which filled the room with the eerie shadows of giant palms and hanging ferns. The fragrance of sleeping vegetation filled his senses and he wandered the length of the room entranced in the stillness.

Just past the pool at the center of the room his eyes came to rest on a long branching spike of twisted orchids. The flowers were white blotched with an intense violet. This is the same orchid, he thought as his mind shifted back to the murder scene. He could see the orchid on the piano in the living room where they had been questioned.

But he also remembered an orchid half tipped over by the front door when they had arrived at Addison's the first time. Were there two orchids or just one? He could not remember seeing the orchid in the hall when they returned from the Mark, nor could he remember it being there when they all left at midnight. Had it been moved? If so, how?

The question obviously hurt his theory that the delivery boy was the hatchet man. If the delivery boy had gained access to the apartment the orchid would not have been left in the hall. Or was it perhaps a decoy, a contrived clue to confuse the issue? Not likely, for its presence did more to point at Ng than point away from her. But why had it been left so carelessly tipped out of its box?

If indeed the orchid by the door was the same as the one on the piano, Addison must have been out when they first arrived. Perhaps he had returned with Broderick and moved the plant inside. Perhaps they had quarreled, Broderick had shot him and then searched his desk. The possibility seemed logical for a moment, but Albert knew it was wrong. Broderick or anyone else would not have had that much time unless all the events happened in rapid-fire succession. Nor could Albert picture the agitated, almost desperate Addison taking time to move a plant all the way from the hall to the living room. If he had moved it at all, it would have only been to the interior hall.

Another possibility entered Albert's mind and he felt a cold chill as he thought about it. Was Addison's murderer in the apartment all along? Perhaps he had already killed Addison and was only waiting for the opportune moment to leave. Certainly the elevator would have given a warning of both the plant's delivery and their arrival if the murderer had been standing just inside the door. Hadn't Patrick said he thought he had heard some movement in the apartment? This theory too seemed valid, except like the others, it did not explain the orchid being moved. It wasn't logical to assume that someone who had just committed murder would take the time to move a plant. Also, Albert had to consider that Addison had been dead for a little while for he knew from seeing men die in the war that death is seldom instantaneous. And Addison looked dead when they found him. The rigors had not yet set in but he was not bleeding, either.

That night Albert's dreams were troubled by the strangely inverted petals and violet blotches of an orchid that seemed suspended in space. He could not place it in the greenhouse or on a piano or in a hall. It appeared up through his subconscious, as a message without context.

CHAPTER 46

ALBERT HAD NOT been following the conversation the next morning when halfway through his first cup of coffee, he turned to Katherine.

"Do you remember an orchid on the table by the front door of Addison's apartment when we arrived the first time?"

The question startled Katherine, pulling her back to the horror of the murder scene.

"An orchid?" she asked, not understanding what Albert was talking about.

"Yes, an orchid," he repeated, as if trying to press something out of her memory. "There was a white orchid with violet splotches, long stem, very twisted petals. It was on the table in the hall. When you sat down it was right behind you. It was tipped out of its box at almost a 35 degree angle."

Katherine shook her head slowly, as if trying to find a mental picture that was just not there.

"What are you driving at?" Patrick asked, trying to understand the significance Albert had placed on the question.

"There was an orchid by the front door when we first arrived at the apartment. Last night I remembered noticing it when I saw one just like it in the conservatory," Albert explained, starting at the beginning. "It was at the front door the first time but I don't remember it being there when we came back over from the Mark. Then I remember seeing it on the piano when Crompton and Key were questioning us.

It was either the same orchid or one just like it. But I think it was the same one because I don't recall seeing it by the door the second time or when we left the apartment at midnight."

He attempted to explain several of the theories, but it was a bit too early for Patrick and Katherine to follow all the implications they entailed.

"Let me get the one in the conservatory," he said, frustrated with his inability to create any enthusiasm.

He returned in a few minutes, carrying the plant in question, the moist clay pot having left a ring on his silk dressing gown. The moment Aunt Louisa saw the twisted petals and violet blotches she recognized the species.

"That's an Oncidium Incurvum!" she exclaimed.

Katherine was sitting with her back to the door and she didn't see the plant until Albert brought it around the table. But the moment she saw the inverted petals she recognized it.

"I know that orchid. It's a South American variety, isn't it?" For a moment she felt her mind go blank. Then she remembered even more. "This is Aunt Gloria's favorite species," she said, turning and looking searchingly at Patrick.

"I remember when I was a little girl my father always sent them to Gloria. One time I was playing with Anna, one of the children of the ranch, and she knocked one over which Father had given her. Gloria flew into a rage, cried hysterically and started beating both of us. Poor Anna avoided the big house for years after that. I had to go out to the casita to play with her."

As Katherine recalled this incident from her childhood, Albert could not help but notice a strange terrifying look come over Aunt Louisa. Her eyes, always so intense and lively, took on a distant quality as if a long forgotten ghost haunted her memory. Neither Katherine nor Patrick noticed this at first. But as Katherine finished and looked across at Aunt Louisa, she could tell that something had happened and she was afraid that her story of Gloria's cruelty had somehow unhinged her. For several long moments there was the most dreadful silence. Then Albert leaned around the back of Aunt Louisa's chair and looked at her carefully.

"Are you quite all right?" he asked.

There was no reply. Then quite methodically, Aunt Louisa folded up her napkin and placed it neatly on the table.

"Sit down, Albert," she commanded. "I am going to tell you all something, something I had hoped to carry to my grave."

Drawing herself up in her chair, she smoothed out the linen tablecloth in front of her with a slow but firm sweep of her hands. She looked *directly at each of them in turn as if extracting a pledge of trust.

"Stanley McMasters brought Gloria the orchids because he was in love with her." She paused for a moment to let what she was saying sink in. She continued, looking at Katherine. "And she was in love with him. Even more so, I would guess."

A puzzled look came over Katherine's face. "What are you saying? I don't understand."

"Katherine," Aunt Louisa's voice came strong and firm. "Listen to me. None of it matters now. But you need to know. You need to know so that woman will never hurt you or any member of this family ever again."

"Know what?" Katherine said, beginning to absorb what Aunt Louisa had told her. "Are you suggesting that my father and Aunt had an incestuous relationship?"

Aunt Louisa nodded. "Yes, Katherine, that is what I am telling you. Your dear mother told me a few weeks before she was killed. Stanley McMasters was the most evil human being I have ever known. He was capable of the most perverse cold-hearted cruelty. He never loved your mother, never showed her the least little kindness or consideration. He only married her for the conquest. He wanted to possess the most beautiful and accomplished woman in San Francisco just as he wanted to possess everything. He married her, then he destroyed her."

"But how did you know about ...?"

449

"Your dear mother came to me a few weeks before she was killed. She was terribly confused and frightened. She told me she was going to sue for divorce on the grounds of infidelity and name Gloria as the correspondent."

Katherine sat quite still for a moment while she absorbed the implications of what she was being told. Yet of all the words Aunt Louisa had spoken, one sentence seemed stronger than the rest: "None of this matters now." Her father was dead and she was at long last completely free of Gloria. She had never really loved either of them, nor had they been capable of loving her. They were both dead to her now and she could not let their depravity touch her. Her father only loved himself and the closest he could come to making love to himself was to make love to his sister! It was a narcissistic relationship that fulfilled both their perverted needs.

"Yes," she said at last, "you are quite correct, Aunt Louisa. I needed to know." Again she paused for a moment before continuing. "I suppose in some ways, it makes everything more understandable."

"What do you mean?" Patrick asked, not quite able to follow her thoughts.

"I mean Gloria's obsessive jealousy and irrational behavior. It all fits. Her hatred of my mother's side of the family, her obsession about my father's papers and the company, even her relationship with Otto."

"Yes, it all fits into place," Aunt Louisa agreed. "Your mother found out about their relationship not long after she married. Gloria, you see, was so dreadfully jealous that she started tremendous rows with poor Elizabeth. It became obvious that she and your father had been incestuously involved before and even after the marriage. Gloria could not let go."

"And mother kept the secret until just before she died?" Katherine questioned.

"Yes, I am not sure why. Perhaps it was because she loved you and there was the instinct to avoid either divorce or scandal. I think it was her undoing. At first she sought revenge in having her own affairs, but then her anger turned to depression. She looked for relief in alcohol and drugs. In the end she couldn't take it any more and he killed her."

Katherine began to weep. "I never thought my father loved me. I never felt a part of his life or that I was ever wanted."

"But why didn't any of this come out at the time?" Albert queried. "It seems to me that …"

"It seems to you, Albert, yes," Aunt Louisa interrupted. "It seems to me also, but there was no point in it. I was the only one who knew." She paused, remembering the terrible dilemma she had faced after her niece's death.

"No jury would have believed it. As Elizabeth's aunt, I would not have been considered an unbiased witness. Everyone in San Francisco knew I loathed Stanley."

Katherine did not hear the last part of this explanation. All she heard were the words: "I was the only one who knew."

"No," she said after Aunt Louisa finished. "You were not the only one who knew." She looked at Aunt Louisa and then at Patrick and Albert.

"Phillip Addison knew," Albert said, slowly putting the pieces together in his mind.

"Knew what?" Aunt Louisa demanded.

"Knew about Stanley and Gloria," he explained, still pondering what it all meant.

"Why would you say that?" Aunt Louisa demanded, sensing that he was onto something.

Katherine and Albert looked at each other in the realization that it would take forever to fill in all the gaps.

"What did you know about my mother's relationship with Phillip Addison?" Katherine asked, ignoring Aunt Louisa's questions.

"He adored her," Aunt Louisa said. "He absolutely adored her, but she was really never romantically interested in him. He settled for being her friend. Towards the end he was one of the only friends she had left. She used to talk fondly of him though, as if he was someone upon whom she could count.

"Yes," Katherine said, "I think he was."

With the image of Phillip Addison tending her mother's grave, tears again came to her eyes. He had truly loved her mother, and he had faithfully guarded her interests for all these years. The piano, the company, her secrets, all these he had kept safe for her by keeping them safe for her daughter. Katherine felt a tremendous sense of gratitude mixed with sorrow as she thought of what Addison had sacrificed.

"You still haven't answered my question," Aunt Louisa demanded impatiently. "Why do you think Addison knew?"

"It is a matter of a thousand and one inductions, Auntie," Albert said. "But it really doesn't matter. It's only a matter of motive. What matters is the orchid. If this is the same orchid that was in Addison's apartment, then we know who shot him."

"Who?" Patrick and Aunt Louisa yelled in exasperation.

"Why Gloria! Who else? Who else would go to the trouble of moving a particularly rare specimen like this, but someone who was inordinately fond of it? Someone who could not bear to see an orchid she loved tipped at a precarious angle."

"But why was the orchid on the outside of the door when we first arrived?" Katherine asked, understanding where Albert was going, but not the path.

"The delivery boy," he said. "He must have delivered the orchid after Gloria shot Addison, and just before we arrived."

"But that doesn't make sense," Patrick objected. "It's all too coincidental to prove anything. If you are saying only Gloria would have sent this particular type of orchid, why would she have it delivered when she was going to see Addison? And why the hell would she send him an orchid anyway? It's simply not logical."

"No, it isn't," signed Albert. "But there you have it. It's all a matter of deduction."

"Anyone could have sent the orchid, perhaps even to incriminate Gloria," said Patrick.

"Yes," he agreed, "but who would go to the trouble of moving it when a man has just been shot in the next room? And who would know Gloria's preference for a species as rare as Oncidium Incurvum?"

Albert could see that Patrick's point had a degree of legitimacy, but it did not dissuade him from his theory.

"We need to find out. Can you call Mike and have him check it out?"

It was around 11 a.m. that Albert was finally able, with Katherine's help, to convince Patrick to call his brother to check out his hunch.

"Mike said he'd get right over to the apartment with either Key or Crompton. He'll let us know this afternoon what they find," Patrick said after hanging up the phone. "He says he thinks we're nuts, but he'll see what he can do. And by the way," he added as an afterthought, "Mike says Madame Ng was with a client in Atherton until almost 7 p.m. the night Addison was killed. You're right, Albert, she has an iron-clad alibi."

There was nothing to do for the next several hours but wait so Aunt Louisa called for her old wicker wheelchair and lap blanket and bundled up against the cool moist December air, she took Katherine and went out through the Italian garden towards the pavilion and greenhouses. The sun, which had retreated almost to its southern limits, still was strong enough to bring the midday temperature into the sixties and fill the freshly washed world with bright shades of green. Beyond the gardens the fields and hills celebrated the return of the wet seasons by covering themselves with an undercoat of new grass. Stopping by the pavilion door they sat for a while, looking back over the gardens.

Addison's murder, the endless questioning and the revelations about Gloria all in rapid succession had taken their toll and Katherine needed a few uncomplicated moments to sort things out. Partly because she sensed this and partly because she was lost in her own thoughts, Aunt Louisa said very little. After a long time she finally reached over and took her niece's hand.

"Katherine," she said very slowly. "There is something you need to know, in addition to what I have already told you. You see, you asked something this morning about your mother and Phillip Addison, about their relationship. I am afraid I did not tell you the whole truth." She stopped for a moment, but they did not look at each other. Instead, they stared at the complex interconnecting patterns made by the Italian garden.

"And what is the whole truth?" Katherine invited at last. She turned and looked at her aunt, who continued to stare out across the garden.

"The truth is often difficult but it is almost always redeeming."

"I think, Auntie, I might guess the truth," she said, squeezing her aunt's hand.

"Yes, I thought you might."

"Do you remember Katherine, the day I first showed you the greenhouse, the day I first met Patrick?"

"Yes."

"People, like orchids, display certain qualities of character they receive from their parents. You could never have been a product of someone as unacceptably contemptible as Stanley McMasters."

Katherine smiled. "Yes, it is as I suspected then. Phillip Addison was my father."

"Your mother turned to him in that difficult first year of her marriage. He was kind and honest and … she needed someone strong and sympathetic after she learned what a terrible mistake she had made."

"But why didn't she …"

"Divorce and marry Phillip? I think she might have—perhaps if she had not been killed."

"And McMasters never knew?"

"About Addison? No. I think he felt he was a stabilizing influence, you see. And he was desperate to keep her quiet. Addison was more of a friend than a lover, anyway."

"You know, it is strange that I never knew, that he never said anything that would indicate …"

"I'm sure he knew," Aunt Louisa said sympathetically. "I think Elizabeth told him; and then there is the company. He would not have wanted to risk losing it for you. That was his primary consideration."

Katherine was quiet for a while. Her brief relationship with Addison over the past few months passed through her mind and she carefully reviewed each contact and conversation they had had in light of what she had learned.

"I think he did know," she thought out loud. "In the end I think he did know, at least intuitively," she stopped again before continuing. "You're quite right, Auntie."

"About what, dear?"

"About redemption. Funny word, isn't it? But you are quite right. I think for the first time in my life, I feel a sense of belonging, of being truly loved. Not just now, I mean, but also in the past. I suppose that was Addison's final gift to me.

The story was much different in the morning room, where Albert retrieved some note paper from the library and started to make lists. Gloria, Otto, Ng, Broderick, Horsley, Addison, and McMasters. There were seven major headings in all. Under each heading he began scribbling the names and events, which connected the seven people.

"Look," he said, spreading the sheets of paper out side by side on the refectory table. "Each one of these people is connected in some way or by some incident to all the others. Now all we have to do is find the common thread."

Albert had no more said these words than in a transparent flash of consciousness, everything fit.

"Yes, of course," he heard himself saying. "Yes, of course."

"Of course what?" Patrick asked impatiently.

"They bring the "O" in on those orchids. Katherine saw it from the beginning. That's why they had to get control of the company. Without it they lose a vital link in their vertical monopoly."

"Of course," Patrick said with a deep breath, as he followed Albert's logic. "I see what you mean. They control every aspect of the drug trafficking. Shipping, distribution, financing, the docks."

"Yes, and I wouldn't be surprised if they don't control production somewhere in Asia or South America. For all we know, McMasters Shipping is only a small but vital cog in some international syndicate. With Otto von Brutmann involved, anything could be possible."

"So anyone of them could have killed Addison," Patrick concluded.

"Yes, any one of them could have killed Addison, or have hired someone to kill him. Perhaps Broderick intended to do it when he went to Addison's apartment, but he didn't because Gloria beat him to it. Broderick would not go to the trouble of moving an orchid, and the rest of them have alibis. The irony is, I suppose, that Addison was murdered to protect the sins of the flesh rather than the sins of greed. It somehow seems more personal that way, I should think."

"You're still absolutely convinced it was Gloria, aren't you?" Patrick said with a stubborn note of doubt still in his voice.

"She had to kill him to keep him from exposing her. She had to find whatever it was that Addison had, a letter of some sort, I would think. That's why the desks were searched and that's why she wanted to get into her brother's effects. It was only by chance that she killed him before one of the others did. He finally must have come completely undone the day he died and they all could see their world come collapsing down around them. But Gloria must have been particularly panicky. The others might have had a chance to survive, with a good attorney disavowing knowledge of narcotics trafficking. But Gloria could not have survived emotionally."

"But any of the others would have searched Addison's desk for incriminating documents after murdering him," Patrick interjected.

"Yes, of course they would have. Horsley and Otto did at the company. My guess is that they were leaving the apartment to Broderick. Ironic, isn't it? Gloria killed Addison because he was going to expose her for incest and drug trafficking. She never knew that he killed her brother."

"He did what?" Patrick yelled in astonishment.

"Oh, yes, I'm quite convinced that is exactly what happened. Stanley McMasters didn't die of a heart attack. He wasn't that sick. He died of a toxin that Phillip Addison used to contaminate the insulin McMasters always used after the first nine holes of golf."

"How the hell did you come up with that idea? You're forgetting there was no indication of poison in the autopsy."

"No, there wasn't, because the pathologists would not have thought to test for them in a million years. Probably couldn't have found it if they had. Toxins aren't your ordinary run-of-the-mill inorganic poisons like arsenic or strychnine. They are products of living cells like snake and spider venom or ricen from castor beans. They are fatal in very minute amounts. The concentration in a tissue sample would be so infinitesimal that it would be impossible to find unless a pathologist knew exactly what he was looking for. Even then they would be hidden among the thousands of organic compounds that exist in any tissue sample. It's the proverbial needle in a haystack."

"But who? I mean what? I mean how did you come up with such a wild theory?"

"Oh, quite simple. It was dear old Beezie."

"Beezie!"

"Oh, yes, Beezie. You see, the day of your wedding Beezie became all muddled between Mendelssohn's Wedding March and Shakespeare's Midsummer's Night Dream. Something struck me when Doug Mackey attempted to explain that Puck, King Oberon's page, put the drop of Love in Idleness in the eyes of the Queen of the Fairies, which made her fall in love with Bottom the Weaver, who was wearing an Ass's head. I happened to notice Addison at the time, and I remembered something or rather felt I should remember something. You know how it is when you know something instinctively, but just can't bring it to the conscious level?"

"No, I'm afraid I don't," Patrick said with a note of genuine concern in his voice. He thought perhaps Albert was beginning to crack under the strain.

"Oh, I'm afraid I am not making much sense," Albert continued, realizing how confusing it all was. "You see, what it was that I vaguely remembered was something Ogden Wallraven said at the Halloween party about chemical warfare research and toxins causing nerve paralysis. One drop is potent enough to kill a herd of sheep. Well, I couldn't get the Wedding March out of my mind. And when Addison prescribed the few drops of Dramamine it all jelled. I remembered that Addison graduated from Annapolis in biochemistry and was stationed at Fort Detrick, Maryland during the war. Fort Detrick is the Army and Addison was in the Navy. My hunch was that it was Fort Detrick where the biological warfare research took place. You see, it was the drop of Love's Idleness, the drop killing the herd of sheep and the drop of Dramamine and the fact that I couldn't get the damned Wedding March out of my head. Well, don't you see? It would only have taken a drop to kill Stanley McMasters and what better way than to put it in his insulin and let him kill himself? Stupid of me not to see it all sooner. That's why I went to Sausalito last Monday. I wanted to see Ogden. I wanted to find out if my hunch was correct."

"And was it?"

"Oh, yes. The Medical Research and Development Command at Fort Detrick is where they did the work on toxins and that's exactly where Addison was assigned."

"This is all very interesting Albert. Fantastic, really, but aren't you forgetting a couple of things?"

"What?"

"Motive for one. Why would Addison want to kill Stanley McMasters now? Granted, he may have hated him, but why now, after all these years?"

"The will, of course. McMasters was going to change his will and significantly reduce Katherine's inheritance. My guess is that she would not have had control of the company under the terms of the new will and that would have invalidated everything Phillip Addison had worked for."

"And you're suggesting that Addison destroyed the new will?"

"No, destroyed McMasters before there was a new will and then disposed of whatever rough drafts might have been around just to make certain."

"And what about proof?"

"Oh, I have no intention of trying to prove anything. What would be the point? It would only mean endless legal complications for Katherine and possibly endanger her fortune to say nothing of her happiness."

"Yes, I see what you mean there," Patrick said, shaking his head.

"But why are you telling me now?"

"Because I trust you and because I'm not so sure Katherine needs to know. At least not just now. She's been through enough."

"And you've known then for three days?"

"Yes, remember when I told you about the puffer fish at Yamamoto's? I knew then. I came very close to saying something, but I couldn't bring myself around to it."

Patrick sat down and shook his head and looked at Albert incredulously. "But this is all guess work. You, I mean, you have no evidence. It's all too fantastic to ..."

"I don't need evidence. The autopsy report mentioned paralysis of the central nervous system for no apparent reason. McMasters' heart condition was not that bad. A toxin-induced death according to Ogden, depolarizes the nerve junctions and makes the cause of death look natural, like congestive heart failure. And Phillip Addison, according to Nigel Sayers, went to Washington, D.C. one week before Stanley McMasters died." Ironically, I suspected it had something to do with the cancellation of those Kaiser contracts. In the end that didn't make sense. Old Rigg was just being conspiratorial. I know Edgar Kaiser and Henry too. Even if McMasters had used Addison to cancel the contracts, they never would have resorted to murder.

Patrick smiled and shook his head. "We may never know then, I mean for certain."

"For certain?" Albert asked with a smile. "What do we ever know for certain? But I'll tell you one thing that should make you feel good."

"What's that?"

"You gave me a lead even before old Beezie."

"I did?"

"Yes, when you mentioned having scorpions the night you took Katherine out to Trader Vic's. It was just after the autopsy came back and it sort of made me think. I remember fellows getting stung by those little devils during the war and well, it probably started my subconscious down the right track."

"Gee, thanks, Albert," Patrick laughed.

Patrick was still not fully convinced of Albert's conclusions when Aunt Louisa and Katherine came back from the garden. For the next several hours, while they had lunch and then sat around the fire in the library, Albert fleshed out his theory concerning Gloria. Neither of them would mention anything about the death of Stanley McMasters.

"I think I'll give Joan Bywater a call and have her find out when our next ship is due," Katherine said after an extended recounting of what they had learned in Hawaii and how it dovetailed with what he had learned from Rigg. "I think we can give the custom's house a few places to start looking."

"We'd better be careful there," Patrick advised. "Broderick might have someone in Customs. We don't want to tip our hand."

"Right you are," Albert concurred. "You might alert Joan not to ask any obvious questions. 'We have scotch'd the snake not killed it.'"

Katherine put in the call to Joan and was pleased to report that Joan had a shipping schedule in her office.

"She says the Kaahupahua, a C-3 type freighter, is due in port at 8:00 o'clock tomorrow morning. It sailed from Honolulu on November 29th, after picking up cargo in Hilo, and several of the other islands."

"That sounds like our ship!" Patrick cried. "As soon as Mike calls, I'll fill him in."

They only had to wait about 15 minutes before the call came down from the city. Albert had been correct. There was only one orchid at the apartment matching his description and it was on the piano. But even more intriguing, Inspector Key had found a card wedged in the side of the pot. "Phillip. So looking forward to dinner this evening. Fondly yours—Gloria and Otto."

Follow-up revealed that a Oncidium orchid had been ordered by Mrs. Otto von Brutmann from Ng's florist at about one p.m. the day of the murder. It had gone out with the late delivery truck.

"Did they get any prints?" Albert asked.

"Yes, there were finger prints on the pot and on the discarded florist's box." He paused and looked at Albert with admiration. "They seem to match the prints on something else they found."

Katherine sensed the tension in her husband's voice. "What?" she asked.

"The murder weapon they found in the trash container in the basement of Addison's apartment. They ran a ballistic check and it's the 32-caliber revolver that shot Addison, all right." Patrick stopped, shook his head and gave Albert a congratulatory slap on the back. "You called it Albert! Key and Crompton are on their way over to bring Gloria Brutmann in for questioning. They only got one print off the barrel but that was enough for a match."

"Did you tell him about the freighter coming in tomorrow?"

"Yep, he's going to fill Key in when he gets back to the hall. He thinks it wise to wait and let Key suggest the best approach. He says once you start talking about the wharfs you don't know who you can trust."

"Good," Albert said, settling back in his chair, feeling confident. "I think we're getting all our ducks in line. This may be our only opportunity. That ship probably left Hilo when Ng and company still felt secure. Now they probably have suspended shipping the stuff.

They would naturally have wanted to lay low for a while, until they gained control of the company."

"I still don't understand the orchid," Patrick said as he paced the floor. "If Gloria wanted to kill Addison, why would she go to the trouble of sending him a plant with a note about dinner?"

"To throw suspicion off herself," Albert said. "He must have told her that he was going to expose the whole bloody mess and she panicked. When she was unable to locate him on Tuesday she became hysterical with fear just as Joan Bywater reported. The orchid was just an attempt to create the illusion of a friendly relationship between the killer and her victim. My guess is that after she ordered the orchid sent, she grabbed Otto's revolver or perhaps one she found at Stanley's. She went over to the apartment and waited for Addison to return. When he did they undoubtedly quarreled. She shot him and began searching the apartment for whatever damaging piece of evidence she thought he might have."

Katherine shuddered at the thought of Gloria lurking behind the locked door with a gun and a corpse.

"So she was there when we arrived?"

"Oh, I'm quite sure of it," Albert continued. "No one would have noticed a shot with the cable cars and traffic on California at that time of day. Again my guess is that the delivery boy or our arrival scared her into dumping the revolver into the garbage shoot. Then she inadvertently took the phone off the hook after you called from the Mark. The ringing would have unnerved her as she made a last frantic search of the desk."

"But why would someone in that much of a hurry stop and move an orchid from the landing to the living room? It just isn't logical," Patrick objected.

"Yes," Katherine sighed, "but it is typical of Gloria. She was a master of dissembling. It's ironic, isn't it? The very item she used to deflect suspicion from herself became the clue that led to her undoing?"

"Yes," Albert agreed, looking at the violet blotches and twisted petals of the Oncidium Incurvum. "Evil always has a way of twisting back in upon itself, I suppose."

Mike did not call back for over five hours. They waited nervously, like pointers for the shoot. At eight they tried reaching him, but without success. Then again at eight-thirty and nine, but still they were told he was not available. By 9:30, Patrick was ready to drive back to the city, but Katherine prevailed upon him to stay and they settled back into the library to wait.

When the phone finally rang at 1:15 it was all over.

"Gloria Brutmann has just been booked on suspicion of murder," Mike reported. "Her prints matched those on the murder weapon. Evidently Key and Crompton had found her alone and she became hysterical when they told her she would have to go downtown for questioning."

When Patrick told them the news, Katherine sank onto the Chesterfield and began to cry. Much of her life had been a nightmare, which had now reached its tragic climax. She needed to mourn the senseless horror of it all so that it could be purged from her soul.

Patrick sat down beside her, put his arm around her shoulder, and held her tightly. No one said a word. Albert looked at Aunt Louisa to see how she was taking the news. She turned her head around and looked directly at him. Her eyes sparkled with triumphant glory. The wickedness she had detested and fought for so many years had finally destroyed itself in an orgy of passion and greed. She had won at last, reclaiming all that had been stolen from her and more. She savored the sweet taste of righteous vengeance. She was not oblivious to Katherine's pain, but she saw it in terms of being necessary and healthy. It was the afterbirth of a past life and she must deal with it before she could get on with the life she was now entering.

It took a half an hour for Katherine to dispel her emotions. She dried her eyes and with a deep breath, sat back and rested her head against the Chesterfield.

"I'm quite all right now," she said, reassuring herself.

"Yes of course you are, dear," Aunt Louisa said sympathetically. "We'll have a cognac. It's been a feverish day."

"Wait a minute," Patrick interrupted as Albert started towards the brandy snifters. "We have a decision to make. Mike has everything set for tomorrow. Key and Crompton are going out on the barge with the federal agents. Mike says we can go too. The Koahupahua is due in at eight a.m. and we should be on the pier by 6:30."

"I see you standing like greyhounds in the slip, straining upon the start. The game's afoot!" Aunt Louisa laughed.

Albert looked at his watch and handed Aunt Louisa a cognac. "I wouldn't miss it for the world," he said. "'Fortune brings in some boats that are not steer'd.'"

Patrick looked at Katherine. "I suppose you should," she sighed. "The suspense will be absolutely marvelous."

"Too marvelous for words," Aunt Louisa laughed. "I'd go if I could. I want to know everything that happens down to the last detail. Are you going, Katherine?"

Albert could see a worried look come over Patrick's face for he had not considered the possibility.

Katherine sighed. The thought of the drama excited the adventurer in her. But something still deeper resisted the notion.

"I probably should go," she said after a while, "but I think I'll decline."

"We'd better get back to the city," Albert suggested. "I'll call Chow-Ling. You can stay with me the night and we won't have to coordinate in the morning until after coffee."

"Fine," Patrick agreed. "I'll have one of my brothers come over at six and wait with Katherine."

"That's not necessary," Katherine complained.

"It is necessary," Patrick insisted. "And we're going to do it!"

Katherine sensed some temper in Patrick's bluntness and it gave her a secure feeling.

"Oh, yes, mein Fuhrer," she teased, holding out her brandy snifter in a mock salute.

CHAPTER 47

*T*HEY REACHED ALBERT'S apartment at 1:30 with the knowledge that they had to be up in less than four hours. Patrick and Katherine fell into bed and Albert retired with Windsor. He had not been home for what seemed like a long time and it was comforting to lay back on his bed and stroke Windsor's ears. He only had one thing left to do and at around 2:15 he woke Charlie Cahoun out of a sound sleep.

"Charlie," he said lowering his voice. "Albert Devonshire here. Listen, pal, it's payback time. Be down at pier 25 by 6:30 tomorrow. Meet me there."

Charlie had the amazing ability to come wide awake out of a whiskey-soaked sleep when he smelled a story. He wanted more information but Albert put him off.

"Trust me, Charlie. Be there."

Too much adrenaline had been pumped into his body to allow him to sleep soundly. His mind seemed suspended on the line between the conscious and subconscious and images from the two worlds mingled. At 5:30 Chow-Ling was at his side with a large mug of espresso and a firm thumb massaging the knots out of his neck. After five minutes, he began to feel alive as Chow-Ling's skillful old hands pulled the vitalizing forces up through the spine.

It was pitch dark as Albert headed the Buick down Lombard and around the hill. The city was only beginning to stir and each sound along the wharf seemed isolated in the overall quiet.

Mike was waiting with Inspectors Key and Crompton.

"I'd like to take my friend Charlie Cahoun along," Albert said when a disheveled Charlie came running down the waterfront. Crompton looked at Key. "I owe him a favor," Albert said.

"Yeah, O.K., as long as he keeps out of the way and doesn't ask any questions."

They met the Federal Customs inspector and were aboard a government launch by 6:30. Huddling together near the cabin, they passed around the thermos of black coffee Chow-Ling had prepared. The bay was gray and choppy. It writhed and foamed among the piers like a great beast in the final throws of death. It was too cold to talk. The scream of gulls pierced the air as they started scavenging the dripping wharf.

They were under way by seven and as they rounded the end of the pier, they could see the tremendous hull of the Kaahupahua through the fog. There was a strong headwind but the tide was with them. Within twenty minutes they were on board.

After the customs officers presented credentials to the captain, they were given full cooperation. It did not take long to find what they were looking for. In Cargo Hold D specially sealed boxes were torn open, revealing a large shipment of orchids from the Lehua Nursery. Unceremoniously uprooted, the orchids revealed large pellets of opium skillfully concealed among the mixture of perlite, volcanic rock and horticultural sand. Vials of morphine and heroin, ingeniously hidden in the hollowed-out sections of compressed tree fern fiber, were also uncovered.

Patrick shook his head as one of the agents cracked open a totem filled with additional bags of raw opium.

"We almost brought one of these home to you," he told Albert.

It took several hours before everyone was satisfied at the extent of the cache and it wasn't until around eleven that the Kaahupahua was allowed to dock.

"You guys can stick around if you like," Mike said as additional agents swarmed aboard. "But from here on in it's all a matter of routine. Paperwork, you know."

"Thanks, Mike," Patrick said, putting his arm around his brother's shoulder. "I think I need to get home. Katherine wasn't feeling well this morning and I could use some sleep."

"I'm afraid that goes for me too," Albert said. "It's been a long few days."

Katherine had just awakened from a nap when they walked into the apartment. She slowly pulled herself up from the davenport. "Well?" she asked, looking at Patrick.

"We have them now," he said, embracing her. "We have them now."

"It's over then?"

"Yes, it's all over," sighed Albert.

Although she felt relieved, Katherine did not seem overly excited by what Patrick told her of the morning's discovery. Chow-Ling, sensing that she was nervous and queasy, had soothed her with an herbal tea and Tai Chi.

"I had to laugh," she told them after they had finished their detective saga. "Here I was, balancing on one foot and trying to achieve harmony while you were out braving the danger and cold. It seemed so absurd. But Chow-Ling has his ways."

"Yes, I know," said Albert, looking over at Chow-Ling, who pretended not to hear the conversation. "I have had over thirty years of Chow-Ling. The outcome is always the same."

Katherine's eyes twinkled as she watched an expressionless Chow-Ling methodically feed Hector a green grape.

"Not twice this day
Inch time foot gem" she quoted.

"Yes," Albert pondered before finishing the saying Chow-Ling had taught him from his youth. "This day will not come again. Each minute is worth a priceless gem."

Katherine and Patrick returned to their apartment on Jones to sleep and waited to hear what would happen next. Albert was too tired to consider lunch and found myself trailing off towards his bedroom. Before he was undressed, Chow-Ling appeared with a large bowl of litchi nut custard and a pot of herb tea.

"Thank you, Chow-Ling," he said as Chow-Ling helped him with his pajamas. "I hope that's the same herb tea that did such wonders for Katherine."

"No," Chow-Ling smiled. "You no have swollen lip."

Albert was too tired to pursue a discussion of Chinese herbal remedies or ask Chow-Ling what he found so humorous, for he had begun to chuckle in a way he always did when he found something profoundly amusing, and knew a secret others did not know.

As they slept the afternoon and early evening away, the police and federal agents were busy at work. By four o'clock enough evidence had been amassed to issue arrest warrants for Madame Ng, Richard Broderick, Chambliss Blackmond Horsley and Otto Brutmann on suspicion of illegally smuggling and trafficking in narcotics. Additional individual charges were pending subsequent to further investigation. Gloria had unwittingly supplied decisive information. Under questioning she had become so completely muddled that she exposed all the major players.

At six o'clock Katherine awoke from a dream she could not remember. Leaving Patrick, she crept out of the bedroom and down the hall. At the end of the living room stood her mother's piano. Pulling the curtains aside, she stood for a while watching a lone white sail fluttering through the dark waters. Slowly it grew larger as it neared the shore. As the sun sank between the twin towers of the Golden Gate and into the Pacific, Katherine sat down at her mother's piano and in the dim light began to softly play a Braham's lullaby. She could not know, that as her graceful fingers moved across the keys, Broderick, Brutmann and Horsley were being taken into custody.

Katherine's thoughts were far away. She could not recall if it had been in her dream or on top of a hill above Potraku Ho-O-Hanau, but she remembered an old Hawaiian named Ekewaka, his garden and touching the bell stone. Then she remembered that Ekewaka had been in both her dream and her waking world and the realization caused her to smile. She remembered also the dream she had had on the night after touching the bell stone.

The god Lono had spread a tapa cloth and bid her lay with Patrick.

Katherine could hear in the notes from the piano the bell stone echoing through to her. Each echo reverberated with the announcement that she was carrying a child.

Made in the USA
San Bernardino, CA
07 October 2015